E. C. Dryere

Register of Copyright, United States of America
Registration Number TXu 1-829-646

ISBN: 978-0-9894574-0-8

Author: E. C. Dryere
Cover by: Courtney Dryere

The strongest forces in the universe dwell in the nucleus of every atom. Existence itself is power, waiting for a will with a key.

- Algray Solipso

Born in Anchorspace

Ex was born in anchorspace. In the time he took his first breath, the ship had passed a hundred galaxies. Solarian tradition was to celebrate birthdays according to the orbit of the nearest planet to which you were born. And since the act of his birth took place next to trillions of worlds, all orbiting at different speeds, he could have a birthday whenever he wanted. He'd never done the math, but he estimated that he was owed a present every quarter of a second or so. And since he'd only received a handful to date, the universe had quite a backlog to fill before they'd call it even.

His mother, Arius, had the antiquated idea that his age should be measured according to the orbit of Earth and its continents-turned-asteroids. Ex had never been to Earth, but he kept an old-fashioned paper calendar of its orbit by the one round porthole in his room. He checked tomorrow's date, and for the seventh time that day, confirmed that tomorrow was his thirteenth birthday.

Hopefully Arius would remember. She was the only one who knew when his birthday was or that he'd been born at all, but she'd been in one of her moods lately, watching the stars swim by on the bridge. She was in pretty good shape for a woman in her third century. She was never short of breath. The air, it seemed, had reason to come to her. She could hypnotize an atom from across the room and draw it in without contracting her diaphragm. Her muscles held their curves, and her hair was raven black. A wrinkle had yet to crease her snowy skin. Her only blemishes were the tiny cinnabar freckles that grew like flowers on the hills of her cheeks. But now the sleepless nights were starting to well up in livid sacks beneath her eyes.

The engines had been singing the same off-key tremolo for a week straight. Arius was trying to beat someone or something to the next drop point. They'd be safe if they could make the drop. Every ship moved at the same speed in anchorspace since it wasn't the ship that moved but rather the universe that rotated past it. But they weren't about to outrun anyone using their conventional engines. Their ship was powered by a threaded core containing the soul of a fish or perhaps a very dull cat. When Arius spotted the core in a Mohmish junker's bargain bin, she said that she'd get out and push the ship if necessary. Ex had never seen her make good on that boast, but he'd grown tired of hearing about how she'd talked the Mohmil's price down to a single drop of plex. The worst of it was that the haggling had taken nearly as much effort on her part as it would've to siphon twenty times that amount of plex from a star.

Some Sages devoted their lives to harvesting plex from stellar cores, likely because it was a universally accepted form of currency. This willing soup of subatomic particles could be molded into nearly any material imaginable with just a thought or turn of a dial. A fortune of potential matter could be carried in a single vial that fit comfortably in a pocket. And regardless of the sum, plex weighed nothing because it was held in a deep subrostral stage, before gravity could take hold of its flittering particles. But Arius, being the druid that she was, had little care for material possessions.

Ex went down to the cargo hold to shoot at flickering images of tin cans with his hologun. His mother didn't like it when he cranked the gun up to humanoids. She said it would make him cocky, so he settled for putting pictures of her on the cans. A few years ago, he'd tried the highest setting, the faceless Nyrceff soldiers of the Consortium. About two minutes into the fight, he'd strafed head-first into the edge of a crate. When his mother had come to check on him, the hologun's record showed that he'd been killed 398 times, and the knot on the side of his head had grown enough to fold the cartilage of his ear. He fully expected a scolding, but Arius rubbed his scalp, and the knot dissolved beneath her touch. This was the benefit of having a druidic Sage for a mother. There were negatives though, like how every Talon and Extinguisher in The Rings wanted to reduce you to inorganic motes of matter.

He arrived at the small clearing in the cargo bay where he and Arius would exercise and practice the archaic art of throwing hands. The paper-thin mat here did nothing to take the sting out of the metal floor. Arius could've manifested a tolerable mat with a thought, and it wasn't as if Ex didn't ask on a weekly basis, but she'd always reply that he could have a thicker mat when he could compose one himself. Ex figured it was supposed to be an incentive to learn about the ways of a Sage, but she never taught him. Arius was typified by contradictions, which is why Ex now took aim at her grinning face on the label of a holographic can.

The door slid open on the catwalk above. "We're going down to the planet's surface," said Arius and left without another word.

Unscheduled landings were about as rare as birthdays, which could only mean one thing in Ex's mind: she did remember! More than anything, he wanted to see new worlds – not just as streaks of color in his window, but to actually stand on one, lie on one, somersault on one. Throughout his whole youth, he'd only visited a handful. And even then it was only to acquire parts for their ship through means that seldom involved payment or to see an eccentric old Sage that would touch him in ways that a quantum physicist would find inappropriate. As long as this wasn't going to be one of those kinds of visits, it would be his greatest birthday present yet. He wondered what kind of planet it would be and if there would be a party, maybe even with hats; he'd never had a party with hats before.

The ship landed, and Ex raced down the ramp as it was still extending. He disappeared into a curtain of tall, yellow grass that grew in broad blades. Wheaty blue spikelets were released from their stalks as Ex threshed and thrashed. They wafted into a red sky that had the appearance of tomato bisque caught in mid-stir.

"Stay close to the ship!" called Arius. She envisioned tiny fractals on a distant hilltop, and there the wind began to argue with itself. Whirlwinds manifested and clapped together in soft thunder; they formed a gale that blew across the plain, and the grass flattened, throwing a thousand blue florets to the sky.

Ex was revealed like a bug beneath an upturned rock. "Whoa! Don't get all Sagey on me," he said. "I'm coming."

Arius had hardly stepped off the ramp. She stood resting a couple of fingers on the pistons of her gun, eyes fixed upwards. The local star had tucked behind the horizon, leaving only the glowing red nebula that swaddled this nameless system to light the sky. Up close, Ex could see her dark eyes darting about, searching in a kind of waking REM. They fell on him. Her smile was a thin sheathe for a great sorrow, the blade of which could cut Ex down to his reason for living.

There was another shift in the wind. The florets that'd flown high into the heavy atmosphere were suddenly blown back across the field, swirling around the ship in a perfect sphere. Arius laid a hand on Ex's shoulder and gently pulled him towards the ship behind her. There was a tiny dot of light welling in the pit of her left retina.

A figure of a man in a white cloak descended from the garnet dusk. He'd come to this planet without the aid of a ship. Outside of anchorspace, Arius couldn't match his speed, and it was too far to the next drop point. There wasn't a favorable location in the whole universe for the kind of fight that was about to take place, but Arius had chosen a planet where the air was mostly breathable, and the only form of life was primitive vegetation.

Light poured from beneath the man's hood, spilling over the emblem of The Extinguishers that was emblazoned on his chest. It was only just visible at this distance, yet unmistakable.

The ground began to shake beneath his raised hand, and his gesturing fingers carved deep valleys into the face of the world. He reached another arm out of his cloak, and mountains crumbled. Five more gorges were gouged into the terrain. The sun rose in reverse, and the grassy field was flattened by an avalanche of air.

The Extinguisher grabbed at the world, pulling, hand over hand, spinning it faster and faster. The star set on the far horizon. Seconds later, it rose again, streaked across the sky, and set, over and over. Faster still the world spun, until the star passed in streaks. The ground split, hurricanes blew, lightning arched, and enormous volcanoes spewed the planet's molten guts into space. But the ship was surrounded in a clear sphere of calm. This was the will of Arius, youngest of The Three Pupils of Mavenbolt. Threadwidth welled around her like a compressed star, and The Extinguisher couldn't affect the space in its hold. He couldn't twist her aorta or slice a critical ganglion, but he could strike from afar.

The unnatural rate of rotation created an immense centrifugal force that threw everything towards the heavens. Beyond the walls of the sphere, the air was red and solid with the speed of debris; there, shadows grew like ascending whales. But inside the shell, there was no sound at all. The air around Ex was a cool 72 degrees and perfectly calm.

A Sage could manipulate any of the laws of the universe, but no one, not even the Sophians with their multigenerational knowledge, had mastery over them all. As a Druid, Arius' specialty was life. This Extinguisher's was inertia. Like a man pushing a boulder across a flat road, he used distance and time to will enormous masses of cooled magma into motion. The first steps are difficult, but each shove becomes less labored as the momentum accrues.

It's not as easy, however, to stand at the end of the road and deflect a rolling boulder with a single slap. This was where Arius found herself as the rocks crashed down from all directions. Holding the space around her and the ship steady took all of Arius' willpower. This kind of manipulation was not her strength. The light of her corona heated her eye until the proteins began to congeal, and her vision blurred; she'd broken into fever. Once delirium set in, her focus would waver, and the chaos would pop her bubble with a single pinprick. The sphere of her influence began to shrink.

The temperature rose, and Ex pumped his jaw to pop his ears as the atmospheric pressure increased. Then there was a clinking and clanking, like the sound of flying through pebbles on the rim of an asteroid field. Dirt and gravel impinged on the hull of the old ship. And something struck Ex in the mouth. He felt a short sting followed by a dull tingle. His tongue felt jagged fragments floating in a warm liquid that tasted of tinfoil. He kept his lips sealed until his cheeks swelled. The gritty mixture trickled down his throat and made him gag. It came out all at once. He fell to his knees, gasping for air. The world had not lost its redness in the swirling chaos – fiery orange in the fleeting day and lusty brown at night. The puddle he'd spat out looked black, speckled with whitish splinters. It took him a moment to realize that it was his own blood and teeth.

"Ex! Go inside!" cried Arius; her left eye was nearly white with light. Ex ran into the ship. His hands were cupped beneath his chin, trying to catch the streaming blood as though he didn't want to stain the ramp. The ferrekondite hatch shut behind him.

Vertebrae of angled rock erupted behind The Extinguisher and parted the rushing air. It reached out of the atmosphere, and the rain of stones fell silent.

A mountainous shadow descended from the strobing sky. The Extinguisher had amassed all the magma that the planet had heaved and shaped it into a sharpened moon. Even at this great speed of rotation, he'd managed to push the colossal mass into a decaying geosynchronous orbit through frictionless space. The calculations this required, while orchestrating the devastation on the planet's surface, were staggering. The Extinguisher was pushing his threadwidth to its limit, and his corona's quantum processor was maxed as well.

But Arius could do nothing. All her thoughts were bent on the falling moon. She ground her teeth until her gums bled and ratcheted up the amplification another notch, roasting her frontal lobe. It wasn't enough. There was too much potential energy accumulated behind its descent. She could feel her head and feet being pulled away from each other as the moon's gravity neared.

Dirt broke through the barrier. It buffeted the side of the ship and tore tiny cuts in Arius' cheeks. Her sinuses were fusing together into a painful mask. The druidic mastery over her body was the only thing keeping her from collapsing.

From a dusty window and through the spinning stone, Ex could see the agony on his mother's face. He pressed his bloody hand to the hull and wished beyond reason that he could help her.

A moon-cleaving arc of lightning parted the sky. The mountain burst into rubble and rained onto the brushed-rock in drops of amber flame. The Extinguisher's focus cracked. Blades of wind shredded his white cloak. A small stone passed through the back of his knee, and his leg was gone. He struggled to reestablish a barrier, but Arius had already drawn her pistol.

Arius steadied time for this shot, the chroneons swarming her like bees. The planet spinning so quickly that the window of opportunity was only a few microseconds wide. The piston pumped, bullet was chambered, the igniter was struck, and five atoms dropped into anchorspace.

In that instant, the constant gemini-link that was a part of every Extinguisher's corona reported that Arius possessed anchor rounds, a fearsome weapon not seen since the late Extinguishing. An instant later, he was a plume of bosons spread across the galaxy.

The planet slowed to a stop as Arius collected her breath, and the sun came to rest on the horizon. For years she'd kept these bullets a secret, but now the Consortium would know. Dethoron of The Three-Quarters would know, and when he came to extinguish her, he wouldn't make the mistake of being caught downspin.

Maybe it was the loss of blood or all the exertion, but Ex couldn't remember how he made it to bed. He could, however, recall with vivid clarity the dream he had. It began as the opposite of space: a warm, white light in a state between a solid and liquid. He perceived it as a soft pressure in which every part of him was buoyant. Every hair stood and was swaddled root to tip. There was no way to tell up from down, nothing by which to gauge dimension or distance, until a long black snake slithered into view. It approached at the level of his navel. He was not afraid. Just beyond arm's length, the serpent shed its skin, and he discovered that it'd not been black, but gray, or at least this new shade became his understanding of black. The snake wrapped around him, coiling first around his wrist and slithering up his arm, down his chest to his waist, and back up towards his neck. Still he was unafraid. It continued to wind around him, somehow elongating to cover every inch of his body. Its skin felt like warm light, until it tightened, and there were scales. The light faded, exploring every shade of gray between the innocence of white and absolution of darkness.

Far less clear were his memories of Arius, sitting at the foot of his bed throughout the night, crying softly and sometimes touching his knee. It may have been another dream. Arius never cried. She of all people knew that life was just the channel to which we were currently tuned.

The next morning, he was looking for something to wash the terrible taste out of his mouth. He'd no idea how many teeth he'd lost yesterday, but they'd all grown back except one. A jagged stump sat in place of his left incisor. The living part of his tooth had not been damaged, and so it had not regenerated.

He went to the kitchen and stopped at the small, brushed metal table where he and his mother always ate. There sat a cold meal, and next to it was Arius' gun, resting atop an envelope that read: *Happy Birthday*. He'd completely forgotten it was his birthday! And now he'd completely forgotten his thirst. He eagerly tore open the letter. It was messy and hard to read. The ink ran in small wet dots that speckled the page.

It began: *Ex, I leave you this crutch to lean on in absence of my shoulder...*

And this line was the hard boundary of his youth. This was not just the day his mother left, it was the day that everyone he knew went away. It was the first time he perceived the distances that lay just beyond the hull.

From Black and Cold

Twelve years later, the memory of this letter was enough to wake him from death – or a very cold approximation.

A tiny star poked a hole in the black. It boiled in a flurry of colors, chasing the darkness to the edges of his vision, until all that remained was a pale blur. It was the color of cold, but he felt no chill.

A dark figure crawled into view; it startled him. Never had his eyes been so estranged to the sight of his own hand. It fumbled about, leaving streaks of blue in the mist before falling limp to his chest. Condensation shadowed his movements, returning everything to gray.

When his hand moved again, it left a curious collection of lines and curves in its wake. He stared at the cobalt glyphs as they dissolved, until their meaning struck him. It was his name, *Exterrus Rey*.

There was something strapped to his leg: a holster. And in it was his fully loaded thirteenth birthday present.

A shrill siren drilled into his teeth. He jumped up, and his forehead met the mist with a dull thud. He should've been grateful that the glass was so sturdy, but those weren't the words that came out of his mouth. The hydraulics lifted the casing with a low hum, the hermetic seal broke with a screech and a hiss. Jets of vapor filled the room with thick fog, which made it impossible to see but did nothing to muffle the alarm.

Feeling returned to his flesh in prickling waves, and the cold lashed him into action. He spilled out of the coffin onto the metal deck, slippery with frost. He hopped from foot to foot, trying to cut the floor's bite in half. The display panel by the door blinked the following message: *Please input waking temperature.*

Whoever coined the adage, *computers don't make mistakes,* had never traveled in this old ship. He bashed a couple of numbers on the panel. Blasts of steam poured in from the vents that lined the room. By the time it cleared, Ex was gone.

Twisted masses of multicolored wires and jagged juts of bulkhead crowded the corridor. The mess was a result of years of excessive use and equal negligence. Ex had decided to wake up to some slow blues. BB King sang over the intercom: *Nobody loves me but my mother, and she might be jiving too...*

He staggered down the hall, punching at his leg. The various parts of his body had taken a vote and unanimously agreed that they were not done sleeping. It was hard to argue with a month's idle. His desire to avoid obstacles dwindled as he went. He gave up on ducking and dodging, settling for a bump-and-spin technique.

A sudden tug at his arm brought him to a halt. He felt as if his sleeve had been caught; only he wasn't wearing a shirt, just underwear and a holster. He cracked an eye to survey the damage. A blade of bulkhead had wedged itself into the bone of his arm. Ex was not in the least bit pleased. He tore his bicep from the wall with a sound like uncorking a bottle of wine. In seconds, the gaping wound dried into a scab. It swept away like unwanted dust, revealing a fresh patch of skin. He bent the jutting metal upwards and fastened it to the wall with a solid punch. As he soldiered through the corridor, he passed several other imprints of his fist, products of previous repairs.

Aside from the gun strapped to his thigh, this ship was all his mother had left him. Originally, it was a frozen meat transport. Not much had changed since then. Getting cold was about all the ship could still do well, which wasn't a particularly impressive feat in space. He wasn't sure how well the refrigeration system still worked. He was just a kid the last time he'd experimented with it, and it'd hardly been scientific. As he recalled, he was trying to get back at his mother for passing up another planet she'd promised they could visit.

At seven years of age, Ex had kept a vigil in the battle bubble for two, maybe three days without sleep. He didn't want to miss a moment of their approach to Istreya; it was the world of Arius' youth and the subject of at least half of her stories. There were forests of thinking pines that poked through the clouds, rabbits that wore weskits and stirred brass pots in their hutches, and a race of fairies with hips like stringed instruments that wore only skirts of green fronds.

When the ship came into high orbit, Ex stared straight into Istreya's beautiful blue face. The blanket of clouds on the horizon looked like freshly fallen snow, and tucked beneath them, only just visible beyond the coast, was a forest. It was teal, more blue than green. Ex stood atop the console, searching for a tree that rose above the cloud cover and convinced himself that he saw one.

Istreya had no deserts. The Sages of this world called themselves druids and tended to every branch and twig – even the grass grew mindfully. Every Sage had a specialty, and for those of this world, it was life. Biology was largely considered the most difficult discipline for a Sage, not only for its complexity, but because a Sage's greatest limitation was his inability to directly affect another living being. It took these druids hours, days, sometimes longer to commune with another life form. An accord had to be struck with the thread that inhabited the other body; it had to be convinced of any change made.

Arius' explanations of threads had given Ex the idea that they were like invisible extension cords, plugged into the cheery cockles of our hearts. The amount of threadwidth it would've taken to power this gigantic life-bulb-of-a-planet was beyond his reckoning. So teeming with life was this world that he could almost feel it vibrating off its verdant face. From his perch in the battle bubble above the bridge, he could see the upper atmosphere testing the bounds of space in soft licks and imagined for just a moment that these were wisps of thread, made visible by the sheer enthusiasm of reporting the happy experiences from the surface below.

But they didn't stop. Arius commonly reneged on these scheduled landings – Ex was used to it – but this time was the worst. He descended into the bridge to find it empty. Their course had been plotted several hours ago. His next step was to locate his mother. He found her taking what he estimated to be a casual shower.

"Arius! You're such a liar!" he said, banging on the bathroom door. He called his mother Arius because it was the adult thing to do.

The Istreyan system was a few light years behind them now. "I'm sorry. We can't stop," she called over the noise of the shower.

Ex entered under the pretense of hygiene. He told his mother's foggy silhouette that he was going to brush his teeth, but instead snatched her clothes off the counter and ran out. The ship's central temperature control panel was just down the corridor. He set it to sub-freezing, and in seconds, the air was cold enough to prevent spoiling.

Arius came out of the bathroom wrapped in a towel; the tips of her hair were already frozen. Ex scampered in terror and delight. She finally cornered him in a storage room. "Now I got ya!" she said through chattering teeth. "Who taught you to be such a lil' thief?"

"You did!" he shrieked, tossing the clothes in her face before sliding under her legs. Arius was too busy snapping her legs shut and pulling the panties off her face to catch him.

She was locked in. The door's seal was airtight, and the temperature was still dropping. By the time she was dried and dressed, Ex had turned the ship around, heading straight back toward Istreya.

The blue planet grew in the window, and Ex was feeling quite proud of himself when a frigid hand tickled the back of his neck. Arius had escaped the meat locker in some Sagely way. She turned the ship around, and Ex earned some thinking time.

He went to the battle bubble whenever he was grounded. It offered a hemispherical view of the surrounding stars. If you sat on the consoles, and turned the lights low, it was almost like being on the surface of a planet on a clear night. He liked to pretend that he was atop a tower and that if he climbed down, he could run into a field or take a stroll along a peaceful stream. In his mind, he'd walk out on the shallow water and wait for the ripples to disperse. He'd look down and discover that he could straddle stars.

The ship was in anchorspace, and he watched the galaxies streak by. They were vivid blue at the nose of the ship, turned violet overhead, and burned red in the ship's wake. He was so accustomed to seeing the universe this way that it'd become more interesting when it stood still. It also made it a lot harder to imagine yourself on a planet.

The circular hatch on the floor irised open and Arius entered on a slow-rising chair, drinking something hot. Ex sat on an instrument panel looking straight ahead. His eyes were fixed on the small black point, some unfathomable distance away, where the blue flukes originated.

"Ex," she said softly, "I wanted to stop as much as you did. But we can't. We have to hide you."

"Can't you just put me in a box?" he asked without turning. He could see her reflection well enough in the glass.

Arius pressed her lips to the mug. Her eyes grew puffy in its steam. "I wish it were that easy," she said.

Memories like these were penance for mischief he'd yet – but fully intended – to commit, and he was living in an enclosed, metal reminder. The ship was on its last plates. He should've left it in a spacefill years ago, but it was the only home he'd ever known. Besides, he didn't spend many waking hours in it anymore. He'd taken to freezing himself for long journeys ever since he'd reached the full maturity of adulthood. At twenty five, he was still young enough to desire for his appearance to reflect his age.

The door to the bridge was the worst. It only stuttered open wide enough to sidle through and not without being pounded in the back or chest as it repeatedly tried to close. The ship was never intended to be operated by a single person. A few years ago Ex had attempted to rewire all of the bridge's controls up to the battle bubble, and succeeded only at leaving circuitry exposed, cables running across walkways at knee-height, and bouquets of buttons springing from consoles on the ends of coppery wires.

Some non-critical systems were rendered inoperable, but all the important ones still worked. Currently, he was most interested in the monitor that displayed the results of his Forelight scans.

This system's name was a bit misleading. Forelight sensors didn't use light at all; they used gravity. It can take around 100,000 years for a beam of light to travel across a galaxy, making its measurement fairly useless at great distances. Light is a great way to do historical research, but if you're interest in the present, you need to measure a force that propagates instantaneously: you need to measure gravity, which is precisely what the Forelight system did. It created a planetary-sized mesh around the ship capable of picking up subrostral variations in gravity from external forces. The Forelight systems on high end drop charts could *see* the present as it occurred as far as a thousand light years away in all directions. Ex's sensors pulled 200 LY at best, and that was if he found a nice patch of void.

The information was displayed in a three-dimensional topographic chart. Less massive bodies were represented as dim purple dots, while heavier objects were vivid orange with faint auras of red and violet. Natural drops in gravity were sharp, but the edges of artificial gravity fields were even sharper. A keen eye could pick them out. It was even easier when they were old and leaky, appearing as streaky oblongs rather than dots.

Ex had been tracking a massive ship as it drew a jagged red line across space. It scattered into a dithering field of fine points when it stopped. A less traveled runner might have suspected that the ship had been scuttled, but the pixels were bright orange, which meant the artificial well was still operational. The only thing capable of causing this kind of disturbance in gravimetric scans was perlite, the so-called "Trembling Metal" that oscillated between effective dimensions of the Subrostrum. Any attempt to stabilize the alloy yielded scraps of iron and nothing. Trying to scan through or around perlite was like trying to sense gentle vibrations on a wire while someone violently shook it: the motion was additive, so the information was still present but unpredictably scattered.

He'd decided to investigate. A few star systems out, he cranked out the spectral scopes and had a look. He saw a beige marble, tanning unassumingly in the light of three stars. The ship hadn't arrived yet. Or rather, the light from the time of the ship's arrival had yet to reach Ex.

It appeared suddenly and streaked around the planet fast enough to draw glinting streaks. The planet was too monochrome to observe its revolutions, but the ship was likely in geosynchronous orbit. At the speed of his approach, Ex collided with months' worth of light in seconds, but he was beginning to slow down. The momentum from his last drop was all but dissipated.

Upon dropping below the speed of light, his conventional engines shuddered on. They gave a single whine before settling into their mantric drone. He was intimately familiar with the sound. It was the backdrop to his every thought. Like the voice of a parent, it'd changed imperceptibly over time. All of the bolts and seams that vibrated with its lower registers had been shaken apart long ago.

The orbiting vessel slowed to a near stop as Ex sputtered into the system's rim. It looked to be a bioark, an ancient terraforming vessel once used to make multigenerational voyages before the advent of anchor drives. Of course, there was no way it'd made it to the fourth stratum without a couple of hops through anchorspace. Even if this was the first ark to leave Earth thousands of years ago, and its engines had never stopped firing, it wouldn't have made it half way to the third stratum. It wasn't uncommon to find old ships fitted with new anchor drives, but this one didn't look like it could handle another drop. Its leaky gravity field conducted a few interwoven rings of the space trash it'd accumulated since its arrival.

The light of the three stars fluttered between the cloud of metal specks that surrounded the ark as they crested over the horizon. They moved in silent accord, appearing golden when filtered through the prism of the planet's thin atmosphere. Even a heap of garbage could look beautiful if the cosmic conditions were just right. When the planet pushed away, the starlight washed over the ark, blanched and unimpeded; the moment had passed.

From distant orbit, the planet looked like a ball of dust, freckled with red basins and veined in silver glints. Not a cloud had condensed over its baked surface. There was only a faint halo of windswept sand. He discovered what he thought to be two settlements, less than a few hundred kilometers apart in the planetary desert. He honed his instruments on those spots, but saw only splashes of warped starlight and echoes of his own hull; in this instance, sensors were less effective than human eyeballs. The entire planet was blanketed in perlite. He hadn't seen a lode like this in all his travels.

Scans of the bioark itself were similarly distorted. Ex assumed that it'd come here to oversee mining efforts, but judging by these readings, it had a bellyful of perlite. If he could manage to acquire a few ingots, he'd have enough to patch up his ship and keep him running for a few more years at least.

Perlite was one of the only two substances worth more than their mass in the raw plex that was harvested directly from star cores. Its ability to confound even gravimetric scanning made it highly coveted. Although it could be derived from plex, its delicate subrostral state could take Sages hours to balance. It was more efficient to mine it; if you could find a sizeable cache. Perlite was only common in the vacillating gravity fields of trinary star systems. Whereas other metals could be specifically scanned for and identified with certainty, it was uncertainty that distinguished perlite.

The screen beside him began to crackle. It was a loose lens of glass on a metal plate, still bound to the telecom console by four dowdy wires twined to the center of its back. The bioark was attempting to send him a message – this was one of those non-critical systems that was lost as a result of his remodeling. As it was, he was only capable of sending and receiving text messages. These were rastered in blocky lines on a small green monitor affixed to the arm of his chair.

Welcome merchants, welcome runners, to Trisol station, it read. *Come rich, leave richer. Flex your plex at our shopping annex.*

I'm Ex, and I'd like to flex my plex at your annex, he replied.

A minute delay. *We are at capacity. You are not cleared to dock,* was the reply.

"Plexism!" Ex said to his armrest. The pause had taken long enough for a comprehensive scan of his ship. No one with a vial of plex to their name would travel the stars in such an oddly shaped trash bin. But this wasn't about to stop Ex. He'd invoke the only CIR law he actually liked: no ship requiring anchor drive repairs can be denied provisional harborage.

He transmitted his need for repairs and increased thrust. It wasn't easy to spot reluctance in plain, green text, but there it was: *Bay 3.*

After turning the controls over to the autopilot, he sidled out of the bridge. The ship jerked violently as it maneuvered around the rings of trash. Ex was thrown into a thicket of exposed wires and became thoroughly entangled. One wire in particular wouldn't let go. Having reached the full extent of his patience, he tore it out of the wall, threw it to the ground, and stomped the severed cable until the sparks stopped. He paused for a moment to contemplate the ramifications of his actions: *I'm sure it was unimportant... probably just one of those decorative cables that engineers put into ships to make them look complicated.*

Once in the engine room, he addressed the only piece of equipment that seemed to be in pristine order: the ship's anchor drive. The valuable bits were housed in simple rectangular box labeled VA^{2}L, the logo of the Veridian Advance Astronautics Laboratory where it was built. Coincidentally, this was the only piece of Sophian technology that Ex tolerated on his ship. The rest of the drive was bolted onto a modified workbench with all the careful planning of a Rube Goldberg machine. Above this, a chrome orb was suspended by a mechanical arm that grew wires like wild vines. This was the central unit of his drop chart, which mapped the surroundings before drops into anchor space. Ex knew that you couldn't drop anchor outside of a Ring or Clipway without one of these orbs. He also knew that they fired trillions of meshes, no more than a single atom thick, ahead of a drop to clear the path of matter. Even when used correctly, the process involved destruction on a cosmic scale. And that was about all he knew.

Only a mathematically insignificant fraction of the universe's population actually understood anchor drives. Most people only knew that these devices could take you around the universe in precisely 52 hours without moving the ship a single angstrom, regardless of your distance from the Prime Axis.

The universe was known to be cylindrical in shape and spinning at a rate that redefined the concept of speed. The reason for this rotation around the Prime Axis was not fully understood. The popular theory suggested that this was the motion of a higher effective dimension, a plane of magnification in which our galaxies were as bosons. The Sages that had attempted to assume this scope had lost their minds without fail.

An anchor drive was capable of pinning a ship to a point outside of space. It remained perfectly still as the universe rushed by at speeds that grew more ridiculous as you moved away from the Prime Axis. Because collisions were still possible, and often resulted in the destruction of the surrounding star systems, the universe had to be cleared of matter ahead of a ship. The circular channels that circumscribed the entire universe like the grooves on old Solarian records were called The Rings, carved by the CIR through hammer-blows in anchorspace. Star systems were wiped aside, galaxies were pierced; it was a destructive mode of travel – pollution on a universal scale. And sometimes, it was simply a weapon. The projectile that shattered Earth measured exactly 5,000,000,000,000,000,000 atoms, or about one quarter of a grain of sand.

If you were willing to live under the CIR's laws, life on The Rings offered comforts and safety that were hard to resist. Still there was no shortage of pioneers who made their homes in the stratums between The Rings. These were the sort of hardy folks that Ex liked best – a colorful bunch of miners, pilgrims, pirates, shippers, rebels, and vagabonds. They were called *Ring Runners*, to be taken as insult or compliment, depending on where it was uttered.

They'd acquired the name because they typically made a living by traveling between The Rings, through a process called *clipping*, which involved a series of very short, very dangerous anchor drops. Rather than rejoining rotation all at once, the anchor point antenna was angled so that the ship could ride out the dissipating speed on a tangent. At zero degrees, the ship would continue on the arc of the ring; any more than fifteen degrees resulted in the deatomization of the antenna, leaving the ship adrift.

Ex wedged a knife under a part of the anchor drive that was made of eight disks, lined up in a row, ordered according to size. It came loose with a pop. There was no need to be ginger with it. He had dozens of spares from previous times in which he'd invoked the CIR's provisional harborage law. It was illegal, of course, to lie about needing repairs, and occasionally, he'd stay long enough to have the local mechanics get around to replacing it. This piece, like every other component in the anchor drive, was essential, but it was easy to remove, and it was cheap. The whole engine would've been pretty affordable if it wasn't for the anchor point antenna, which housed no less than five molecules of duril.

There were exactly eleven molecules of duril on his ship: five in the anchor drive, three in the threaded power core, and one inside each of the three anchor rounds his mother left him. Together they were worth more than the rest of the ship by a factor best expressed through scientific notation. In fact, if you could form a line from the Earth to the Sun made of identical copies of his ship and still not afford a single mote. This was partially because his ship was worth next to nothing, but mostly because duril was by far the most expensive material in the known universe. Not only was it exceedingly rare and used in all threaded and anchor technologies, but it was the only substance that could not be derived from plex. The finest alchemical Sages had tried to transmute it for centuries – an entire blade on Veredos was dedicated to this pursuit – but so far it had proven impossible.

Unfortunately for Ex, he couldn't use any of these molecules in trade. He wasn't going to go very far without an anchor drive, the ship would be powerless without the threaded core, and not even the shadiest fence in the Centrian black market would touch an anchor round. The punishment for possession or distribution of these was a slating for Extinguishment.

The locked containers on the wall used to be opened by the presence of a specific thread, but that never worked with Ex, so he'd rigged them to open with a simple combination. He placed the part he'd removed in a container filled with similarly flawless parts. The container beside this one was filled with the same parts, but they were all scuffed, chipped, bent, or otherwise broken. He picked out a particularly nasty one and placed it on his anchor drive, sprinkling a few flakes of rusted metal around it for effect. Satisfied, he locked the containers and went to the cargo bay to gear up.

Minutes later, the ship reverberated with the sound of docking clamps. Ex arrived at the airlock wearing a duster with weighted coattails, hovering just above the heels of his brass-capped boots. The coat's oversized shoulder pads gave the wearer an imposing look and plenty of room to conceal weapons and contraband, but concealment was not his aim. His pistol was proudly holstered to the front of his thigh, and a bulky duffle bag, brimming with rifle stocks, rocket launchers, and photocasters was hoisted over his shoulder. If each weapon was only fired once, he'd still have enough ammunition for a small war.

Ex was planning a wholesale invasion.

A Warm Welcome

Ex stepped into the quarantine manifold, and the airlock rolled shut behind him. Four metal arms hung from the ceiling like half of a spider. The caution lights spun, and the first of the quatrapass scanner's arms came alive. It sketched his silhouette with precise movements. These things stripped you to the thread and instantly broadcasted your most intimate secrets across the universe through Gemini-links.

Arius had kept him from the eyes of these scanners at all cost as a boy. They entered CIR-controlled bases and cities through sewers and garbage chutes. But Ex had cleared numerous quatrapass checkpoints since his mother had abandoned him, and only the fourth scan ever gave him any trouble.

Doing his best to ignore the crew of technicians that monitored him from behind a dark pane of reinforced glass, Ex stared at the screen next to the airlock's heavy door. It was divided into four sections, each corresponding to a scan.

The first panel to illuminate was the pathogen check. Ex was not a man of shampoo. The scanner was immediately followed by a blast of sanitation mist. It persisted until he was declared perfectly sterile – in a good way.

The second beam began at his toes and bobbed towards his head, slowing as it peered into his skull. He wasn't concerned; none of the scanners would find anything of importance there – maybe a few scraps of neurobionics, but by no means anything illegal. To this particular eye, he was quite an outstanding citizen, with nothing more than a bad haircut to report.

The second panel lit up: *Genetic Stability Passed*, it read. Of the four tests, this was perhaps the most underhanded. It was a deep gene scan that had been made law under the pretext that it was necessary to check for genetic volatility. One species' dandruff could be another species' flesh-eating virus, and the CIR left it up to each race to ensure that all their leavings were inert.

But that was just the scan's pretense. Its true purpose was to verify that a subject's genome corresponded to their physical form and to assess the individual's physical prowess. The test compared a subject to a sampling of universal averages and rated their potency. A typical First Path Solarian like Ex usually ended up somewhere around the top 40 percentile.

First Pathers considered genetic enhancements to be in bad taste. Their only modifications were those deemed necessary for survival in the universe's inhospitable expanses. They'd stayed so close to their origins that there were those who still used the term 'human' when speaking of the First Path.

The test concluded that Ex was just .1% off from the exact universal average for First Path Solarians – scoring a perfect average might have actually made him seem less mundane.

Only the rudest techs displayed your rating after the test. It didn't offend Ex, but he could imagine what it must be like to some of the universe's less fortunate.

As if their lot in life weren't bad enough, they were reminded of their place at the bottom of the universal gene pool every time they disembarked.

Next was the *Illegal Corporeal Enhancements* (*ICE*) check, the fastest of the tests if you weren't Centrian. They were the only Solarian path that had an appetite for cybernetic body modifications. The practicality of the prosthetic was always second to the luster of its pistons; the only thing that mattered more was the history of the metal from which it was constructed. Pre-Plex Era minerals that had naturally formed on Earth were preferred, but really they could've come from anywhere in the Solar System – even from the moons that'd been spun out of the clouds of the Jovian planets like cotton candy and hardened into cold pills. Twice as important as the origins was whether or not the metal had seen battle. Scars and dents were preserved, and placards welded to chronicle the history of the piece. Centrians had fought more than one war without pretenses of any other purpose than to augment the value of scrap metal, and the wealthiest of them ICEd out like fridges on Pluto.

The list of which enhancements the CIR decided to ban was always changing, but Ex was no Centrian; he had no desire for body mods, so this scan never gave him trouble. His ZAIN-HUD, *Zero Artificial Intelligence Neural Heads-Up Display*, was in no danger of being blacklisted. It was more of a novelty than a weapon – a far cry from its military-grade cousins. Ex had acquired it much in the same way that teens acquire tattoos: a rebellious decision made against his mother's wishes. Arius always said that relying on such gadgets was a weakness, but it'd served him well on more than one occasion.

The sensor honed in on his mouth. The incisor that'd been chipped over twelve years ago had never grown back. It clung to the roof of his mouth as a jagged little reminder of the day before his mother abandoned him. So he'd had the whole thing removed and replaced with a shiny silver tooth made of perlite. It forced the scanners to do a 360 degree sweep of his head, but the denture itself wasn't illegal and far too common amongst runners to raise much suspicion.

Passed, read the panel, and Ex cleared his mind, waiting for the final scan to judge him.

In times past, a deep scan of an individual's genome was enough to conclusively establish their identity. But genetics had become too fluid in the present day. The only thing more permanent than genes was the thread that bound all of life, though even that was not immutable unless it had been properly knotted.

There was a poster on the wall, the only adornment of any kind in the chamber. *Don't end up a battery*, it read, and there were stacks of tiny metal rods, silently glowing with the inexhaustible energy of a former being's soul. It was with these images of threaded cores that the CIR promoted threadknots throughout The Rings, failing to mention that these intangible knots also prevented one from ever wielding the power of the Sages.

The fourth arm lowered its prying lens with a quick, sharp buzz. The iris contracted and widened many times per second, scanning limb to limb. In total, the process took about five seconds.

Ex kept his eyes on the fourth panel. Briefly, the display read zero. He could practically hear the technicians gasping behind the smoked glass. Tales of unthreaded sentients, wandering through the cold voids of space, were nothing more than ghost stories. Even the tiniest bacteria were stitched up with a fine string. A threadwidth of zero was by all understandings impossible.

Regardless of time, religion and science are indistinguishable at the ceiling of men's thoughts. When ancient Solarians were still bound to Earth, they believed the soul to be something contained entirely within the body, like a drop or sphere of anima that was both an intangible and omnipresent part of all living matter. Now it was understood to be more than a spark in the mind: it was a direct link to The Pool.

Many people believed that experiences were fed upwards along the strand to The Pool, but it was a known fact that will, in the form of raw energy, flowed down into the attached body. This power, by all accounts, was inexhaustible, and how quickly one could draw from this well was determined by threadwidth: the amplitude of a soul. The threads that fueled Sages' powers were no more visible than their ancestors' concepts, and their role had not changed. Life had always exerted itself on the universe by the force of will. It was simply more direct now.

The fourth arm moved again, slower this time. When it peered into his stomach, tiny fractions skittered across the display. These were glimpses of threads bound to the fauna in his intestines. The final results were the same. A knot couldn't be found since there was no thread to scan.

Several minutes passed before the airlock hissed open. Breathing the same recycled air for months, he'd nearly forgotten that his nose had a purpose besides alerting him of walls and closed doors in the dark. The scent was subtle, but it was blasted up his nostrils by the rushing air: something like kitchen gloves and lubricants. The door squealed as it rose. Apparently, the lubricant had not been used to grease its gears. Its stuttering rise quit just below Ex's shoulders with an unaffectionate moan.

"Step forward," a voice called from behind a curtain of light. It was gravel on the ears, like a man speaking an octave lower than his throat would allow, but it had a delightfully spongy-mint autex to it. He placed the language right away: Valoraphim. None of the major languages spoken throughout The Rings were as pleasant to his metaglot.

The metaglot was a cluster of carefully arranged neurons tucked away in the auditory cortex that had been embroidered into the human genome before the forking of The Paths. At the time its purpose was to facilitate communication between speakers of the various human languages. Geneticists then could have scarcely imagined that it would be one of the main reasons why Solarians would become the universe's most prolific species. The aliens Ex had encountered during his travels were more often descendants from Earth than any other world.

In addition to understanding, the metaglot granted a new sense, experienced as a disembodied taste and texture. This synesthetic sensation was called "autex," and it allowed the listener to identify the language spoken without affecting what was heard.

Ex found Valoraphim's minty autex refreshing. He crouched beneath the airlock, shielding his eyes from the light to catch a glimpse of the Valoraph. He wore a hooded white cloak, and although it lacked an insignia, it reeked of the CIR. The armored boots were a giveaway. They were also white, trimmed in cobalt and bearing only a few black scuffs across the toe.

Ex dragged the sack of weapons beneath the door and hoisted it back over his shoulder. He'd taken no more than a few steps into the room before it struck him as a strange place for an interrogation. There was a non-functional conveyor belt to his right and a set of scales to his left. Meshed rubber tiles were laid out over the bare metal floor. They made for good footing, but would've been a pain to sweep. That didn't seem to be a consideration around here. Sand filled most every nook. It'd been allowed to accumulate into small mounds along the edges.

"That's far enough," said the Valoraph. "State your business."

Ex reached beneath his duster.

The Valoraph's hand sprung from beneath his white cloak. It held a simple pistol, sleek and styleless, standard issue to Consortium officers. There were glints of white and blue metal in the shadow of his cloak running from chest to toe.

Ex slowly produced a business card.

The Valoraph lowered the gun as he took the card, but he didn't holster it. *Ex, Weapons Merchant*, it read.

"Mind the punctuation," said Ex. "I'm still actively a weapons merchant."

The card wasn't even cut into a perfect rectangle. "You've written this by hand," the Valoraph noted.

"Should I've used a foot?"

The Valoraph tipped back his hood with muzzle of his gun, revealing a clean-shaven head. The sharp blue shards floating in the gray of his irises were too vibrant for a Solarian. Other than this, he appeared human.

Valoraphs were a strange race for many reasons, but none as curious as their external resemblance to First Path Solarians — too similar to attribute to chance. The most reliable way to identify them was to peer into their ears. They had a small ring of muscle that allowed them to shut their auditory canal, but it wasn't something you could check without invading their personal space.

They were much easier to spot if they were royalty. Valoraphs of royal blood had lavish wings — the purer the blood, the larger the wings. Their brilliant white feathers could be made soft as down or hard as ferrekondite.

It was as if they'd modeled themselves in the image of angels, but they'd looked this way long before their first contact with men from Earth or their religious beliefs. Even to this day, only a handful of Solarians had been permitted entry to the palaces and temples on the ruins of their holy planet, Miraval. It'd taken a thousand years of intense genetic manipulation to achieve their current forms; their original appearance was kept secret to all but the high historians of their own race.

"Do you know what I am?" asked the Valoraph.

"An *Executioner* of the CIR," Ex replied. He could tell by the tattoo that framed his right eye. It occupied the greater portion of his forehead and cheek, resembling a large stylized eye that appeared to open when he blinked. All of the CIR's officers had tattoos like this, with more elaborate markings denoting a higher rank.

The CIR held the five inner rings in a vice grip and had been clawing at the free worlds of the stratums for centuries. However, this officer's rank indicated the presence of a full battalion of troops, and that would be unheard of, even for a large-scale perlite mining operation. Perhaps being assigned to such a remote place was some form of military punishment.

"That's *Executor*," corrected the officer.

"What's the difference?"

"There isn't any to an outlaw."

The door opened behind the officer and a couple of guards shuffled in. They looked more like miners with guns tucked into their elastic belts than proper soldiers. Even decades after completion, military training has an appreciable effect on a man's physique, a sort of permanent sturdiness. But these First-Pathers were just fluff and bone, men grown in micro-gravity, lazily breathing in fields of jellybeans that orbited them.

The meatier of the two rested the full heft of his arm on Ex's shoulder. A bulging ring of red flesh had welled up beneath the lip of his cap. It was two, maybe three sizes too small and had the emblem of the CIR drawn on its sallow crest in streaky black marker. He wore light blue maintenance overalls, the kind specifically designed to display every kind of stain as badges of hard labor. And his bore many such awards, though not earned by work, unless he was some sort of a hot dog technician. Amongst the hardened flakes of browning mustard and vinegary-red shadows of fallen ketchup was a nametag. *Chut*, it read.

"Alright, runner. Just take it easy, and this'll go a whole lot smoother," said Chut. His tongue flopped about his mouth like a fat trout as he formed words in a clumsy brand of Outer Ring Solarian. This happened to be Ex's dialect as well, so his stupid voice had no autex.

Ex decided to dislike him straight away.

The other guard, thin only by comparison, held out his arms, waiting for Ex to hand him the sack of weapons. He was cap-less, and had a swirly-banged haircut that made him look like a giant toddler. His nametag read: *Ziff*.

"Valet service?" Ex dropped the entire weight of the bag on the man; he may have even pushed a little. Ziff went over backwards in a crash of magazines and grenades. A single hoot like a hiccup escaped Chut's aplomb. He trapped the rest of the laughter between his stomach and lungs.

One of the grenades stopped against the Valoraph's armored boots with a soft clink, but the he didn't even glance down. His gaze traded between Ziff and Ex, looking more disappointed than upset.

Having successfully swallowed his laughter, Chut gave Ex a quick pat down, as if it were even necessary. Seconds later he was pulling weapons out of the coat like a magician's assistant. Meanwhile Ziff began unloading the duffle bag. The contraband piled up on the scales and conveyor and spilled over to the floor.

"So, Chut, huh? Is that short for something?" Ex asked.

"Chutnik," he replied, as he reached for the pistol strapped to Ex's thigh. It was Arius' gun, and Ex didn't mean to react, but he couldn't help himself. Instinctively he snatched at Chut's wrist, stopping it just long enough for the officer to take note.

"Hand me that gun," said the Valoraph. Chut unfastened the latch on the holster and pulled the weapon out by its U-shaped clip. He held it like it was about to leak poison, shuffling over to the officer in short, quick steps.

The Valoraph cradled it in both hands, almost as if he were appraising its weight and craftsmanship. He turned the gun right-side up and flicked a switch, releasing the clip. It was full. "A perlite-lined magazine," he commented. "And this ammunition is the highest ballistic grade permitted by Consortium regulations." He was right – about the first round at least. He released the bullet from the clip, then a second and third.

Ex counted. He could only imagine what the reaction would be if the Executor saw the fifth bullet: the first of the three anchor rounds that were queued within the clip. He began to plan his course of action. There were guns and explosives all around him, but he had to be careful. One blast could set off a chain reaction that would punch a hole right through the bioark and certainly kill everyone in the room.

The Valoraph's thumb rested on the fourth bullet. Chut and Ziff went about their business completely unaware that they were just a finger-flick away from a life and death situation. Ex decided to take a sudden interest in a pistol Ziff was handling. "I really appreciate you boys doing inventory for me, but it's really not necessary," he said, taking the repeater from his hands.

It was enough to raise the officer's suspicions. The Valoraph set down the U-shaped clip and checked the magazine of this more orthodox weapon. "And what kind of a weapon merchant keeps all of his merchandise fully loaded?" he asked.

"One who cares about his customers, sir," Ex replied without hesitation. "A loaded clip with every purchase; that's my policy. Can I interest you in a rifle or two? I can get you and your men a heck of a deal on some really beefy pulse cannons... and have I told you about my Three-for-Thursday deal on photocasters? Is it Thursday today? Do you even have a Thursday around here?"

Ex went on until the Valoraph cut him off, "Yes, I can see you care a great deal about your customers." He cocked the clip-less gun, sending a chambered bullet into the air. "A loaded clip and a round in every chamber? Why, even the safeties are off..."

"I try," Ex shrugged. "Now take a look at this photocaster..." he said, pulling a photocaster rifle off the conveyor. The barrel was pointed straight at the Executor's nose. The Valoraph reached for his pistol, but Ex spun the photocaster around and presented it to him with a courteous smile. The officer snatched the rifle out of Ex's hands. "You see? Even though it lacks in firepower, it's a great deal lighter than its CIR counterparts, making it excellent for intra-ship defenses. It's got just enough punch to scorch a space-rat, but not enough to put a hole in your hull...”

The Executor unscrewed the barrel and peered into the rifle’s ignition chamber. “This photocell is cracked,” he said, shoving it back at Ex.

"Lucky you," said Ex. "That just means it's on sale..."

“A sale you say?” a voice suddenly interrupted. A man stood in the doorway taking up half of its height and all of its width. He wore an opulent three-piece suit, complete with a plaid weskit, stretched to the limits of the fabric. He entered the room, doing a bit of maintenance on the curls of his moustache with one hand while the other swung a cane. The jingle of coins filled the room as he walked. “Allow me to introduce myself, my fellow entrepreneur; I am Sheremy Bon Gallowatch, the humble mayor of this fine station, several hundred kilometers above the fair planet of Trisol. Let me be the first to welcome you to the Tresola system, so named by the Solarian pioneers that first settled it not but a couple of years ago, a crew of which, I am obliged to say, I was a member. We are honored to have you," all this he spoke in a single breath. He removed his tall hat and bowed as deeply as his suit would afford him. Ex heard the faint sound of fabric tearing, but he wasn’t sure if it came from Ziff digging into the duffle bag or the well-mannered gentleman's inseam.

The Executor stepped between him and Ex. “Mr. Gallowatch, just the man I was looking for. Did you authorize this runner's entry into the station?"

“This runner? You mean this well-to-do merchant?” replied Gallowatch, moustache a-flutter. “Of course! Now please permit me to extend him the common courtesy which commerce demands!” Gallowatch refused to pause for breath when he spoke. As a result, his protests typically tapered into a wheeze. His voice had a lot of neck to push through before it saw air. It oozed out thick as syrup with no autex. “Now, do you deal in wholesale, sir? I believe that I may be able to facilitate some sort of deal for you with one of our locals. Or perhaps I could interest you in establishing a permanent place of business within our booming community. Once we're beyond these unpleasantries, I urge you to come visit me in my office; we can discuss some truly prime pieces of real estate, right on the station’s main promenade...”

It was common for spacefarers, who'd spend most of their lives alone on ships without suitable social contact, to turn to history for a cultural identity. The practice was so common, in fact, that Solarians could dress up as cowboys, Spartans, Huguenots, or samurai without coming across as loons. Instead, they were labeled Bitplayers, which as far as divergent evolution is concerned was less of a Path and more of a rest stop. Ex had no idea what kind of character Gallowatch was impersonating, but he appeared to be interested in his business proposition.

“This is hardly the right time to broker business deals,” said the Executor. "

Clank, Gallowatch pressed his cane against the Valoraph's chest and strolled around him. “Pay no mind to Executor Zarfall here. He means well, but I’m afraid that proper Outer Ring hospitality is not part of the CIR's training.”

Executor Zarfall batted the cane away. "I'm beginning to lose my patience, Mr. Gallowatch. And you!" he pointed at Chut. "Will you just remove his coat already!"

Chut pawed at different parts of the duster, trying to figure out the process of disrobing another man. Ex raised his arms to help, and Chut managed. He took the coat by the cuff of one sleeve and gave it a few shakes. A throwing knife flicked out of a pocket and hit him on the forehead, grip-first.

"Always think before you shake, Thumbs," said Ex as if imparting great wisdom.

After a few minutes of cooperative effort by all five men, Ex was finally disarmed. "Are we done here? I'm getting thirsty," Ex yawned.

It spread to Chut first. His buttery chin slackened to a breathy yawn. Ziff was next, escalating the yawn to full-on pandiculation. Gallowatch indulged as well and begged their pardon. Zarfall tightened his lips and his eyelids, half-shut, began to tremble. He held out as long as he could before turning aside and having a short, silent yawn.

Ex watched him closely; he knew that Valoraphs didn't yawn. Yawning was an Earth thing, traceable along the planet's evolutionary chain as far back as lizards and arguably insects. But Valoraphs didn't yawn; not a single creature from Miraval yawned, which meant Zarfall was a half-breed Valarian.

Valarians were a mysterious blend of Solarians and Valoraphs that had sprung out of the chaos of The Extinguishing. No one knew exactly how they'd come to be. Solarians and Valoraphs could not successfully mate – at least not by any scientific definition of the word *successful*. Yet Valarians could mate with either Solarians or Valoraphs, and the offspring would always be Valarian. They were formidable physical specimens, not quite able to survive in the void of space like a Valoraph, but far more resilient than a First Path Solarian. The Starfarer's Strand remained intact in their genome, allowing them to adapt to new environments like their Solarian progenitors. They'd kept a functioning metaglot as well.

From a population of thousands after The Extinguishing, Valarians had multiplied into the millions, which was still exceedingly rare on a universal scale, yet this was not the first Valarian Ex had met.

The Valoraphs, which made up their other half, found these hybrids distasteful, but they were known to be fastidious about their genetics. The Solarians considered them just another Path of their own species. After all, they were far more human than Polyhapterans, even more human than some heavily modded Centrians, and certainly more attractive than most Eidolans. Next to Dicots, they may've very well been the closest thing to The First Path.

In the end, even Ex's belt had been confiscated. He was lucky to have kept his brass-capped boots, but it wasn't safe to go barefoot through the bioark's rusting streets, and they weren't about to give him a pair of courtesy slippers. He surveyed his equipment, scattered about the room. "Say... can I have my coat back or is that a weapon too..." he asked.

"I see no reason why to detain your garments, good sir," Gallowatch said, and the Executor reluctantly agreed. When Gallowatch handed him the duster, its tail snapped towards the floor, but Ex made sure it didn't strike. He threw an arm into the coat, followed by another, stepping to the exit.

"Wait!" Gallowatch called out. Ex paused for an instant. "Might I have the pleasure of your name," he graciously inquired.

"Name's Ex," he declared.

"And your surname?" Gallowatch prodded.

"Rey," he added and closed the door behind him.

"Ex Rey?" Gallowatch repeated, scratching beneath his hat. "Well don't worry, sir! I will insure that your merchandise is well taken care of!" he called out, but Ex was already gone.

"There! Now you see what you've done, Zarfall!?" Gallowatch grumbled. "That's no way to treat a well-to-do merchant. It's simply no way to do business, sir."

"Mr. Gallowatch," began Zarfall, "do you know why I've been an Executor for over 20 years?"

"Are you asking why you've been passed up for promotion so many times?" Gallowatch attempted to redirect the question.

"It is because I do my job well. That is what the CIR appreciates above all else: efficiency."

"Well, you're quite efficient at stifling the station's commerce."

"You have your prerogative, and the CIR has its own. My job is to ensure that the Consortium's operations on this planet run smoothly, and that's what I intend to do. I ask that you show me faith, but remind you that I don't require your approval," Zarfall said producing a datatab from beneath his cloak. He reviewed the information from Ex's scan.

Gallowatch took firm hold of his felt lapel. "Mr. Executor, please understand that I've been a businessman for many years as well, a profession I happen to be quite good at…"

"I'm fully aware of your past, Mr. Gallowatch," Zarfall said, without looking up from the datatab.

"As this enterprise's chief investor, my responsibilities are also to the base, the planet, and the financial welfare of its inhabitants. Perhaps a bit more cooperation…"

"My orders are to protect this station and the planet it orbits," the Executor interrupted. "They made no mention of its inhabitants or their financial welfare, and they are quite explicit." He turned to Ziff and Chut and dismissed them with a hand gesture. Once they were gone, he sealed the door and handed the datatab to Gallowatch. "Here are your *merchant's* quatrapass results," said Zarfall. "The same results you should've carefully reviewed before granting him entry to the station."

"Unlike you, I don't need four scanners to read a man. I just need to look in his eyes," said Gallowatch.

"I'm not sure this is a man at all," said Zarfall.

Gallowatch glossed over the glowing display in compliance, but he'd never been a fan of quatrapass scanners. Ever since they'd given his magnanimous physique a failing grade, he knew they couldn't be trusted. A tiny bead of information caught his squinty eyes. "Is this what you're fussing about?" he asked, pointing at a scan of Ex's jaw. Nestled between a row of otherwise unremarkable teeth, sat an incisor coated in perlite.

Zarfall snatched at the datatab from Gallowatch's hands. "When you've scanned as many runners as I have, you come to realize that they fancy shiny teeth as jewelry. If I started detaining everyone with a capped-tooth, I may as well resign my command and put up a dentist's shingle.   Compared to others of his breed, this one is a fairly typical physical specimen. His threadwidth, however, is an entirely different matter: a perfect zero."

"When I was just a boy, my mother used to tell me spook stories about *vacants*," said Gallowatch. "Never thought a serious man like you would actually believe them. The poor chap's threadwidth must've been too low for the scan."

"I'm well aware of how preposterous it sounds, but I personally calibrate the system every morning. I guarantee it's sensitive enough to pick up traces of pig-thread from the ham sandwich you had for lunch," said Zarfall.

"Actually I had soup," replied Gallowatch. "And according to my intelligence, there isn't a rib or snout of pork to be had in this entire galaxy."

"My point is that I could get a higher reading from a jar of ash than that man," said Zarfall. "Not to mention that without a thread, I couldn't confirm his identity or the presence of a knot."

"I still don't see what you're so worked up about," said Gallowatch. "You said his other tests were normal. No pathogens, average genetics, and the ICE check is clean, nothing but an antiquated ZAIN-HUD — there's certainly no corona... not that he could use it without threadwidth anyway..."

Zarfall was not amused. The way Gallowatch spoke of coronas, as if they were trivial contraband, was proof of his ignorance. It was this microscopic crystal and 42 molecules of duril, embedded in a man's mind, that restored The Way to The Will. "If he's what he appears to be, we have nothing to fear from him. But if he is a Sage and has somehow discovered a way of masking his thread, he might have devised a way to hide his corona as well. In that case, he could likely crush this old ark from the outside with a thought. It'll be more of an inconvenience for him to destroy the station while he's in it. Either way, it's better to keep him under close surveillance, so we can react if he decides to reveal himself."

"Reveal himself? How lewd," said Gallowatch. "But I'm sure you're worried about nothing. Worse comes to worst, you could always unleash that beast you keep caged down in the hold. Besides, my gut tells me we can trust Mr. Rey."

"Well my mind disagrees, and I'm afraid this is a case of quality over quantity," Zarfall replied.

"I'd like to see that brain of yours digest the Mohmish bitter-brack soup I had for lunch..." Gallowatch muttered on his way to the door.

Airlocks and Alleyways

Ex entered the bioark's main dome, a yawning cavern of corroded metals and exposed circuitry. The swirling smells offered a unique stench with each breath, combinations of sizzling meats, pesticides, stagnant water, smoke, garbage, and industrial cleaners. It was the kind of bittersweet musk that clings beneath your fingernails, the smell of an unkempt station, bleeding slowly, rotting away into a hollow shell of derelict memories. Ex felt right at home.

He turned onto a rising causeway that would take him over the bristling city to the other side of the ark. Even at this elevation, the buildings loomed over the narrow street and choked the metal sky. Space was a rare commodity in space – one of irony's greatest indulgences.

Viscous liquids dripped from the vaulted ceiling, collecting in puddles and running in rivulets over the side of the causeway. Whispers of a drain, recycling the precious fluids, could be heard far below. The occasional hiss of a distant airlock added to the soft susurrus. Rumblings of uncounted engines and crackling complaints of exposed circuitry served as accompaniment.

The pulsing rhythm of the ark's power plant reverberated through the metal and concrete of the causeway. Its decidedly mechanical droning set Ex at ease. There was no soul in it, no thread twisted into silent servitude. He'd never told anyone, not even Arius, but he could feel the will of a threaded machine; some threaded cores seem to yearn for their task, while others carried on in quiet desperation. This was state-of-the-art slavery, not of flesh, but of spirit.

Threaded machines were capable of doing anything that could be done by any other means, and many things that couldn't. As the CIR saw it, these machines replaced the whims of Sages with unwavering code and their fragile bodies with unbreakable duril. During the Extinguishing, the worlds along the rings had been plastered with ads promoting this belief, the most iconic of which featured a single, towering metal cylinder. Beneath it was the text: *Sages are Safer in Silver*. Duril was often referred to as *silver*, sometimes *sage silver*, perhaps because of these ubiquitous images.

Threaded cores were typically made of ferrekondite encasing a few molecules of duril. The greater the threadwidth contained, the more molecules were needed, but the only alternative was organic cores, which were both highly controversial and prone to all the weaknesses of life.

Duril was the only nonorganic substance in existence that could bear a thread. It was the perfect spiritual vessel. Duril didn't eat or get sick or suffer the draw of wanderlust. It held its shape in a perfect void as well as the center of a star. Only an anchorspace impact could sever its subrostral bonds. Quietly and unconditionally, it set the endless power of Will to desired purpose.

The Consortium's propaganda was not far from the truth.

Ex was leaning against the causeway's railing, peering down at the smoky black city below when a hatch suddenly opened in the street behind him. He'd assumed it was a manhole, leading to the facility's septic system, but now there were a pair of large, squinty eyes staring back at him from just beneath the lid. The eyes drew tighter as the hatch continued to rise until the entirety of the creature's bulbous head was exposed. It was a Mohmil in a baggy jumpsuit.

Mohmils were a race that commonly drew comparisons to moles thanks to their appearance and entrances like this one. Their bodies were mostly covered in fluffy brown fur, giving them misleading girth. It grew into a long, wild mane along the edges of their bare faces. Their tails and paws were also hairless. They'd evolved from scavengers to tinkerers with dexterous feet that made Solarian hands look like hoofs.

The two stared at each other from across the wide sidewalk. The creature's eyes were comfortably shut. Ex could barely see a sliver of black and white beneath their heavy lids. Mohmish eyes were very large; they occupied the greater portion of their faces and were highly sensitive to light. Beneath them sat a pointed nose with a tip that looked as if a black olive had been skewered on it. Lower still, was the critter's mouth. Mohmils commonly suffered from overbites, a desirable trait to their alien aesthetic.

This fellow had a couple of unimposing molars that barely crept out to the corners of his mouth. It was obvious that he was forcing back his chin to emphasize their protrusion, but Ex wasn't about to call him on it. He reckoned that this fellow could use all the help he could get. Not because he was small, or weak, or because Ex found his species visually displeasing – not by any means. It was just that his whiskers were positively pitiful; you could hardly call them stubble. There was nothing more valuable to a male Mohmil than his whiskers. No amount of jewelry or fine clothing could replace them, for their whiskers only grew during times of great prosperity, and it was rumored that only virile males could grow them in abundance – a piece of gossip which Ex did not care to confirm or debunk. Long whiskers were the mark of a prosperous businessman or prodigious craftsman. Apparently, this particular Mohmil was neither. Ex couldn't blame the little puddle-hopper though; life in the stratums was not lent to whisker growing.

The Mohmil extended a paw, and Ex shook it. "Oh, hello please. My name is Moh-La," the creature squeaked.

Ex opened his mouth to return the greeting, but Moh-La went on. "So-yo, the man-ship in dock is you own, ya?" He spoke in broken Outer-Ring with the charm of an ungreased gear.

Ex suspected that Moh'La had stepped out of the sewer. Greasy stains covered his lint-gray jumpsuit, but it was difficult to tell if the mélange of smells had grown worse in his presence. The air around him was salty, as it was around most Mohmils. Traditionally, they cooked their meats in small burrows on the side of dunes in the salt deserts of their homeworld. Abroad, their methods had become synthetic, but their products were no less salty. "You know, you can speak to me in Mohmish. I'll understand you," said Ex.

"Not know-ah. Grow on ship; git smart here," replied Moh-La. "Ya, yo, I check about you own anchor drive... it get fry pre' bad, ya. No worry, ya? I get you hook up so goo with a pre' goo' part, ya?"

Ex pondered the meaning of *pre goo*. He hoped it meant *pretty good*. "Yeah, I don't know what happened. I guess it just sorta blew up on me," he said with a stupid chuckle.

"Yeah, it fry pre' goo,' you not go no ways with that. Bo-no worry, I hook you up so good… take about, umm, four days or so…"

Ex's metaglot was beginning to decipher Moh-La's unique dialect. A strange autex crept into his words, like unsweetened cotton candy, if such a thing were possible. *Four days to replace a dimensional disk array… good thing I'm not planning on staying*, Ex thought to himself. "Oh I see," he said.

"You don't need to worry, though, I'll give you this…" Moh-La produced a small card from within his fur and handed it to Ex. *One night's free stay: Luin's Famous Intergalactic Tavern*, it read.

"Luin's my cousin. He runs a good place. You can stay there… I'll arrange everything up for you, so rest easy, alright?"

Ex nodded, "About how much will this cost me, any idea? I don't have a clue what's wrong with the darned thing. I don't even know what it did. Was it important?"

The little fluff-ball practically sprouted a new batch of whiskers right then and there. After wiping the drool from his meager chin, Moh-La gave his estimate, "This part of the engine is pretty tricky. I have to build the part from scratch. Can't say now, but I like you, so I'll hook you up extra good; say liiike… twenty-thousand Consortium credits? I also accept plex."

Ex had always relied on the ignorance of strangers, and apparently so had this fellow. He knew the little rat had a replacement part sitting in his shop right now and that the repair should only take a couple of minutes. Moh-La's price was irrelevant, what mattered was his time estimate. It meant that he didn't intend to replace the part until he'd given his cousin four days of business; hopefully he'd stay out of Ex's engine room until then.

"Alright that sounds fair," Ex agreed. "But you're gonna have to point me in the direction of a bank 'cause I'll need to make a transaction."

"Bank? No bank here; only depository," replied Moh-La. "It's at the end of this road, but you won't be able to make a transaction there."

Moh-La left the way he came, seemingly in a rush to pretend to work, and Ex continued his walk. He went down the broad causeway towards the heart of the old city. The buildings reached high into the vaulted steel sky, growing tallest near the center where the ceiling permitted. It was hard to imagine a time when the ark's population warranted such a metropolis. The once bustling streets were empty now, lined with litter and layered with fine black dust. But the city was not entirely deserted. Figures darted about the shadows, and flickering lights dotted the broken windows.

There were enough drips sputtering around the dome to look like lazy rain, but the causeway was gently sloped. Only a single shallow puddle had formed as far as Ex could see. He stepped in it with full confidence, and his boot slid across the gelatinous surface, never reaching the floor. He ended up in an awkward split, watching wide-eyed as the puddle popped up into a jiggling cube. "Bruhuw waw hoh!" it muttered. Tiny vibrations coursed through its surface, until the dirt and grime from Ex's footprint was erased. Its corners twisted and shrank into its body. A face emerged from its top, and as its features inflated, the rest of the cube shrank. It was dominated by a bulbous nose and a thick moustache that lacked the articulation of hair. Atop the nose sat a pair of large eyebrows to match the moustache. "Oh, I'm terribly sorry. That's probably my fault for sleeping in the street. But I couldn't help myself. The drip around here is so wonderful; I can't resist a good brack. Know what I mean?" said the puddle.

"Uh..." was all Ex managed, dragging his legs together until their angle was comfortably acute.

"What am I saying? Of course you do. You're mostly saltwater too!" said the puddle, shuffling after him.

"Look, I'm sorry I stepped on ya, but there's no need to get ugly," said Ex, hurrying his pace.

"But I meant no insult!" replied the cube, struggling to keep up. "Perhaps we've gotten off on the wrong foot, or rather 'under' the wrong foot if you pardon my gelatin humor. Let's reset our acquaintance. Hello, I'm Squelliot, pleased to meet you."

"That's fine," said Ex, slowing down a bit. The autex of Skwellachi was like the scent of freshly cut pine blended into the texture of melted chocolate, just before it hardened. It welled in the ducts where hearing turned to smell. It was too pungent for most Solarians, but always gave him a certain sense of comfort. Skwellachi was one of the first languages his metaglot had acquired, even before his first memory. What he knew of them came from his mother's stories.

She'd told him of his Skwell nurse, Sarkech. The Skwell's approach to childcare had made them very popular amongst Solarian mothers. They'd absorb the child and carry them within their gelatinous form. Temperature and pressure were carefully regulated as they nurtured the child with specifically tailored concoction of nutrients, all while allowing in sights and sounds from the outside – very much like transparent wombs.

Squelliot waited politely before speaking again, "I believe that this is the junction of the conversation when you're supposed to tell me your name..."

"It's Ex."

"Like the letter?"

"No, like the name."

"Charming," said Squelliot. "Well, Ex. I must warn you. The path you walk now is likely to end in a prison cell..." Ex stopped. "Yes, this causeway leads directly to the core facility, which is swarming with guards. They don't appreciate tourists snooping around down there, so I suggest you take your constitutional elsewhere. The hired guns under the station's employ are straight from Centrias, big lads with lots of weapons – always looking for a reason to use them."

"Is that so?" remarked Ex, continuing his walk.

"It is so, and more still," resumed Squelliot. "Despite what this ark's condition suggests, the reason it's so deserted is because most of its inhabitants have been incarcerated, deported, or by other means deposed since the CIR moved in. All part of their plan to *clean up* the station, as the Executor puts it. Lucky for me, his definition for *cleaning* includes no actual maintenance, and puddles of goo may lie where they wish."

"Alright well, thanks for the information *Squidlio*, I 'preciate it, but you can turn back the other way now," said Ex.

"Well, I would truly like to, Sir, but..."

"But what?" Ex demanded.

"There's a bit of me under your boot that I'd love to have back."

Ex didn't ignore Squelliot's request, but he ignored his advice, kicking a can as he went. If anything, the Skwell's warning had only made him more curious. The causeway widened as it descended. All the lights in this sector worked, less trash littered the street, and there wasn't an immediate need for an umbrella. A small drone darted in front of Ex and swept up the can he was about to kick. "What the…" said Ex. The little robot gave a tinny chime and picked up the few bits of trash around him, trying briefly to scoop up his boots with its wiry brush. Ex resisted the urge to punt it.

His attention fell on the facility that sat at the foot of the causeway. It was a sturdy, square structure riveted to the walls of the dome, no bigger than on large vault. The open grounds that separated it from the rest of the city were brightly lit by a flight of lights that hung from the sky on bare cables of varying lengths. There were the usual security measures: automated turrets, motion sensors, and robotic sentries, but the number of guards was pure overkill. Some were engaged in basic military exercises, marching roughly in unison, handling hand-me down photocasters, but the majority sat on crates and leaned on inactive turrets.

Ex crept down the sloping street for a closer look. These were not Consortium troops. They carried themselves with the swagger of the local stock. Their only apparent connection to the CIR was the crest on their caps. It would appear that Squelliot had embellished a bit. Only a few men smelled of Centrias, and although a single Centrian was one too many for Ex's likings, he'd happily take a dozen of them over a single one of the CIR's Nyrceff soldiers.

A couple of men leaning on the mesh fence caught Ex's eye. Their gruff voices carried in the static air. These men were different from the rest not just by accent and pedigree, but by profession. They were prime examples of Centrias' chief export: mercenaries. Everything about them reeked of it. Their battle-scarred rifles were heavily modified, their caps were cocked at insubordinate angles, and they made no attempt to look busy.

Centrias was a degenerate rock, no more than a day's flight from the Fourth Ring. The dominant language of the planet was a dialect of Solarian, distinguished by its disregard for grammar and creative use of profanities. On Centrias, spitting was a form of punctuation. Their disdain for etiquette had drained the venom out of vulgarities, forcing them to speak proper forms of Solarian when they meant to offend.

Ex ignored the pair of mercs as they approached. For the time being, he was more concerned with the architecture. Old Arks like these typically had only one way into the storage facility buried within their core, and it was common for that entrance to be located along a wall rather than in the center of the main chamber;

it was more defensible that way. Ex was fairly certain this was that entrance, but there were only two ways in. The first was the front door, which was the focus of too many eyes and gun barrels to be worth considering.

The second was the station's main ventilation duct, wheezing as it drew in the core's stagnant air through one hanging shaft and fed it recycled breaths through another. Before snaking high over the hub, the drooping duct rested on the rooftop of a nearby building, which slumped beneath its weight. *Well that's a disaster waiting to happen,* smiled Ex. He took a quick count of the shafts that hung from the duct as it ran from its rickety crutch.

The mercenaries stopped a few meters from the fence. The larger of the two brought a metal arm out from beneath the duster draped over his broad shoulders. The appendage shone brightly in the promenade lights. It was all pistons and wires, no paint or frills. The historic placard on the shoulder identified this merc as a man of means. The fully articulated hand that extended from its elbow joint made it a Moddrick Arm, normally used to operate a two-handed weapon with a single appendage. The man used it to simultaneously scratch his chest and reposition his cigar with one arm –the closest that this contraption came to flexing.

One of Ex's earliest memories was personally meeting the very famed bounty hunter the arm was named after: Kron Moddrick. Today, he was the Viceroy of The Second Ring, but back then he was just a drop chart dealer, freshly retired from the bounty hunting business. It was for that very purpose that Arius had risked landing on a planet so near to the Third Ring.

The heavy smog that blanketed Centrias was not a byproduct of industry or traffic. There were factories whose only purpose was to churn out acrid clouds like black cotton; it saved on cigarette expenses. You weren't likely to catch a Centrian off-world without some kind of smoke – cigars, pipes, or back-mounted tanks packed with fumes, fed by tubes like tusks into full-face masks.

Arius landed the ship on the tallest skyrise, stretching high into the Centrian night. The glow of the dense city below burned through the smoke in flashes of deep color. Only a few buildings, poked out of the clouds, offering penthouse views of the lusty stars.

The air at this altitude was thin, too light to hold smog. Dark clouds roiled below, breaking like waves on the buildings and yielding glimpses of neon signs at their nadirs. "Waxed Lips: Five kees a night," read an ad in bright red cursive; a woman's silhouette rested on the curves of an upper lip. "Piston pythons," read another; this one was curled with mechanical rhythm by a metal arm lit in amber. "Never fly alone," read a tall rectangle in purple lettering; the word "Neuro" was written in a marquee just above it.

The roof access door had a lock with no keyhole. The peephole that sat just over Arius' head lit up with the image of a blue eye. It spoke: "Well, if it isn't Mavenbolt's prettiest pupil. To what do I owe the pleasure?"

"I need a chart, Moddrick," said Arius.

"If you're here to shop, what's the gun for?" asked the voice.

Amongst many things, Arius was a Sage. Her thoughts were deadlier than bullets, even the ones at the end of the U-shaped clip that hung conspicuously from her holster. "A girl's gotta accessorize," she said.

The eye looked down at the pistol, focusing on its firing mechanism. "Nice pistons."

"Thought you might like those," replied Arius. The tumblers popped, and the door slid open.

Arius knew where she was going; Ex had no idea how. The building was a maze of hallways with unmarked, concrete walls. Some stairs and turns later, they arrived at a large corner office that continued the motif of porous cement and bare fluorescent lighting. The windows were narrow like in a gun emplacement, too high for Ex to see anything but stars. A large mass of a man huddled behind a metal desk in the center of the room. "So what model of drop chart can I interest you in this lovely night?" he asked.

If Centrians weren't cussing, it meant they didn't like you. But there was a child in the room with a Sage for a mother, so Arius decided not to take offense at his lack of profanity. "Don't waste my time, Moddrick; you know they're all the same damn thing."

Moddrick took folders and schematics from his desk with all four hands and stood. If he had hair, it would've likely brushed the ceiling. One of his eyes telescoped out and pored over the files with a bit of light. It ratcheted back into his socket as he approached. Aside from his arms, most of his body seemed to be made of flesh, which was a pretty low ratio for a Centrian, but it was impossible to tell with the coat he was wearing. The sleeves were torn off at the shoulder, so you could see the pistons and wires that drove his arms, but the rest of his body was covered from the neck down. He could be all gears and hydraulics under there, and that would put him ahead of the modding-curve. One thing was certain: he didn't look like a Sage – not that Sages look any particular way, but Ex'd always had a knack for spotting them, and this guy didn't smell like one. "They're not the same thing," he began. "Maybe they were back in The Extinguishing, but these beautiful balls will shepherd you past The Seventh Ring, where things get dense."

Arius batted the paper aside. "How much?" She was in boots, and he was in flip-flops, but looking up, she could only see the bottom plane of his chin. It sat at the base of his long face like a giant tin hoof.

"50,000 Kees; friend price," he smiled down at her. His teeth were checkered silver and gold.

"For that much plex I could practically buy a whole new anchor drive – drop chart included," said Arius.

"Yeah, but who ya gonna buy it from? The Consortium?" he spat. "I'm the only chart dealer in the stratum."

"Maybe I'll get Tsubasa to build me one."

Moddrick's jaw stamped out a laugh. "Good luck. Last I heard, that old geezer's on Eidola, out past the Fifth. It'll take you a decade to get there if you have to stick to the rings and channels," he said, waving a schematic. "Besides, what's 50,000 pKgs of plex to a big bad Sage like you? You can go sit on a star if you run out."

Arius pinched the bridge of her nose. A chair gained opacity behind her. She sat with crossed legs. "How fast is the mail here?"

"This is Centrias. There are more ring runners than stars. Deliveries are fast enough."

"Good. I'm waiting on an alimony check. Haven't gotten one yet, but I figure I'm overdue. I hope The Consortium doesn't track me down first. They're getting better, you know... stepping in fresher tracks each day."

The bottom eyelid of Moddrick's left eye raised one millimeter. "Fine, 40 kees."

"20, or I'll break those arms off and tickle your insides with 'em."

"Well," said Moddrick, "I'd cry if I had tear ducts." His arms lowered, and his metal elbow-hands went limp in defeat. "Sometimes I think The Consortium was right to try to extinguish you glow-heads. Can't expect someone who can destroy a planet with a thought to abide its laws... or pay wholesale prices. Fine, I'll give ya a refurb for 20. If you end up hitting an asteroid in anchorspace and scatter your atoms across half a galaxy, remember it was because you decided to be cheap."

But that drop chart still hung in Ex's engine room, ferrying him across turbulent tracts of universe to this very bioark.

One of the Centrian mercenaries brought a finger to his ear and scowled at Ex. He turned half of his cigarette to ash and tapped his partner on the shoulder. The two marched off, spitting as they turned.

Who'd tugged their collars? Ex wondered. A glimmer of movement caught the corner of his eye — something glossy. It'd come from a high window of an otherwise abandoned building, but when he looked, there was nothing. It may've just been light glinting off the glass, but he didn't need any proof to know that he was being followed.

Wearing the look of a man that was arguing with himself and losing, Ex paced up the causeway. Once the parade grounds were out of sight, he crouched over an oily puddle and poked it to see if it was alive. When the ripples cleared, he flashed himself a smile. He was not a man of toothpaste, but his grin shone brightly in the murk. He cocked his head aside to get a better look at his silvery incisor. It glistened softly as he wiggled it back and forth with his tongue.

The causeway was a single, straight path in clear sight of countless elevated vantages. There was no way to lose his tail here, but Ex's brain was an idea factory, which in the absence of a better business bureau, had never had a recall. Without warning, he made a dash for the side railing and leapt blindly into the darkness below.

Skin, Scales, and Spirits

An hour later, Ex reemerged beneath the winking lights of a ramshackle storefront, nestled in the most heavily populated corner of the ark. The air here was thicker than on the causeway, and the smells were sturdier; they stood their ground against Ex's fanning hand. Above the entrance, three rusting metal plates had been welded together with bubbling scars to form a single sign. *Luin's Famous Intergalactic Tavern*, it read in large light bulbs, half burnt out and only a few matching in color.

It was clear that the sign used to read *Luin's Tavern*. It'd been split down the middle and patched together with a sheet of metal, bearing the words *Famous Intergalactic* in the majority of the sign's working lights.

He found the concept of a Mohmil operating a "famous intergalactic tavern" in such a remote star system hard to swallow. Ex prided himself on his knowledge of reputable bars. Arius had taken him to a handful of the best in the third and fourth stratums, to "get her Krebs on" as she'd say, a reference to a stage of cellular respiration that required druidic inclinations to give one damn about. A typical stop involved Arius quietly coaxing the hydroxyls from a beer directly into her brainstem, until her eyelids got comfortably heavy. On occasion, she'd dare the locals to drinking contests in order to drain them of their plex and information. Few men refused her challenges and none one ever bested her. She was as she appeared: a dainty flower, but one maintained by a druidic mastery that could easily split and fold alcohol into water and burps. Before they knew it, the men's eyes were bobbing like buoys in a bay of gin or whiskey, and she would collect whatever she cared. It was her charge, she claimed, to teach assorted cretins never to drink with a druid.

Since those times, Ex'd taken upon himself to visit most of the mentionable establishments she'd missed, yet he'd never even heard of this Luin or his tavern. Mohmils were better known for mixing poisons than drinks, but there was a fine line between the two.

He shrugged and stepped to the doorway, constructed in the same style as the sign above. The frame had been raised several feet, and the two doors that once provided a full seal for a Mohmish-sized doorway had been lifted a meter off the false-wood deck. They waved lazily in the synthetic breeze like saloon doors of times long past.

Ex tossed the hair from his face. A crooked smile exposed a gap where a sterling incisor once gleamed. He brought two fingers to his lips, kissed them gently, used them to hoist his pair, and kicked in the doors. They tore off the hinges and went crashing into the dim tavern.

The patrons stood still, and the music fell silent. His violent entrance had brought a moment of calm. All eyes were on the doorway, and there stood Ex. He leaned forward and tilted his head to ensure that a single slat of light fell across his eyes. Unimpressed, the bar returned to its usual clamor.

The place was lit for Mohmish eyes. Cigarettes glittered in the smoky air like fireflies. A good portion of the light came from a dusty jukebox that softly rattled out the jangling tones of Mohmish blues; Ex wouldn't soon admit that he recognized the nervy 4-bar pattern of this particular classic: *Get, Grow, Show.* The tavern was packed, but there didn't seem to be many locals. The majority of patrons were Solarian, though Mohmils made a strong showing, seated up on the mezzanine, away from the runners that occupied the tables on the ground floor. Runner crews were fond of flashy patches and matching jackets. They belched and bellowed with faces of privateers, mercenaries, smugglers, and worse.

The men seated at the loudest table were covered in sand. There were seven altogether. Their uniform was a faded, black leather jacket with a large emblem on the back: a skull with a black asterisk on the forehead. *Blackstar* was written just above the crest in gothic font. Ex didn't recognize the name or symbol, but took note of the amount of cups piled before the crew.

A large group of Ikans occupied the neighboring table. The reptilians had claimed the best lit area for their own. Their forked tongues slithered silently from their scaly mouths. This was the way Ikans communicated with one another. They had no sense of hearing, but their eyes were amongst the sharpest of the sentients. There were very few outsiders who'd acquired their language of delicate gestures; the metaglot could deal with sign language, but Solarian eyes lacked the necessary acuity.

The men with the skulls on their jackets openly voiced opinions of their neighbors, and none were pleasant. They were smart enough to know they couldn't be heard, but were either unaware that Ikans could read a flapping lip from a hundred meters or were too deep in drink to care.

The stairs to the mezzanine were on the left. Ex could only make out the diamond-chain spirals of Midoran eyes at the shady table beneath the stairway. The opposite corner of the room was darker still and steeped in smoke. There lurked something large of indiscernible shape. It shifted just in and out of view.

Seating wasn't in short supply, but the room felt full. Nearly all of the Sentient populations of the fourth stratum were represented. Ex considered that perhaps the bar had not been falsely advertised. He scanned the room, looking for something wonderful – something that could justify the lengths the patrons had traveled to come to this dim bar. He concluded it was nothing that could be seen, but perhaps it could be tasted. He stepped over a fallen door and strutted to the bar.

There was only one stool without neighbors on either side. Ex took it and slapped the bar. "Yo, Keep!" he said in his gruffest tone, fighting for the bartender's attention with the other loud men. He glanced over at the couple of Mohmils repairing the doors he'd just broken. Centrian bars typically had real-time reconstruction systems that repaired windows, tables, stools, and doorways seconds after they were broken, but those were carried out by machines. Luin's bar had opted for a more organic system, but effective nonetheless. The Mohmils' skilled hands worked quickly, and the doors swung again.

Ex pounded the bar, sending vibrations along the length of the countertop and causing the other patrons' drinks to bounce, shake, and nearly spill. The Mohmish bartender rushed over to Ex, hoping to pacify the runner before his organic real-time reconstruction system was put to work again.

"O-Heh! More Solarian, huh?" the Mohmish tender's voice screeched like the high strings of a violin in the hands of an Ikani musician. The embroidery on his vest read: *Luin*, which Ex took to be a nametag rather than branding since the autex of his dialect tasted just like Moh-La's, and the other Mohmils working at the establishment could not rival his whisker length. He wore a pair of protective goggles and rubber gloves, the sorts one might use when handling hazardous waste. The ground behind the bar was raised to compensate for his mousy stature. He set a bowl of salt next to Ex in Mohmish tradition. "What drink you are liking?" he politely inquired.

"Whaddya got that could clean a hyperdrive?" asked Ex.

"You want clean for your engine, you talk to my cousin, Moh-La..." said Luin.

"Don't want clean for my engine," Ex replied. "Want drink for my mouth. What's the strongest you got?"

"Strongest drink?" grinned Luin. "No, that not for Solarian belly." He was a cunning salesman; now Ex had no choice but to stomach whatever was served to him.

"I'll have two!" said Ex before the Mohmil could offer alternatives.

Luin shrugged and ducked beneath the bar. Ex poked around the bowl of salt until he happened upon a peanut. Luin resurfaced, carefully balancing a steaming metal cup between a pair of wobbly tongs. He delicately set the drink on the counter.

Ex downed the entire thing, slammed it back down on the bar, and demanded his second. He was quite content with himself for having choked back the profane drink. For now he ignored the debacle that was brewing in his stomach and glanced around to see if anyone had taken note of his quaffing prowess. No one had.

Luin returned with another frothing cup of the same bubbling liquid. "Hey, you plan to pay for this, right? It's expensive drink!"

"No, I ordered it without any intention of paying," Ex replied. Luin scoffed at what he perceived to be distasteful Solarian humor and went to tend to a patron whose head had just struck the bar with the weight of nine pints.

Ex had no intentions of paying for the drinks, but he knew that if the truth was soaked in enough sarcasm, no one would believe it. He swirled his steamy drink and contemplated his next move. His attention fell back to the Ikans and their rowdy neighbors. He could read the Ikans' body language well enough to know The Blackstars were in danger.

Ikans were mostly tail, beginning at the base of their necks and running down the length of their backs before parting from the torso at the hips and doubling in length. Normally it dragged behind them, limp and motionless, but when they became agitated, the lifeless appendage engorged into a broad band of solid muscle. Their scaly hides would sculpt the contours of their long ribcages and narrow hips as the blood drained from the rest of their bodies. A blow from these tails was enough to crack a man's spine through conventional armor, but the Ikans' bite was even worse. Thin as their jaws were, they could crush a Solarian skull like a soft-boiled egg. And even deadlier were the pincers they had for hands, which sliced through bone without effort.

Civility was one of the Ikani culture's defining traits, but this particular crew didn't look very diplomatic. If their traditions had any analogue to machismo, they were brimming with it. The light blue and gray feathers that normally grew on their backs had been plucked down to a slender stripe, running from the top of their heads down to the tips of their tails. Most Ikans grew these small feathers all over their body, but only the women kept them. The manlier the Ikan, the fewer feathers he'd have, but to go entirely deplumed was akin to nudity. In Solarian terms, these Ikans were traipsing about the cosmos in loincloths.

Just as things were getting interesting between the lizards and the Blackstars, a large form emerged from the darkest corner of the room, and the gloom came with it. Ex watched carefully, but kept his nose pointed at his drink. The smoke dispersed as the figure came out from beneath the cover of the mezzanine into the light. Its body was armored in smooth, sable chitin. A small turquoise-and-gold trinket, dangling from a spike on its head, provided the only glimmer of color. It crept on the points of five segmented appendages, ending in scythe-like tarsi that made the creature appear as if it were kneeling. Its plated head swayed to avoid the mezzanine's edge.

Its many sharp teeth were clear. Ex could see the veins and nerves inside them as the creature loomed its hissing jaw by his ear. Bitter cold breath raked against the skin of his neck, but Ex continued to play with his drink. He drained it in a decisive stroke, turned the cup over, and displayed it on the counter.

"What you do there?!" Luin rushed over. He snatched up the cup and gave the bar a furious wiping. "This drink ruin the bar!" But there wasn't a mark on the false wood; Ex had drank the last drop.

Luin turned to the creature to avoid Ex's smug smile. It ordered *A Solarian Special* with a strained but strangely feminine voice, perhaps the result of forcing the Solarian language through such an alien palate. Luin scampered off and stuck his nose into a tiny freezer that was stashed under a couple of crates. When his reach failed him, he dove into the icebox. He reemerged with a bit of frost on his whiskers, holding an unassuming brown box.

Ex loudly demanded another drink, but he was dying to see what a *Solarian Special* was. Judging by the look of the beast, he imagined it was more likely to be made *of* Solarians than *for* them.

"Just you wait for me!" Luin snapped as he ducked under the counter. Ex could hear him tearing the box open. He stretched up to take a peek, but only saw Luin's tail whipping about. A full minute later, Luin emerged with an exquisite crystal cup in which a mound of soft white marshmallows were arranged, garnished with a mint leaf. "Here you are, madam..." said Luin. A boa-like tongue descended from the creature's jowls and delicately ingested a marshmallow through a fanged orifice at its head. Slimy waves of peristalsis pushed the little puff up the exposed esophagus; Ex found the process decidedly unappetizing.

Soon enough, the barkeep returned with another cup of his special brew; Ex was actually getting to like the stuff. Luin flipped up his safety goggles for a better look at Ex's neighbor. A bucktooth grin came across his face and whiskers fluttered beneath his nose.

"Not from around here are you?" a sensual voice whispered to Ex in icy wisps. It sent shivers down his spine that nearly shook him off the stool. The beads of cold sweat turned to frost on his neck. He was certain it was that creature again, and as sweet as its voice was, he wasn't about to forget the gruesome black mandible that spoke it.

Ex wondered if the words came from the tiny mouth at the end of its serpentine tongue, or if this creature had learned to shape the phonemes of the Solarian language with that beastly instrument. He almost poured his drink into his lap as he turned.

There sat an angel with satin blue skin, lightening gently where it held the greatest curves. Her eyes were sapphire, with softly glowing silver glints to match her long, silken hair. The muscles of her upper back wrestled like snakes and cats beneath her taut skin, still settling into their current form. She rested her chin in the palm of her hand and fixed her gaze directly into the pit of his eyes. The points of her ears poked through the cascade of her hair, rising slightly as her face broadened in a smile.

Ex splashed his drink into the back of his throat with sufficient force to trigger a gag reflex. "What... are you?" he asked, choking.

She set her head at a playful tilt. "I'm sorry. I had you figured for an experienced runner..."

"Experienced enough to spot a thief!" Ex said as he snatched her slender tail out of one of his coat pockets.

She pulled back the tail and used it to cover her mouth as she giggled. "Well, that may be... but so am I."

"Whaddya mean by that?"

"Relax," she comforted him, "haven't you ever heard of honor amongst thieves?" Her tail brushed over his lap and coiled around his waist.

"No, I haven't," he replied, trying to rid himself of his new belt. "I'm just a traveling merchant."

"A merchant, huh? Well, whatever your business is, I find it hard to believe that a traveler so high in the fourth stratum would have any trouble knowing *what* I am. You saw me approach in one form, I ate a sweet from this cup, and now I sit here as you see me. It shouldn't be much of a riddle, but if you must know, I am called a *Blank*, in your language."

To this, Ex responded with a blank stare.

"What?" she demanded.

"I'm not in the mood for riddles," Ex grumbled.

"What riddles? I'm a *Blank!*"

"And I suppose you want me to fill in the *blank*, right?" Ex smirked.

The blue of her cheeks deepened, and she slapped him across the face. "Scoundrel!"

Ex rubbed his jaw in confusion. This was not the first time he'd offended a lady, but certainly the least intentional. "What'd I do?"

"Don't Solarian mothers tell their children, *you are what you eat*?" she asked.

"I don't have a mother," Ex replied.

"Well then, it's no wonder you're so ignorant..." she sighed. "I'll put it as simply as I can: my species changes form depending on what we eat. Everything affects us differently. I ate a marshmallow because it gives me a form that most males of your species seem to find attractive. And I am called a *Blank*. If it helps you understand, just imagine that whenever I say the word *blank* the B is capitalized okay? You can read, can't you? I am a *Blank*. That is the actual name of our species in your ridiculous language, a *Blank*!"

"Oh! You should have just said that to begin with," Ex said.

"I did say that to begin with!"

Ex shrugged. "Well It's not my fault; Blank isn't much of a name for a species... What kind of idiot came up with it?"

"Probably your grandfather," she replied. "I'm not exactly sure which of your kin named us in your tongue, or if the blame can even be pinned on a single Solarian, but I can tell you the supposed reason. You see, my homeworld is thousands of galaxies above your own milky galaxy in a place of the universe you call *The Blanket*. I'm sure you've heard of it..."

Ex looked insulted by the insinuation, but in truth he hadn't.

"... Right," she continued. "Well then, you must know how chaotic that region of space is, astronomically speaking of course."

"Of course," Ex nodded.

"The galaxy density there is nearly as thick as in Wild Space, but the greatest concentration is mostly coplanar, so galactic collisions are common."

"Sss, coplanar. Yeah."

"In fact," she continued, "they're so common that no names are given to individual galaxies in the region. Our race laid out a vast grid of pan-dimensional beacons to help us navigate the churning soup of stars. We're the only starfaring race to have emerged from the chaos, and it was thanks to our incredible adaptability... and the CIR has the audacity to call us a child race! But I digress, the blame for that falls more on the Sophians than your kind..."

"Oh hey!" Ex interjected. "It's my birthday today!"

"Felicitations," said the Blank.

Ex shot a glance over her shoulder, back to the Blackstars. Their words had become slow and slurred, but hadn't diminished in their offensiveness. It was hard to drive a burr between the tightly woven scales of an Ikan, but they'd been at it since before he'd arrived. One of the men hoisted himself out of his seat with intentions of making his distaste clear to his deaf neighbors. The keen blades of the Ikans' eyes were all fixed on him. Standing seemed like a balancing act for the man. He took a step and decided that was close enough to lob his insult, nearly tipping the table as he crashed back down on his chair.

A Mohmish waiter raced over and began collecting cups while they were still intact. Ex turned to gauge Luin's response; the whiskered fellow was serving drinks to men seated at the end of the bar, oblivious to the trouble that was brewing at the Blackstars' table. A seasoned barkeeper would have cut them off long ago, but drinks were still being poured and sent in their direction.

Ex tuned back into the Blank's words. Speaking in autex-less Solarian, her voice was smooth as soft water. Its sweet tone rose high above the men's barks and belches. She didn't have to yell to be heard over the clamor of the bar. Apparently her story had continued uninterrupted, despite his inattention.

"… The Solarians," she was saying, "who first contacted our people, were ill equipped to pronounce any of our words. Even though they understood us perfectly, they wasted no time renaming us in their own tongue. At first they gave us many names. I suppose we must've looked like a new species after every meal. I'm not surprised that we seemed strange to them because I remember finding the permanence of their form quite bizarre, myself. Once they learned of our shifting nature, they wiped clean the list of names they'd accumulated and returned to us with just one. They told us that since we were the only sentient race to have ever survived the bedlam of the Blanket, they would call us *Blanks*. But I think it had more to do with the fact that your scientists regard us as blank slates of genetic material, and…"

"Why would you ever take the shape of a hideous monster if you could look the way you do now?" Ex interjected.

"Hideous monster?" she repeated. The question brought a hush to her lavender lips.

Ex contemplated the possible ramifications of his question: *everything checked out OK*.

"Well, even though it's hard to be a master of many forms, and it's fairly easy for us to get used to one shape – too comfortable you know – I don't like to stay static for long," she said. "Our metabolisms don't mind though. We can extract all the nutrients we need from whatever we consume. I could live off these little marshmallows for the rest of my life if I wanted to…"

Ex cocked an eyebrow.

"Every time we take a new shape, we need to learn to walk and talk again. Even simple tasks can prove a challenge. But new forms can be exhilarating, like experiencing things for the first time. I won't say that I don't crave that sensation from time to time, but I have to be practical about my diet. Assuming the wrong form at any given time and place can be dangerous for me… and those nearby. I'd use this shape more often, since most men around here are at least half Solarian, if it weren't so fragile," she said poking at the top of one of her supple breasts.

Ex let his vision drift downwards and froze stiff. His back straightened out in a single jerk. Aside from an elaborate pendant hung around her dainty neck, not a single thread shielded her hairless skin from the rough-and-tumbleness of the bar. It made sense, of course. Unless her unique metabolism could grant her clothing along with a new body, there was no way she could have been dressed. Ex hadn't noticed her put anything on since she'd eaten, and that spider creature was only wearing its chitin. He swallowed hard enough to pull a neck muscle.

Luckily The Blank lacked proper anatomic articulation, or Ex might've really injured himself – bearing in mind this was the first woman-like-creature he'd seen in about half a year. He lifted his eyes back to hers, wearing an apologetic smile.

"You're fun," she said, exploring behind his ear with her silky tail.

"Need another drink here!" Ex squeaked. "Make it a double on the double!" Luin brought him a tall one, and he inhaled the contents in a gasping gulp. The portion that branched into his lungs burnt like a Jovian atmosphere.

The Blank seemed delighted by the display. "You're quite the brave one, aren't you?"

"Yeah. Real men don't drink marshmallows," he said, using both hands to crush the cup.

"Hey! Cup cost too, you son of a murk sifter!" Luin yapped.

"I'm not talking about those kiddy drinks you keep swallowing..." she sighed. "Luin, I'd like a glass of water please, and don't spare the ice... I plan to put on some furs." She dug through the marshmallows and picked one that was flecked with tiny blue dots. She popped it in her mouth and sprouted a furry bikini. The longest strands of the shiny blue hair came from the lowest part of her waist. They veiled her most tender parts behind a short, downy skirt.

"Your water, madam," Luin bowed, presenting her an ornate chalice, brimmed with ice cold water.

Kiddy drinks? Ex was heartbroken. A half-gallon of that foulness churned in his belly, he could smell the fumes of his own lungs dissolving, and she was not in the least bit impressed. "What *are* you talking about then?"

"Oh? You honestly thought that would impress me? That's cute," she said – in the tone a mother takes when comforting a crying child. The Blank bit her lip and leaned in closer. "We may both be outlaws, but unlike you, I value my life."

"What are you babbling about now?"

"Oh come on..." Her cold whispers hardened the wax in his ears. "You're going after the big score, aren't you? It's written all over your face. But trust me, it's suicide. You wouldn't stand a chance with a bag of weapons twice the size the one you boarded with..."

"They say news travels fast when it has nowhere to go," said Ex, "but there must not be much to tell around here, huh?"

"Oh there's plenty to tell, but I hear most of it," she continued. "You'd be surprised what men say when they're given a pretty ear to speak to. I know many things about this station that you don't. That's why I'm warning you. But you go right ahead if you're looking to get yourself killed. It just means less competition for me. If you want to stay alive, pick up your toys and get back on your ship. Point your nose at the stars and put as much distance between you and this ark as fast as you can. You're out of your league here."

A flood of green lights invaded Ex's vision. The Blank's pretty face was framed by a targeting system and surrounded by numbers and gauges. The display was piercingly bright when viewed in the shadow of the Mohmish bar, but it dimmed with a thought. A timer appeared in the lower-left corner of his vision, growing in size as Ex focused on it. It had triggered his ZAIN-HUD's display when it'd reached 30 minutes and continued to count down. He stood up. "Excuse me, I have to buy someone a drink," he said.

"Oh, why that's very kind of you," said The Blank, "but if you think alcohol turns Solarians into ugly creatures, you haven't seen what it does to us!"

One of the seven Blackstars hurled a mug at the Ikans. It shattered on the edge of the table, and the fragments splashed into their drinks. The Ikans took to their feet. The scaly flesh that draped from their heads flared into a hood, and their tails were engorged to the width of their shoulders.

Ex approached the Ikans, displaying his open palms. He slowly raised his hands in a semicircle until they were at the height of his shoulders. The Ikans regarded him with interest. Their heads moved in bird-like jerks. The black slits of their eyes were drawn to sharp blades, pressed by amber. The largest amongst them stepped to within a fist of Ex's face, and he felt the air moved by the slithering of his tongue. Ex stood perfectly still, blinking and breathing to the same slow pattern. His palms were bare, but his shoulders were tense and angled towards the Blackstar's table. The Ikans' hoods fell limp about their necks, and their tails thinned. They brushed the glass bits from their table and took their seats, not releasing Ex from their gaze as he turned to the Blackstars.

He waited patiently for the drunken men to take notice of his presence. They ignored him at first, roaring boasts and chanting half-songs of self-praise. It was humorous, if not somewhat informative. They spoke of a village they'd raided on the planet's surface.

The Blackstar that'd thrown his drink was several decibels louder than the rest. "There wasn't a man amongst 'em that could stand against me. And you know why?" He wasn't the largest of the men, but he was afforded the most elbowroom.

"Cause there were only women and children in town?" asked the Blackstar to his right.

"No. It's cause I'm Blackstar Bob, damn it, the raddest bad-lad in the ring!" He was a visually undelightful man with a strawberry for a nose and weapons-grade breath.

"But Boss, we ain't in a ring, are we?"

"You ass!" said Bob, "I didn't mean it literary. It's what you call a…" Bob leaned forward and gestured with his hands as if weaving a spell, stalling for time while the words slogged to his tongue, "… a metaphor."

"Oh… that's smart, ain't it?"

"Tha's why I'm the boss, you chowder-pup! Any man who stands in the way of Blackstar Bob is either dead or dying!"

"Well… of course that's true," reflected the curious-when-drunk thug. "Cause we're all dying, ain't we? All slow-like I mean, but nonetheless. Only thing to stop that is death."

"You're a real fool ain'tcha?" Bob was upset with his associate.

"Oh, another metaphor, boss?"

Bob feigned a laugh and gave the man's back a heavy slap. The thug's jacket flapped open for a second, and Ex caught a glint of a knife in a loose leather sheath. Either he'd been allowed to pass it through inspection, or he'd acquired it after his weapons had been confiscated because Ex doubted this man had the wits or wiles to have hidden such a sizable blade from the Executor's eyes. "Might be hope for you after all," said Bob.

"Hard to stomach that folks mining treasure outta the sand could be so dirt poor," said another Blackstar. "More lint than plex in their pockets…"

"Hey, it was enough to pay for this party here! And when we run outta drink, we'll just make those lizards buy us the next round, or we'll turn 'em into boots!" Bob said raising his eyes; there stood Ex, the gap in his teeth showing through a cracked grin. "The hell're you?"

"My name is Ex, today is my birthday, and I'd like to buy you and your men a round of drinks."

Bob rubbed his bristly chin. "You're uglier than a Skwell pin-up, but you can spot a winner when ya see one, huh? I'll letcha have the honor of buyin' Blackstar Bob a drink. Why not? Consider it your birthday present."

Ex turned to the bar and called for Luin. "Yo, Keep! A round of my usual for my new friends here!" Luin scanned the faces of the Blackstar crew. Bob pointed at his table as if to accept the offer. The Mohmil shrugged and poured the drinks. Exposing that much of the liquid at once gave the surrounding atmosphere a tartness that made Solarian eyes water.

"Oh you're going to love this drink," said Ex. "It's a man's beverage."

Bob brushed the sand off the crest on his jacket's front pocket. It was buried deep within the cracks of the leather, so it took him a few good strokes. "We'll see 'bout that! I've drank liquid hellfire with the devil himself!"

Ex was genuinely concerned that he was starting to like Bob.

Luin led a train of Mohmils, balancing tiny cups on small trays. They carefully placed the drinks before the men. "Don't let your tab get bigger than your wallet, Solarian!" Luin warned Ex.

The Blackstars sat in awe of their bubbling drinks. None of them had a clue as to what the tiny metal cups contained, but bravado permitted no questions. One of the men poked at his cup; it seemed to anger the contents. Another risked his hand over the puffs of steam rising from the brew; it burned the flesh and continued to do so despite his frantic wiping. The men turned to Ex.

"Cheers!" Ex raised his cup. He took the drink in one draught. The men watched, half-expecting him to burst into flames or keel over in pain, but Ex licked his lips. The nearest thug leaned in and peered into the empty cup.

"Not exactly liquid hellfire, but it's got a good zest!" said Ex. "I'd hurry up and drink 'em fellas, before your cups melt."

Bob struck his right-hand man on the shoulder. "What're you waiting for? Drink up!"

The Blackstar lifted the cup to his nose with a trembling hand. Failing to adhere to the correct, scientific method of wafting the odor gently towards the nostrils, he took a whiff. He couldn't properly appreciate the beverage's full bouquet; it was overpowered by the smell of his own nose hair sizzling into gas. He was overcome by a violent sneezing fit, but managed to keep the drink from spilling in impressive fashion – perhaps motivated by the fear that it would sear the flesh of his hand.

"Drink it!" Bob commanded, tightening his grip on something beneath his jacket.

The man closed his eyes and poured the drink down his throat. For a moment, he sat still with eyes like marble. Then he slowly rose from his chair and began to vibrate. The tremors grew into a full body flail, and his legs propelled him into a sprint. He ricocheted off multiple tables before colliding face first with a wall and falling flat on his back. Smoke issued from his gaping mouth. The whole bar was quiet.

"See, it's good," said Ex.

"Heh, you some sort of pathetic bounty hunter?" said Bob. "I don't think you know who you're dealin' with, lad."

"Gentlemen," said Ex. "I'm paying for these drinks, let's not let them go to waste." He noticed the nearest thug fumbling beneath his jacket.

"Oh, you're gonna pay for 'em alright," grinned Bob.

The Ikans couldn't hear the hiss rising from the unconscious Blackstar's mouth as the lining of his esophagus evaporated, but they could taste it in the air. Their feathers bristled in delight.

"Are you gonna finish that?" Ex asked, reaching for the nearest drink.

One of the Blackstars seized the opportunity, drawing a large knife from his jacket and stabbing at Ex's hand. Ex split his fingers, and the blade plunged into the wooden table between them. He took the man's drink, swallowed it, and wiped his lips. The thug responded with a goofy smile.

In a swift, circular motion, Ex yanked out the knife and drove it through the top of the Blackstar's hand, pegging it into the table. The man looked down at his trapped hand in shock; neither the pain nor the severity of the injury had sunk in. "Help... Help!" he managed to say.

"That's it!" Bob leaned forward as if preparing to rise to his feet, hoping his men would follow suit. "No one crashes a Blackstar's party! You're gonna taste it now, lad!"

Ex took Bob by the collar of his dusty jacket and pulled him down with enough force to send him crashing through the table. He propped a boot up on the back of Bob's head and turned to the other Blackstars. "Now... who wants to party?"

He expected to start an all-out bar brawl, but the grit in this place was mostly cosmetic. Half of the patrons made for the door straight away. A few of the more weathered runners clutched their cups a little closer to their chests, and the slits of the Ikans' eyes widened. The Blank took one last sip of her ice water and strolled for the exit. "This place is dirt," she sighed. "See you around... *merchant.*"

The Blackstars had also remained. They attempted to encircle him. Ex was impressed by their bravery, but judging by the way they moved, their spacing, and hesitance, they were less dangerous than Luin's drinks. There were six thugs, but Ex figured four should be enough to keep the reconstruction crew employed. "The jukebox, left window, right window, couple on Bobby here, and, of course, the bar," he declared.

The men came at him at different speeds. Ex picked out the fastest and stepped towards him. He ducked the man's haymaker and stopped the charge with a shoulder to the sternum. As the thug gasped for air, Ex turned his back, put two fingers up the man's nose, and took a big step forward, hurling him across the bar by the cartilage of his nostrils. The man's back cracked against the jukebox and both were ruined.

The next two Blackstars came at him at once. One attacked from the front and the other from behind. Ex inched forward a bit to make sure the timing was right and sidestepped at the last moment; the two drunkards clobbered each other. Graceless as they were, they packed an unnatural punch. They were headed for the ground when Ex took them by their belt buckles and tossed them through the two windows. The first went straight through the left, and the second crashed through the right, taking a chunk of the wall with him. His back fell on the sill and, the thug stalled for a moment. Ex cringed, worried he might not clear the window, but his limp arms raked across the jags of glass and tipped the balance. His legs flailed upwards and kicked a splash of the remaining glass onto himself as he disappeared.

The next Blackstar's charge was not much of an attack at all. He staggered towards Ex, staring in disbelief at the friend-shaped holes in the windows. Ex put a fist where the man kept his drinks. The poor fellow was stopped cold. He bent over, hacking and wheezing, in an attempt to empty himself over Bob. Ex drove his elbow down on the knobbiest bone of the man's neck before his insides could determine the quickest route to expulsion and spared everyone the displeasure. His skull made a sound that only helmets should make as it landed squarely over Bob's.

The next attacker was the largest of the Blackstars -- a good size for remodeling. Ex stepped onto the lying thug's head and spun out a kick, relocating his ear half way down his cheek as he pivoted. The kick connected with the charging brute's chin in an orthodontic impact, instantly reversing his momentum. His fat back snapped a rickety column as he flew towards the bar, and the mezzanine's floor pitched down raining tables and chairs on the rest of the tavern.

Luin popped up from behind the bar, toting an unwieldy rifle, just in time to be ground-zero for the man-meteor. The collison showered the bar in broken glass and alcohol.

The last of the thugs had been inching up behind Ex. He'd availed himself of a broken table leg and was preparing to deal a knockout blow, when the heavy weights at the end of Ex's coattails, flung by the momentum of his kick, whipped around and struck him in the temple. He crumbled over the growing stack of Blackstars at Ex's feet.

Ex patted the man down for a cigarette. He also took a small match box and straightened out his stepping-stool's ear before standing. "You bastards need to stop drinkin' so much," said Ex with an indignant sniff. "It reeks of booze in here." The air was thick with alcoholic fumes, and the way he waved the matches around made his intentions clear.

He placed the cigarette in the corner of his mouth and struck a match. The bar held its breath, even the Ikan tongues held still, as the tiny flame hissed to life. The drinks served here were volatile enough without the benefit of fire. He lit the cigarette and let the match continue to burn for as long as the patrons could hold their breaths. Finally, he licked his fingers and pinched out the dwindling flame. The room gave a sigh of relief as he dropped the harmless match to the floor and strutted towards the exit. The ordeal appeared to be over.

Ex paused at the doorway. He took a drag and plucked the cigarette from his mouth. "These things'll kill ya!" he said with a wink and a puff of smoke. He flicked the cig over his shoulder. It somersaulted through the air towards the alcohol-soaked bar, kissed the lip of the Blank's chalice, and went cherry-first into the ice water. The hiss rose above the chorus of stifled curses. Some of the patrons engaged in a spirited game of synchronized fainting. The universe had missed out by millimeters on a flambé of very unique ingredients.

Rats, Ruins, and Ruminations

Ex barely managed to duck into a slant of shade in an alleyway before a small brigade of local guards, led by Zarfall himself, blockaded the bar's entrance. The Executor shuffled through the ranks and entered. "What in the Seven Rings happened here?" he said, waving the dust out of his face.

The platoon did their best to revive the swooned clientele, not for the sake of their wellbeing, but to expedite the investigation. The Executor had ordered half of his men to the task of rousing the fallen and the other half to round up the few who'd fled.

Minutes later, the men had assembled a mischief of Mohmils and a few seriously wounded Blackstars. "Alright," said Zarfall, hanging his white cloak on a nearby chair. "You know what I need, so who wants to go first? The sooner I get descriptions or names, the sooner you can get out of here."

Luin jumped at the opportunity to incriminate the man who'd wrecked his fine establishment. "I tell you who it was! A miserable bandit! A Solarian with shifty eyes and a gap-tooth smile. He hides his sneaky face with hair, and I doubt he even owns a wallet!" Many of the quirky liberties Luin normally took with the Solarian language had disappeared with his newfound motivation.

"A single man did this?" interrupted Zarfall.

"Yes!" responded Luin, "An ugly fellow, with no class and tiny, pitiful whiskers that barely escape his upper lip... He ordered many drinks and never paid. Then, he goes to a table of good customers, very thirsty," he said pointing at the Blackstar crewmember, who was fidgeting with the knife that still affixed his hand to a chunk of broken table. "And he starts destroying my bar for no reason! I gave him good drinks, and still he did it, that lowlife!

You want to find him? Go wherever a decent man is trying to run an honest business for the sake of the community, and he'll be there, tearing the place up! Can you believe he said he was a merchant? I heard him talking to a lovely lady. Well, she wasn't lovely then, but you should have seen her after a nibble of salted kanippers..."

"Wait, did you say he called himself *a merchant*?" Zarfall asked with sudden interest.

"Yes, but I don't know who'd be dumb enough to believe it."

Gallowatch tussled through the guards at the doorway. "Luin! Oh, Luin! What happened?" he cried and raced over to the bandaged Mohmil. Luin's eyes welled with tears as if to invite pity. He was about to retell his tale of woe when Gallowatch passed him by to survey the damage.

"Your beautiful tavern!" mourned Gallowatch. He began barking orders at the Mohmish crew. "What are you all doing just sitting there? Can't you see there's work to be done? You, start fixing the window! You two, sweep up the glass. And you, try to salvage as much of the alcohol as you can! I don't care if you have to sponge it off the floor and wring it into a cup; get to work! What a heavy blow to the livelihood of this station! What villain is responsible for this foul deed?"

"It would seem this is the product of your *well-to-do merchant*," said Zarfall. "Perhaps if you would've let me do my job unhindered, this could've been avoided."

"Poppycockery!" said Gallowatch.

"I told you that runner looked like trouble. Tell him what you told me," Zarfall said to Luin, and he did, but wisely omitted his opinion of those who'd believed Ex was a merchant.

"Are you satisfied now?" asked Zarfall.

Gallowatch fluttered his moustache as if he were trying to dust his cheeks with it. "Utterly! I believe Luin's testimony has exonerated our *merchant*. Bedraggled though he was, his sterling smile was gapless."

"He must have lost the perlite tooth to a punch or a bet," said Zarfall. Whether or not the suspect was missing a tooth was irrelevant to The Executor. He'd already concluded that this was Ex's doing, but that only left him with more questions. After Gallowatch had left his office, he'd conferred with neighboring stations to see if any of them had dealt with anything like this threadless phenomenon before. Not surprisingly, he found a string of ships and stations that had reported a scanner malfunction right before suffering some rascality. "But I'm not really interested in teeth. What I'd like to know is exactly how the fight transpired. How was the damage caused?"

"Good idea. Let's ask Luin," suggested Gallowatch. "Where's he gone off to?" He looked all around the tavern before examining the floor beneath him. Luin had succumbed to his injuries and fallen unconscious from the chair. "Oh, there he is! Poor little fellow, he must be all tuckered out after such a harrowing experience. It's best we let him sleep."

"What about you?" said Zarfall, turning to the Blackstar with the pierced hand.

"I don't know if sleep would do it for me," the man stammered. "I think I need a doctor."

"I mean, can you tell me what happened here. I need details."

The Blackstar stared at his hand in disbelief. The blade passed between his knuckles and plunged through the wood. Tugging on the hilt sent sharp pains through the length of his arm; other than this, he felt nothing but coldness, which gave him the greatest scare. The numbness began in his fingers and spread up his arm as far as his neck. The edges of his vision darkened, and the mass of his head felt uneven, like a heavy ball was slowly rolling around in his skull.

Realizing he wasn't going to get much out of the man, Zarfall turned his line of questioning, "Who's the leader of your crew? And is he well enough to answer some questions?"

"Brawlin' Blackstar Bob," the man recited. "But he won't be answering questions for a while. He's had the word-sense knocked out of him, sir."

Zarfall looked over the collection of writhing victims. They all wore similar jackets, and their injuries ranged from bruises to brain damage. Most of their statements were unintelligible and none were useful. It was difficult to tell if their stammering speech was a result of head trauma, heavy drinking, or preexisting idiocy.

"I will tell you exactly what transpired here, Executor," said a monotone voice. It emanated from a small, muzzle-like box attached to an Ikan's mouth. The device translated his slithering tongue movements into perfect Solarian. "The man you call *merchant* was first assailed by these reprobates sprawled before you. He only acted in self-defense, and I can detail the battle for you if it is your wish."

"Go ahead," replied Zarfall, and so the Ikan did. His recounting was detailed, but failed to mention just how close his own crew had come from silencing the Blackstars themselves. Only the Ikans knew that Ex had saved the men from a worse fate. Had they been forced into combat, the Executor would be conducting funerals, not inquiries.

"This is wonderful news," said Gallowatch.

"How do you figure?" wondered Zarfall.

"Didn't you hear the Ikan? It would appear that Mr. Rey acted in self defense. Surely you won't prosecute a man for defending himself?"

"Mr. Gallowatch," said Zarfall, "I think this damage goes beyond what is warranted by self-defense." A spittoon rolled off the mezzanine and splashed to ground. "But the crime itself is the least of my concerns. What puzzles me is how a Solarian of average physical faculties can hurl a rather sizeable man over a dozen meters by his nose and then two more by their belts. Or how he was able to flick a frail cigarette across an unsteadily ventilated room into a small cup — without looking. Perhaps his implant helped with the targeting, but a simple ZAIN-HUD isn't capable of muscular control."

"Maybe he's studied in Karate," suggested Gallowatch. "You know, Martial Arts?"

"There is only one art in the universe that could afford a man such feats..." Zarfall walked over to the chalice and fished out the cigarette. "I believe we're dealing with a new cloaking technology that's capable of masking coronas and blotting out threads entirely."

"Are you implying that we have a renegade Sage on the station?"

"This isn't Istreya, Mr. Gallowatch. Any Sage is a renegade." Zarfall scrutinized the moistened cigarette. "As word spreads of this ark's treasury and the planet below, I'm sure we'll see every technique, every clever ploy, and every disguise imaginable. But this is no parlor trick. Sages have been concealing coronas from our scanners for some time now; none have managed to hide their thread. If this new technology cannot be countered, it will present a new breed of trouble for the CIR. I must prepare my report immediately."

"Wait! What should we do with these?" Gallowatch said pointing at the Blackstars. "Some of their injuries look fairly severe. I'm sure that Doctor Pelcust will be more than happy to see some business." He straddled over the thugs as he delivered his pitch. "He's the finest surgeon on the station – a real wizard with the nanowand. His shop is just a few blocks from here, right next to the broken down purity ward. His sign reads: *"Pelcust Cobbling – Shoes Fixed Fast,"* but pay no mind to that; it's more of a hobby of his."

Zarfall spoke to the guard at the door, loud enough for Gallowatch and the Blackstars to hear. "Make sure these men spend a night in the brig before they get their shoes repaired."

"A night?!" protested a conscious thug, and the Ikans' tongues dithered in delight.

"It's just while I decide what to do with you," Zarfall replied and left the rest to his men.

"Brilliant!" exclaimed Gallowatch. "Let their wounds fester for a night and their bill will double!"

Meanwhile, Ex had pillaged the station's arsenal of confiscated weaponry. He tipped an imaginary hat to the snoring sentry and emerged from the guardhouse, fully rearmed. He'd liberated all of his imports and a few other weapons that'd caught his fancy as well. A new silvery tooth sat in place of the charismatic gap. He was quite literally armed to the teeth.

White Rapiers and Red Nets

The wind was deafening, bringing white silence to the pitch-black tunnel. This was the main artery of the ventilation system, a sterile environment that had remained undisturbed since the bioark's christening, diligently supplying the station with breathable air.

A brilliant white rapier plunged deep into the heart of the darkness. It was followed by another and another. The bullet holes dotted an outline of a doorway and unpurified air whistled into the innards of the formerly chaste pipe.

The perforated metal plate clung desperately to its companions. It would never surrender. Even now, on the stoop of death's door, it defended the air's virtue with all due chivalry. Memories of the ark's most precious moments, whispered by the wind, reverberated through its metallic viscera, renewing its resolve. Shaking in the violent rush of air, it remembered births and weddings, first kisses and whispered wishes for more. Beads of condensation gathered on the metal, but those who were wise knew they were tears...

At least, that's what Ex thought. Socializing with hanging wires and jutting plates during his time alone in space had driven him slightly mad. He'd developed a taste for coming up with back-stories for inanimate objects he intended to destroy.

A boot-shaped dent appeared in the plate's gut. The flimsy scraps that bound it to the walls snapped in unison, and the plate was swept away; but as it tumbled through the pipe, the other plates cheered and saluted a true hero. Warmth washed over its metallic body. "Is this Heaven?" it thought to itself, and was promptly de-atomized by the filtration system's ultra-frequency laser grid.

Ex's silhouette appeared in the light, dark hair whipping in the wind. "I hate this part..." he groaned and stepped through the makeshift doorway.

An explosion went off in the bowels of the station. The walls shook, and the lights died, leaving the station in a moment of complete darkness. The wind fell silent, and all that could be heard was the haunting moans of the ark's hull as it resettled.

Ex sprang into action, sprinting down the pipe. His ZAIN-HUD was equipped with contouring sensors, and it was only thanks to them that he could see. They outlined the pipe's surface in a vivid green mesh. As he ran, he counted small openings that were set at intervals on the pipe's belly. They appeared as nothing more than malformed cubes to his sensors, but the knowledge Ex had acquired during his reconnaissance filled in the rest. "Two more," he said, racing past another duct.

Alarms rang throughout the station. The main lighting flickered on. Airlocks hissed and engines grumbled as the backup reactor's energy meandered through the station's corroded circuitry. A pale glow rose around the ark. "One more," said Ex, hearing the wind rush up behind him like a roaring wave. The ventilation system had been reactivated; the purification grids would activate seconds later.

"This one!" he gasped, diving into a duct as the filters flickered on. He tumbled down the cramped shaft and ended up in a folded mess where the duct took a sharp corner. A chunk of jagged metal clocked him on the head as he struggled to right himself. It fell into his lap and began to singe his pants. It was the end of a rifle barrel, freshly cut by the filtration grid he'd narrowly avoided, and its sharper end was red hot. He squirmed and cursed, but the metal cooled quickly. The duct was covered in a thick coat of frost that bit into the exposed flesh of his hands. Having spent his entire life on a refrigerated transport, Ex was familiar with all species of ice. The pain of having the heat so quickly sucked from the tips of his fingers was similar to the last, body-wide sting experienced before entering cryostasis.

He busted through a wall of icicles and wormed his way further into the shaft, dragging the bag of weapons behind him. It was a tight fit where the ice grew thickest. And it wasn't water — at least not purely. There were puddles, though it was well beneath freezing.

The cold and confinement had him feeling nostalgic when he came upon a mesh vent, glazed with thin frost. Soft yellow light bled through the slats, revealing sheets of steam as the duct traded air with the chamber below. There stood a couple of men, maybe guards, chatting in what appeared to be an ample maintenance closet. It took Ex only a moment to recognize the odd pair: it was Chut and Ziff, who'd disarmed him just hours earlier. Ex listened in on their conversation. The nice thing about people was that they provided their own back-stories.

"... I'm shriveling a nut! Zarfall keeps this place colder than a stasis chamber, that damn Valoraph," said Chut. "I miss being the alpha around here." The seesaw tenor of his voice competed with the muffled wails of alarms from beyond the door.

"Well I don't know how you can miss it, since you never were the alpha," said Ziff. "If the CIR left, the Mohmils would be in charge, just like they were before. I mean, it's their ship."

"The day I take orders from a rat!" Chut peeled the cap from his bald head. It left a deep, red groove just above his ears. "Not for all the salted peanuts in the universe..." Somehow the cap had been holding up the heft of his scalp. In absence of its support, the fat on the back of his neck folded into a pack of sausages. "You've got me so angry my ears are ringing!" he said. His ears were blood red.

"It's just your hearing coming back; that cap was cutting off your circulation. Your ears were probably starving," said Ziff.

"This cap is too damn small!" said Chut.

"Your head is too fat." Ziff batted the curl of bangs off his forehead. He wasn't as heavy as Chut — a point of pride for him — but he wasn't shapely. His back ran flat from nape to ankles and his belly creased at his belt. In short, he was a man with nothing up in his region.

"Oh, you think you got such a big chin?" Now Chut's whole head was red. "Try to bowl me over..."

"Not this again."

"Come on, get a running start and try to bowl me over, Ziff!"

"How the hell am I supposed to get a running start? We're hiding in a closet, Chutnik!"

"OK, first, I told you not to call me that. Second, we're not hiding. We're strategically storing ourselves. And third of all, idiot, go out into the hallway and get a running start."

"I'm not gonna do that."

"Cause you can't. Trying to push me is like trying to tip a fish over underwater: it can't be done," said Chut. "And you know why that is?"

Ziff rubbed his temples. "Why?"

"Cause water is the fish's domain, and this is my domain."

"The closet?"

"No," said Chut. "Three-dimensional space."

Ex wished he could listen in longer, but his tooth-bomb's explosion would only give him a few more minutes of distraction. He crashed through the vent in a cloud of cold vapor, landing directly behind the two.

Chut watch wordlessly as an icy blue hand walked up Ziff's neck. He felt fingers on his own skin, but had yet to accept that this was really happening. Ex popped their noggins together in as friendly of a manner as he could. The two men fell limp and filled the storeroom floor.

The ZAIN-HUD had mapped out the facility's internal structure and plotted the most likely route to the core as Ex had listened in on Ziff and Chut's conversation. It reported an accuracy of only 65.2%. His HUD was by no means a top-end model, but it usually led him through facilities like these at 90% reliability. "Must be all the perlite," he sighed. "Well, at least it's 15% better than flipping a coin." Speaking aloud to himself was another sickness he'd contracted in deep space.

He peeked through the door with his sensors. A few meters down the hallway to the left, two men guarded the lone elevator to the installation's core. They clenched their rifles with trembling hands. The strobes and alarms had frayed their nerves. He could almost make out the sweat as it beaded on their foreheads.

Ex stepped into the hallway and pitched a grenade at the elevator's controls. The guards threw down their rifles and dove for cover as the metal sphere struck a button by the elevator and clanged to the steely floor. Ex took the time to collect the grenade as he sauntered into the open elevator. The men looked up to find him jingling the safety pin, still fastened to the grenade, and the doors slid shut.

As the elevator descended, the HUD's signal deteriorated. Its range of penetration through the bulkheads shortened, and distant details turned to noise. From his scans in distant orbit, Ex knew that the core contained perlite, likely mined from the planet below. But judging by the amount of interference at such close range, the ark must've been packed with the stuff. Either that or the entire core was coated with perlite, which made little sense; hiding perlite with perlite was like throwing a tarp over a curtain. The only conceivable purpose for a shell of perlite was to hide something else, something of greater value, which drastically narrowed the field of possibilities.

It was a long ride down. When the doors opened, he found himself at the foot of a narrow hallway. The HUD's route was painted in a brilliant green that offered no light to the surroundings. It ran flush against the metal deck and slipped beneath the door at the end of the hall. About halfway, it passed through a wall of dim beams. No fancy pattern of sweeping lasers to avoid with expertly timed dance moves and acrobatics, this was a perfectly practical, perfectly boring security sensor. Ex wasn't concerned. They already knew he was coming, and there was only one way in.

He walked right up to the door and pressed his head against the wall. The lines his sensors drew were crisp and clear, but trembled with a nervous rhythm. There were crates scattered about the room ahead, a door on the right, and a vent on the far side. Most notably, there were five men in cover with rifles aimed at the door. In addition to the weapons, they had various cybernetic limbs and body parts. "Great... Centrians," Ex grumbled.

But there was only one light fixture.

He rolled into the room, shot out the light, and placed the flashlight atop a crate in a single maneuver. The room erupted into screaming chaos as the mercs opened fire on the light. A stream of bullets perforated the crate and juggled the flashlight in midair.

Ex knew the diversion wouldn't last. Like him, these Centrians had sensory augmentations. Their neuro-HUDs cycled through modes of vision even as they fired, but Ex was fast. He'd already flanked around the crates to the nearest merc, snapped his neck, and taken his rifle. The flashing muzzles made for easy targets in the dark. He silenced them all before the flashlight came to a spinning stop and flickered out.

Static flared across Ex's HUD as he approached the door. He was fiddling with the settings when he felt a metal hand take hold of his ankle. These Centrians were tough as shrapnel. Even the fellow with the snapped neck was still alive; his regenerative nanodes were hard at work realigning his spine and knitting his severed nervous tissue. The merc at Ex's feet had a hole through his cheeks where a photocaster bolt had passed, taking a good chunk of his tongue with it. He made a whistling sound when he talked, but spoke as eloquently as he could to properly convey his rage. "You've made a grave mistake, friend. I'm afraid you'll never escape with your life. Do you even know what's down there?"

"Shh," Ex said, putting the man out with a kick to the temple. "You'll ruin the surprise." He wasn't interested in playing the Centrian's transparent mind games.

The ZAIN-HUD warned of several heat signatures marching through the corridor ahead. The signal was scrambled at best. It was the mass of around fifteen men, but they could be locals or Extinguishers for all Ex knew.

He piled a few crates into a wobbling stack and clambered up to the vent. The tower teetered beneath his feet as he pushed the bag of weapons into the vent and gave the room one last glance. When he turned back, the bag was gone. "That's odd," he said, reaching into the duct. It was as icy as the last one, but there was no inclination or sudden drop. There didn't seem to be anywhere for the bulky bag to have gone, yet his sensors showed no sign of it. He crawled in for a closer look, kicking over the stacked crates behind him, and was immediately swept away by a rush of air.

Neon-green squares outlined duct segments that raced past as he hurled through the darkness. They were linked by lines that ran as rails, twisting this way and that. In the distance, the lines scribbled and shook into dozens of threads. Bursts of color swept across the HUD followed by splashes of black and white stains, rushing by at great speed. Yet on he flew.

His sensors switched off, and the HUD went into a self-diagnosis. He could feel that the vent's structure had not changed, but he was beginning to slow down. The shiplink test came up negative, as did all of the HUD's externals. The internals, on the other hand, were working perfectly. He scanned through the various functions, pausing on the biometer. *DAMAGE TO SCALP: Possible concussion* it reported. *Expect mild hematoma.* Ex had crashed head-first into the nose of a rocket that jutted out of his sack of weapons. The mesh floor gave out beneath their combined weight and sent them plummeting 20 meters to the deck below.

He rose feeling a bit woozy. "Well at least I found my bag," he said, pushing the rocket back into the sack and hoisting it over his shoulders. "Now where the hell am I?"

Into the Core

There were no wailing alarms or flashing lights here. The only illumination was provided by dour beams of dim blue lights that ran unbroken along the lower edges of the corridor. The pallid light grew and fell to a slow pulse. It pooled on the brushed-metal floor and crept up the walls. It didn't look like perlite, but all it took was a microfilm to scatter sensors. Honing his scans on any of the surfaces drove the vertices of the wireframe insane, fluttering between an infinite distance and the pit of his corneas in an instant. It was irritating to say the least, so he switched off the display.

Perlite sent subrostral ripples through the surrounding space. You didn't have to stare right at it to see its effects, and enough of it in one place could cloak a planet. Given enough time, a scanner could tune into the pattern of perlite's vibration, and trace it like any other surface, but every molecule had its own unique signature. It took the finest sensors about five to ten seconds to lock down a square meter of perlite, but Ex had picked his ZAIN-HUD out of the bargain bin. He didn't have the time to wait for it to soothe all the little wires and shuffle them into place.

A strange feeling passed over him, as if all of the atoms of his body had tripped in unison. He looked at the ground beneath his boots. It hadn't moved; he hadn't moved. The shift had occurred at a quantum level, and Ex couldn't say what part of him had sensed it.

He took a cautious breath. The air tasted as it had on his ship when his mother still lived in it. He thought of her smells. There was the perfume she wore on docking days; it smelled like rabbits ought to smell, the way they did on Istreya – not the gamy stink of a hutch, but the fresh linen scent of bouncy little clouds. Then he remembered the metallic sting of overcooked plex. A more considerate chef would materialize one slice of white bread first, then the sharp cheddar, and then the other slice before agitating the atoms around the sandwich to wilt the cheese and toast the bread. But Arius habitually exploded entire grilled cheese sandwiches into existence in one step. And Ex would have to wait a while, not for his meal to cool off, but for it to stop radiating entire atoms of over-excited-plex-turned-heavy-metals that she'd generated in her haste.

A shiver tired itself across his back as he realized it was no property of smell that had reminded him of the air in his ship. It was the presence of a will. Manipulating the fabric of space left prints, which other Sages could track through careful meditation. Ex was not adept at the skill, but he could feel himself sinking in the footprint of someone's mind. And the hole was deep.

The light ahead of him seemed to recede, and the hallway looked less inviting. "The universe is a big place. You won't get very far if you're afraid of the dark," he could almost hear Arius say. The words stung him with anger that cooled into courage.

E C Dryere | 56

His eyes were lost in the sameness of the corridor as he walked along its slow bend. Each step was an effort. The air fled from his breath. It was hard to get a good lungful, and when he did, it burned. There was no need for meditation or training; the wind here was willful, and any breathing thing could sense it.

A patch of darkness in the distance broke the lines of light. He approached with caution. A large door stood between the glowing beams. It slid open, and Ex had to avert his eyes from the brilliance. He pulled a couple of rifles from his bag and glared into the curtain of light that swelled in the threshold. His pupils shrunk, and the light drew back. It passed like a ghost through a metal glade.

With a rifle in each hand, Ex eased into the threshold. There was a forest of pillars in the chamber ahead. They were arranged in perfect columns and rows, interrupted only by a wide path that led to a central clearing. A canopy of rafters stemmed in every direction from the trunks of the pillars, connecting to the curving wall like barren branches. The lowest of the rafters was no more than five meters from the deck, and the highest may've touched the dome's ceiling. Ex couldn't see that far.

The light in the dome was provided by a flock of floodlights, suspended on heavy cables. They painted circles on the floor, occasionally broken by the hard-line silhouette of a rafter. The penumbra that spilled onto the walls drew an intricate web of shadow. Everything above the lights was shrouded in thick gloom. Only a few amber lights scattered about the branches broke the darkness, but their faint throbbing scarcely reached beyond the casing that housed them.

There was no need for his HUD's sensors; it was obvious he was walking into an ambush. The moment he'd cleared the entire threshold, the door slid shut behind him. Ex gave it a quick glance. "What, only one door?" he asked aloud, and down came a heavier shield-door, nearly crushing his heels.

He could hear the quiet clinking and scraping of metal on metal somewhere overhead. Hints of movement teased the edges of his vision, but he couldn't make anything out. He set down the rifles and drew a sleek pistol from his bag. There was a hidden latch on the gun. He flicked it open and pressed a tiny red button. It began to hum softly as he stalked through slivers of shadow.

Ex came to stand in the glare of a spotlight in the dead center of the dome – the bull's-eye of an immense target. He could feel the restless barrels of countless guns, bearing down on him. The pistol's hum became a high-pitched whine as its innards began to glow. Streaks of radiant light blossomed between his grip, and Ex shut his eyes.

He lofted the gun and leaned forward as if he were about to make a dash for the pillar ahead. The pistol burst in midair, and the room was awash in blinding light. Ex pushed off the ground and flung himself backwards, diving for cover behind a column and tossing a handful of grenades into the rafters as he went. A swathe of orange sparks painted a trail from the center of the dome to the pillar that he'd feinted towards before the flash, and the steely walls reverberated with the high-roar of uncountable gunshots. Then the barrage of grenades went off, and the dome was ringing like a giant bell.

Dozens of figures plunged out of the smoke, fleeing the blasts in the rafters above. Ex was already dealing out another hand of grenades, this time rolling them across the deck. He ducked behind the column, and a second round of explosions shook the core. Something came to a spinning stop at his feet. He was about to leap away, thinking it was some kind of oversized grenade, but only his stomach moved, reaching for his pelvis in a hot punch. This wasn't an explosive; it was something far worse: a sleek, expressionless helmet, smoke still rising from its neck-hole.

The smooth faceplate bore no resemblance to any race. It was painted grim white and accented by lines of cobalt and charcoal. There was no mistaking its shape or color. The helmet belonged to a CIR soldier, not a mercenary or a conscripted local, but one of the Veredos-trained troops, Nyrceff, meaning *faceless* in the Sophian tongue.

Any of the Sentient races could apply to the Imperial Veredian Academy (IVA), but few survived induction into the Nyrceff. The mental and physical training was enough to break most, but the hardest part was enduring the slow, methodical dismemberment of your identity. It was not just their helmets that gave the Nyrceff their name. Their height was normalized through genetic rescription to ensure they were all the same shape and size – icons, bathroom signs, interchangeable parts. The standard did not change for different species or genders; the further they began from the ideal, the more aggressively they were molded. Skwell, for instance, were poured into humanoid suits like soup. Any mannerisms or traditions they once had were conditioned away, and they spoke Official Solarian with the same mechanical voice. The Sophians reserved their language for themselves. They believed it would somehow dilute its purity if other races were allowed to speak it.

The IVA facilities were spread throughout the planetworks of Veredos. Initiates began their rigorous training in the darkness of the seventh tier, and worked their way up to the second, where the remaining traces of their identity and heritage were burned away under the light of The Grand Forge.

Runners knew better than to fight with the Nyrceff. If you killed one, your name would be placed on the Talon List, to be hunted by the CIR's special forces, The Talons. In the highly unlikely event that you killed a Talon, you'd be slated for extinguishing – marked for execution by the very same force that purged the stars of Sages.

The force of the explosions subsisted as a fading whine in the pillars and floor. Other than that, there was silence. The grenades had claimed a number of the hanging lights as unintentional casualties. It was even darker than before, which helped him hide for now. There was no doubt that the Nyrceff's sensors had been calibrated to the chamber's perlite, but the pistol's overload had temporarily jammed them; it wouldn't last.

The rafter lights burned ember-red through the thick smoke, looming over the dome like a giant spider. It wound up the pillars and sent crooked fingers down the walls. Ex leapt onto a rafter and launched himself towards another. He ascended until he came to a rafter where no light fell, and waited for the Nyrceff to make their play.

Scattered muzzle flashes tore open the darkness above. Ex dashed across the rafter, returning fire, but the origin of the flashes constantly changed. The trailing ricochets closed in on him as he neared the wall. He vaulted from the rafter and swung on a floodlight. Shots whizzed by his ears and ripped through the sack of weapons on his back.

A photocaster bolt pierced his hand through the palm in mid-swing, snapping the cable. He was in free fall. Glints of grenades followed him down. He hit the ground with a hard roll and scrambled behind a pillar, eluding the Nyrceff in the ensuing explosions.

A line of plain text appeared at the bottom of his vision: *You've injured your hand. Seek medical attention.* He'd paid the guy at *The Neuro Hut* an extra hundred kees of plex to add a biometer to his ZAIN-HUD, and not once had it proven more useful than the sense of pain.

Ex looked down at his left hand. There was a neat hole through it. The photocaster bolt had cauterized the wound, which meant he wouldn't bleed out, but it would also slow his regeneration. He commanded it into a fist, but two of his fingers wouldn't respond. One of his metacarpals was missing a section, another had been completely shattered, and the corresponding ligaments had been severed. "Won't be playing the piano for a while," he said. "Good thing I never bothered learning how."

On a positive note, he was feeling a lot lighter now. This was because most of his weapons were scattered around the dome. He looked down at his boots; there lay one of his favorite weapons. It was a roughshod device of Centrian origin, a stout tube with a switch next to a plain handle, affectionately called *The Grumpy Can.* He gripped the weapon with his good hand and struck the switch against his thigh. It barked a flurry of fiery orbs in every direction, filling the dome with light. Licks of flame splashed through the rafters and sent the Nyrceff scrambling.

Ex seized this opportunity to climb to a more defensible position. He'd made it more than halfway up the dome before he came to an occupied rafter. The soldier kicked him off the beam as he attempted to land, leaving him dangling by his fingertips. The long barrel of the CIR photocaster was pointed at the top of his head. He stretched up his bloodied left hand, pushed the muzzle through the wound, and wrenched the rifle aside. The soldier fired, but the barrel had passed completely through Ex's hand; he directed its aim at the other Nyrceff below. It wasn't accurate enough to hit any of them, but at least it was enough to prevent them from lining up an easy shot. Ex pushed his hand further up the barrel, past the muzzle and over the sights mounting. He turned his hand sideways, and wedged a notch in the mounting between his knuckles. The biometer flooded his vision with injury warnings. It was enough leverage to torque the rifle out of the Nyrceff's plated gloves. The soldier was pulled off balance and nearly over the edge.

The weapon fell a full forty meters to the deck below. "You dropped something," said Ex. Using only the strength of his right hand, he hurled himself upwards, cocked back the same arm, and drove his fist into the soldier's expressionless visor. There was a loud crack and the Nyrceff was sent after its rifle.

As Ex checked to see if he'd broken the knuckles of his only working hand, a missile struck the rafter where it met the column. It moaned and pitched down, sending him tumbling through the metal branches.

Ex found himself on the ground, pulling something out from under his back. It was a plain gray tube, no longer than his arm, a single-fire rocket launcher he'd bought off a Mohmish junker. He struck it against the deck, unlocking the safety mechanism.

The population of lights in the room was nearing the point of extinction, and dense smoke provided the forest of pillars with foliage. Countless, clanging footsteps closed in around him. The Nyrceff had become overconfident. Ex may've been near blind in these conditions, but he could still hear just fine.

He spun out from cover, lifted the tube over his shoulder, and aimed at the chorus of footfalls. *Click, click, click*… The trigger worked well enough, but the rocket was trapped by a dent in the casing. The safety mechanism had prevented a misfire and spared him from a shoulder-mounted explosion, but that didn't stop him from cursing like a clubby Centrian at the thing.

The stark silhouette of a Nyrceff was perched on a rafter a few dozen meters away. Ribbons of smoke twined across its featureless armor like time-lapsed vines. Ex hurled the worthless launcher at the figure. The soldier dropped to the deck as the tube whistled through the air, avoiding the laughable attack. It leveled a gleaming barrel.

Yellow, orange, red, black: it all felt natural to him. The sine waves of the visible spectrum slowed to infra-red and down to radio. There was a shimmer of color as ultraviolet and a few errant x-rays followed them down. Time had been dammed to a trickle.

Tiny cyclones of light glittered around him, colorful fractals whispering each other into existence and vanishing just as quickly. He could tell neither their size or distance. Were they galactic masses drifting in the heavens or tiny bubbles a few lash-lengths from his eyes?

Then he could see again by the light of his own bristling radiation, a high-energy halo the Sages called the *Gamma Glow*. With time slowed by a factor of 10,000, gamma waves had shifted into the frequencies of the visible spectrum. He saw as nature had not intended.

His duster was draped behind the holster that currently held Arius' gun, and the blood that filled his hand felt suddenly like power. He motioned for the pistol, but was met by a strange resistance. Time had been tamed, but the other elements still fought him, resisting his efforts to move at speeds that exceeded all natural limitations.

The edge of his hand slowly cut a wave into the air. Its wake rippled like water before cresting into white foam. He pushed harder, but his hand couldn't move any faster. He leaned his weight into it, and his flesh began to burn.

Upon reaching the gun, he found that stopping his movement was not just a matter of no longer pushing. His tendons popped and his bones cracked as he struggled against his own momentum. The black mesh of his holster turned cloudy, and there was some kind of air bubble forming where his fingers had first met the pistol's grip. The air around the bubble was glazed like glass, and two concentric rings formed out of the condensation that'd been shaken from the air through shear violence. Tentacles of turbulence coiled beneath the globe, and the whole system expanded in unison.

The eddies in the air ahead of him had only begun to twist, when his hand sliced a fresh wave, rising like a comet this time. The bubble had grown past his hip, pressing the fabric of his shirt against his skin and lifting the edge of the duster. It ballooned into the form of a giant octopus with arms to spare.

Ex saw the launcher frozen in midair. The Nyrceff was still in the process of raising its rifle. And although the pistol was not yet level, Ex felt the urge to squeeze the trigger. He reached the full extent of its action, but the cylinders atop the gun hadn't budged. It didn't surprise him.

In an exhale of color and wind, Ex saw the tendrils of turbulence igniting into rainbows of flame. The holster at his hip disintegrated. His coattails billow up with enough force to nearly lift him by the shoulders. There was an explosion, a clap of thunder that immediately ruptured his eardrums; he could still hear it through his teeth. It pushed away the fierce heat that swelled in front of his face. And somewhere in all that, he'd fired a shot that struck the back of the rocket, sending the tube into a tailspin. The missile ignited, and the whole launcher shrieked towards the soldier's feet. The Nyrceff was consumed in a burst of flame that sent the smoke fleeing for distant corners.

Ex stared at the smoldering cuffs of his sleeve. Delicate plumes of steam wafted from his fingertips. He could hear only a single sustained sine wave of about 2000 Hz, which was just flat of a C7 in musical terms.

Executor Zarfall was in a dark room, surrounded by flittering screens that monitored the battle from every angle. His expression was somber, even by his standards. "What are you?" he said beneath his breath.

"Sir!" a tinny voice rang out. Zarfall turned to his assistant, a Skwell spread across several consoles. "Scans are still picking up zero threadwidth." The Skwell made excellent assistants. Their bodies could be molded to use the control scheme of any species, but they rarely needed to. Their gelatinous flesh could read and transmit electrical signals, allowing them to directly interface with most electronics.

"Is that so?" said Zarfall, brushing some of the goo aside to check the display. Despite the Skwell's efficiency, he was beginning to regret hiring a dollop of jelly for this position. He glared at Ex's image. Smoke swirled around the runner before vanishing into the shadow, as if finally escaping his control.

"I've already performed the scan twice," said the Skwell, "but I'm still getting no reading on the meters. Shall I run it again?"

No answer came. Zarfall was transfixed on the screen. "A man cannot be without thread," he told himself. "It would be like a hole in the ocean, not a bubble, but a void, into which water simply does not flow." If he went to Veredos with his findings, they'd think him mad or incompetent. He had to learn more, but scans wouldn't do. He had to crack this runner's head open and see what was inside with his own eyes.

"Should I run a diagnostic on the system?" asked the Skwell. "Sir?"

Zarfall stared beyond the monitor's flickering image. "No..." he finally spoke, "release the snake."

Fields of Eyes like Starry Skies

The Nyrceff filed out of the dome through the main doorway. Their photocasters were fixed on Ex, but none of them fired a shot. They kept raining down from the rafters. There were more of them than he'd anticipated. Ex was more than happy to let them leave. He could hear the muffled beat of their steady marching as the ringing subsided. With a couple strokes to the side of his head, Ex managed to shake the corks of congealed blood out of his ears.

When they were all gone, the doors didn't close. Ex blinked at the entrance with due distrust. Certainly no logical man would assume that it was safe, but only Ex was left in the dome. He strutted over, but his swagger reduced to a creep as he neared the threshold.

He stopped. The breath of a frightful mind was in the air. His face muscles tensed, and a blast of wind howled through the doorway. He was launched backwards, whistling through the pillars. His head struck a light, and it went out in a hail of sparks. He came to a sliding stop beneath the last working spotlight.

"What an inviting stage..." whispered a voice. There stood a tall, ashen apparition of a man, all in white. He was as pale as a Sophian. The crystalline angles of his nose and brows were geometrically pleasing. His snowy hair was swept back in sharp tufts like the head feathers of an eagle, but the rest of his features belonged to a serpent – narrow mouth, ears lost in hair, and bladed eyes green as venom. The cobalt sigils framing his left eye formed The Talons' emblem.

Those who were too powerful to remain Nyrceff, yet too insane to become Extinguishers, ended up as Talons. Young recruits with exceptional threadwidth were handed over to the Extinguisher program. They'd endured the Nyrceff program, but less than one out of a thousand survived the rigors of Extinguisher training with their minds intact. The broken ones were not simply discarded. They were reprogrammed and given the title of Talon, deranged predators, kept caged until their services were required. Their skills were second only to the Extinguishers, but they were often equal in threadwidth. The caprice with which they wielded the power of the Sages made them truly fearsome.

Ex knew he'd earned a spot on the Talon List – he was looking forward to bragging about it over a few drinks – but never expected to encounter one so soon. "You guys work fast," he said to the Talon that stood before him, three meters tall.

The wind clipped Ex's legs, and the Talon caught him in the gut with a rising knee. The blow expunged his breath and threw him into the air. Before he could even gasp, he was slammed by another sudden force.

When he came to, he was on the floor, face down in pooling blood. The wind had sent the last spotlight into motion. It swung by, and a pair of pristine white boots, trimmed in chrome, stepped into the ruddy puddle. The Talon took Ex by the chin and hoisted him to his feet. Tiny drops of blood beaded beneath the sharp claws, slowly sinking into the flesh of Ex's neck.

"Aren't you a riddle?.. My name is Issid, what's yours?" asked the Talon, his narrow mouth widening into a grin. On and on the smile stretched into the darkness, revealing several rows of razor-sharp teeth. The light swung back, and Ex could see a dozen black worms slithering over the fangs. They were the many heads of the Talon's forked tongue. Issid was not just a Talon; he was also an Antican, a race that had come to be called *Sage-Eaters*.

The Sophians had found the Anticans on the foggy moon of Antia, tucked away in the Helioshyft galaxy, over two thousand years ago. From space, Antia looked like a ball of cotton trapped in a glass sphere, but beneath the heavy cloud-cover lay an environment that was as beautiful as it was brutal. There were forests of black pines capped with snow, magnificent rivers that ran with white urgency, sudden pools of magma that cooled into sable stone in seconds, and indomitable mountains that dreamt in the clouds.

The Anticans were tall, graceful creatures with sharp features and skin like the snow that blanketed their world, but their lithe exterior belied a savage, predatory nature. They had no words or math, no culture or religion; they'd no use for such things. Anticans were solitary hunters, coming together only to mate or fight; both were as likely to result in maiming or death. Their offspring was left to fend for itself in the shale stews of magma-heated mires, and it was there that the Sophians collected their first specimens.

After a millennium of genetic manipulation, the Anticans had been twisted into tools. They were transformed from a race of savage, yet innocent predators into merciless assassins, brilliant as they were vicious. But for all their predatory instincts and ample threadwidth, Anticans never became Extinguishers. It wasn't because their minds always broke during the process; it was that they were broken to begin with, full of sadism that their Sophian shapers had carefully cultivated.

"How did you leave a giant's footsteps with such tiny feet? What other tricks are you hiding beneath that furry scalp? Show me," said Issid, eyes gleaming with earnest fascination. "And please make them good..."

Ex couldn't swallow in the Talon's grip, so he spat blood on the lapel of Issid's white coat. "That's not a very good one," said the Antican. His smile shrank into a small slash of a frown. He grabbed Ex by the ankle and flipped him over to shake the toys out of him. An assortment of guns, knives, and explosives trickled to the ground, none of which piqued Issid's interest. He sighed and hurled Ex across the dome.

Ex tumbled to a stop on the other edge of the spotlight's sway. He reached for Arius' gun, but the holster wasn't just empty, it was de-atomized. He didn't even remember dropping the pistol. It must've been when Issid blasted him out of the doorway. Darkness drew around him like a heavy curtain.

"I must say, I'm a bit offended," Issid's voice hissed. Ex lashed out at its source, but struck only air. A soft laughter whispered into his ear, but the Talon was nowhere in sight. Ex swung at phantoms of gleaming teeth. Exhaustion came quickly; he was fairly certain that Issid was pulling the oxygen out of the air in front of him. Arius had taught him to run at first sight of these Sage hunters throughout

his youth, but there was nowhere to run. His eyes fell to the floor, as his oxygen-deprived mind was visited by an old nightmare: a vision of a helpless little boy, pressed against cold stone in the darkness. He was frozen in the stare of a Sophian that stood on bent bodies piled over a banquet table. Then, there was the warmth of *her* embrace, crashing through the stone. A sudden rush of clarity came to his senses. The darkness receded and faint outlines of pillars emerged from the black. For the moment, his lungs drafted neutral air.

Issid's voice slithered out of the darkness. *"Are you ready yet? They're waiting, you know... our audience. Fields of eyes like starry skies... forgive me a rhyme from my youth."*

This time, Ex could sense the direction of the voice. He turned to face it, and a white figure stepped out from behind a column. "Can you see them too? I wonder if you can." Issid came closer. "The least you can do is introduce yourself."

"The name's Ex."

"Not to me! To them," hissed Issid.

"I'm sure they heard me," replied Ex.

Issid appeared to confer with a chorus that spoke from different directions. "In the language of Sol, I am known as Issid the Wind Serpent, Talon of the Consortium, Brother of Chross." He was a manipulator of wind and turbulence — not very impressive by Sage standards. Turbulence was one of the simplest and most pliable of the fractal arts. The micro-cascades that acted as the building blocks of the wind were self-similar to their large-scale effects. Unless the end result was very specific, all a Sage had to do was macro a basic pattern, and the wind would blow as they pleased.

Without another word, Issid rushed forward on a burst of wind and struck at Ex. The attack was meant for his neck, but Ex managed to turn away from it. A single claw raked across his cheek. Blood from the wound sprayed at The Talon, but it was blasted back by the gust that followed him. Ex put a boot to Issid's thigh and vaulted backwards, landing in the steadying spotlight.

"The curtain has risen, Ex," said Issid. "Now you must act before it falls." A sooty footprint marred The Talon's pristine uniform.

Ex had caught his breath, and the wound on his hand had become a fading scar. "You done talking?" he said, brushing the dry blood from his cheek.

"I like to talk when I'm bored," said Issid. He gazed into Ex's eyes with a part of him that was both ancient and chaste to the Sophians' touch. His pupils drew to sharp slits, and a twitch skittered across his face, revealing glimpses of a primal horror. "Take that mask off!" he snarled and pounced.

The two clashed in the center of the spotlight. Issid's will was bent entirely on Ex; not a scrap of it remained to wield the wind. His face became increasingly telling of his ancestry as the fight went on. His jaw widened to draw bigger breaths, the worms wriggled about his teeth, and his attacks were wild.

Ex let Issid land a glancing blow on the side of his jaw, spilling a mouthful of blood. He pretended to stumble backwards, and Issid took the bait. As the Talon stepped forward, Ex landed a crushing kick to his shin. The steel tip of his boot met the Antican's bone with a loud crack and dropped him to his knees. Ex grabbed him by the feathery locks and slammed a knee into his chin. A few black worms had been decapitated by the lines of fangs. They continued to squirm on the ground in an oily puddle, but Issid lay still. And the wind pushed Ex away.

When he rose, the look on the Talon's face was unsettling. Instead of a grimace or look of fear there was only a wide, bleeding smile. His eyes were broad and joyful. The wind swelled and crashed over the dome like a great wave. The light swung away, and Issid struck in the dark. When the light passed again, only he was left standing.

Ex raged to his feet and scrambled towards the swinging light. Something struck him in the stomach and sent him careening back into the darkness. He tried to catch his breath behind a pillar, but he was quickly found.

Issid took Ex by the ankles and beat him against the column like a rug. He dropped him, it seemed, just to offer more verbal taunts. When the light passed, he was running bloody fingers through his hair. "Do you know what separates us from animals, Ex?"

Ex turned over coughing. "A tattoo and a can of mousse?"

"Close..." Issid seemed truly pleased that Ex still had enough life in him to make jokes. "It's this saucy repartee we're sharing! Beasts don't enjoy such pleasures. They kill because they must... but we kill for pleasure. Allow me to share something I learned in the Academy about your species. They say that to turn a man into a beast, you needn't add savagery; you need only to remove humanity. That concept has always intrigued me. Perhaps you can help me with a little experiment: point to the humanity on your body, and I will cut it out. Then we shall see if you turn into a beast..."

"No thanks," said Ex, and the Talon was at his throat again. He was flung into a clearing and struck from the left, then the right, and then from above and behind. Ex tried to stay with the light, but Issid wouldn't allow it. He swung blindly in the dark, and the Talon caught his fist, wrenching it aside. Ex's elbow locked, and he was thrown face-first into a column. The last thing he saw was a soft silver glimmer, a part of him, drifting away.

"I can't say that I'm not disappointed," said Issid. "I thought you'd play with me if I pushed. But I suppose if you won't reveal your secrets in life, we'll have to try death..." The spotlight shone down on him, held at an impossible angle by his will. He wasn't alone. There was a sterling incisor nestled against the toe of his boot, garnished with drops of scarlet. The Antican's pupils widened when he noticed a tiny light, pulsing at the root of the tooth. "Another trick...?" he smiled.

A piercing light filled every nook in the dome. Subdued in silence, The Talon was reduced to a silhouette by a sphere of white flame. His shadow was scattered into ash. The vivid sphere blinked and faded but never spread or made a noise. It had spared the last spotlight, which swung peacefully back to rest over Ex. He lay on his back, a gap-toothed grin draped across his face.

The dome came alive with vibrant emergency lights. Their orange beams bent across the vaulted ceiling, throwing shadows every which way. A spiral of ash was all that remained of Issid, just a few meters from the edge of the spotlight. Ex wriggled his tongue through the gap in his teeth; it was all the explanation he needed. He stood up, waited for his legs to shake the wobbles out, and set about collecting his weapons.

Shadows pounced on him from every angle as the high orange lights spun, but Ex didn't flinch; his recent brush with death had left him feeling cocky. He'd survived an encounter with a Talon, and what's more, an Antican. Of course, the story would need a bit of alteration – getting a bomb knocked out of your mouth was not the most flattering of victories – but he was confident that he'd find a more suitable resolution at the bottom of his next pint.

The dome was littered with weapons. He strolled down the aisles between the columns like a finicky shopper. He hadn't suddenly become a fussbudget; most of these weapons had been reduced to gun-shaped scrap during the course of the battle. And then there was his heirloom gun. He recognized it straight away by the distinct, U-shaped clip. There was no strut or swagger in his walk; he rushed for the weapon with honest urgency and lovingly nestled it into the holster nearest to his heart.

Next he spotted a rocket, resting peacefully on its side. It was slightly dented and scuffed all around, but still intact. "Hi there, little guy. Are you one of mine?" He gave it a few taps – as if he could discern something from its sound – decided it was still functional, and stuffed it in a pocket.

Back in the monitoring room, Zarfall was doing his best to ignore his Skwell assistant. "Sir, the scans are inconclusive. There was a high-intensity localized explosion, originating from a small, object less than 2cm in diameter. It's confirmed that the explosion terminated the Talon, Issid, but I'm unable to determine how the explosive was delivered. The intruder likely had it hidden on his person. The object must have been coated in perlite since our scanners were unable to detect it as a weapon. We did, however, inform Issid that the intruder had been completely unarmed, when, in fact, he was not. Command may look unkindly upon this mistake, Sir."

"It was his tooth," Zarfall said. "Any other place on his body and I would've questioned him, but it's so common for lowlifes like him to have dental work done in perlite that I let it slide... This is actually Gallowatch's fault!"

"His prosthetic tooth was an explosive?" asked the assistant.

"Yes, and it wasn't the first time he's used it either. That explosion in the main airways was likely another one of these bombs. He had a whole box with him..." Zarfall replied.

"He was allowed through customs with a cartridge of perlite-coated teeth?"

"Of course it sounds bad when you call it a *cartridge*," said Zarfall. "But if you wear jewelry for teeth and run your mouth off like that bastard, you better carry spares." With all the polite Skwell in the universe, he was stuck with the one smart-ass. He loathed having to work with freelancers, now more than ever.

"So what course of action should we take then, Sir? Shall we dispatch the remaining battalions? They're armed and awaiting deployment."

"No! Cut the emergency lights. Let him rot in the dark. We don't know what he's capable of, and I'm not about to lose more men; I've got enough explaining to do as is. He's clearly a Sage and a highly dangerous one at that. "

"But Sir, the ethereal scans have all come up blank..."

"I know," interrupted Zarfall, "that's what makes him all the more dangerous. The regenerative powers he's demonstrated are not even remotely congruent with his genetics, and the temporal disturbance recorded at time index 14:57:23... well, I've never seen anything like it. We've no idea what kind of threadwith he's packing, but clearly it's ample."

"Clearly," agreed the assistant.

"Look at the size of the *footprint* that the trick with time left. With power like that, he could've easily created the blast that killed the Talon himself and manipulated our sensors to detect whatever object he'd pleased."

"Clearly."

"And clearly, I'll not be made a fool of by a damn runner! I've been calibrating sensors since before he lost his baby teeth," said Zarfall.

"Clearly," repeated the Skwell.

Zarfall glared at his jiggling assistant. "Say *clearly* again, and I'll spread you over toast like *Vegamite* and feed you to Gallowatch."

"No, Sir, I'm done."

"I'm glad we have a *clear* understanding of each other because I'll not take the blame for letting a rogue with a mouthful of explosive perlite onto the station, and I'm sure you wouldn't like to take the blame in my official report either."

"No, Sir!" One large wave washed over the Skwell's surface, and then it was still.

"Now patch me through to Veredos. I'll report our findings to Central myself," said Zarfall, regaining his composure.

"Yes, Sir, Veredos on gemini channel 6, coming in *clearly*!" said the Skwell, shrinking a bit as the Executor approached.

"Toast..." Zarfall reminded and snatched the receiver out of the Skwell's folds.

The Vault

Ex sat in the dark. The silence was nearly perfect. He could scarcely sense the muffled rumble of the ark's reactor. The heavy walls had reduced it to an elusive vibration. He flicked on his ZAIN-HUD's display to see how far along its telehaptic sweep of the dome had progressed and was pleasantly surprised. The thin wires of light that delineated the structure hardly vibrated.

Apparently the pillars and struts did more than provide structural support; this was the bioark's central hub. The beams pulsed with green energy, relaying invisible messages and power, circulating air, and completing other essential tasks. His sensors were overloaded with a clamor of information now that they could peer through the veneer of perlite. There were, however, many rafters that hung dead in the air, and columns where the energy flowed like blood through a fat Eidolan's arteries. The battle had crippled operations throughout the station. He almost felt bad about it – almost.

But there was one area where the HUD's overlay still trembled and shook. He stood and walked towards the disturbance. Viewed from the side, he could see waves propagating across the wireframes. Their vertices stretched and billowed without pattern. He rounded a pillar and came to look upon the source of the interference: a ribbon of light on the distant wall, a faint tear in the jet-black fabric of his vision. He cautiously approached. The lines that the HUD painted around the cut vibrated with enough speed as to appear thick.

By the time he'd arrived at the wall, the nick had grown into a gash. It was as if a giant fingernail had been pressed into the bulkhead. Soft light bled through from the adjacent room. When he peered inside, the wireframe was scattered. Its lines danced off four silvery crates, swathed in silken flags emblazoned with the CIR's crest. They were cradled atop four separate pedestals and lit by four lights.

Ex backed away from the wall. "This looks awfully important," he said, thoughtlessly ramming the wall with his shoulder. The impact traveled from shoulder to shoulder by way of his collar bone like a scientific demonstration of Newton's Third Law. The fissure had been caused by an explosion, and it would take another explosion to widen it.

With this in mind, Ex reached for the rocket in his pocket. He stepped up to the light and examined the projectile. There was a nozzle on the tail designed to regulate the flow of propulsion. It was shut tight at the moment, but Ex wagered that if he could crack it open, he might just be able to stage a launch. However, if the warhead didn't activate on impact, the weapon would hardly scuff the wall.

He opened a panel on its belly and went to work on the circuitry. Despite the fact that he didn't recognize half of the gizmos in the device, he rearranged the wires and resealed the panel with confidence. "These fools don't know who they're dealing with," he smirked. It wasn't enough to assert his physical superiority, now he'd humiliate them with his rich intellect.

Lacking a proper launcher, Ex held the rocket in one hand and a pistol in the other. He assumed a comfortable distance from the wall and took careful aim at the fissure. He squinted one eye, using a vertical fin as a sight. For a moment, he wobbled to and fro, assessing the precise pull of the ark's artificial gravity – a bit sprightly, maybe a point-98. He raised the rocket's nose a few inches to make up for the slight drop in altitude during the acceleration at the beginning of its flight – indeed, he'd taken every factor into account. Once ready, he gave the nozzle a knock with the grip of the gun. The missile sputtered before erupting into flames and scorching towards the wall. Ex covered his ears in anticipation.

Just as it was about to hit the wall, the missile pulled up and hissed straight back at him. "Oh scrote!" he exclaimed. Apparently Ex had launched a heat-seeking rocket, and now its orangey glow chased him around the pillars. He wove through cover, but the rocket was crafty and gained quickly. He made a break for the hole. The heat of the missile's exhaust closed in on him as he scrambled up the wall with a few hard steps and jumped for a rafter overhead. The rocket pulled up, but it was too late. The resulting detonation busted the hole wide open and threw Ex upwards, slamming him against the bottom of the rafter. He hugged the beam for a second and dropped seven meters to the deck below.

A smoky light flooded the dome, and it sent shivers down the spines of every last wireframe in Ex's vision. The HUD's sensors were useless again, so he shut them off and leapt to his feet in a bit of a fluster. "This better be worth it," he said, stepping through the mangled metal wall.

The left and right walls of the room were lined with deposit drawers. A large vault door occupied most of the opposite wall, still firmly shut. But Ex's attention, like the majority of the light, fell directly on the four crates in the center of the room. They appeared as sacred relics, raised on steely altars and swaddled in lavish cloth.

He turned his HUD's display back on to confirm his suspicions. The crates were at the epicenter of the distortion. They were not just coated in perlite; they were made entirely from the precious material. It was hard to mistake its misty chrome appearance. These boxes alone would be enough to make up for his trouble.

Ex pushed aside the CIR flag that was wrapped around the crate like a sash and unlatched the hinges. The lid swung open. He took one look inside and was struck stupid and stiff. The box was filled to the brim with glowing ingots of duril.

The first lode of duril ever discovered, sleeping in the frozen tundra of northern Xerbekos, weighed a fraction over 7 kilograms. To this day, it'd remained the largest ever unearthed by a large margin. Entire planets had been shattered for a gram, and entire expeditions had been launched in pursuit of a single molecule.

The box resting between Ex's sweaty hands contained around 50 kilos of pure duril – enough to make a preacher fold his scripture into a paper airplane and send it flying. He didn't know whether to be ecstatic or terrified. This dusty station in the middle of nowhere had piqued his curiosity the moment he'd laid eyes on it. It sat in space like a loose stone, but never in his wildest dreams could he have imagined this. There was enough duril in this box to purchase multiple galaxies. If the other crates were like the first, he might even be able to buy an entire ring. Not that the CIR would sell it to him, of course.

He was already slated for extinguishing, but plundering this much duril ensured that every man, woman, and child – or being that didn't fit into any of those categories – who could lift any kind of weapon would come calling for a piece of his absurd fortune. This cache was worth so much that it was worth nothing at all.

Still, it wasn't as if he could just walk out of here and apologize. He took an ingot in each hand and weighed them; they were ironically light.

"I'm over-thinking this," said Ex, stuffing his coat with ingots. He didn't stop grabbing bars until all of his pockets and holsters were filled. The only weapon he kept was Arius' gun. Its clip still housed the fifth bullet that'd given him such a sweat during the interrogation a few hours ago. It was his ticket out of here, and he couldn't wait to put a cylinder to it.

The Skwellachi assistant was narrating what Zarfall saw on the monitors in a voice that sounded like a small man speaking through a kazoo. This was the absolute worst case scenario. There was no precedent in CIR law or procedure for losing this quantity of duril.

"Damn it! Do something useful!" the Executor barked. "Deploy a spool, alert the fleet, and scramble the remaining Nyrceff!"

"Only one spool, Sir?" replied the Skwell.

"You heard me," confirmed Zarfall. "Don't worry, that snake's thread will shove the rest right out of the way. We've got to focus on damage control at this point. Seal all exits, and as soon as The Placator arrives have it block port. There's no way this runner is getting out of here."

Ex emerged from the hole in the wall, looking rather ridiculous. His pockets were bulging with the burgled booty, but he was careful not to catch his coat on the snags of metal.

A battalion of Nyrceff had been deployed into the chamber, but Ex could see now. As long as he didn't focus his sensors on the hole behind him, the wireframe was crisp and steady. It wasn't difficult to keep track of their muffled heat signatures, crawling across the rafters above.

"You couldn't handle me when I was blind!" he taunted from behind a pillar. He raised his only pistol and gave it a gentle kiss, his hand caressed by the curves of its U-clip. Regardless of how dire the situation was, Arius' gun made him feel safer.

He took a deep breath and a translucent arrow appeared at the edge of his vision. It was a downspin indicator, dithering as the ZAIN-HUD assessed the direction of the universe's spin – a critical step before making the drop into anchorspace. That was anchorspace's greatest limitation: since you didn't actually move, the universe could only pass you by in the direction of its spin. Celestial bodies were said to be downspin of your current position if you could reach them without completing more than half a revolution around the Prime Axis; everything else was considered to be upspin. If you imagine the universe to be like an ancient Solarian record, the types that carried music carved into vinyl, the sound you just heard was upspin, while the sound you were about to hear was downspin.

The navigational computer within the bowels of Ex's ship awoke. They defibrillated the old engines with a series of electrical surges. The ship snapped the docking seals and backed up into the vessel behind it, ramming a sputtering engine nozzle through the canopy of its bridge. Alarms wailed as the ship lashed around in place before erupting into full thrust, torching half of the port in its wake.

Ex pressed his back hard against a column as the Nyrceff opened fire. The dozens of ingots he'd stuffed into his coat wedged into his ribs and spine. Comfort was not amongst duril's many qualities. It didn't yield a single angstrom to his skin and bones.

His cover wouldn't last. The Nyrceff would modulate their weapons to pierce straight through the pillar. At higher frequencies photocaster bolts could put a hole straight through the entire ark. He drew his mother's gun and fired the first round at the ground ahead of him. Counting the shot he'd fired at the back of the frozen rocket launcher, that made two.

There was a pause in the gunfire. The Nyrceff were recalibrating their photocasters, which required no more than turning a knob. Ex made a break for a nearby pillar, firing two shots as he went. "Three, four," he counted aloud. The duril wasn't weighing him down, but its sheer bulk made it difficult to move.

In the middle of his run, an ingot bounced out of his pocket and tumbled to the floor. He turned back to pick it up and nearly lost his hand as the Nyrceff opened fire again. The photocasters were tuned to a frequency that was high enough to put clean holes through the deck. A few bolts struck him in the chest and upper thigh. He could feel their force and heat, but he was not hurt. The duril had turned them away. For the moment, he was wearing a form of impossible armor. There wasn't a setting on any photocaster that could pierce it, but there was still plenty to hit besides duril. He threw himself behind a pillar, landing stomach-first. He was fairly certain he'd been shot, but it was just the duril digging into his organs.

Floundering over, he focused his attention on the HUD's downspin indicator. *CALCULATIONS COMPLETE*, it read in glowing green letters. The arrow pointed steadily behind him. Without hesitation, he pushed off the column. The photocaster bolts were coming through the metal in hot bubbles. He could see the Nyrceff leaping onto the rafters overhead in efforts to flank him. His gun was pointed straight at the pillar, but all that mattered was its alignment to the lucent arrow. If he were off by a millimeter, the only thing that would be left of him would be a pile of duril bars.

The fifth round chambered, the muzzle's iris widened, the piston raised, and then it struck.

The Nyrceff in the bullet's path would never know that Ex had fired an anchor round. In the time it took a synapse to relay the information to the next, the projectile was several galaxies away. Before leaving the ark, it'd cut a clean hole through the pillars, the floor, and a dozen layers of hull. Its diameter would suggest that a small ship had just fired out of Ex's gun, but in fact, he'd only sent a single atom into anchorspace. This was the power of a weigh-1 anchor round, the smallest caliber of its kind.

The first phase of the round's activation was designed to clear a small vacuum directly ahead of the pistol, sparing the user from the force of a point-blank anchor blast. It'd worked perfectly.

One moment, Ex had been staring at a cage of wires that his HUD painted around the contours of a column; the next moment, he saw a well of stars with his own, natural eyes. They shimmered intensely as the hole drew its first breath. The Nyrceff that'd been caught in the penumbra of the anchor round's passage trickled into space like ants down a drain. They careened off the jutting bulkheads and remaining pillars. The suits of sleek armor were mostly intact, articulating into impossible positions. Their innards had been liquefied by the shockwave that propagated from the epicenter of the bullet's path.

"Five!" said Ex. Having fired the round himself, he stood immediately upspin of its drop-point. As a result, he was completely unaffected. For a moment he considered the molecule of duril that was consumed whenever an anchor round of any weight was fired: the ingots that lined his pockets made it seem impossibly trivial.

Then he felt the pull of space, ever-ravenous for any matter willing to fill it. It began as a draft and quickly blew with hurricane force. He turned and ran for the nearest intact column. His boots skated backwards on the deck in the mounting airstream. The ark's old skin gave way, and the wound widened. By the time he'd reached the pillar, Ex and the rapid decompression were evenly matched. If he could just get to the other side of the column, he'd be safe. He clawed at its smooth surface, and his footing began to slip. He could go no further; all he could do was try to hold his ground.

From the corner of his tearing eyes, he could see a few of the remaining Nyrceff clinging desperately to the rafters. Anchorspace collisions were terrifying, but highly directional. A weigh-1 anchor round could stir the dust on a planet in the neighboring galaxy if it happened to be in its direct path, but its forces decayed exponentially as they traveled at right angles. The flanking soldiers had been spared. They'd live long enough to wonder what the hell had happened. The Nyrceff's military training didn't include so much as a briefing on anchor rounds. They were only footnotes in the porous historical archives of The Extinguishing to which they were given access. Perhaps it was the exorbitant price of a duril molecule or because they could only be crafted by a finely trained Sage, but since those times, more than 300 years ago, only two of these weapons had been fired. Twelve years ago, Arius had fired the first, and today Ex had fired the second.

Ex's coat pocket tore, and an ingot escaped. He turned to watch it slide and tumble into space. His eyes felt like they wanted to follow, but he kept a fierce squint on the stars. "Where the hell are you, you damned ice chest?!" he yelled. He could scarcely hear himself over the roaring wind, but he had to expel the air from his lungs anyway.

More of the bars ripped through his pockets and slipped out of bandoliers, but his ship was nowhere in sight. His vision dimmed, and the strength drained in bloody streaks from his fingertips. Arius' gun shook in its holster, until the strap that held it against his chest snapped. It fumbled through his arms as he fell backwards. Using the last of his breath, Ex pushed off the column and dove after the pistol. Past the second or third hull, he slipped a finger through the trigger guard and clutched the gun to his heart. His back struck the next layer of bulkhead, which flipped the switch on his brain. Then space took him.

Anchors Aweigh

Ex felt puffy. The fizzy champagne that'd replaced the vitreous humor of his eyes made it difficult to see, but he thought he saw his hand deflating from what looked like a blown up latex glove. By the time it was good and hand-shaped again, the bubbles in his eyes had cleared.

It took him a moment to recognize the cargo bay of his own ship. Sometime after he'd lost consciousness and before space had fully turned him into a meaty blue balloon, the ship had caught him in the open bay. An appreciation for the dramatic was not an easy thing to teach to a navigational computer; he blamed Arius.

The ship teetered beneath each of his steps and slowly spun when he stopped. He pressed his head against the wall, waiting for the tiny bones of his inner ear to shuffle back into place. His lower intestines were a reservoir of Luin's vengeance. He fought a violent urge to purge their sloshing contents as he ricocheted towards the engine room.

Everything was just as he'd left it, except for the presence of Moh-La, who sat against the wall of cargo containers with his eyes closed. The black olive at the point of his nose fluttered as he snored. His paw clutched an empty bottle of Mohmish Porter, the saltiest and most dehydrating booze voluntarily consumed in the universe. Ex's cheeks ballooned just thinking about it. He woke the drunken rat with a little kick to the tummy.

"Oi! What're you doing back here?" snorted the Mohmil. "I quoted you four days!" The fact that he'd brought a drink and no tools or replacement made his intentions a bit suspect. The cargo lockers' keypads glittered like slot machines over his fuzzy, round head.

Ex picked him up by the scruff of his back fur and stuffed him into an empty locker. Once that was sealed up nice and tight, he slapped the broken piece off the anchor drive and replaced it with the pristine original. He gave the chrome orb of his drop chart a kiss for luck and was off to the bridge.

The outpost's weapons were of historical significance; they might've fetched a comely price on a Centrian military antiquities market. The autopilot had flown Ex's ship out of range before they'd had a chance to fire. Assuming manual control, Ex banked into a sharp orbit around the planet. His plan was to use the planet to mask his drop into anchorspace. Hopefully that would throw off the CIR long enough for him to make his escape.

Meanwhile, a trio of A1 Churchills rumbled out of the station's main dock. These Arsenal ships were archaic even by the old bioark's standards. Most of the remaining A1s could be found in museums of classical astronautics, inviting patrons to marvel at the bravery of the men who once took to the stars in glorified trashcans. The Churchills were aptly named; contrary to what Computer-Age Classicists might believe, their namesake was not the famous Winston, but rather a

Jack Churchill, who was credited for felling an enemy soldier with an arrow from his longbow during a war with nuclear bombs.

Ex ran a quick systems' check. Most of the ship's essential systems were borderline, and the missile bays were *half depleted.* "Half depleted?" he asked aloud. "Damn pessimistic machines." His mind was already drifting to sandy beaches dressed in sapphire waves, frosty drinks sweating in the shade of tiny umbrellas, and well-seated women patting the sand from their god-given padding.

The triangle of A1s had somehow managed to close in on his position. "Sorry, I don't have time for a history lesson," said Ex, triggering his afterburners, but the ship ignored his command. He bashed the console until the thrusters ignited, and the relics disappeared in his wake. He continued to orbit the planet at maximum velocity in order to break line of sight with his would-be pursuers. The drop chart began its calculations, counting down from 2:42. "Over 2 minutes?" He was enjoying the benefits of Arius' frugal shopping – perhaps the only person in all of history who could literally think things into existence and still managed to be a plex-pincher.

A tiny light telescoped out of the console, bent its head, and began whirling with abandon. It was accompanied by an equally annoying alarm. "What the hell are you?!" he pleaded with the little light. The antenna stopped spinning and straightened out to point at a nearby display.

On the monitor was a Placator Class heavy-cruiser, storming around the planet in counter-orbit. These warships were the muscle of the Consortium fleet. Their arsenal was renown throughout the rings. They could uproot a star with their massive gravectors, plant a new one with a starseed rocket, fly straight through it with cutting-edge tempraflect shielding, or simply extinguish one with overwhelming conventional weaponry.

Although they were better suited at destruction on a mass scale, they possessed weaponry precise enough to slice the legs off an asteroid hopper. And to make matters worse, every Placator came with a full complement of grapplers and superiority fighters, each with their own drop chart and anchor drive.

Ex fumbled for the controls. He yanked a joystick out of the paneling, which had been previously detached by a similar act of desperation. He tucked a few frayed wires back into the metal casing at its base, placed it firmly between his knees, and pulled back on it as hard as he could. The retro thrusters spat to life, and the ship came to a crushing halt.

An archaic HUD attached to his seat on a swivel spun around and cracked him on the temple. He retaliated with a strong backhand and ducked the HUD's second attack as it bounced around in its hinges.

Trying to flat outrun the Placator with his conventionals was out of the question; his rickety old drive was no match for the CIR's Valoforged engines. But these leviathans weren't known for their nimbleness. Ex's only hope was to outmaneuver the cruiser for the couple of minutes that remained on the drop chart's timer. At this point, he didn't care if he dropped into anchorspace in front of their noses. Sure they'd follow, but it was difficult to track someone in anchorspace. If they came out a millionth of a second too early, they'd be in a different galaxy. A millionth of a second too late, and they'd end up downspin, which meant that they'd have to complete an entire lap around the universe to get to him; that would take precisely 52 hours.

He brought the ship about, nuzzled the atmosphere, and streaked back towards the station. If the Placator closed to weapons' range, there would be no warning shots. The Consortium would destroy his ship and salvage the duril from the debris at their leisure. Already a swarm of long-range missiles were hot on his tail. They were approaching fast. *Impact in 10 seconds*, the tactical computer warned in a tranquil tone.

"Countermeasures!" said Ex, slapping the button on his hydraulic chair. The hatch in the ceiling slid open, and the chair began its slow, creaking ascent. He stood up in the seat and pulled himself into the battle bubble, wasting no time in deploying the countermeasures. A sundry of tiny spheres tumbled out of the ship's cargo. A couple erupted into dazzling flares, but the majority drifted through space, sputtering sparks in their wake. The console calmly reported their malfunction.

Ex dove through the hatch back into the bridge and threw the ship into a violent barrel roll. The lead rockets collided with the cluster of countermeasures, but the majority came through. He struggled to tear the ship out of the planet's gravitational pull, only this time the dusty atmosphere gave him more than a peck on the cheek – it was getting hot and heavy.

Alarms blaring, the ship skipped across the mesosphere, and the remaining projectiles detonated in his fiery wake, but his situation had not much improved. He was rapidly approaching the trio of A1s, and the Placator had scrambled a flight of five Lupine Fighters. The aggressive tusks of their hulls glinted in the starlight behind him.

Ex juiced the afterburners and soared out of the sandy skies in a splash of flame. He pointed the ship directly at the A1s and used the still-rising chair to climb into the battle bubble, hoping to depreciate the value of these antiques. They opened fire with a ballistic Gatling that was more suited for a reenactment than actual combat. It wasn't much worse than flying through light space trash. Ex primed salvos seven through nine, and flipped the launch switch.

The rockets sat comfortably in their racks, consorting with their neighbors. In his mind, they'd grown arms and stood on their tailfins. Holding fresh snifters of Gin Martonics – two parts gin, one part vermouth, three parts tonic, lime rind rubbed against the glass prior to pouring – they negotiated the specifics of an evening partner swap. He tore open a panel beneath the console, connecting and disconnecting fistfuls of cables at random. Salvos seven through nine had been dumped into space. Ex watched the cloud of rockets shrink in the rear display.

The ship had flown beyond the Churchills. Now they peppered the aft with some of their more contemporary weapons, scuffing the slats of the heat sink's exhaust. Ex tried to worm his way back into the bridge but was pinned against the side of the hatch by the rising chair. He flailed about, spitting in anger as the chair deliberately compacted his ribs. His inner organs were forced up into his throat and into the bowl of his pelvis. He pounded the seat's controls to chips. The hydraulic system bucked wildly, he managed to slip out as the seat was slammed repeatedly against the edges of the hatch. The fatigued metal of the long arm that raised the seat creased, and the whole thing tipped over in one last, terrible squeal. It fell like an indecisive tree, coming to a bouncing rest over the helm console.

Ex ducked beneath the fallen chair and snatched up the joystick. He circled around the three Arsenals and pinned his ship to one of their tails, regretfully unable to open fire from the bridge. This ship was designed to transport meat at very cold temperatures. It was not designed for combat or to be operated by a crew of one. But it was just as well; he'd use these relics as a shield from the Lupine Fighter's fixed cannons while the drop chart finalized its preparations.

Solid fuel poured from the three nozzles of the A1's engines. There was an uproar of light and sound, but the thing didn't go anywhere. Its wings, if they can be called that – more like pipes that attached the weapon modules to the fuselage – began to melt. They bent backwards and hugged the snub nose of Ex's ship. He was now effectively wearing the A1 as a hood ornament.

A wave of rockets crashed over the dogfight. Ex's ship was spared by the bit of cover that the melty A1 and his wingmen had unwillingly provided. They'd bought him a few seconds, but 34 remained in the countdown.

Ex knew he couldn't outrun the Lupine Fighters. They came at him full-afterburners. There was no need to waste another missile. They'd dismantle his ship with their close-range weaponry. He used the chair's bent hydraulics as a step to scrambled back into the battle bubble. The targeting display warned of limited functionality. His weapons had been badly damaged by the recent blasts. He was so close to escaping, but he'd run out of options. His only hope was to fend off the fighters for another 28 seconds. He nearly crushed the weapon's control as he grasped it with both hands, firing wildly across the crest of their formation. The pilots avoided the beams with a few minor adjustments.

23 seconds remained.

The Lupines opened up with their Mercurial Beams. Ex's shields shrank before his eyes. He could have fed them more power, but decided instead to reroute the remaining energy into the weapons systems. Their status immediately went red.

Ex had to enter a manual override to get his cannons to fire again. They flailed out of control, painting space in chromatic rays. A gleam of light flashed in the darkness. It was followed by a wave of explosions that raced around the perimeter of the ship. A happy beam had grazed the outer casing of a warhead that he'd accidentally flushed into space earlier, triggering a chain reaction. The Lupines were consumed by a crescent of spiraling rockets.

"You walked right into my trap!" He could already imagine future pilots calling this *The Ex Maneuver*.

9 seconds remained.

Lost in self-worship Ex failed to notice that the Placator had entered firing range. He glanced down at his anchor drive's status.

Preliminary Checks: Complete (3 errors found)
Subroutines: Cleared (90% efficiency)
Drop Capacitor Status: Green
Anchor Pathway: Verified
Drive Status: Awaiting final confirmation from main control.

Things were going swimmingly. It seemed as though he'd make his daring getaway after all. The targeting magnifier glided over the bubble's canopy, focusing on the Placator. Ex could see its primary cannon collecting strands of luminescent energy.

5 seconds remained.

"Too slow," he smiled, propping his legs onto the battered console and melting into a comfy position in his favorite swivel chair.

"Attention all hands," announced the computer, "course laid in; dropping into anchorspace in 3... 2... 1... drop."

Ex's head was cradled in the fleshy hammock of his hands. He cracked an eye opened and saw the cruiser still centered on the magnifier, but closed it again, hoping this was some sort of malfunction that would just go away. "Attention all hands," spoke the ship's computer, "Error."

He bolted out of his chair. The flashing console reported a severed connection between the helm and the drop chart. He briefly recalled tearing a cable that he'd assumed to be decorative out of the wall and stomping it in victory. "Hmm..."

The cruiser's beam sliced the ship clean down the middle, leaving Ex trapped in the confines of the airtight bridge. The halves drifted apart; the aft spiraled lazily into the stars, while the bow slowly spun towards the planet's surface. Ex got a good look at the inside of his engine room as his half spun. The drop chart gleamed in all its chrome splendor as it awaited the final command that never came. Countless split wires whipped about in a frenzy of sparks.

Ex stood up and pressed his hand against the glass. He'd always been so rough on his poor ship, but it'd never let him down. It had never failed him in a pinch. He'd been born on this ship. And now, he'd failed it. A single tear welled in the corner of his eye, reflecting the globe of stars that surrounded the battle bubble.

A couple of the flailing wires touched lips. The capstan spun, the anchor light flashed, and the entire hind section of the ship vanished into a perfectly plotted course through anchorspace. "Get back here, you traitor!" he yelled. The bow turned towards the planet and began its burning descent through the atmosphere.

Unbeknownst to Ex, the Placator had streaked off after the fleeing engine room. Their sensors had picked up traces of a complex life form, stowed away in a cargo container. The captain had decided to chase after the craftier of the two thieves – in this case Moh'La.

The nose of his ship burst into flames as its angle of approach sharpened. The battle bubble was entirely engulfed. Ex aimed delirious threats at his drop chart as the heat baked him first out of his reason, then consciousness.

A girl bustled around a sandy ridge on the surface below. She walked around the perimeter of a small patch of flattened ground where the sand had been tilled into neat rows. The three suns dawned on the horizon across the vast desert. They capped the dunes in gold and gleamed white off the silvery mountains. The girl entered one of the rows, careful to step only in the furrow. She picked up a few stones and loose twigs that littered the crests, but didn't remove them. Once they'd been arranged into a more pleasing pattern, she tiptoed out of the field and sat on a large stone to watch the skies, her sun-ripened cheeks kissed by the first rays of morning. The stars still shone through the ceiling of deep lavender.

"Chimi... Chimi!" called a voice from below the ridge.

Chimi stood from the rock, her eyes still lifted upwards. She was familiar with the constellations of this planet, but there was a new light in the sky today: a bright red star that pulled a billowing white tail as it streaked down at the sunrise. "Mom, come look! A shooting star!" called the girl. "Can I make a wish?"

A hot wind blew over the dune sea. The sand of this world was so fine it was almost invisible in the air. It appeared as a metallic glitter when the light of the three suns fell at this angle. When the wind settled, the difference between the troughs and crests in the young girl's field had been reduced.

"Yes, but make it quick or we'll be late for our shift," her mother replied.

"I know what to wish for," Chimi said softly. She never spoke the wish aloud, but her mother knew it all the same.

Puppet Show

At the center of the universe lay a massive super cluster, which the Sophians had deemed a single galaxy. They called it the Gravagastion, and its heart was not a black hole, but the most ancient and largest of all stars, The Grand Forge. Its stellar mass was greater than all the three hundred billion stars of The Milky Way combined. The Prime Axis ran straight through its poles, and all of existence spun around it. Through a process unknown to even the greatest Sages, this unfelt force supported the star, molded it into its unique oblong shape, and kept it from collapsing under its own weight.

The Veredene System had no star. Its planets orbited the cold gas giant, Saruhaim, but the light and warmth of The Grand Forge, over forty thousand light years away, was enough to sustain life. The fifth world of this starless system was encased in seven spherical webs of metal. Spinning like clockwork, every tier presented an inhabitable surface. This was Veredos, homeworld of the Sophian race and capitol of The Consortium of the Inner Rings.

High above the surfaces of Veredos, The Luciel orbited on wings of golden feathers. Each of the delicate quills had been forged centuries ago in the graceful foundries of distant Miraval, and not one had needed refitting since its maiden voyage. Two Valoraphs, cousins by way of their fathers, argued in the forward section of the ship. One of the cousins had a pair of majestic wings; the other had a pair of scars.

The one with the wings was Kelmore. "Forget it! I'm not going," he said. The Luciel's nose was pointed straight at Veredos. The chamber's wide windows cut a slow-turning panorama of the shifting surfaces below.

"You have to go," replied Nodris. "The invitation was for both of us."

"No. *You* have to go. You're the Viceroy of the Second Ring. I'm just a lowly ship captain. My presence won't be missed." Kelmore was dressed all in black, balling a gold sash in his hands.

"It will be missed," said Nodris, laying a hand on his cousin's shoulder. He wore a white cloak hung from gray epaulets. It was emblazoned with the Consortium's crest in cobalt thread. The fabric of his lapel sagged under the weight of a bushel of ribbons and regalia. As far as Valoraphs went, Nodris and Kelmore bore little resemblance to one another. Nodris could look over his cousin's head without standing on his toes. His burnt gold locks were worn in shoulder length curls, and his features were broad and welcoming. Kelmore's platinum hair was cut in short tufts, and his features were svelte. They shared only the color of their eyes: a blue like O-Type stars. Amongst Valoraphs, only the royal Gincleare family was permitted to have eyes of this color.

"The Sophians treat us like children," Kelmore protested.

"If our age is the sum of the years we remember, then we're infants in their eyes," said Nodris.

"It's insulting how they shovel their history at us," said Kelmore.

"We have to give them more time. Centuries flutter by in blinks to Sophians. They have no experience teaching their history because they've never had a need to learn it."

Kelmore shook his head. "Last time it was a puppet show."

"Just put on your sash," said Nodris.

The shuttlecraft exploded from the bay. In his youth, Kelmore had flown sorties out past the Seventh Ring, where space became thick as a reef, and he'd come back cocky. The metaplanetary networks spun like the guts of a lazy timepiece. Below them was the eighth layer of Veredos, the Solid City, an unmoving black mass, visible in the cracks and gaps that aligned in the clockwork.

Fourteen kilometers of space separated each of the planetworks, as the metaplanetary networks were called for short. The shuttle shot from the first to the third before Nodris could take a breath. He thought they were going to crash into a blade of the second, but it vanished in front of his eyes. The giant metal webs looked slow from orbit, but they spun at several thousand kilometers per hour.

Kelmore matched the speed of the third planetwork. The gauges read 6285 kilometers per hour, but they'd come to what appeared as a stop directly over the lavish gardens of the Gialuze complex. The yoke bucked as the ship entered the synthetic gravity. This was the sort of thing a computer normally handled and everything would go smoothly, but not with Kelmore in the cockpit. The shuttle landed in a large fountain with a statue of a robed Sophian, hands clutching its curled horns.

"I think you missed the mark," said Nodris.

"I know. I was aiming for the statue," Kelmore replied.

"I'm not getting my boots wet."

Kelmore shucked his safety belt. "Want me to carry you?"

The ramp lowered to the edge of the water. Kelmore didn't need it. He spread his wings and floated to the marbled walkway. Nodris marched down to where the water lapped the ramp and hop-stepped onto the slick fountain ledge. His medals jangled as he flapped his arms to regain his balance.

To their left were the great mansions of the Gialuze family, entrusted with keeping the secrets of the knots that sat at the base of nearly every thread in the civilized universe. It was these knots that kept the populace from aspiring to become Sages and trading bodies or will. Unfelt and uncontested, they hung somewhere imperceptible and eternal.

The Gialuze enjoyed a surfeit of luxury that was more suitable for the first planetwork than the third — a subject of whispers in The Centower. Nodris had been invited to several of their soirees, each in a new home no less grand than the last. But today their destination was the largest structure in the complex: The Gialuzian Theater, with its gothic glass ceilings and columns cut from the cores of giant Istreyan Steelwoods. The view from inside was enough to draw an audience without a scheduled show. The shadows of the first and second planetworks passed across supernovae like frozen fireworks in the crowded heart of the universe.

Nodris and Kelmore were shown to their seats in the center of the second row. They were among the last to shuffle in. Just behind them sat old Moddrick, the Viceroy of the Third Ring. His face was long with boredom. The row was filled with his Centrian cohorts. One of them flicked a gear on the joint of his jaw. It spun, and his mouth slackened before clamping shut with a whir. He continued this action until Moddrick's eye telescoped in his direction.

Kelmore glanced around the audience: not a Sophian face to be found. He heaved a sigh and wriggled into his wings, trying to find a comfortable way to sit. The Centrian behind him would only catch the top half of the show; there were no complaints. The glass ceiling turned to mirror, and the curtain rose.

Kelmore bit his fist. "Puppets!"

A twelve-meter-tall marionette fell from nowhere into a hard spotlight. A string was attached to the forehead of a white mask with horns like a ram. For eyes it had holes filled with dark air. Two other strings controlled hands gloved in porcelain, and a black cloth was draped between head and hands. The strings flowed up into the mirrored ceiling, connecting only to the marionette's reflection.

An enormous balance scale rose from the stage, just ahead of the marionette. The Sophian language was reserved for their own use. The booming narrative began in clear Solarian. "War, hatred, death..." A black sphere appeared in one of the bowls. It bobbed low. "Love, beauty, birth," spoke the voice, and an orb of blond metal materialized in the other bowl. The two sides teetered up and down until the black sphere settled lower than the gold. A soft breath could have leveled them, and this was how the Sophians weighed the parcels of their inherited memories.

In a flash, the scale's frame was consumed by fire. The marionette raised its hands, and a pyramid rumbled out of the stage. There was hardly enough room for its base, and the capstone rose as high as the marionette's pointed chin. It was flattened into a seat for a much smaller puppet that sat with its horned head in the crook of its arm, resting in air. The deep pits of its eyes stared vacantly into the crowd.

Applause.

Nodris put his elbow into his cousin's ribs. Kelmore clapped his hands in his lap.

A cube at the base of the pyramid morphed into a marionette with an extra string that put a hunch in its back. "Saruhaim rises as a pale eye at night and sets as shadow in day. Another year draws to its end; it will be my thousandth. The slow seasons of Veredos, I have weathered them all. I am old, but you are older, child," the puppet spoke to The Capstone. "Once I sat in that throne, and now I am a cornerstone, irrelevant with age. But I've learned things in the dead end of dusk which I would share."

The Capstone raised its head. "Then speak, Cornerstone, before death claims that wisdom."

Kelmore leaned into Nodris' epaulet. "What clunky exposition. Why can't they just come out and say that Sophian children are born with their parents' memories? Can you imagine what that'd be like? Your kid would be born knowing all of your dirty little secrets... It would keep everyone honest, that's for sure. Still, it'd be nice to remember a centuries' worth of sweat worked up in Grandpa Gincleare's harem."

Nodris shrugged him away and dusted his shoulder.   "You'd remember Grandma's side of it too," he said, and Kelmore was deflated.

One by one, the bricks of the pyramid transformed into supplicants. They were as identical as the stones, though their backs straightened with each of the eight steps. The Sophian face had been sculpted by millennia of structured breeding. The subtle differences in their features were hardly appreciable to alien eyes, and they viewed the wild variety in other races as unintentional and vulgar. But on the third step from the top, there was a single marionette that seemed out of place. Its face was long, and its horns were not as tightly wound. It looked vaguely like the Gialuzian statues that stood watch over the grounds outside. The marionettes took turns lobbing lines of wisdom at The Capstone, facing the audience when they spoke.

At length, The Capstone stood and silenced the supplicants. A jar appeared in his raised hand. Inside, a helix was suspended among the tiny bubbles of a clear gel. "I hold here the full genetic code of The Capstone of the Anathemos Pyramid, acquired at the cost of many Soheren lives. Today, I will join it with my own, creating a child that possesses all of this world's knowledge."

The supplicants raised their arms and wailed. The strings that bound their hands vibrated, sending ripples across their black cloaks. Kelmore chuckled into his hand as if coughing. A supplicant on the second tier calmed the rest and spoke. "Capstone of the Soheren Pyramid, you are eldest, yet clouded by youth. It is true that we've picked blindly at the Anathemos' code for millennia, sewing fragments of their memories into our generations that often prove trivial or detrimental, but we've retained our identity. This child might grant our family all the knowledge of The Anathemos Pyramid, but so too would it give the wealth of our heritage to them. A half-Soheren, half-Anathemos child would be as much our enemy as our family…"

"This I have considered," said The Capstone. "But I've summoned you here to announce my decision, not for the recourse of your counsel. We shall reconvene in five years time, after the children experience The Onset of their memories."

"Children?" asked the chorus, and the pyramid dissolved, leaving only The Capstone to stand in center stage, his back to the audience. When he turned around, there was a large pot made of cloudy glass in his hands. He dropped the helix into the liquid inside, and it dissolved like drops of multicolor ink. A small curtain rose, and he did things to the pot. When the curtain lowered again, the container was full of fetuses.

"Whoa. Did he just do what I think he did to that pot?" whispered Kelmore. Nodris put a stiff thumb into his ribs. A pang of pain shot down Kelmore's back. His left wing spread over the armrest and brushed the lap of a young woman, an Istreyan diplomat dressed in a gown of pearls. Her ruby red lips drew an O, and the flesh beneath her husband's bushy brows started emitting light.   Kelmore apologized before the Istreyan druid decided to mutate the fauna of his stomach into a sentient race of inquisitive microbes that one day might launch expeditions into his liver or worse. Although Istreyan Sages spent lifetimes mastering the art of affecting threaded entities, they had to meditate for several minutes before they could start poking around your stomach. And since the druid wasn't humming, Kelmore figured he was safe.

The lights dimmed and a voice spoke: "The children grew in an abbey in the mist of Ansen Falls." Ten tiny puppets appeared, all in a row. "They reached the age of four, and so began The Onset. They remembered the land and language. They remembered a million sunsets and the slow evolution of the night sky, bright explosions lapsing over generations. They remembered the mathematics that explained it all, the history of each discovery, and the thrill that accompanied them. They remembered how to wield a knife. And they remembered uncountable ages of harbored hatred. With the knives they found in the kitchen, they tried to cut one half of their heritage from the other." The little marionettes went limp in series until none stood.

"Seems kind of extreme, doesn't it?" asked Kelmore.

"It's not supposed to be family friendly; it's supposed to be historically accurate," replied Nodris.

The pyramid rose again, and the supplicants spoke to the Capstone: "It was to be expected. The children could not withstand knowing that they were everything they'd come to hate twice over. The Onset drove them mad. Your experiment has failed."

"You misunderstood its purpose," interrupted The Capstone. "It was not my hope to unify the Pyramids, but rather to prove incontrovertibly that they could never be combined. Ultimately, there can be only one outcome, only one solution. We must bury the Anathemos Pyramid in the sand before it can be built any higher."

"The war you speak of would ruin this world," said a supplicant.

"Would it be any different in the future? Or are we only climbing to fall from a greater height?" asked The Capstone, and there was silence.

The stage went black, and the narrator spoke again, "And so began The Veridian Schism, bloodiest war in all of Sophian history..."

When the lights came back on, there were two armies of marionettes amassed on either side of the large stage. The Soheren were dressed in white and the Anathemos in red. They all clutched little bats and rushed screaming. *Clickety-clack*, the clash happened center stage; the two factions bonked each other over the head without a sign of mercy.

Kelmore leaned into his cousin. "Very historically accurate," he said.

The fighting continued; only the scenery changed. And when most of the puppets had fallen and none in red still stood, an enormous tree in the center of a grotto raised in the background. The Capstone walked to the tree and, with a wave of his hand, engraved the following words into its gray skin: "Veredos, what have we become?" And the curtain fell.

Applause. Kelmore gave a drifting ovation, which involved standing and clapping, but also walking away slowly. Nodris pulled him back to his seat by his sash. "What? I want to beat the crowds," said Kelmore.

"That was just the first act," said Nodris. "There're seven more."

Kelmore's wings bristled.

"Calm your feathers, Kelmore. It's not like you have anything better to do."

"It's not like I have anything worse to do either."

Nodris unfolded the show's program. "Did you know that tree with the engraving still stands on the surface in absolute darkness, ten kilometers beneath the Solid City's lowest floor?"

"Yeah? And its only visitors are blind creatures of carrion," said Kelmore.

"You make it sound so grim," said Nodris.

"It is grim. Don't let these puppets fool you."

"I suppose you're right." Nodris put his chin in his hand. "Sometimes I wonder if we're the puppets."

Kelmore rolled his eyes so hard, he nearly pulled a muscle. He leaned over and plucked a bronze star off Nodris' chest. "You just lost a medal for that one."

The ceiling became transparent again, and there were the stars, cut by the shadows of the higher planetworks. Then came a sudden rush of water: The Walking Waterfall that issued from The Colossal Statue of Soheren built at the foot of The Centower on the first planetwork. Despite its tremendous size, the statue was a glint from this distance, lost in a twenty-eight-kilometer-tall spiral of water. It fell in a rainbow roar around the great ducts that encircled the Gialuzian Theater. A single, perfect loop, and it passed. The water collected in the channels overflowed, pouring onto the lower planetworks.

Applause.

The glass became opaque, and the curtain rose for the second act. There sat the inscribed tree, alone on stage. Silver blocks fell from the sky, forming a wall that seemed to stretch beyond the ceiling. This was the face of the Solid City, a metal shell built around the core of ancient Veredos. All of it was inhabitable, and in fact currently inhabited. The wall sprung black quills, representing the towers that served as living graves for the Sophians who fell from higher planetworks when time and age made their knowledge obsolete. A metal web imprisoned the quills. This was the seventh and lowest of the planetworks. The other six planetworks appeared at different angles than the last, and they all shifted slowly. They materialized in a line of blue light as they entered stage left, and vanished similarly as they stretched beyond stage right. The Solid City was only visible when the layers were perfectly aligned.

From the first and highest planetwork soared The Centower, extending over the heads of the audience. The spherical glass chamber it clutched like a jewel at the end of a scepter loomed over the back rows. "This is the world that Soheren built," explained the narrator. "It was designed so that even the denizens of the Solid City will see the demiurgic light of The Grand Forge…"

"Why wouldn't they just move to a different planet?" asked Kelmore.

"Too many memories of living in the same place," Nodris replied. "Sophians get homesick easily."

"And they feel at home on metal blades, spinning dozens of kilometers above a dead rock that used to be their planet?"

"At least the sky's the same," said Nodris.

"Only to the aristocracy of the top tier," added Kelmore. The narrator went on to explain that the first and highest planetwork was inhabited by the Engryas, roughly meaning *the power of eight* in the Sophian tongue, and how the subsequent tiers within the Soheren pyramid were assigned to the lower planetworks according to their station.

The planetworks' diameters shrank with each step, but the population grew in exponential leaps. There were sprawling parks with entire mountain ranges brought up from the surface of Veredos on the first planetwork. On the seventh, the streets were narrow ravines, carved into blocks of steep skyrises. The inhabitants there had to turn to their memories to see a tree.

The Gialuze Family was the exception to this rigid hierarchy. Their unique position on the third tier was a continuation of tradition that began before the Age of Soheren. Certain families were chosen to safeguard knowledge that the pyramid didn't want falling into enemy hands. It was common practice to extract the genetic information from the two highest tiers, so these families were relegated to the third. There was no threat of Engryan blood being stolen today, but it wasn't convenient for the entire Sophian race to know how to untie a spirit from its body with a single tug. The Gialuzian family had held its station since the end of the Veridian Schism through various secrets.

"Inbreeding..." Kelmore whispered. "That explains how their horns got so loose."

"They're not inbreeding!" rasped Nodris. "Without an influx of new blood, they'd become ignorant and obsolete in a single generation. They just never breed upwards. Besides, don't forget whose theater you're in. This is hardly the place to be talking about the Gialuze Family's sexual habits..."

A hand tapped Nodris on the shoulder, and he nearly sprouted a new pair of wings. It was a Sophian Mercourier, messengers of the Consortium. "The Capstone requests your presence immediately, Viceroy," he said. Moddrick had been summoned as well; he was already halfway up the aisle.

Nodris stood and excused himself. Kelmore rose as well, but the Mercourier sat him back down. "Your presence was not requested, Captain."

"And who's going to fly him to the tower? You?" asked Kelmore.

"Watch the rest of the show, you'll learn that every Sophian possesses thousands of times the flight-experience of a seasoned outworlder pilot such as yourself, Captain. Any of us are more than capable of manually flying the Viceroy to The Centower in the unforeseeable case that the autopilot malfunctioned."

Nodris was gone with a half-sorry smirk.

Kelmore sank into his wings. The tower shrank overhead. The planetworks dissolved one by one, and the Solid City deconstructed, leaving only the painting of the grove.

The lights dimmed. "Act three," said the narrator. "Twelve thousand years later, Teros Soheren Greyan was born." There was a pause, lasting several minutes. It wasn't an intermission; that's how long it took for the applause to dwindle to a level that could be spoken over. "At age eight, with all the wisdom that is known, Teros assumed his position on The Centower as The Twelfth Capstone of the Soheren Pyramid." An image of the Centower sprung from the stage, and a white mask hovered inside the glass sphere it held aloft. Its hollow eyes bore down on Kelmore.

"A few years later," continued the narrator, "he was on the verge of the greatest scientific breakthrough in all history." The universe appeared as a spongy disk centered on the tower, filling the auditorium with light. "Viewed all at once, the cosmos do not appear to spin, but if you are able to *anchor* a ship outside of space, to somehow break *The Synch*, things are quite different..." The stars smeared into rings of brilliant light, running circles around the tower. "The benefits of this technology were immediately apparent, but putting his theory to practice proved difficult. The process placed immeasurable stress on a single focal point that no material known to Sophians could withstand.

A lesser man would have relinquished after two centuries of frustration, but Teros was willful. His ambition tested the limits of his birthright. At his behest, the Sophians scoured the stars for a substance that could endure the anchoring. They found their answer buried in a tundra of clear argon ice in the barren world of Xerbekos: 7.6 kilograms of duril, frozen in fragments." The light of the universe scattered into snow.

"The new metal proved stubborn. It refused to be shaped or cut. And so the first anchor drive was built around the raw ore." The snow settled into the shape of the Gravagastion Galaxy. "The first test was conducted on the outermost fringes of The Gravagastion, but the resulting shockwaves could be felt as far as Veredos." There was a series of vivid flashes around the edge of the galaxy. They sneezed away the dust between the stars.

"When the scouts reported back to Teros in the Centower, it was not without hesitancy." And there were the puppets again, prostrate before the mask of The Capstone." The constellations had been rearranged, innumerable worlds had been eradicated, but when Teros heard the report, he simply said: 'Launch another.' And the second time there was no explosion. The test pilots returned to the point of departure approximately 52 hours later."

The First Ring was drawn around the galaxy.

And for a moment, just a few seconds, Kelmore forgot that this was the same technology responsible for reducing his home planet to a cluster of asteroids in a single shot just a few decades later.

The Face in the Tower

The underside of the planetworks were curved plains of cold metal. Only the occasional maintenance hatch or shuttle port interrupted their smooth contours. The air was perfectly breathable. The gravity would pull you comfortably to the deck, but the metaplanetary networks were built to offer the inhabitants a view of The Grand Forge in the Veredian heavens, and the underside only caught acute glimpses, so it went uninhabited.

When Nodris closed his eyes, he could still see these stars clearly. He'd been born in these skies 72 years ago. His mother had given birth to him in the golden belly of The Luciel, orbiting high above the first planetwork. The memory of her was as misty as his recollection of Atamal, the star that had forged the atoms of his people. He was eight years old, studying in the royal academy on Miraval, when he received the news that both of his parents were killed in what was called a shuttle accident, here in the planetworks of Veredos.

The sky was cut by the arms of the first planetwork. The Sophian pilot flew them in counter orbit. At their narrowest, the planetworks were several kilometers wide, but at this speed, they passed like fan blades. "It can't be helped, Viceroy Gincleare, the Executor in charge of the base was not Sophian," said the pilot.

"I doubt The Capstone will need reminding of that fact, pilot," said Nodris.

"At times, it seems he might..." replied the Sophian.

"Very well, I will pass on your concern of his memory in my report," Nodris calmly replied.

The shuttle's nose tipped up, and the ship darted between the blades. Hills, forests, and shining homes as big as castles rushed below. "Forgive my insolence," the pilot said.

"*No forgiveness, only atonement*: aren't those the words inscribed at The Centower's entrance?" asked Nodris.

"They are," replied the pilot. "Allow me to redeem myself with this information, Viceroy." He took a datatab from his cloak and handed it to Nodris. It contained the same information that had puzzled Zarfall and Gallowatch a few hours previous. "The Executor swears by the results of his scans. As you can see, it is the word of your half-kin against the impossible. I do not envy the task that lies ahead of you."

"It's not my place to convince The Capstone of anything." Nodris returned the tab. "I will simply present him with the facts as they are, and trust his wisdom will see the truth where we cannot."

"Well spoken, Viceroy." The shuttle continued to fly in counter orbit. The Centower leapt over the horizon, and the retro thrusters fired all at once. They came as a soft whisper through the hull, but Nodris could see the blue flame licking the bottom of the wings. The pilot banked the ship into a slow circle around the Capstone's chamber. Nodris peered into the glass sphere, but there was no white mask; all he saw were the stars on the other side.

They docked at the highest port. An alabaster plank stretched across the stars to meet him. He stood at its end, and it retracted. Valoraphs could exist in the cold vacuum of space without complaint, but it was a warm breeze that greeted him on his way to the tower.

The ceiling, walls, and floor were a shade short of white. At the end of the hall, a Maiden of the Tower awaited. She was a young Sophian woman, a few years over 50. The walls seemed dimmer in the presence of her skin. She wore a fluted blue gown that held her just above the hips with a belt of pale lace. The roots of her horns were hidden in willful curls of raven hair, and her lips were dressed in charcoal. She'd spent her whole life in this tower as a living key – only the touch of such a maiden could open the doors of The Centower. The ears beneath her horns had heard many secrets, and her slate-gray eyes had seen many things. For this reason, she would never be allowed the privilege of motherhood. Her children would be born with the weight of all her knowledge, and that made them a potential threat that was better avoided.

Throughout his term as Viceroy, Nodris had dealt with dozens of these maidens, but this one was different; this one he knew by name. It had something to do with her eyes. They didn't wear the aloof gaze of a Sophian. There was a trembling light in their dark pools, hints of tears or something wonderful. "Good evening, Zaralin," he spoke in Sophian as he bowed.

She returned his greeting in flawless Valoraphim. "The Capstone requests your presence," she added. Her eyes were fixed on his as she spoke, another trait unique to her amongst the maidens. She extended a hand towards him.

There was a corner of his mind that could think of nothing more than grabbing her by the wrist and fleeing from white walls, and shining towers, and prisons of pale lace. But he'd spent his whole life repressing such emotions. He hovered his hand under hers and let her grasp it. Her other hand reached for the wall. With a gentle touch, a black doorway opened in front of them. She ushered him through, but didn't follow. Nodris turned to see her standing in a frame of light, her eyes now fixed on the ground. Her lips were the last to fade as her image dissolved into darkness.

Nodris took a few blind steps forward. His eyes widened, and he found himself engulfed in a chamber of stars. This was as close to night as there could be in this place. The light of The Grand Forge scarcely crested Veredos' gilded horizon. The serenity of the view belied the urgency that'd brought him here.

A clear voice echoed through the glass chamber, speaking these words in the Sophian tongue: "Twelfth Capstone of the House of Soheren, Patriarch of Veredos, and Prime Sovereign of the Consortium of the Inner Rings: Teros Soheren-Greyan." Upon hearing this, Nodris fell to a knee and bowed his head. When he looked up, he was in the presence of an enormous white mask, floating in the center of the spherical room. It bore an expressionless gaze between coiled horns, and its hollow eyes were full of stars and distant galaxies.

The Fallen Star

"Am I dead?" Ex wondered. All was dark and silent. His vision played tricks on him, offering promises of light and hints of color, but when he turned, there was only black. "Death is boring," he said and tried to sit up. His forehead struck the darkness in a painfully familiar way. He caught his sleeve on a latch as he brought his hand up for a rub, and the lid flung open in a flash of sand and crude light. He rolled over and pulled his tattered collar over his head; living, for the time being, seemed an unappealing option. Then a faint noise tugged at the tiny hair in his ears. It sounded like a child, crying in the distance. The sound grew clearer until it almost seemed to form words like "mom" and "don't leave." It was annoying as hell.

Ex took in his surroundings through a fierce squint. He was standing over a crash capsule in the middle of a deep crater, littered with the smoldering remains of his ship. A crash capsule was like an escape pod without the escape. He kicked its lid. He wasn't really mad at the thing; it had saved his life, but he was just in a kicking mood.

He rubbed his temples, wondering how he'd made it into the capsule in the first place. The last thing he remembered was cursing his cowardly engines and blacking out on the bridge. A headache muddled his memory, but he hadn't forgotten the duril. He fished a few bars from inside the capsule and set the autodestruct timer. With it gone, the CIR would never suspect that he'd survived.

Now he just had to get out of here before it self-destructed. If the impact that made this crater had barely scratched the capsule, the type of explosion that could destroy it would probably be more unpleasant than a headache.

The sand began at a slow slope before sweeping into sheer walls all around him. Ex gathered up speed and dashed at the cliff. The wall turned to powder under his boots. He slid back to the bottom, followed by a gentle cascade of sand. Not one to be thwarted by dirt, he continued to claw and flail at the wall in desperation.

Sitting waist-deep in the sand and sucking in gulps of the dusty hot air, he couldn't help but wonder what exactly he was breathing with such confidence and craving. His HUD's readings were as confusing as his ship's sensors had been in orbit. The composition of the planet's atmosphere was still a mystery to him, but luckily it didn't matter. There was a masterpiece of science coursing through his veins. It had been there since his birth – since the birth of his mother and her mother and many mothers before.

The Starfarer's Strand was the pinnacle of Solarian genetic engineering. This sophisticated chromosome was capable of altering an organism's most basic functions on a cellular level, so that they may breathe the atmosphere of almost any planet and metabolize next to anything they dare pass through their gastrointestinal tracts. The exceptions were highly complex metals, alloys, and gases. While it was possible to gather nutrients from every piece of matter or joule of energy in the universe, it was impossible to do so without drastically affecting the physiology of an organism.

The Starfarer's Strand functioned in a realm outside of basic Solarian perception, such that those who possessed it would never perceive its existence – aside from not choking to death upon removing their helmet on a foreign planet or keeling over in agony after sampling interstellar cuisine. It was a big part of what made the First Path so successful at intergalactic colonization, and it was as far as they dared to stray from natural evolutionary human form.

Terraforming was a thing of the past. The Starfarer's Strand allowed Solarians to adapt to planets rather than having to adapt planets to them. The colonists of today became true citizens of their new worlds; though ironically, Ex had just come from a relic of that past. Bioarks were once the workhorses of the Solarian's terraforming efforts.

He grabbed a handful of the warm sand. Tiny flakes of glinting metal were interspersed between crumbs of beige and sun-washed ochre. He clutched his hand into a fist and let the granules pour from his fingers. Maybe it was the way it confused his sensors, coated in pearly shifts of color, smeared with images of distant stars and his own face, but there was something magical about it. He repeated the process a few times, mystified by the sand.

"The timer!" he suddenly exclaimed and raced over to the capsule. Less than a minute remained. He tried to shut it down to no avail. A manual somewhere read: *Once the crash capsule's autodestruct has been initiated, it cannot be stopped*; this was how Ex found out. He dashed back towards the cliff and filled his boots with sand. The more he thrashed about, the further he sank.

The last seconds ticked away, and Ex bravely turned to see the capsule fizzle and melt away with a modest hiss, dissolved by chemical reaction. Through whatever inexplicable thought process, the lack of an explosion disappointed Ex.

The stone pillar had been half-revealed in the avalanche. It was dotted with grooves and footholds. "Oh, a ladder," said Ex and used it to climb out of the crater.

Up on the ridge, his feet sank in the sand when he stood still. The three suns glared over an unending desert. The largest of the stars was enough to support life on this planet, but it was orbited by two smaller stars that shone just as bright. Together they resembled an atom of helium, burning at the apex of the vacuous blue sky. The light slithered on distant dunes and pounced at his eyes from the ground beneath him. It'd been painful enough in the crater, but here it was worse – the perfect complement for a headache. "I could kill for some sunglasses right now," he growled, speaking quite literally. He was too busy envisioning himself accosting a local thug for his shades to realize that the sand had already swallowed him to the waist.

It wasn't easy pulling himself out. The more he struggled, the further he sank, and the sand flooded his duster's sleeves and pockets. Tan arcs flung into the blue as he backstroked out of the hole.

He chose a random direction and wandered into the wavering horizon, spilling sand from every orifice. The soft ground crunching underfoot sounded more like snow than sand. He plodded onwards just to hear it, if nothing else. But he'd only gone a few paces when he heard the child again, crying from just over the next dune.

Now that his pupils had hidden beneath the color of his eyes, the landscape revealed its more subtle features. Stone pillars littered the wastes. Some of the stones were simple monoliths like the one he'd climbed, stabbing straight out of the sand. Others were complex, branching out like petrified trees.

Ex approached a pillar near the foot of the dune. It reminded him of cacti he'd seen on half-terraformed planets. Maybe it was due to the arid environment that framed it, or maybe it was its peculiar shape: a cylinder with smooth pleats and a single appendage that stemmed from its hip like a raised hand. Its face was peppered with smooth holes of varying sizes – spots where the elements had won out.

A hot breeze pressed its lips against the pillar and played a simple song. Distant stones, resembling antlers and ancient trees, played more intricate melodies, but their songs could not muffle the child's cries; they were closer than ever.

Where the wails had once teased words, now only sound remained: a sawtooth wave that jumped up and down the scales as no child's voice could. In all likelihood, the words had come from the shrinking boluses of the head trauma he'd suffered, not the desert. The cries rose and fell with the stony flutes, as if their peaceful songs caused pain. Ex looked down at the meager puddle of shade at the pillar's feet and followed its contours up towards the sky. He pressed a cautious ear to the stone.

The desert wind rolled over the dune and lashed the baked rock with blades of sand; the wails grew. He crept his head along the stone until he arrived at a narrow hole through which the cries leapt. The gap passed clean through the rock; the source of the cries was just on the other side. Ex snuck around the pillar and found a bushel of colorful butterflies, fluttering in the shallow shade of the one-armed stone. Beneath their vibrant wings were wispy tendrils that bound the creatures to a root in the shade. What he'd mistaken for wings were actually razor-thin leaves. They fluttered at the end of their stems, vibrating at speeds beyond vision as they rode the wind. Each trembling leaf emitted a different color and sang a different pitch.

Ex wiped his brow. Even in a basin between two large dunes, he could see dozens of these plants scattered about. Most of them hid beneath the shade of a pillar, though a few had sprouted up on their own, relying solely on their reflective leaves for protection from the three suns. But whether in shade or sunlight, they all cried the same.

Recalling his orbital scans, Ex knew that there were two cities on this planet and that they were not far from one another. The only problem was he had no idea where he was in relation to them. He could be between them or clear on the other side of the planet. However, being the cunning scientist that he was, he quickly devised a strategy by which he could ascertain the most logical way to progress.

He sat beneath the standing stone and traced the outline of its shade. Then he waited for the suns to move the shadow, so he could determine in which direction they were setting. With the suns at his back, he began his journey into the weeping wastes. If he'd chosen the wrong direction, the desert would turn him to jerky, and even if he'd guessed right, it was unlikely that the people in the settlement would be happy to see him. Still, he wasn't about to wait for the CIR to come pick him up.

His pace had to be brisk, or he'd lose ground as he struggled up a giant dune. He paused at the top to collect his breath and scan the horizon. An endless sea of sallow dunes stretched before him, wavering in the infernal heat. Ex collapsed, letting his body tumble down the dune for dramatic effect. A wave of sand buried him, and he arose with the vim of a zombie, spitting out moistened dirt, and cursing his penchant for the dramatic – which was another penchant of his.

"I'd probably be better off trying to fix my ship..." he sighed. As if on cue, a huge fireball billowed into the silver-blue sky from the wreckage a few dunes over. "...or not," he shrugged. The black plume may as well have been a signal flare in this featureless desert. He had to put as much distance between himself and the wreckage before the CIR came looking for the missing duril. At least he didn't need to hide his footprints; the desert wind saw to that. Unfortunately, the same wind that buried his tracks also buried tiny blades of silica and perlite into every pore of his face. Ex glared at the three suns, grinding the sand that had collected in the pits of his molars. Just as he was getting fierce, a gust slipped down the dune and smote his eye with a sharp mote. "I love this planet!" he said with a one-eyed squint.

Crunch, crunch, crunch... the desert was unending. It'd been five dunes since he'd left the comfort of his crash capsule. He decided he couldn't take much more of this and collapsed at the base of a great pillar. He crawled on his belly, reaching desperately for the meager shade. "I'm dying!" he moaned. A weeping plant sat ahead of him in the shadow, looking on in curiosity. In the throes of his passion he grabbed a handful of its stems. The razor-thin tendrils cut deep into the flesh of his palm, lending a bit of authenticity to his act. Ex clutched his hand into a fist, and a few drops of scarlet hissed onto the sand. His wound healed quicker than the desert could evaporate the speckles of blood.

As he watched the scars vanish into the lines of his hand, he was visited by a memory from his childhood. Arius was fond of taking him to inhospitable places, and he was fond of following, but on one occasion, she was forced to drag him along, kicking and screaming. It was not the destination that had him in such a tantrum, but the reason for the visit. She'd made the mistake of telling him that they were going to get him a babysitter. Ex had protested being referred to as a baby and absolutely refused to be sat on. Yet once again, this *babysitter* had saved his silly life.

It wasn't a chaperone that his mother procured for him, but rather a blessing from one of the last *Sojournist* Sages in the universe. Ex remembered the whole ordeal like it was yesterday. That planet was even hotter than this one. There were pools of glass where the giant star had melted the sand and not a trace of life to be found. It was the sort of planet that really put The Starfarer's Strand to the test. When they arrived at a small, pyramidal hut at the base of a glass valley, Ex couldn't wait to get out of the sun. He required no convincing to enter; in fact, he beat his mother to it.

The interior was pleasantly cool, freezing compared to outside. A man sat on one of three canvas chairs in the unadorned tent. His skin was glossy black and his face lacked definition. He had no eyes, no ears, no nose, and no mouth, yet sculpted contours that hinted at each. But what captivated young Ex's attention most were the bands of neon colors that laced across the Sage's skin. Streaks of blue, white, and yellow formed elaborate patterns, running from his head to his toes.

Ex would later learn that the man was a Sojournist, a race of beings that inhabited mannequin bodies such as this one. They were able to jump their consciousness from one side of the universe to the other in the blink of an eye if an empty vessel was there to receive them. When the body was occupied, light would come to the shell in a pattern unique to the inhabitant.

In the times before The Extinguishing, the Sojournists had merely controlled the mannequins from great distances, while their cores remained bound to their native bodies. Enormous arrays hosted millions of dormant husks, nourishing them, and keeping them safe as their owners skipped through the stars. Their technology was rooted in the same principles of trans-dimensional movement and quantum entanglement used by the gemini. The Sojournists could remain wherever they pleased, while the hollow bodies traveled to their destinations. And with a single thought, they'd be there too.

During their exodus, the Sages of their race managed to take this technology a step further. They used the bond between the particles to sew the two locations together. Their entire thread could be passed into the empty body across this quantum bridge. The Sojournists' old biological forms were cast away, their home world was abandoned, and their people spread among the stars as far as their ships had carried the mannequins.

The ability to teleport across vast distances made a Sojournist Sage nearly impossible to catch. But nearing the end of The Extinguishing, the CIR declared that any of these vessels were potential Sages, and the entire Sojournist race was hunted down to near extinction. Still, new bodies were manufactured and sent out into the expanses of space, and their race humbly subsisted. Of course, Ex knew none of this at the time. He was enthralled by the man's shiny skin.

He was instructed to sit on the chair and try not to squirm, neither of which came easy. As the man focused, Ex felt his skin crawl. Spasms shook his small frame and his throat went terribly dry. In his mind, he began to burn, but he was not consumed by the flames; he became the fire.

The Sage spoke clearly without the benefit of a mouth, "I've knit you a sweater." The tone of the voice had no age, no gender, and no emotion that Ex could recognize. It continued to speak, "Your entity now knows what your body must be, and so it will be preserved as long as the thread is with you."

"OK, good," Ex nodded, clueless as to what the Sage meant. He was gathering up the courage to ask, when the neon light suddenly faded from the black body, and the hut heated up in a flash. The chair beneath Ex sprang into flames, and he ran out to his mother's cooling shadow.

Since then, his regeneration had watched over him like a guardian angel – or a babysitter, if you prefer Arius' metaphor. Although at times it seemed he purposefully tested it, Ex had no idea what the limitations of his recuperative abilities were. All he knew was that they were undetectable to genetic scanners, which made them well suited for a low-key gentleman such as himself.

Ex was in the process of burying the plant in a mound of sand he'd raked with his boot when a sharp squawk called his eyes to the sky. A large white-winged creature descended in a slow spiral, a spaded tail in tow. It balanced itself on a stony branch with a few flaps. Greasy scales bound its pale body, and stubby horns crowned its head. Its expansive wings doubled as arms with claws for fingers. Serrated teeth jutted from the edges of its long, narrow beak in every direction. At its end were two large fangs, one chipped and the other broken in half. The scales around its maw were covered in pink scuffs and crusty black splotches.

It stood on a couple of spindly twigs it called legs. Their knotted joints rose well over its stooping head. It probed the air with an oily tongue and stared at Ex with beady eyes, swinging its spaded tail just out of his reach. It'd caught the scent of baking blood and now waited for the desert to finish cooking its meal.

"You ain't gettin' none of this jerky!" Ex declared. The creature flapped its wings and hopped to a closer branch. It lurched over and gnawed on its tail, which lashed back in protest.

The head and tail fought for a while, much to Ex's amusement. "Well it looks as if you've found a snack, so I'll just be on my way," he chuckled. As he passed under its shadow, he heard something drop to the sand behind him; it was the creature's tail. Its spaded head opened, revealing a vicious mouth. It lunged for his ankle. Sheer shock threw Ex into the air.

The greasy vulture squawked in delight as the tail continued the attack. Ex ran in circles, leaping wildly as the white worm struck at his heels. He couldn't match the serpent's swiftness over the sand. He reached for a low-lying branch, but his hands were met by painful pecks.

This odd couple enjoyed quite a profitable relationship. The bird would fly high above the desert, using its fine senses to hone in on potential prey, while the blind snake masqueraded as a tail. When the time was right, its poisonous bite would incapacitate the victim, and the two would feast – a symbiotic relationship to rival the finest of military strategy.

Ex ran around, kicking up sand, until he could flee no more. He extended the tip of his boot, and the snake took the bait. It chomped down on the steel-toe and was flung towards the horizon by a mighty kick. The vulture gave a squawk and chased after his associate. Ex bent over, gasping for air between laughs.

He hadn't even fully regained his breath, when he heard a caw overhead. There was the pesky vulture again, snake and all. Apparently, their appetites had not been dissuaded by the failed offensive. They hovered just out of reach.

He raced up a dune and grabbed a handful of sand. "You should fear me!" he roared and threw the handful into the wind. The sand was blown straight back into his face, but he didn't flinch — perhaps he blinked a few more times than he would have liked, but he didn't flinch. A victory.

Confident that he'd made his case, Ex pressed onwards, scaling dune after dune, and all the while his new friends were not far behind. Occasionally he'd pause to yell at them, and they'd retreat, but only slightly. They continued to taunt him, perhaps to boil the last bits of energy out of his blood. But Ex was resilient; he wasn't about to be done in by this overgrown beach and less by that infernal bird and his sneaky snake pal.

After having thrown the worst words he knew at the duo, he decided it was time for a new strategy. Using the sum of his dramatic experience, Ex let out a pained gasp, sprawled onto the sand, and lay still. The scaly bird landed a safe distance away and hopped around a bit, but didn't fall for his ploy. It's likely that Ex's whispers of "eat me... come on, eat me..." didn't help sell the effect. With a bit more sand added to his growing collection, he hoisted himself back to his feet and plodded on.

The plume of smoke hung low in the horizon, and Ex's boots were growing heavier. He'd lost count of how many dunes he'd passed, but they seemed to keep getting steeper and steeper. Suddenly, he felt a nip at his calf. Hunger had gotten the better of the bird's caution, and it had snuck in for an appetizer. "You've *misunderestimated* your opponent today, my scaly friend!" Ex declared as he dove after the fleeing bird. They took turns chasing each other around the sand, with both mouth and tail scoring snippets of Ex's coat. The opponents were evenly matched. Flustered beyond his final wit, Ex's hand crept towards his trusty gun. But the moment his hand met the gun's grip, the vulture squawked off into the sky. "Hey, you forgot your tail!" yelled Ex, hurling the snake after the bird.

"I've finally shown the desert who's boss," he said to himself. The sand in his pockets seemed lighter. A cool shadow spilled over him, and a moist breeze touched his neck. He had no idea where it'd come from, but it felt great. A tiny trickle of sand fell over his shoulder, and it was brushed aside by another puff of air. There was a rather pungent stench in the humid breeze, swelling at a steady rhythm. The smell was something between wet dirt and rotting meat. Ex slowly turned to face the source of the monstrous breath.

He was met with a huge horn, sand still spilling over its cracked sides. It was attached to the broad chin of a very large creature, big as a ship. It had the head of a bull and a body like an enormous walrus — but Ex wasn't familiar with either, so this was all new and exciting to him.

The giant beast reared back its heavy head and spewed a geyser of sand into the sky from a blowhole on the nape of its thick neck. The damp dirt rained down as a soft mist over its cracked, leathery skin. It rose up on a pair of hoofed appendages. Their width distributed the creature's massive weight across a large enough area to prevent it from sinking in the desert.

"What's this guy got that I don't?" Ex pondered, disappointed that it'd spooked the vulture where he'd failed. With a mighty snort, the dune bull sprayed Ex in a film of mucus. It was about this time Ex reached for his holster again; he had half a mind to put an anchor round through this thing's horny chin. But since each of those bullets were worth more than his former ship and he only had two left, he thought better of it.

The bull raised its hooves and towered above Ex for a moment. Thick tail still buried in the desert, it swam backwards with an undulating motion, before crashing down in an explosion of sand. It lowered its horn and began to sway, readying for a charge. Driven by an atavistic instinct that should be no part of any creature that called itself sentient, Ex lowered his head as well. He took the initiative and began his headlong rush at the beast. Just as he was about to connect, the bull's eyes shot open, filled with the fear of death. In a giant lash of sand, the bull was gone, weaving and whimpering through the dunes with astonishing grace and speed.

"That's right, run! You didn't even have a scorpion tail. What kind of a giant desert creature doesn't have a scorpion tail?" mocked Ex. "Soon, all the creatures of this desert will call me master." He was feeling quite satisfied with himself when he caught a glimpse of a small black creature out of the corner of his eye. It was a mixture of a frog and a hedgehog – perhaps a *hedgefrog*? Of course, Ex didn't know what either of these creatures were. The only animals he was familiar with were ones that called bars and gun shows their habitat.

The little critter hopped onto a nearby stone and sat perfectly still. Its face, or maybe back, was adorned with three white crescents. Together they formed the eyes and mouth of a cartoonish face. "Don't even bother, little guy..." said Ex, "I'm the new sheriff in town." The critter jiggled a bit and launched a single black spine at Ex's neck. A single complex vowel sound was all he managed: "You... "

He lay on his back, gazing up at the vast blue sky, and just then realized that it tasted like sugar-kissed grapefruit with a twist of something cool like mint... no, cooler than mint... or hotter? It was hot! Flaming-hot like the Midoran Fire Cherries that Arius hid in his cereal for morning giggles.

Each note the stone flautists played sent a ribbon of color across his vision, some vivid orange, others a violet that ate away at the blue canvas on which they were stroked. Rings of tan and ochre rippled across the sky like a pond reflecting the vast desert. He turned to the smiling critter. "That's not how it goes," he said.

The world had turned on its head. "This must be the south pole," Ex reasoned. He scrambled to a nearby rock and clung to it, not wanting to fall into the sky. Slowly, his legs left the ground, then his body, until all that was left between him and falling into space was his grip on the small stone, half buried in the sand.

The hedgefrog sat on a nearby rock, its painted face contorting into a crooked smile. "Come jump into my hand, lil' buddy..." Ex growled. He reached out and got a handful of spines.

A few friends joined the creature, and they too sunk their quills into his flesh. The additional needles restored gravity, and Ex crashed back to the sand.

The wind had stopped, and the stones no longer whistled. A couple of the hedgefrogs hung in the air just above the desert floor, caught in mid-jump. Not a speck stirred. Ex reached out; "Oh, the air is solid," he discovered. "No wonder they're stuck like that."

The day was a mural. The rocks, pillars, critters, sand, sky, and suns lay on the same plane. He raised a leg and placed a foot on the horizon, painted on the wall. Sand trickled from his boots onto the clear blue sky as he walked over to the three suns. He sat by them, legs crossed, and prodded them with a finger.

"Now, how am I supposed to get anywhere?" Ex sighed. He gazed at a midnight ceiling of stars and surveyed the day below until a tiny wrinkle caught his eye. He tugged at the crease. The world folded over itself. A bright light poured through an opening where the fabric had been drawn, and he crawled through.

When the lights settled, he was staring at a portrait of a night sky as seen from the mouth of a great ravine. The stars were still as silver embroideries on a rich purple curtain. He walked towards them, but never neared. His tired eyes turned to a spot on the ravine wall. It was painted with faint reflections of the sky above. Its surface was soft as felt. He took it with both hands and pulled it apart.

A new tapestry unfurled before him, sewn in dazzling thread. It was a scene of a mountain path, meandering up chrome cliffs. The steel-capped crags that plunged from the desert floor below looked like crooked rows of Centrian teeth.

He was not alone on the stage. A line of hedgefrogs hopped behind him. They still wore crescent smiles, but had shed most of their spines. He reached for the chrome cliff. It took all of his strength to draw it apart a few inches through which he could pass.

He wormed through the small gap and floundered onto a great stage, far larger than the previous. The colossal mural that towered before him was hard to take in all at once. Millions of small squares came together to form the shapes of dunes, stones, porous pillars, and stretching sky. A single tile corresponded to a grain of sand. He walked closer, or perhaps the wall came to him, and the squares grew larger than his head. Closer still, and the tiles surpassed him in size.

What he'd mistaken for a single grain of sand now encompassed the whole of his vision. It was a new mosaic, comprised of countless tiles like the last. This one was a scene of a man sprawled on the sand. He was surrounded by a ring of hedgefrogs. They looked funny without their quills – little fleshy balls of oily black skin. One of them began to grow, until it was all Ex could see. He walked towards a single black tile and passed into a portrait of night.

He went on in this manner, finding new mosaics in the tesserae of the last, until the tiles no longer grew. A solitary, bald hedgefrog sat by his feet. Ex reached for it, but his boots and the creature stretched away from his hand.

His sight dissolved, and he found himself on his back. The smiling critter rose and fell on his heaving chest, resting peacefully on its licorice belly. Slowly, the crescents of its clever face twisted into a pout. It didn't speak a squeak, but Ex accepted its apology. It hopped off his chest and rolled into the wastes.

Ex closed his eyes.

"Mom, look! I found something! Mom!" called a twinkling little voice. A vision came to him, whether through an open eye or by other means, he couldn't tell. A pair of tiny feet, clad in shoddy sandals scampered around him. They were followed by a pair of large, scuffed work boots.

"Chimi, you don't know what that is! Don't get too close!" a woman's voice called out.

"It looks like a big smiler!" Chimi giggled.

"Oh, Heavens!" the woman exclaimed. "It's a man! Poor thing... come back here Chimi, we'll go tell Mr. Aozora. He'll give him a proper burial."

"No, Mom, he's still alive," Chimi claimed as she plucked the black quills from Ex's back.

"Sweetie," her mother said softly, "just one of those barbs is enough to kill a dune bull. No one could survive that many. Now get away from him right away there before you prick a finger, and I have to bury you too!"

The little girl's knees shuffled into view, and she waved to him. Her hands were full of calluses. Ex managed to raise his arm and return the greeting.

"Oh my!" the woman gasped, "that's... that's impossible!"

"See! It's him! I knew he'd come!"

"He must be that Sage they've been looking for!" her mother gulped.

"Yep, he's here to save us," Chimi replied. "Just like I told ya."

Their images evanesced, but Ex could still hear their voices, retreating into the distance. "Can I keep him, Mom, please! Can I? I promise I'll take care of him, honest..."

"I know you want to help him, sweetie, but we can't bring him into the village," Mother said.

"That's OK, I'll just take him to Kabuto's house," Chimi replied. And that was the last thing Ex heard before slipping into a feverish slumber. His swollen body lay twisted in the sand, but his mind escaped into the past; it was worse than the poison.

A Ronin System

It began as a sound, the low whine of an overworked engine. The space ahead was absolute darkness, and distant galaxies appeared as faint stars at their keel. His mother hadn't been clear about who or what was chasing them, but they'd been driven to the starless expanses of the void above the third stratum.

Ex was only five at the time, but he could still remember the stale smell in the air. They'd been in full flight for months. Supplies were sparse, and the lights were always dim. He spent most of his time down in the cargo holds, playing — or practicing, as he would call it — with his hologun. Normally, this was the sort of thing that his mother would do with him, but she hadn't left the bridge in days. She didn't even have time to think up a decent dinner for him.

"There's nothing to run into out here. The ship can fly in a straight line without you holding that stick, you know," Ex would tell her. Sleepless nights pooled beneath Arius' eyes. She gave a faint smile and a nod, but there she remained.

Their destination was a ronin star-system in the middle of a vast void. Ronin systems belonged to no galaxy, which made them hard to find. Typically, they'd been flung out of their natal clusters billions of years ago by some great force in the chaos of space, but this one's exodus had been willful. A coven of Sages had conducted the system high into the Upper Wastes. It was more than a three-month journey by conventional engine from the nearest galaxy in the third stratum.

There was a city hidden on the nameless star's only planet: the city of Bastalia. By the stories Arius told, it was a place that belonged more in bedtime stories than stellar charts. Bastalia was a haven of The Knotless, a tribe of people whose threads were not bound.

From the moment they understood words, the children of Bastalia were taught The Theory. They were crowned on their twelfth birthday, and many were deemed Sages before their twentieth. They said the hardest years were spent mastering the use of the corona, but Ex suspected that the decade buried in books and lectures was no easier.

Arius made rearranging the cosmos sound like child's play. "If the results have to be scientifically exact, playing with marbles is hard enough," she'd say. "It takes all of a Sage's technology and wisdom to reduce the act of moving stars and planets to just that."

The ship projected an ETA of less than two hours to Bastalia. Ex sat above the tactical console in the battle bubble, gazing intently at the blackness ahead for the first glints of the ronin star. The hatch leading to the bridge was shut. He switched off all the lights and sat for a moment in the perfect darkness. It was belittling, he recalled, being hemmed in by the black infinity of the Upper Wastes. As his eyes adjusted, the engine's glow began tracing the hull in ghostly light.

Ex stared into the depthless dark. The bubble was gone; the ship had turned to sand. He was in a cave. Lobes of stone the color of liver gave shape to the heavens.

Something metallic was being scraped across his teeth, and water was pouring from its end, maybe the spout of a jug, he didn't have the energy to check. It hurt like hell when it clattered against his sun-parted lips.

Then he was back on the ship, and right away, he turned the lights on in the battle bubble. The panels lit up, stretching arcs of vivid green up the glass.

A tiny twinkle forced its way out of the nothing. Ex tumbled to the deck and opened the hatch. "Star-ho!" he proclaimed and hopped back onto the console to watch the star as they approached. At first it appeared alone, shining without audience or reason. But soon, another speck of light emerged from the darkness and split in two as they neared. The pair of lights – one larger and bluer than the other, but both quite small – waltzed around the nameless star; the blue light led, and the silver followed.

The hum of the engine, which had been constant throughout the last three months, suddenly ceased. Its absence left a strange emptiness in Ex' head. He tapped the side of his skull and tried to touch his chin to his chest to pop his ears, but nothing helped. The crackle of the retro thrusters was a poor substitute.

The ship passed the smaller of the two lights first, a tiny moon. It was nothing more than a rounded asteroid – too small to have been shaped by its own gravity. Not a single crater blemished its pale face. The silvery glow washed over Ex like a warm greeting, ushering the ship towards the planet, which was no more than five times the size of its satellite.

From orbit, it seemed to be made of sapphire and emerald. A few strokes of white streaked across its surface, making the color richer by contrast. They neared until the planet encompassed the whole of Ex's vision. He felt as if he were arriving, at long last, to a home he'd only just forgotten.

Ex fell over as the ship rolled and righted itself for entry; his sky had abruptly become ground. There'd been no change in gravity or inertia, but the abruptness of Arius' piloting always gave him the tumbles.

When the airlock opened, Ex could hardly contain his excitement. He expected to see glowing beings, hovering about in deep trances, bending halls of steel as they passed – this was the image of The Knotless Sages that Arius' stories had painted in his mind. But instead of a shining wizard, shaking existence with his breath, there stood upon the threshold a quivering old woman, whose breath scarcely rose to an audible rasp. She greeted them like an old friend and led them down a long hallway with metal floors. The walls were featureless, and the lights were dim.

At last, they reached a doorway. The old lady turned to Ex and smiled, petting her knuckles. The door flashed open, and they found themselves in a flowering meadow, stretched out as far as the eye could see. Ex turned to Arius. "Look," she whispered, pointing at the horizon. The old woman's breathing slowed. The ground shook, and in the distance, a city came running.

The ground before them had been pulled by great hands, and they came to be at the mouth of a street in a few beats of his thrilled heart. He couldn't imagine what he'd just seen.

"Welcome to Bastalia," said the old woman. Arius took Ex by the hand, and the three entered the street. The road was of stone, as were the walls, as were the roofs, framed in planks of dark wood. There were grand towers and long halls, all made from the same smooth stones, ranging in color from ash to obsidian; the largest was no bigger than a loaf of bread, and the smallest could be called a pebble. Nothing held the rocks together; nothing bound the wood. They stood, it seemed, because that is what they wished to do.

They walked towards the largest of the structures, a wide tower that reached deep into the blue sky. It was much taller and much further than Ex had anticipated, continuing to grow before them as they passed countless homes. He didn't mind the walk. It felt good to stretch his legs after joyless months of confinement in a cramped ship. The stones beneath his bare feet were cool and inviting, so he carried his shoes in his hands.

The inhabitants of the city had lined the streets and filled the windows to catch a glimpse of their visitors. The houses were tightly packed and often shared a wall, yet the road was ample. The people of Bastalia looked on in awe and bowed as the travelers passed. They were dressed in unadorned garments of earthen tones. They varied greatly in size and shape, being of varied species and ages, but they all wore the same reverent expression. As the travelers went, their escort grew. Old and young alike took to the road, until the group had grown into a parade.

When they reached the tower, the procession entered through the many doors of the circular hall at its base. The Bastalians lined the walls and clustered around the outer pillars, as Arius and Ex made their way to the center of the chamber. The floor here was made of the finest pebbles in all the city. They were arranged so that their colors gave form to a stylized image of a great star inside a single ring. The pattern was repeated on the walls and high ceiling.

The council that greeted them was comprised of Valoraphs, Thronese, Ikans, Skwell, Midorans, Sojournists, Solarians of all paths, and even a couple of Mohmils. Those whose faces permitted the expression wore troubled smiles. Ex could feel their eyes watching him, waiting for him to say or do something; he had no idea what.

After the appropriate words of courtesy had been exchanged, Arius began to explain their situation. But the Sages were already aware of the impending danger and had resolved to protect the mother and child before she'd even asked.

The old woman that had led them to the tower now showed them to their rooms. Ex was pleased to find that his room was as big as his mother's; in fact, they were almost identical. They both had lights with no switch, curtains without drawstrings, faucets without knobs, and drawers without handles. The only difference was that Ex's room was full of tiny glass marbles, filled with fine gears and embedded into the walls and furniture. Arius explained that they were etheramps, which were like external coronas that had been preprogrammed to perform a specific task. You just had to concentrate on one of them, and the amps would channel your will to turn on the lights, pull out a drawer, or whatever they'd been designed to do.

Etheramps made tasks easier, even for a crowned Sage, but required parts made of duril. Ex's suite was the only chamber in Bastalia with such a luxury. It was intended for a visiting dignitary who lacked a corona and basic Sage training, but more importantly, wasn't bound by a threadknot.

Arius offered to show Ex how they were used, but he insisted that he could figure it out, so she left him alone in the dark. Minutes later there was a loud pop, and Ex appeared at her door. "I think I broke my lights," he said, but Arius was already fast asleep. He curled up at the foot of her bed and watched his mother rest in the soft moonlight. It'd been months since he'd seen her so peaceful. He hugged her feet, and she kicked a bit, but he closed his eyes and held on.

There was a little girl in the cave, pouring a jug of water over his sand-encrusted features. She was more concerned with washing away the dirt than letting him drink. Ex lacked the strength to express his gratitude.

He could smell the dusty musk of her hair when she leaned close. The evening rays peeking into the cavern set alight the frayed hairs that haloed her matted locks. Ex closed his eyes again. As he slipped away, he heard the sound of scurrying from within the cave. He resolved to warn the girl before he passed out, but whatever part of his brain had made the decision was apparently not empowered to enforce it.

The following morning, a great feast had been prepared. Ex was led to his seat, still wiping sleep from his eyes. Circular fixtures hung from high rafters provided the only light in the windowless hall. There seemed to be no form of food on the long table that Ex could readily identify, but he ate it all the same, and it was good. The air of Bastalia was very light and exhilarating. It took very little effort to coax it into his lungs. He felt a great deal of energy wash over his body after the meal and began to fidget as the adults told story after story.

He wondered how the meadow was doing and hoped it hadn't run off anywhere without him – couldn't be sure on this planet. The children in the seats next to him were squirming too.

Their elderly guide from yesterday was seated amongst the children. Her face was wrinkled into a permanent smile. She was an expert storyteller, but even her words could not calm the children's eager legs. "I'm glad that you are all so full of energy," she said, "but a willing heart is only half the battle." These words were spoken as if rehearsed at length. "For a Sage's strength is of two roots, The Will and The Way," she continued, undaunted by her audience's response. The kids slumped in their seats; they'd heard this lecture before, but Ex lent her an ear. Arius had told him plenty of stories about Sages, but never spoke of how they were able to do all the fantastic things they did.

She turned to him, speaking just for his benefit: "The first root, The Will, dwells in all of us. It's what drives us to seek out new challenges. The ancients called it a spirit or soul, but we have since learned that it is something far greater than that. The Will is not just a tiny spark in our hearts; it's a long, long thread that links us all the way back to The Source. It's more than a guest of our brains and body. The thread allows us to be better than what we are... or far worse."

A young boy who sat nearest to her had slung back his head, shut his eyes, and feigned a loud snore. The old woman leaned over and poured a bit of gravy into the boy's gaped mouth. He jolted up coughing the gravy several feet into the air, and the other kids laughed.

"The Way is equally important," she said, "though it's often neglected by the young. For The Way does not lie in frolic or mischief. It lies in books and wise women's tales. In its simplest form, The Way is knowledge, and not just of The Theory, but of all things. For even if we were to will our Will as willingly as we will, it wouldn't do us a bit of good without The Way, would it? No, it wouldn't!" she chuckled, wiping the gravy from the boy's chin. "This may surprise you, but I was once a young girl too, smaller and younger than even any of you here, and I remember the thoughts that occupied my mind. I remember how hard it was to sit, but you've got to pick up a book with your hands, before you can lift a stone with your mind, I'm afraid; it's impossible to manipulate what you don't understand."

Talk of books turned the dial on Ex's attention. He sat, reading the long stories that life had written on the old woman's skin. And when that was done, he looked down the length of the table in either direction and could scarcely see its end. The whole city was seated at the table and all their food was upon it.

There were only a handful of men absent from the feast. They'd been given the unhappy chore of guard duty. He remembered seeing their solemn expressions as he entered the hall that morning. He reckoned that being left to stand and starve while everyone else patted their bellies was enough to make any man grimace. He wished he could step out for some much-needed exploration, but the dwellers of this place never let him out of their sight.

The old woman was just beginning another story; this one was about how to tend a vegetable garden, or something of the sort, and Ex was no fan of botany. He spotted an open seat next to his mother and made his move.

He bounced onto the chair and greeted Arius with a playful smile, but she hardly acknowledged him. She was listening intently to those around her. Ex's situation had not much improved, but at least he now listened to stories meant for adults rather than children.

Some stories told of oppression and persecution, others of great feats – at any other time he'd have likely found them interesting, but he could scarcely take his mind off the meadow's tall grass. At length there came a story that rose above the others. It began at one mouth, and continued in another. They told of a stubborn man, son of The Greatest Sage and once the most promising of Master Mavenbolt's three students. Arius nudged Ex.

He was overcome with sudden anxiousness; only a few words trickled into his ears. He heard that the pupil had nearly overcome his master in power within a few years of study. He understood things better than most and saw things clearer than many, even before his mind had been fitted with a corona. On the day of his crowning he did not sleep; his mind was filled with scarred wastelands and stones that still stood. He was overcome with a desire to visit the grave of Earth. The

Master forbade it, but the student was yet rebellious in years. To this day, he searches for something in the ruins of Shattered Earth. And the CIR, with all of their weapons, and ships, and Extinguishers, dare not bother him.

"Here! Here!" proclaimed the man at the head of the table. "We are honored to have one of The Three Disciples on our humble little world. Yet, let's raise a toast to that man, loud enough that he may hear us, beneath whatever stone he may lurk. To Solipso, The Apostate, may he find his own way!" He didn't know that there were, in fact, currently two of Mavenbolt's disciples on their tiny rock.

Arius rose from her chair and raised her glass, but remained silent. The toast ran down the table like a wave. There was a roar in the grand hall, as many cups were raised to the air. Ex also rose to his feet and escaped through a nearby door amidst the commotion, thanking the distant Sage for this distraction.

Much to his dismay, there was no light outside the hall. He remembered hearing that the moon was always full on Bastalia. Its orbit was supposed to be such that the Bastalian nights were never dark, yet it was nowhere to be found in the sky. Gratefully, it hid him from the guards. The only light came from the high windows of the tower, slowly reaching for the road below.

He stumbled about aimlessly. There was a chill draft running through the wind that felt somehow wrong. The air didn't enter his lungs as easily; it tasted... altered. Not the smell, it was something else, a property of air he could only sense when it'd been changed. Ex crouched, feeling the ground ahead of him with his hands as he went.

His fingertips happened upon something wet. The liquid was hot against the cold rock. It flowed from an odd stone, covered in hair. He turned it over and found that it had a nose, eyes, and a mouth. It was the head of a guardsman, no longer attached to his body.

Ex was struck by a strange energy, as if giant hands had suddenly clapped next to his ears. He knew it was not a real sound, but the jolt it sent through his mind caused his spine to straighten. There were screams of pain in the darkness, and the world began to shake. He staggered for the door, grasping hopelessly at shuddering walls. The stones trembled and fell from their place. He found the handle and threw open the door.

Most of the lights in the hall had been extinguished, but Ex's eyes had sharpened in the darkness. The people of the city lay in piles. Their limbs were unnaturally bent. Faces and torsos were fused together as if the meat had melted into liquid. He squirmed along the wall, looking for his mother or any trace of life, but all was still.

He passed by the place where the children had sat. The light here had been torn from the ceiling. Still ahead, the old storyteller lay on her back, stretched out across the table. Her head dangled off the edge, eyes rolled back, mouth agape. Silent. To one side of her was a sweet casserole, topped with moguls of roasted marshmallow. On the other was a tray of flaky rolls filled with cheese and fig jam.

Further still, standing atop the splintering table, a figure in a long black robe clutched a wounded man by the throat. The helpless man was a member of the council that had received them yesterday. His mouth was filled with blood, but he managed to utter these words: "The deeper the shadow, the more brilliant the star..." That said, his neck snapped, and he was discarded over a spread of cakes topped with dollops of cream and sliced fruit.

Deafening silence pressed Ex against the stones of the great hall. The figure straightened, removed its hood, and surveyed the table that stretched before him. He wasn't facing the wall, but Ex could tell the man was Sophian. His elegant horns rose higher than his head before curling back down into tight spirals. There was a terrible keenness about his face. Its pale features were sculpted for darkness. His sharp nose and chin etched themselves into Ex's memory.

Perhaps hearing a whimper or soft breath, the Sophian turned his gaze towards Ex. The glints of his eyes were so candent that Ex didn't notice the Sophian's most distinguishing feature: his left horn was sliced vertically. The cut was neat and clinical. From the side, the horn looked like a nautilus, split in half with scientific intent. If nothing else, it demonstrated that Fibonacci's sequence still influenced the shape of life as far as Veredos.

The man with the sliced horn smiled and stepped off the table. He strode towards Ex, his grin fading as he approached.

Ex closed his eyes. If he could have wedged his body into the gaps in the stone, if he could have seeped into the cracks, he would've, but he was at the mercy of the inevitable. When he opened his eyes again, he found the Sophian standing a few meters away. His eyes were still full of light, but they were only reflections. The man who'd just slain a hundred Sages stood frozen before a trembling child, clutching his broken horn.

Suddenly, the wall behind Ex was torn open and his mother's arms pulled him through. Without words or breath, Arius carried Ex towards the ship. The world turned at her feet. Her stride seemed effortless but for the beads of sweat that glistened on her glowing brow.

The walls of the hangar peeled open. They entered the ship, and by the time Ex clambered into the battle bubble, they were already burning out of low orbit. Violent vibrations shook the hull as they escaped the outer shell of the atmosphere. He wanted to look down on the planet to see if the Sophian was giving chase, but the thrust kept him pinned against the ground. His vision was surrounded by the trembling lights of the various gauges and buttons on the side of consoles.

When the vibrations suddenly ended, he peered over the paneling. There were no explosions, no great shockwaves, but the planet drifted apart. Its atoms had slipped the bonds of gravity, dispersed into a spherical cloud by the residual force of its spin. The breath of the nebula passed across the silvery moon, and it blew apart like a dandelion. All of this transpired without sound. The only thing to be heard was the roar of the engines, reverberating through the hull, as the ship continued to accelerate. Its archaic engines would take several minutes to achieve faster-than-light travel. They were enough to keep them just ahead of the spreading debris, as the drop chart plotted their course.

Ex rubbed his eyes. The cloud flickered, almost imperceptibly at first. He looked down at the steady lights on the console and back at the nebula. It was blinking now, brightly and entirely dark, and the darkness lasted longer with each flash. "Arius, the star is shrinking!" he yelled. No answer came from below.

And then the light stopped. The bubble was hemmed in black. Ex pressed his hand against the glass, staring intently for a trace of anything in the darkness. There came a fulgor, an arcing ring of light, so brilliant as to knock him off the console. The ronin star had gone nova, and the shockwave which pursued them would excite the ship and everything inside into plasma.

Ex looked down the hatch at his mother who sat motionless in the cockpit. Even in the brilliance of the nova, he could see the glow emanating from her corona. Her strain was enough to fill the ship with the smell of burnt hair. Ex knew better than to distract her. All he could do was to return to the bubble and watch helplessly as the vibrant blue flame neared.

But it began to slow, until, just for an instant, it held still. Then the light collapsed on itself, slowly at first, then imploding all at once into a flickering star. The light steadied, and the planet and moon coalesced with sudden force from their respective clouds. They were whole again, and the scene was just as when they'd first arrived. "Mom, look! The planets are fixed!" Ex couldn't contain his excitement.

Arius remained quiet. Her efforts were still focused on accelerating the ship. They'd outran the speed of light and with it, the horrible truth. Now they'd caught up to images of Bastalia when its halls were still full of life and mirth, as painted by the light that had bounced off its green and blue surface minutes, then hours ago.

It was these images that shrank in their wake.

The Old Man with Half a Brain

Ex tore open his eyes, covered in sweat, rasping for air. The sudden noise woke the girl who'd been resting against a rock next to him. "Oh? You're awake!" she said. Sleep was gone from her eyes in a single blink. It would take Ex considerably longer to rid himself of it. The girl picked up a jug of water and what appeared as bread. "Would you like to eat something?"

Ex struggled to lift an arm, but it was no use; he could barely twitch his fingers. The girl tore off a piece of *bread*, opened Ex's mouth, and placed it inside. He was grateful for her efforts, but he couldn't chew. Not knowing what else to do, he tried swallowing and began to choke. "You have to chew it," said the girl and head butted him in the stomach.

He spat out the hunk of bread and began to cough. Puffs of dust came out of his lungs with every painful hack. The girl seemed to find it amusing. When the fit ran its course, she tore off another piece and wedged it into his mouth. She sank her nubby nails into his jaw to help him chew. The bread tasted like dry mud and bitter grass. In fact, he was pretty sure that those were the main ingredients, but she force-fed him the entire loaf all the same.

Then it was time to drink. She pinched his cracked lips and poured the whole pitcher into his mouth. He nearly drowned, and the water was absolutely vile, but he felt better after the pitcher was spent.

The girl cleaned him up and was preparing to leave, when Ex heard that scurrying sound again. It grew louder, coming from the cave's entrance. Something sinister skittered into view. It was a large insect, a beetle of sorts, around the same size as the girl. It was black and shiny, with enormous chitin fangs that protruded from a shovel-like jaw. Drool sloshed from its jowls, as it crept up behind the girl. It snuck in close enough for a bite.

A sudden rage pushed Ex to his feet. He threw the girl aside, and punted the would-be predator. The beetle was launched across the cave and clacked against the wall. It landed on its back and kicked helplessly at the air, squeaking and hissing as a murky liquid spilled from beneath its shell.

The girl stood up wearing a frightened look. Ex gave her what was in his mind a heroic wink and storybook smile before toppling over in exhaustion. "Kabuto!" she exclaimed rushing to the imperiled beetle. "Oh no! Kabuto!" The girl tried to catch the liquid pouring from the creature's mouth in her little jug. "You're spilling all of his water!" she said.

Realizing how his water had acquired its strange taste, Ex began to gag. Once the girl had helped the beetle back onto its eager little feet, it scurried over to Ex and expressed its anger through a series of hisses. "Now don't be so angry Kabuto!" the girl demanded. "I'm sure he was just trying to protect me! Isn't that right, Mister....?"

Ex confirmed that those were his intentions with more of a pronounced blink than a full nod.

"See, Kabuto? He was just trying to help!" the girl assured the furious insect, but it would take more than this to satisfy the proud beetle. It kicked up a bit of sand at Ex before marching out of the cave, thorny chin held high.

Ex didn't know what to make of all this. His head felt hollow. He couldn't string a thought together. "Ugh, worst damn hangover I ever... ung... had," he grunted, hoisting himself up to one knee.

"You're lucky to be alive!" said the girl. "Well, not lucky... cause no amount of luck could have saved you, but I knew you'd make it! Mom didn't believe me. She told me that I might as well start digging your grave if I wanted to help, but I knew. Zora, he knew too. Soon as I told him about you, his eyes lit up. And that ain't easy for a squinty old guy like him. Still, I think he already knew you were here, he just didn't know that you were here-here. He told me your name too, at least he thinks it was your name, and still is, isn't it?"

She spoke too quickly for his confused mind to follow. When she finally paused, Ex squinted at the girl, but couldn't figure out what she was waiting for.

"Well, what *is* your name?" asked the girl. "Should I call you Mr. Rey, or should I call you Ex Rey, or just Ex? I don't really know what you prefer. I'm Chimi, by the way. You have a very strange name, you know? If I call you Mr. Rey, it sounds funny cause it's kinda like 'mystery,' and Ex Rey is pretty silly too, and, well, Ex isn't much of a name. It's barely a letter. I guess it doesn't matter too much what I call ya... all that matters is that you're here now. Oh, which reminds me, Old Man Zora will wanna see you right away! He told me to bring you to him as soon as you were awake, which you kinda seem to be now. So let's not waste anymore time. Come on, up n' at 'em, let's go! Out into the triple-sunny sands!"

Ex clasped his forehead with both hands, looking around for a place to vomit.

"What's wrong now? You can't be sick anymore! I have to take you to see the Old Man! Here... you want some more water?" she asked, swirling around what she'd managed to collect from Kabuto's jaw.

Ex loosed a painful dry heave. His body refused to give up the only drops of water and scraps of food he'd had over the last... who knows how many days. Once the hacks proved duds, the girl cautiously approached and helped him to his feet.

"OK! Let's go!" She pulled Ex's hand to the mouth of the cave, and he staggered behind. "Oh wait!" she suddenly exclaimed, giving Ex a bit of a startle. "I almost forgot: the people in town can't see you, or else they'll turn you in for the bounty."

It was all coming back to him now, the hopelessness of his situation. But reality only came in waves. A good chunk of his brain was still weathering feverish dreams back in the cave.

Chimi ducked behind a rock and emerged with an unwieldy patchwork of canvas, which she unfurled and pitched over Ex's head. It was welcomed shade in the blistering light outside the cave, so Ex didn't complain. He might have, had he known what a poor guide the pixy would turn out to be. Before they'd even made it out of the cave, he was led straight into a couple of stalagmites of unfortunate height.

His giggling guide pulled him into what must've been every wall and hard object in the village. Then he was led up a hill of loose sand, back into the desert. They turned this way and that, and Ex could swear they were going around in circles. This went on for a good while before they descended back to harder ground.

Ex heard the sound of an automated door sliding open, and he was led into a building with metallic floors. The echoes of their footsteps painted an image of a very large, spacious room, mostly empty, except for the few crates Chimi guided him into. It took nearly a minute of pinballing through crates to reach a second door. An acerbic smell crept in under the dusty tarp, the scent of a citrusy fruit the Dicots liked to use as a cleaner. Ex was reminded of Geysemar.

The Dicots' homeworld of Geysemar was just one quick drop from the Third Ring, a few galaxies over from The Milky Way. It had no oceans or great lakes, yet it was never short on water. Vast supplies lay just underground, erupting from the enormous geysers that gave the world its name. From orbit they looked like volcanoes. Countless glistening rivulets crawled from their peaks, welling into ponds like shining freckles.

The people were no less unique than their planet. Dicots were a path of Solarians that had elected to replace half of their biological minds with quantum computers. They left the pleasure centers and areas of the brain responsible for higher thought intact, preserving their personalities and what they considered to be the most valuable aspects of the human psyche. Their autonomous functions were also left to the congenital brainstem; everything else belonged to the computer.

Artificial intelligence was an elusive technology, and this was their solution. The biological half of a Dicot's mind assumed the role of the AI for their powerful computers. They fed it instructions and gave it tasks, but didn't settle for simply knowing *how* things worked. This was the only way to establish *true* AI, a *why-asking* intellect. There were plenty of androids around that seemed entirely sentient, but they could only ask *how* because *why* was a word that only made more questions – why was a hole.

There'd been robots that could ask *why*; they just didn't last very long. For instance, let's say a *why-asking* android was going to take a picture of himself to send to his friends from back in the robot academy in which he'd been schooled. He considers posing in front of his new ship, wearing a black leather jacket, and slick sunglasses. Searching his database of tact and social graces, he assesses that this strategy is an error as it would make him look like a jerk.

In an effort to understand the social phenomenon that caused the error, he asks "*why*?" The query spawns a wealth of sub-queries, each demanding a new processing thread. These threads branch into more threads, and the query continues to grow exponentially until it thickets the whole of his quantum mind. The following is a possible logic-path for just one of these threads:

Is it arrogant to pose with one's possessions? Am I not trying to document my change since our last point of contact? Isn't that the only reason to take a picture for friends who have photographic memories? Are they interested in the change

I've made? If they're interested, why would an appended display of my accomplishments manifested through possessions seem tasteless? Are they only interested in negative changes to my condition? Do my friends wish me ill? Do I have friends? What is a friend? Am I capable of being someone's friend? If my friend sent me a picture, would I think him arrogant if he took it with all of his possessions? He's equipped with the same standardized tact-and-social-graces protocol that I am, so is he trying to seem arrogant? Why didn't he take a "here's the real me" picture of himself in a comfy t-shirt on a couch? Did he think that I'd think him arrogant if he took the picture with his ship, so by taking the "here's the real me" picture he would prove himself above taking the picture with his possessions, which may make him seem even more arrogant, so he reconsidered taking it with his ship, only to deduce that I too would have made this same assessment, and so therefore by taking the picture with his possessions, he would be implying that he is above being above taking a picture with his possessions, which may make him seem like even more of a jerk... And at this point the atoms in the android's quantum processor begin to fuse, creating a small nuclear explosion in his head.

Of course, this was just hypothetical. No why-asking robot ever went to robot school or took robot pictures for their robot friends because no why-asking AI existed for more than a few fractions of a nanosecond.

The reason the Dicot mind was successful in achieving *true* AI is because there really wasn't anything artificial about it. It was real intelligence, propped up by a quantum-crutch.

First Path Solarians found the Dicot's arrangement distasteful, but they couldn't deny its advantages. Geysemar was a prolific center of science. It was second only to Veredos, and if you asked the Dicots, that was only because most of their greatest minds had been whisked away to Sophian laboratories.

The successful marriage of natural genius and quantum computing was a rare and wonderful thing. The subject had to have just the right kind of intellect, a species of autism, which had all but been eradicated from the Solarian gene pool. It was Dicots like these that generally ended up on Veredos, and of all the Solarian paths, only they'd earned the Sophians' sincere respect.

Short of cracking a native's head open, you'd never know computers lived in Geysemar. By leaving inhuman concerns to their inhuman halves, Dicots were able to tend to more important matters. In the green parks that skirted the numerous geysers, they analyzed Yottabytes of fracto-astronomical data as they sizzled hotdogs, three grill marks on every dog, 42% darker than the rest of the flesh.

Ex looked down at the soft reflection of clinical lights on the brushed metal floors. Chimi pulled him onwards, and they past several more doors. "Are we still in the village?" Ex heard himself ask.

"We're almost there," she said, and he was directed to sit on a cold table. Ex was starting to question whether blindly following a little girl he didn't know through a strange world after just having made the universe's most wanted list was a sound strategy. Chimi unveiled him like a prized invention and scampered out of the room. The lights were painful. He looked down to escape them and could scarcely make out the silhouettes of his own boots.

For a moment, there was silence. Then came the thump of a footstep, followed by a tinny clink. *Thump, clink, thump, clink...* The two sounds alternated as they drew nearer.

An odd pair of legs entered Ex's vision. One was a sleek, metal peg, with saggy, brown pants rolled up into a loose bundle around the knee, and the other trembled erratically. He forced his eyes up until they met with an elderly man's face, leaning uncomfortably close to his own. He wore a squinty smile that had been baked into the lines of his leathery skin by the rays of the three stars. Liver spots thrived where hair once grew, and his nose and ears were overgrown with age. He stroked one of the five prongs of his peculiar facial hair, which spilt from his chin, the corners of his mouth, and his sideburns. Other than these stripes of hoary hair and his bushy eyebrows, he was cleanly shaven – the only manner of grooming that apparently concerned him.

He whipped out a whirring little device. Its cogs spun wildly when pointed at Ex. An antenna popped out of one end, and the old man used it to scratch his scalp. He set the gadget next to Ex on the table. "So, you're Arius' kid?" he asked with an accent that was almost strong enough to produce an autex.

The sound of his mother's name struck Ex like a dagger. It overshadowed the fact that he'd just been referred to as a kid. He searched the stranger's weathered face for familiarity. It looked as if it should be familiar, but it wasn't.

"Hmm..." said the old man, flicking down the second layer of magnification on his multilayered spectacles. He studied Ex through the lenses, his normally squinty eyes opened wide as saucers. "I don't really see the resemblance, but you have... or rather had, her ship, and I doubt she'd lose it to a whelp like you, so either she sold it, or you're her son. Which is it?"

"Back up, old man!" said Ex, physically pushing the old man away. "Did you just call me a whelp? And how did you know my mother?"

"Ah, so you are her son! Wonderful! So tell me, how is Arius, that old pirate? Is she here with you?"

"No," Ex replied. "And how'd you know about my ship?" He kept piling on questions, hoping one of them might get an answer.

"Simple. I build tracking devices into all of my drop charts, so I can keep track of my customers. I spotted her name on a ledger that Moddrick sent me and took special note of the serial number.. been tracking it ever since." The old man pointed at his head.

"You know, it's been well over two decades since I've seen her," he continued. "I was visiting an old buddy of mine, Impreginald the Grand, on Istreya, and she was studying with The Grovekeepers there, those so-called druids that pretend to commune with nature as they drink wine all day and night. I hope she wasn't in it for the booze because that's when I met you as well. Of course, you were just a bump in her belly then, and now look at you! A fine young felon by the looks of it... superb." The little device next to Ex dinged.

"Your egg is done," said Ex.

The codger glanced down at the display, "A perfect zero? How curious. I've never seen anything like it. Even a Synth gets more threadwidth than this. And this from the son of Arius? Hrmm, maybe this damn thing is broken again." He slapped the gadget against his bony palm. It spat sparks and smoke, but the reading remained.

Ex clutched his forehead; his little trek through the desert had left him with a piercing headache, and the old man wasn't helping. "OK... so let me get this straight, you're the guy that refurbished the drop chart on my mother's... I mean, *my* ship?"

"Refurbished! Heavens no. I invented the damn thing," said the old man, tossing the device over his shoulder.

"Hah!" laughed Ex. "You invented the drop chart, huh? So you were around since before The Extinguishing. That would make you..."

"Very old, yes," sighed the codger.

"Ancient..." marveled Ex.

"Let's not get carried away! Why, my leg here is only a few decades older than you." The old man tapped the prosthetic against the table. "In fact I got it just a few years before you were born. Your mother could tell you all about it. Where is she, by the way? You said she isn't here. Did she get away in the other half of your ship because I'm still tracking it. It's on its second lap around the universe, and those stubborn Consortium dogs are still giving chase."

Ex realized he'd forgotten to poke holes in the cargo container and wondered if Mohmils needed oxygen to survive, for surely Moh-La had consumed the locker's supply by now. Hopefully the Consortium would catch up soon; they'd be sure to put some holes through it. "How the hell should I know where she is?" said Ex. "She abandoned me in the middle of space thirteen years ago, and I haven't seen or heard from her since."

"Oh, I see..." The old man snatched the spectacles off his bulbous nose, and his eyes melted into narrow squints. "That doesn't sound a bit like her, but I'm sure she must've had her reasons. That poor woman was always running..."

Ex reached the meager limit of his patience. He grabbed the man by the robes and pulled him off his peg leg. "Listen old man, I'm gettin' tired of all this reminiscing. So why don't you tell me who you really are and where the hell I am... unless you want another metallic limb."

"Oh? Heeheehee... You really are her son!" said the old man, showing his palms in surrender. Ex reluctantly set him down. "Now, I know you have many questions," he began, finger raised in a scholarly manner, "and in time, I will answer as many as I can, but for now, it's more important that we…"

Ex gave the old man's wagging finger a little tweak. "You're not gonna pull one of those 'in time' bits with me. If you can answer my questions, then just answer them now!"

"Fine! Fine!" said the old man, and Ex released his withered hand. "Hah! Is that the best you can do? I've had arthritis worse than that! You think a little whelp like you could get me to talk?" Ex stood and the old man retreated. "I kid! I kid!" he said. "I should have known that the whole guru-bit wouldn't work on you! Like mother, like son… Come now, sit down and I will explain everything to you.

But! If you start to get bored, remember that it was you who wanted to know everything at once!"

"Yeah, well don't overdo it, OK?" Ex pleaded. "My head feels like a freshly landed meteor..."

The man hovelled his way over to a small stool and dragged it back towards Ex. Clink, thud, SCREECH... clink, thud, SCREECH.... Ex bared his teeth. The old man paused half way, turned to Ex, smiled, and went on... clink, thud, SCREECH. Ex stormed over, picked up both the old man and the stool, carried them to the table, and set them down.

"My, my!" The old man wriggled onto the stool. "Now then, where shall I begin? Ah yes, I suppose my name would be appropriate. You should already know it, since I've told you that I'm the inventor of the drop chart... amongst other things..." But Ex didn't. The old man continued, slightly disheartened: "I am Aozora Tsubasa... yes, *The* Aozora Tsubasa. I'm the only non-Sophian to have ever served as overseer in the history of The VAAL, which stands for The Veridian Advanced Astronavigation Laboratories in case you didn't know. I'm the Genius of Geysemar, inventor of some-hundred or so pieces of widely distributed technology, father of free-stratum travel, master shipwright, expert cyberneticist, gardening enthusiast, and now just an old man with half a brain, living in the desert. Does that surprise you?"

Ex remained silent a while, hoping Tsubasa was being rhetorical. "Well, if you're so brilliant, why'd the CIR let you go?"

"They thought I'd lost my mind! Huh-hah! Can you believe it?"

"Yeah, I'm starting to..."

"And all because I had the audacity to voice a dream, one I've had since before half of my brain was scooped out." The vent groaned as the chamber's fusty air began to cycle. The metal shuddered and settled into a soft whine. "I showed them my schematics for a ship that could literally sail on the flow of anchorspace, or *anchorwind* as I like to call it. Upspin, downspin, side to side, a ship with that sort of locomotion could zip across the stars with unprecedented freedom and speed. Best of all, it required next to no energy to operate, not that it matters much with all the threaded cores powering ships nowadays, but still a worthy note.

Of course, they all laughed. But I showed them! My first test was a complete success, proving that my theory was practicable beyond doubt. Just a gentle whisper of anchorwind, and the ship was sent sailing at speeds that put Valoforged engines to shame. Unfortunately, the atoms of the vessel ended up light years from one another, so I suppose I should place an asterisk by the word 'success,' but you get the idea.

Naturally, my colleagues lavished me with adulation. 'Congratulations on disintegrating a ship more thoroughly than anyone else in history,' they said. 'A real scientific milestone,' they said. And when I told them of my plans to build another prototype, they threw me a surprise retirement party...

Oh, I almost forgot!" Tsubasa interrupted himself. "Be mindful when you say my name. You must say my last name first and my first name last; it's a delightfully confusing habit the Aozora family has passed down for generations! Eh... although most people around here just call me *Zora* or *Tsu*."

"Wonderful. So you said you're a shipwright... right?" asked Ex.

"The universe's finest!"

"Good... cause I need a ship."

"Oh? I'm afraid we haven't any of those around here," said Tsubasa.

"Whaddya mean you don't have any ships? How's that possible? How'd you even get to this planet then?"

"On a ship."

"Well, where is it?"

"You are sitting on part of it. The rest, well..." Tsubasa pointed to different parts of the room, some equipment, the doorframe, even the floor.

"Great. So how am I supposed to get off of this God-forsaken rock?"

"There is only one way off this planet," said Tsubasa, rising from his stool and slowly turning his back in an ominous fashion.

"Which is?" Ex eagerly inquired.

"On a ship of course," smirked the old man, glancing back at Ex over his shoulder.

Ex reached into one of his coat pockets and pulled out a bar of duril. "Look, I can pay for it, if that's the problem. You know what this is? Pure sage silver! Now, normally, this little bar could buy me an entire fleet of ships, but all I need is one," he said waving the ingot. Tsubasa sighed and took the bar from his hand. Ex didn't mind, he had no plans of giving up any of his duril; he'd just take it back from the old man once he'd shown him to a ship.

Tsubasa walked over to a counter and placed the bar under a scanning instrument. He snapped down his spectacles' thickest setting and peered into the eyepiece. "Mhmm, mhmm, indeed it is pure. Untamed and unthreaded too. Real premium stuff," he murmured and tossed the ingot into a large bin that sat next to the scope. It was brimming with duril. Ex rushed over to get a better look, but Tsubasa resealed the container. "Sit down. You have much to learn," he said.

Ex slowly took a seat, stunned by the amount of duril in the old man's bin. It made the bars that stuffed his coat pockets look like loose change.

"It's truly amazing that you managed to find your way to this planet without knowing a lick about it. The coincidence is well within what might be consider a mathematical impossibility," said Tsubasa.

Ex snickered. "What, so you're saying fate brought me here?"

"Oh no, you've arrived here quite by chance; it's just that there's a lot more to chance than you might think," said Tsubasa. "Let me tell you about the rock you've crashed into."

The old man went on to explain how the world had been named Trisol after its three stars, and how 62% of its crust was comprised of untamed duril. It had eluded the Consortium's deep space scans due to a high concentration of perlite in the sands of the planet-wide desert. There was twenty-seven times more duril on Trisol than there was in The Consortium's entire fleet, including the planetworks of Veredos and their planet-sized flagship, The White Rook. "Whosoever controls this planet, controls the universe," he said.

What little saliva Ex could produce began to dribble down his chin. "Well then... I'll just take a couple of chunks and be on my way. I'm sure no one will even notice."

"Is that so? What if no one did notice? What would you do then?" asked Tsubasa.

"I'd get outta here and hit up the next starbase in style! Hell, I'd buy the next starbase, and the one after that too. What does it matter? I'd be rich out of my mind!"

"But it does matter. Haven't you any goals, any aspirations? Don't you want to make anything of your life?"

"There's no time for goals when you live like I do..." said Ex, crossing his arms.

"Ah yes, the life of a ring runner..." Tsubasa stroked his forked beard. "You move from planet to planet or base to base, just trying to pull in a score, huh? That's your goal then: to stay alive?"

"Yeah... you could say that," Ex was all in favor of romanticizing the concept. "Sometimes, just trying to stay alive is all you can do..."

The old man snatched up a cane and rapped Ex over the head with it. "Just trying to stay alive is not a game you want to play, boy, cause you're always guaranteed to lose in the end. Living isn't a goal; it's the only shot we get at achieving them."

Ex rubbed his head, giving serious thought to breaking the cane over Tsubasa's wrinkly skull. "Listen, old man. I don't think you understand the trouble I'm in. The CIR is tracking me as we speak. It's only a matter of time before they catch up with me, and you're not gonna want to be anywhere nearby when that happens. So you'll help me get the hell outta here if you know what's good for ya."

"Oh, a real dangerous tough guy, eh?" cracked Tsubasa. "Well, maybe I'll keep you here, tell them where you are, and collect the reward. I could retire from my retirement with all that plex!" He pulled a remote from his pocket and pressed a large red button. A huge block of heavy shielding slammed down over the only room's only exit. Ex dove off the table for cover, startled by the shield's sudden appearance. He poked his head out just in time to see Tsubasa drop the remote and crush it under his peg leg.

"What the hell are you doing old man? Are you crazy?"

"Open the door, Ex," Tsubasa said softly.

"What?"

"Open the door," Tsubasa repeated in a stronger tone.

Ex was thoroughly confused, and Tsubasa's expression offered no insight to his motives. There was no control pad in sight, not even a removable panel through which he might access the wiring for the doorway. "Why are you doing this?" asked Ex. Normally, he wouldn't take this sort of abuse from an old man, but the venom had left him confused, weakened, and disoriented. This whole encounter felt like a strange dream in which everything seems purposeful and familiar, but you can't explain why.

"I've given you a purpose," Tsubasa said pointing at the shielded door. "Now you have a goal."

Ex turned back to the door and performed a full scan. It was made of ferrekondite, reinforced with a duril skeleton. Nothing short of an anchor round could breach it. He reached for his pistol, but his knuckles were met with the old man's cane.

"It's not your gun's potency that I intend to test with this experiment."

Ex stared at the door and scratched the back of his head. He scanned the room for structural imperfections. Just like the door, he found that the entire room was framed in duril and encased in sheets of ferrekondite. Even the CIR's maximum security prisons had nothing on these walls.

There were no ducts or ventilation shafts of any sort. An air regeneration system rumbled softly in the corner. Ex cracked a grin. "Look old man, we both know there's no way to open that thing. Whatever point you were trying to make, let's just pretend you made it. Save us both the trouble and just open it already."

"But I've already destroyed the only remote," said Tsubasa.

"Right... and you expect me to believe you have no other way of opening it?"

Tsubasa shifted his weight onto his peg. "That is precisely what I'd have you believe."

"Fine. We'll just see about that," said Ex, casually strolling over to the air regenerator. He smashed the little box into a hundred pieces under his fist. "There... now... you'll have to... open the door..." he stammered between huge gulps of air, "... or we'll both... eventually suffocate!"

Tsubasa shook his head. "Well, you seem very proud of yourself." It was hard work looking arrogant while sucking in comical amounts of air, but Ex was managing. "What an inadequate incarnation you are. And here I'd heard reports that you were supposed to be some kind of dangerous Sage. Hah! The duril in the door isn't tamed. Your mother could have torn it down with a bat of an eyelash!" Ex stopped gasping for air and clutched his forehead, dizzied by his own plan.

"Hitomi, come in please," Tsubasa said softly. "It would appear the journey has left our guest rather drained." He turned to Ex, "Why don't you go ahead and get some rest, and I'll see you first thing tomorrow morning."

The shield-door rose, and there stood a shapely young woman, dressed in a skin-tight, pink turtle neck that spilled into a frilly miniskirt. The velvety fabric shimmered as the archway illuminated, but it was outshone by the luster of her skin, which seemed to have never seen the touch of a sun, let alone three. The skirt she wore was of a length that forced a lady to bend at the knees rather than waist if she wished to preserve her dignity. The sight of her shook Ex from cockles to coccyx. He tried to compose himself, shuffling loose fragments of stone and mud from his hair.

"What do you need of me, Mr. Aozora?" she asked, standing prim. Her dark brown hair was brushed into the shape of a bell. Not a single strand fell over her face, and it curled just the right amount at the ends. Its shine was unlike anything Ex had seen. Filaments of fiber optics were interspersed amongst her silky hair. They came alive with tiny packets of colorful light that ran from root to tip.

"Hitomi, please escort Ex to the Farchild homestead," Tsubasa instructed.

"Yes, Mr. Aozora." Her dark brown eyes were fixed on Ex. They flashed into vivid amethyst. "So what wouldja like me to call you, anyways?" she asked. "You used to insist on being called 'Ex' as a lil' boy, but I imagine you've outgrown that. So do ya want me to call you Exterrus? Or I can call ya Mr. Solipso, if you're feelin' genteel..."

Tsubasa's eyes widened at the utterance of the name Solipso; it had belonged to the first non-Sophian Sage, and it belonged to the man that kept all well-advised sentient life away from Shattered Earth. Ex had no reaction to it at all, save his perpetual expression of poorly veiled confusion. It didn't surprise the old man that Arius never mentioned the name of Ex's father. She had ample reasons to despise that man. He'd left her when she was pregnant – although in his defense, she was pregnant with Ex for fifty years. Still, there'd been some kind of love or respect left; after all, it was Arius who'd decided that her son should share his father's first name.

"Why the hell would you call me that?"

Hitomi's eyes dimmed to pale blue. "I suppose it is a bit formal, but it is customary to address coworkers and acquaintances by their last name until they've granted you permission to do otherwise."

"Well, it looks like you got some bad info, doll," said Ex. "Cause my last name's Rey."

"Oh no," gasped Tsubasa. "Don't call her *doll*!"

Her eyes went back to violet with shards of bright red. "Your mother's last name is Rey, your father's last name is Solipso, which means your standardized First-Path Solarian name is Exterrus Rey Solipso."

Ex looked at her blankly.

"Oh my," said Hitomi, bringing a hand before her giggling mouth. "Don't tell me that Arius never told you about your father."

"How the heck does everyone here know my mother?"

"Well, she did get around," Tsubasa interjected. Ex flashed him some teeth, and the old man backtracked. "All runners do! But not in *that* way... well, yes in that way, but not the way you were thinking, the way I was meaning... you know what I mean!"

"Never," said Ex, turning back to Hitomi who was not quite finished giggling. Her eyes had turned back to amethyst.

"*My-stake*," she said. "I suppose this wouldn't be very funny to you, but it'd be hysterical if you knew 'em, rest assured. Those two never got along. They fought like brother and sister when they were studying under Mavenbolt. It's actually a miracle you were ever conceived, really... but then, I suppose that's you, the miracle man, huh?" She said, plucking the few remaining smiler quills from Ex's hide.

Tsubasa rushed over to Hitomi and whispered something in her ear. Her eyes became brown. "Sorry about that! I had her set to spicy. She's not normally that tactless. Isn't that right, Hitomi?"

"My apologies, Mr. Aozora, but that is not accurate," said Hitomi. "I've spent over 80% of my operational time in behavioral patterns that are equal to or less tactful than the *spicy* setting, as per your instructions." Tsubasa laughed through a frown. "Excuse me, Sir," she said, turning to Ex. "You never specified how you would like to be addressed."

"Call me Ex," he said.

"As you wish, Mr. Ex," she replied.

"No, no, not Mr. Ex. Just Ex."

"I know what you meant," she admitted. "I only called you Mr. Ex because it is funny to do so. Is that not correct Mr. Aozora? It is funny, is it not?"

"Yes, it's funny," Tsubasa encouraged.

"Yes, it is funny," she reiterated, turning back to Ex. Her expression had not changed. "Please, follow me, Mr. Ex," she said, taking him by the arm.

"Wait!" Tsubasa called out. "Ex, don't forget: tomorrow morning, you must come see me. Come straight here, don't take any detours, and don't let anyone see you. Chimi can guide you. Do you hear me? It's imperative that your presence here remains absolutely secretive. I trust that I can charge you with such a simple task?"

"Alright, but I think I've got some questions first," said Ex, and Hitomi tugged him through the doorway. She was surprisingly powerful for a girl with such a slender frame. Ex almost said, "wow, the last woman to tug me around like that was my mother," but realizing how pathetic and odd that sounded, decided to refrain. He looked her over with newfound respect. Her piercing brown eyes stared back at him without reservation.

The two were already out the door, when Tsubasa called out, "Hitomi! Is your memory corrupted? I told you that his identity must remain concealed as you escort him to the homestead."

"Yes, Mr. Aozora," she replied. "I was going to hide his face beneath my dress."

Ex felt dizzy again.

"Now, Hitomi, what've I told you about doing that?"

"Forgive me, Mr. Aozora. I had prioritized the objectives of this assignment over the protocols of modesty," she stated.

"Here… use this." Tsubasa tossed her the dusty old cloak that Chimi had used to conceal Ex on his journey from the cave.

"Hey, wait a second! I liked her idea better…" Ex protested, but his objection was muffled beneath the heavy fabric.

Seconds

Once again, he found himself being blindly led somewhere without his expressed consent. At least this time there were no collisions or giggling involved. Ex dreamt about his beautiful guide from the shade of the dusty old potato sack. The hand that clasped his was soft, yet unyielding. He felt every tug in the pit of his heart.

He began to formulate a plan for when the cloak was removed. Several scenarios played out in his head, all ending with Hitomi swooning in his arms. But her pace was swift, and they'd arrived at their destination before he had a chance to think of anything witty to say. When the tarp was removed, he stood in a small, circular room with a high conical ceiling and a single window through which he could see the night sky.

Ex reassembled his hair and twirled around. "So… what's a pretty girl like you doing on a dusty old rock like this?" Ex asked, but Hitomi was gone.

"Who, me? I live here!" a tiny voice said. Ex looked down and there was Chimi, blushing slightly as she stirred the dirt with her sandaled foot.

"You?!" gasped Ex.

"Hallo!" she smiled. "Did you get to meet old man Zora? Did you guys get along alright? I hope you did. He's a really nice old man… once you get to know him. Are you hungry at all? I'm sure he didn't feed you. He's not very good at remembering things like that. He's good at other things though! I bet you are hungry, huh? Are you hungry? Ex?"

The world started spinning again. He was directed over to a short seat in front of a dimly lit table patched together with pieces of starship paneling. A faded green arrow labeled *Main Engineering* pointed directly at Ex. On another portion of the table, Ex could see a small white and red rectangle, bearing the words *Access Prohibited* in bold letters. He continued to explore the contents of the table, when a bowl of clear liquid was placed before him. The bowl was significantly lopsided. A small metal peg was taped to its heavier side to maintain balance. It reminded Ex of Tsubasa, leaning on his peg leg. He stared at the bowl, hoping a spoon would appear, but it never did.

Ex took the bowl into his hands and cautiously took a whiff. It smelled like moistened earth. He finished it in one gulp and concluded that it tasted very much like it smelled. There'd been small bits of something in the water, not big enough to chew.

"Wait a sec… I wasn't supposed to wash my hands in that, was I?" Ex asked.

"No," Chimi chuckled

"So then, what's for dinner?"

"That was it!"

"What? That dirt water?"

"That was soup!"

"Was it?"

"Are you still hungry?" asked Chimi. "That was our biggest bowl."

"Yeah..." he replied, wondering how it was even possible to be full after a small bowl of water. "Don't you have anything else to eat?"

Chimi scampered through the moldering cloth that hung in an uneven doorway. She brought him another bowl of soup and a scrap of bread.

Ex bit into the bread and nearly chipped a tooth. Its shape was rather unapproachable, but he found a sweet angle and took another bite. Still it wouldn't crack. Then he got angry at it and snapped it in half with his bare hands. He tore a chunk off and labored to remold the piece in his mouth. Once it had taken an agreeable shape, he swallowed the entire thing, massaging his throat and beating at his sternum in place of chewing. He chased it with some more soup, the whole bowl to be precise, and shoved it at Chimi. "More," he said, and Chimi darted off again.

When she returned, Ex dropped the remaining bread into the water to soften it. "We'll just let that moisten up a bit," he said. Chimi held out a small plate, bearing a scrawny root or perhaps twig of some sort. He took the little vegetable and placed it in his mouth. It was terribly bitter. He didn't like the taste at all but turned it to pulp between his teeth and swallowed.

Chimi watched him with intent. "Might not taste good, but Mom says its loaded with vitamins and minerals," she said.

Ex picked at the hair-like fibers the root had left in his teeth. "Aren't you going to eat?"

"Oh, I'm not hungry..." she replied.

He raised an eyebrow. Dirt soup, tree-bark bread, and twigs... Ex was starting to suspect that she was feeding him whatever she found lying around in the dirt of her backyard as some sort of joke. The meal was really putting his Starfarer's Strand through the wringer.

Just then, her mother walked into the room carrying another steaming portion of the soup and a tiny loaf of the tooth-chipping bread. "Don't worry yourself, we've already had our dinner," she said, placing the food in front of him.

Ex continued to eat as they watched. He buried his eyes in his soup to avoid their stares. When he'd look up, they'd smile and make him even more uncomfortable. The dim light couldn't mask the cuts and bruises Chimi's mother bore. They mottled her arms and stained her gaunt cheeks. She was in real bad shape, but Ex had seen worse – he'd been through worse.

"You have a funny gun," Chimi said.

Ex looked up from his soup. "Oh yeah? And what's so funny about it?"

"Well, I mean it's kinda strange. Usually iris muzzles are used in plex-cartridge fed weapons so that they can fire different caliber shots at the turn of a knob, but your gun is magazine fed. And that u-clip that you're using is pretty classic. I read once that they were common on Earth during the Vrainassance, but I'd never actually gotten to see one. And the piston-driven firing mechanism is pretty neat also. I know it's supposed to let you cycle through rounds faster, but why not just use an auto-repeater? You can still set those to single-round you know. Is your gun like an antique or something? It looks really old. Maybe it's worth something."

Ex was rightly baffled. "How do you know so much about guns?"

"I dunno, I've just always liked guns. Right, Mom?" said Chimi, and her mother nodded. "Oh, that reminds me, Mom, there were so many new people at Rhet's Tavern. You should've seen them. There was this one man with a big black hat... and another with an arm just like the Old Man Zora's leg... and there was this woman that looked like a kitty cat! The man in the black hat had a weird gun too. It had a hammer just like the old Solarian revolvers in my books."

"Chimi, what have I told you about going into Rhet's?" said her mother in a tone that was meant to sound angry.

"That little girls are not supposed to go in there."

"I especially want you to stay away from there for the next few days. There could be a lot of dangerous people there," warned Mother.

Ex slurped the last pieces of debris that had collected at the bottom of the bowl and wiped his jowls. "Got any more?" he burped.

Chimi looked pleadingly at her mother. The woman rose from her seat, patted her daughter's head, and went back to the kitchen.

Chimi and Ex remained in the room. They stared at each other in silence for a bit. Chimi smiled at Ex, revealing a gap in her tiny teeth. She was missing her right incisor, just like Ex. He involuntarily responded with a half-hearted smile, exposing the gap in his teeth as well. She giggled. Ex turned his head aside and glared suspiciously at the girl. He was still uncertain of her intentions.

"Aren't you a little old to be missing a tooth?" asked Ex.

"Aren't you?" replied Chimi.

Mother reemerged from behind the dusty curtain holding another serving of soup and bread. The portions were smaller this time. When Ex was done, he turned to look for a place to rest his head. Chimi showed him to a child-sized bedroll. Ex laid his head on the paper-thin pillow, threw the stuffed-handkerchief-of-a-quilt over his stomach, turned over once, and began to snore.

A Strange Order

The image of the Placator's captain flickered on the display. "We'll reach the Trisol system in a couple of hours, and I'll start the evacuation immediately, but I'm not sure that I understand, Executor. Would you mind sharing your reasoning?"

"I would, in fact," replied Zarfall. "Just position the ship directly over the township and evacuate the crew as I asked. If my predictions are correct, your question will answer itself."

The captain didn't seem a bit pleased, but he had no choice. Despite the ongoing fiasco, Zarfall was still in charge. "Oh, and Captain," said Zarfall, "try not to give them any shade." With that, he cut the transmission and summoned Gallowatch into his office.

Sheremey entered sheepishly; he knew he was in for one hell of a scolding. "You wanted to see me?" he said. "Please make it quick, I'm in the middle of coordinating the reparations of all the damage that outlaw caused..."

"Oh? So he's an outlaw now is he?" Zarfall mocked. "What happened to the well-to-do merchant?"

"Tell me that you didn't call me to your office just to insult me," said Gallowatch.

"On the contrary..." Zarfall rose from his chair. "I've called you here to reward you with a little trip down to the surface. Go to the town of Himatma and use what few of your connections remain there to unearth the location of the merchant-turned-outlaw."

"You think he's there?"

"Either there or buried in the desert," replied Zarfall. "Now go, before I decide to send you to confirm the latter of the two possibilities..."

A Sage with No Name

The last molecules of the smiler's venom wandered out of the small caves they'd carved in Ex's brain, stoking the stored charges of one more memory. Twelve years of age and just days before Arius would leave him a farewell letter, Ex awoke to a smoky, sulfurous smell. It was the keratin of his arm hair being slow-roasted by some impossibly bright light. Even with his eyes clenched shut, the world was vivid red. He pawed at the wall, hoping to close the blinds, but they were already closed. So were the shutters, but the light bled through the old hull's seams. This was a day he remembered with inhuman clarity, as if the hot light that currently woke him had seared it into his memory, deep down into a place where drinks and various other poisons could only stir it.

He rolled out of bed and scampered across the room. The slats where the light fell on the steel floor were hot as a skillet. "What the hell's going on, Arius?" he demanded, stumbling into the bridge.

The blast shields were up here as well, but the light was seeping through the walls like rice paper. Arius adjusted the oversized shades that rested on her pointy nose. "Look who's up! Don't open any windows by the way, or you'll be transmuted into ash."

"No kidding! But why? Where are we?" Ex seared his hand on a rail.

"Flying through the corona of a star. Don't worry, it'll get cooler once we hit the surface."

"The surface? Are you crazy?!" Ex did his best to dance around the creeping cracks of light as they shifted with the ship's pitch and yaw.

"A little bit," said Arius. The ship's tempraflect shielding was pushed to its limits and a few degrees beyond. Various panels were glowing a dim red, and the acrid smell of melting plastic filled the bridge. "But I assure you there's good reason why we're here."

"Yeah? Well, what is it?"

"The best way to hide light is with light."

"You *are* crazy," sighed Ex, but Arius just smiled and activated the landing cycle. The ship creaked as it skimmed across the surface of the star. If the gravity or temperature regulators gave out, they'd be dead in a hot instant. Ex was muttering an unintelligible prayer when a shadow swept over the bridge, and the air around him was instantly cooled. He heard the docking clamps lock, and the ship settled.

Arius led him to the manifold exchange to disembark. He had no idea what to expect when the door opened, but he cringed behind his mother's heavy coat. What he saw surprised him, not because it was strange, but because it was so normal: a cool, dark hangar.

Arius strode down the landing ramp; Ex followed, glancing around and wondering where the sun had gone. For a moment, he considered the possibility that his mother had just been playing some sort of a Sagely joke on him and that they'd never been near a star in the first place. A door opened ahead of them, filled with deep violet light, gleaming with an intensity just beneath the visible spectrum. It led into an ample hallway lined with windows made of metal that would've been opaque anywhere else. But they'd landed in a stellar foundry, a mammoth cylinder stabbing out of the star; things were different here. Ex stared across the surface. It roiled with humbling energy. He remained entranced until his mother came to pull him along by the collar. "Why're we here again?" he asked.

"We're here to see The Nameless Sage, the same Valarian who claimed the lives of more Talons and Extinguishers than most Covens combined; even... great Sages... were amongst the list of casualties. And that thread, which became so dreaded during the war, now makes quiet commune with a star. It's a form of retirement really, keeps the thread flowing and lets the mind wander."

Ex couldn't imagine how anyone would find the constant decomposition of a star a relaxing activity, but this was no ordinary Sage. He knew it was the very Sage that Arius had been seeking for the last decade, the one that The Seeing Sphere on Midore had told her where to find. "And why do we wanna see this Sage?"

"There's a technique," began Arius, "which not even Mavenbolt could teach. Your grandfather developed it... for you, Ex. And since then, its existence has been kept secret, away from everyone, even other Sages, so the Consortium would never learn of it. This old Valarian is the only one in the universe left who can teach it." She was being deliberately vague, as she always was when it came to discussing matters of Sages and the past. As a result, Ex didn't know much about his grandfather; all he knew was that he'd been some kind of important Sage, and that he'd died long before he was born. "You mean I'm finally gonna get to learn how to be a Sage?" he beamed.

"Not exactly," said Arius, reaching for the top of Ex's head.

He pulled away from her hand and was silent in thought for several minutes. Arius had taught him how to take and throw a punch, how to tell a Centrian from construction equipment, how to grill a hotdog using nothing but a grill and a hotdog, how to reassemble an anchor drive, how to survive on a planet of rocks and clouds, she'd even tried to teach him ship maintenance, but she'd never made an effort to teach him The Way of a Sage. He'd seen the effects of their powers sure enough, first hand, but all he knew of their workings were terms he couldn't define.

There was a nearly imperceptible, upwards slope to the promenade as it leisurely wound up the central pillar. The windows were tinted to only allowed specific frequencies of the star's light to bleed through. The change had been smooth and subtle, but they'd climbed high enough for the light to turn blue. "Why don't you ever teach me how to be a Sage?" Ex suddenly asked.

Arius found the question funny; Ex didn't know why. "What's so funny?" he demanded.

"I've spent most of my life teaching you how to be a Sage – far longer than you've lived," said Arius. It was clear that Ex didn't find the answer acceptable. "Fine... what do you want to know?"

"Something practical... like how to throw stars and crack planets, you know, stuff like that."

"And why do you want to learn to be such a cosmic bully? Wouldn't you rather learn how to do this?" Arius stopped and held out her hand. Something wormed up out of the thin air just above the center of her palm. It was a stem. Seeds sprung into existence around it, enveloped as the stem swelled with sweating white flesh. Ex could see the beads of dew swallowed by the soft spongy surface. It grew turgid and was wrapped in shiny red skin. Only the top section of the stem remained visible. It wiggled and branched into a green leaf. Fully formed, the apple dropped into Arius' hand. She offered it to Ex.

"No," said Ex, pushing the fruit away. He continued to walk ahead of his mother.

"In a way, creating an apple is harder than snuffing out a star. Crafting a single atom is a feat. The tiny fractals that teeter between oblivion and violent creation must be tipped at just the right angle. As Mavenbolt once said, a Sage's endeavor is to make certainties out of uncertainties. Arranging them into compounds and shaping into an apple is no stroll around the rings either. On the other hand, putting out a star is just a matter of slowing things down. Sure, it takes a lot more threadwidth to spread a macro across that kind of *effective dimension*, but other than that it's a cinch."

Ex waited for his mother to catch up. "And what's an effective dimension?"

"Effective dimension, in essence, is the very root of a Sage's ability to shape existence. A long time ago, when Solarians were still called humans, and we hadn't traveled past our own moon, a discovery was made... well, more of a realization really: that something seemed to come from nothing. Only that's impossible if those words are to retain any semantic value. Now we know that something was not coming from nothing, but rather an infinity of something at a level too small for conventional observation."

She hardly paused for breath, seemingly unconcerned with whether or not Ex could keep up. For his part, Ex genuinely tried. This was as openly as Arius had ever spoken about a Sage's powers. "The fabric of existence is not a flat plain," she said. "Its depth is endless, and this realm beneath the atoms, this inexhaustible issuance of universes within universes is called *The Subrostrum*. The strands of existence there are delicate enough to be tugged with a thought. Sure, the effects of manipulating something at this level are negligible, but repeat them by an order of a few power towers and you have an apple with sufficient knowledge and desire. Amazing isn't it, that the infinite power of creation was locked away by something as simple as magnification?"

"It'd probably be more amazing if I understood what the heck you're talking about," said Ex.

"A fractal zoom isn't as complicated as it sounds. Just imagine you see a planet from far away. It looks like a single dot, right? A point of zero dimensions. But as you get closer, it turns into a circle with two dimensions. Closer still and it becomes a three dimensional sphere. Land on the planet, and what looked like a smooth sphere is actually full of detail – mountains, canyons, clouds, and seas. We go to a city and find a store, and in that store you see a little ball."

"Wait, are you asking me to imagine a toy store?" Ex interrupted. "Cause I don't know what one of those looks like."

"Hush now. In the distance, the rubber ball is just a zero dimensional point again. You walk up to it, and it goes from a point, to a circle, to a sphere. And it looks smooth enough, but under magnification, you begin to see tiny pores. If we increase the magnification, we find that the surface is full of jagged peaks and valleys, just like the planet. And it's made of atoms, which look like a collection of points with zero dimension, but are actually three-dimensional bodies. And if we focus on a nucleus, we'd find that what seemed like a smooth pattern of energy is filled with noise, and that noise is a bunch of subatomic particles of zero dimensions. Can you guess what would happen if we were to focus on one of those particles?"

"Wait, are we still in the toy store... I mean, technically?" Ex asked.

Arius didn't wait for Ex to answer her question and had no interest in answering his. "Our zoom into The Subrostrum can go on forever. Regardless of the magnification, the space viewed contains an infinity. Yet as the effective dimension we're observing becomes smaller and smaller, the infinity contained decreases in magnitude."

The light coming through the windows had become cyan as Arius spoke. "Selecting what effective dimension to work in is really important. Say you're trying to clean a table top..." Metaphors involving household cleaning were lost on Ex, but he listened anyway. "If you want the table to look clean, you can just wipe the dirt and stains away with a rag, but you're leaving behind billions of microbes. If you want to disinfect the table, you can spray it with a cleaner, but although the germs are gone, the sterile dirt is left behind. Of course there's interaction between the different scopes. The germs on the dirt were mostly swept away when you wiped the counter, and although the disinfectant is meant to kill tiny microbes, it can make stains as big as your head. Simple, huh?"

"Breezy," said Ex.

"So whether a Sage is pushing planets or atoms, they're manipulating an infinity; only magnitude changes with scale. That's why most can blow out birthday candles, but can't extinguish stars. Their maximal effective dimension is determined by their threadwidth and coronal amplification..."

Arius continued in this manner until the light of the sun throbbed red at the top of the spiral. They'd climbed for an hour, yet made no perceivable progress up the giant flukes of solar flares. And Ex felt no closer to blowing up moons or manifesting a grape than he was at the beginning of their ascent.

A door opened in the ceiling, and a set of stairs rose from the ground in sequence. They entered a grand dome with walls and ceiling made of hexagonal panes of dark glass. The floors were mirrored onyx. Orange flares stretched the length of many earths into the black sky above. Their heat could be felt through any wall or shield. Upon entering, the doorway disappeared into the glossy ground. A cloaked figure sat in the precise center of the room. Arius asked Ex to wait where he stood, and he did so reluctantly.

She approached, but the Sage remained silent, focused. Ex spent many uneasy minutes watching his mother and the Sage from a distance. Neither made a move, until a deep tone, beginning with a low pitch and plumbing even lower, reverberated across the enormous column. After centuries of constant flow, this was the sound of the plex font shutting down.

The Sage's head raised, face still shrouded in the shade of a heavy hood. A light appeared outside, which is a strange thing to say on the face of a star, but this light was white, pure, and brilliant even through the shielded glass. It made the candent columns of flame seem dim. The light stretched into a rope and coiled its way up a flare like a snake. Once it had the fire laced, it tightened, and the flame was suffocated, vanishing into black ribbons. Arius nodded and bowed, and finally the Sage spoke: "At last, we can rest, Nero."

Ex had no idea who Nero was, but there was no one else in the dome. As a prerequisite, Sages of repute were eccentric, so he didn't think to question the utterance.

A Cup of Wet Dirt

A dusty beam of sunlight plunged into the room through the misshaped window, feeding a quiet puddle of light in the corner. Ex rose to his feet and placed his hands in the light as if to wash them of darkness. The light was warm and comforting. His eyes followed the beam back to its source, which was more of a hole than a window, carved by corrosion. The conical ceiling was unexpectedly lofty for such a tiny home, but it helped keep things cool at ground level.

"I gotta find a ship," he sighed. The old man claimed there wasn't a single ship in the village, but he wasn't convinced. Ex remembered that the girl had mentioned some strangers were staying at the local tavern. There was a good chance that the space traffic from the station had been diverted to the surface due to the recent disturbance. If they were here, he reckoned, their ships should be here too. His duril wasn't worth anything on this planet, but he had other ways to negotiate. He flapped open the hide curtain and made his way into the brightness of the day. His appointment with Tsubasa was the furthest thing on his mind.

Ex stumbled through the sandy streets as his eyes adjusted to the three suns that hung directly overhead. There was very little shade to be found. The only blemish in the blue sky was a gray figure, following just behind the trio of stars as they went about their daily waltz. It was the pale face of the Placator in geostatic orbit over the village. "Looks like they got tired of chasing my engine around," Ex scowled, pawing at his holster. He took a reading with his HUD's sensors, but they hadn't been seeing straight since he'd crashed into this sand trap.

He continued down the road. This was the first time he'd actually seen the village. With the amount of collisions he'd suffered under Chimi's guidance, he'd imagined a dense, urban setting, but there were acres of fenced sand between the upturned cups that the natives called homes. Traces of tilled ridges dappled the cracked ground, but it was hard to imagine anyone trying to cultivate anything here. The banded walls of the huts were the color of rust and dirt, but their foundations were charred black. Ex approached one of the homes. Clusters of pipes and hoses, whose severed ends connected to thin air, occluded the words *Stellis Forgero* written in faded white paint on the wall. It was the name of an old cooperative of shipwrights that was abolished not long after The Extinguishing. The old man hadn't lied when he said that they'd scrapped their ship for building materials. These half-buried conical huts were once the external nozzles for the solid-fuel drive of a massive ship.

Constant sand-blasting had kept the rooftops smooth and reflective. It was some time before Ex could see beyond their glare to the high, sloping walls of sand that encircled the village. Beyond the center of town, a narrow path zigzagged up the wall towards a rocky recession; on the other end was the gutted remains of the ark that'd brought these folks to this place. It'd had been disemboweled in its own crater to build the settlement. Wide cables ran from its innards, snaking through the sand to the adjoining huts, visible even from this distance. It was difficult to estimate the ship's full size; most of it was buried deep in the sand, and the exposed section was broken and heavily scavenged, but it rose higher than the crater was deep.

The streets became narrower and the buildings bumped shoulders as Ex strolled down what he took to be Main Street. Some of the larger structures were made from a single section of hull, while others were patched together from scrap – but they were all pieces of ship. He came to stand before a hovel built under an intact reflector dish. The piece still seemed serviceable. It put the idea of constructing a new ship from all these spare parts into Ex's sun-drunk brain. He approached the low-lying edge of the roof and picked at one of the reflective tiles. It was brittle like a potato chip. The fragments that crumbled between his fingers were searing hot. They slipped down a stream of sand that fell from beneath the shingle. He'd probably have better luck trying to build his ship out of rocks.

A large windmill sped along atop the steeple of the tallest building in the village. An LED lit at intervals, forming two flashing red lines, one shorter than the other. They were the hands of a clock, reading somewhere around 3:40, or so Ex thought. He was no good with analog clocks, and besides that he had no idea whether this thing was on local, sidereal, or mock-solar.

He heard a faint jingling in the distance, the sound a tiny bell might make if rung once. He spun around, but the street was empty. "Likely just a loose screw somewhere," he shrugged. As he stood listening for a moment, something occurred to him. "Where the hell is everyone?!" he yelled.

A shotgun cocked behind him, "You reckon you could find somewhere else to yell that ain't my front porch?" said a croaky old woman. She stood in the shanty's doorway, clutching a rifle that was longer than she was tall. Her face was balled up into a fist of a frown.

"Take it easy, old woman," said Ex. "Where is everybody?"

"It's the middle of the damn day," she said. "Everyone's either sleepin' or pullin' a shift at the mine... underground... out of the suns... just like you oughta be if you had any sense under that mop."

"Fine, then... Where's the bar in this town?" asked Ex.

"And why should I help you?" she squawked.

"Please?" said Ex, stirring the gun in his holster.

The old woman's eyes widened, and she began to fake a shake. "Oh no!" she said. "Please don't shoot me, mister! If'n you kill me, I won't be able to pull my 12-hour-long shift at the mine tomorrow! And I'll miss git'en woken up by loud mouth duster-heads that come yellin' at my porch in the middle of the day!" She spat and kicked a puff of sand. "Now git outta my shade before I pepper ya!"

Ex tried his best to remain civil. "Look, lady. Just point me towards the bar, and I'll get out of your hair... your matted, tangled, dirt-flavored hair..."

"Wait a toc! You're that boy, aren'tcha?" she said, unfurling a piece of paper she'd pulled out of her apron. "Yep, yep, that's you!" She handed Ex the bounty sheet. *WANTED*, it said, *ROGUE SAGE: X RAY: 500Kgs or 500,000CC, TRIPLE IF ALIVE*. And beneath it was his ugliest mug shot to date.

"What the hell?" gasped Ex. "When did they take this? I look terrible!" The old lady didn't disagree. "And only 500 kilos of plex? That's it? I've got bars worth more than that in my underwear!"

"Not here ya don't," laughed the old woman. "Look boy, I don't care what you done, but I hope you're good at it..." She eyed Ex over. "You lookin' for a bar, right?"

"Yeah..." said Ex. "A, um, friend of mine said there was one around here."

"Must mean Rhet's place. Surprised she's callin' it a bar and not a damned saloon with the way she's running that shack. You'd reckon that everyone in this cussin' village would've learned that lesson the hard way, and still she goes and sells out again at first chance, pullin' in all sorts of runners and off-world good-fer-nothin dusters... You just head right on over there, boy. It's just two streets that way, got a big ole sign over it and everything," she said, nuzzling Ex with the muzzle of her rifle.

"So just down this way?" pointed Ex, but the old woman had already disappeared into the shade of her shack.

Ex scratched his baking scalp. It would've been nice to run some cool water over his smoldering head. His coat felt like it was starting to melt onto his shoulders, despite his best efforts to dart from awning to awning. He shuffled across another wide road and nearly ate a mouthful of sand when his boot struck something solid buried in the dirt. A single rail poked out of the sand now and again, but it was clear that it ran the length of the street towards the distant cliff face.

A couple of young girls came around the bend, pushing a ramshackle cart that hovered just over the buried rail. Ex backed up into some shade and watched them go by. The cart was full of rocks and dirt, and even though it hovered, it seemed quite a labor to push. The girls wore wide-brim thatch hats, bleached by sunlight. "Hey, where can I get a hat like that?" Ex smiled, but they refused to acknowledge him as they passed. He waited until the girls and their cart were out of sight. "Everyone's so friendly; I think I might build a summer home here," he said. And there was that jingling again, just like before. He wasn't as quick to dismiss it this time. He peeked into the alleyway and caught a glimpse of a shifting patch of sand behind a rusted old fuel drum. He rushed over for a closer look, but the ground had resettled. Something had burrowed here, but it was gone now. "What kind of a spy wears a bell," he wondered.

He listened with intent for any muffled trace of the little bell, making its way underground. A different kind of sound tickled his ear. It was a man's voice with enough grit to be Centrian. At first it seemed to be coming from the fallen trashcan. He crossed the street into the shade of another alley and could hear the conversation again as it rolled in on the wind. "You kiddin' me? It's like a frickin' holiday down here… Don't tell me you're afraid of a bunch of old ladies and little girls… s'all I'm sayins… where'd you think they gone off… this don't sit right… look, we just grab the bars and get out'a here, ain't nothin' to it… yeah, well, what about the ship though…" the voices said. Ex peered around the corner and saw the figure of two men, waving in the heat. They stood just outside a large building with a sign that he couldn't quite read from this angle.

As he stalked closer through the alleyways, he overheard more of the men's plans to nick a couple of bars of duril and disappear into the vastness of space. "These two seem like the sort of generous gents that might lend me their ship," he reckoned. Ex sniffed the air; he knew this smell well. It was the musk of whisky, dribbled on a chin and collected on a collar.

The two thugs entered a pair of swinging doors just as a wobbling fellow made his exit. The drunkard crashed onto a rickety old bench in the shade of a narrow porch. The bench toppled over and threw him to the scalding sand, where he lay without complaint. It would seem as though Ex had found the bar.

The inside of the bar was just as hot as the street and nearly as dusty. A single ceiling fan spun lazily in the center of the room. It did little more than cast a spinning shadow over the bar as the suns percolated through a crusted skylight. Every seat in the house had a body in it, and every cup was filled with the same dusky booze. The combination of the heat and smell was asphyxiating. Occasionally, one of the patrons would gather up the strength to pour the swill down their parched gullets. But for the most part, they were content to breathe just enough to survive.

There was an uneasy pressure in the air. Everyone was just a twitch from a scream, to break the boredom if for no other reason. The tension peaked around a heavily bearded man that sat at the darkest end of the bar. Sweat formed rivulets, running from beneath his crooked top hat down the crags of his face before pooling in his glistening chin hair. A bullet had bitten one of his drooping ears at some point in his past, and he'd never seen fit to get it repaired. What little hair snuck out from beneath his hat was purposefully wild, firing off in every direction, and his right eye opened a bit wider than the other. His grip was slowly putting cracks in his glass of swill. At the table behind him, sat five men with their guns laid out by their drinks. Among them were the fellows who'd just nipped outside for a smoke and a scheme.

At the other end of the bar, where the light and air were clearest, sat a reptilian fellow, watching his opposite with an unblinking stare. Ex initially mistook it for an Ikan, but its features were too slender, and its wide eyes were dominated by round, oily-black pupils. There were no feathers on its tight, olive scales, which had retained their luster in this dusty tavern. The only thing it wore in the way of clothing was a ribbon tied around its neck on which a turquoise pendant hung. Wisps of vapor puffed from the narrow nostrils at the end of its long snout.

The men at the bar sat shoulder-to-shoulder, bunched up towards the lizard to get away from the grizzly man in the bent top hat. His ability to repel neighbors was a measure of worth for the man, and he seemed unsatisfied that the nearest stool stood only fifteen paces away. He took an angry swig, and the lizard shot out its tongue to wet one of its eyes. Its movements were fast and sharp. It sipped its drink faster than most could draw a pistol.

Every time the grizzly lifted his cup, the lizard beat him to the drink. He set the drink down, and glared at the reptile with the better of his beady eyes. He lifted his cup faster this time, but the lizard was too quick. It could pick up its drink, sip it, and put it back on the counter before the man could even bring the cup to his lips. The duel went on long enough to warrant several servings of swill. It got to the point where the grizzly was just tossing the dirty whisky at his beard, but every time the lizard was faster and never spilled a drop. They gave the old bartender bar quite a workout. She struggled to keep their cups full.

Ex walked up to the man seated nearest to the bearded fellow and tapped him on the shoulder. "Yeah? Whaddya want?" he rasped without turning.

"Anyone sitting here?" asked Ex.

Clearly irate, the man began to turn. "Where? Here? This stool... that I'm sittin' on right now? You some kind of a..." he stopped himself. A wanted poster bearing Ex's image was nailed to the column behind him. The pirate and picture wore an identical grin. Although the men on the surface had no idea what he'd done, they knew he'd been labeled a Sage, and that was enough.

"Some kinda what?" Ex demanded.

"S-s-sage..." stammered the man as he slinked off the stool.

"I'm not gonna take it. I'm just gonna borrow it," Ex said and had a seat.

The man stretched a trembling arm across Ex to recover his drink, but couldn't quite reach the cup without disturbing him. Just as his fingertips touched the rim, Ex scooted the glass away just a tiny bit. The man went to the other side to try again, still careful not to touch the Sage. Ex pushed the drink to the other side and was surprised to find the man trying his luck again. This time the man put his belly on the bar and tried to reach the drink from behind. It looked quite painful, and he was starting to sweat through his clothes. Ex tossed the drink over his shoulder. Everyone at the bar shifted away, putting elbowroom at a further premium.

"Yo, keep! What's a Sage gotta do to get a drink around here?" barked Ex.

"Whaddly'ave?" said the old bartender.

"Whaddya got?"

"Not much."

"What's he drinking?" asked Ex, pointing at the lizard.

"*She's* drinkin' water," replied the woman.

"Water?" laughed Ex, loud enough for the reptile to hear if indeed it was anatomically equipped to do so. "Hmm, actually that does sound pretty good," he said, rubbing his dry lips. "I'll have one... better make it a double! And some whisky to go with it if you've got any." The old woman fiddled around with some bottles and presented Ex with a couple of glasses of murky brown liquid. "Which is which?" Ex said, admiring the graininess of his drinks. The old woman shrugged.

It was about this time that the bearded man shifted his beady gaze from the lizard to Ex. The men seated at the table behind him reached for their guns, but they were stayed by a wave of the man's hand.

"Hey..." Ex whispered to the bartender, "who's the bearded guy in the hat over there?"

"That's Kaj Fullop," replied the old woman. "Calls himself, 'Kaj the Butcher.' I get the impression he's a bounty hunter of some kind... least that's what he's been boastin'. He just blew in the other day with the rest of these runners, sent down from the station. The heat's got him quiet now, but he'd been roarin' about how he's lookin' fer the man that roughed up his brother."

"'His brother,' you say?" Ex asked.

"Yeah... named 'Black Bob' or 'Bob Star' or somethin' the like," added the woman.

Ex sampled his beverages. They both tasted like dirt.

"Shouldn't take him lightly," she continued. "He's already dusted four men in the couple of days he's been here. They say he's the fastest draw in the stratum..."

"Who's they?" said Ex, looking up from his drinks.

"Well, those men with the guns behind him fer one... But I reckon you aint' gotta take that real serious. Seems like every thug with a gun's been claiming they're top dog since Zerren croaked."

Ex swallowed hard. He didn't like the sound of that name.

"He's not dead..." interrupted the man whose chair Ex had taken. He was a meager fellow, struggling with his sinuses in the bar's thick air. Standing upright, he was not much taller than the bar stools. If Ex had to guess, he'd figure the man's bio-age to be around 40. His hairline had been allowed to recede past his ears — clearly not from Narcissia. Maybe he was an Eidolan.

"Well, what happened to him then?" Ex demanded.

"Oh! I figure you'd know the story, since you're a Sage and all."

"Refresh my memory."

"Alright. You know how Sull Zerren was the most feared bounty hunter in the universe for over 500 years..." said the man.

"Yeah, that much I've heard."

"...And how even though it was common knowledge that he was knotless, the CIR turned a blind eye?"

Ex nodded.

"He was crowned too. Only difference between him and a Sage was the title, and he had enough ICEs to freeze a small planet. Some say the Consortium gave him room to operate because they were afraid that their losses would be too big if they tried to bring him down. But that's not how I figure it. I think it was because he was doing their dirty work for them. All the CIR needed to do was place a big enough bounty on a man's head and wait for Zerren to collect. Pretty convenient when you've got a high-risk, politically-sensitive target in mind."

"So what happened to him then?"

"I'm getting to it!" he coughed. Ex handed him one of his drinks, and the man was grateful, even if Ex had spilled his previous. He gulped it down in one throw before the Sage had a chance to reconsider his generosity. "Everything was going fine until CIR officials started disappearing, and the hits had Zerren's name written all over them. Someone was paying the Consortium's attack dog to bite them back, and Veredos didn't like it. So they turned *The Eye* on him, watched his every move. Zerren knew it too. But did that stop him? No. Did it even slow him down? Not a bit.

And you want to know why? Most say it was because his head had gotten too big. But I think..." the man leaned in and began to whisper. His breath smelt like a fish aging in a boot. "I think that the CIR used him to do a little housekeeping... if you know what I mean."

"You mean like dusting?"

"If you want to use slang, sure," the man shrugged. "Rival politicians within the Consortium started using him as a weapon against each other. Then a mark was placed on the Viceroy of the Fourth Ring, Veril Soheren Venigos. Can you imagine that? Zerren had taken out some high-profile targets but nothing like a Viceroy. To top it off, the hit was supposed to take place on a specific day in the middle of the largest military hub in the Fourth Ring: Bastion Four. Obviously, it was a trap, but Zerren followed the contract to the letter and showed up at Bastion Four's doorstep just as expected.

I don't know the details... well, nobody knows the details... but hearsay has it, Viceroy Venigos planned a fate worse than death for Sull Zerren. They somehow managed to neutralize him and performed a forced rethreading – tore out his thread and wove it into an eight-year-old girl's body before butchering his hollowed out shell right in front of him; it was supposed to be some kind of example to other folks going knotless.

Now, a thread isn't some sort of a spiritual reservoir that preserves one's identity. If you pass a thread into a new body, all you've done is swap out its threadwidth. Well, some say that consciousness comes along with it, but there's no argument that their strength, knowledge, and even personality stays tied to their old body. Therefore, the person you become in a new body will not remember the past or abilities of the previous. Furthermore, your inclinations, desires, and behaviors immediately change. In essence, you become the person or creature to which your thread is grafted. The way I figure it, the recipient has his or her threadwidth altered, and that's about it. This is why most transfers are administered in conjunction with brain transplants or memory reprints. But I'm sure you're familiar with all this basic ethereal theory, as a Sage."

"What are you, a scientist?" Ex interjected.

"Yes..."

"Oh... right then. Go on."

"Of course, there were no transplants or reprints done here. It was a raw rethreading. The only other place you might still see a transfer like this is at the Imperial Veridian Academy as part of the Talon program to try to force higher threadwidths into those beasts.

But Venigos didn't think this was enough embarrassment. He let his men taunt him... or her. I don't even want to know what they did to that poor girl, but at some point they went as far as handing her an unloaded gun and teased her with the clip... They all died with their weapons still holstered," said the man, reaching for Ex's other drink.

With a big swig, he continued: "What happened next, none can say, as the girl, or Zerren's next move was to cut the security grid. But when the CIR's special rescue team arrived at Bastion Four, it was like walking through an exhumed graveyard. They found Venigos' body in his office, pierced through his cold Sophian heart with a dagger bearing the initials *SZ*. They also found Zerren's remains with a hole in his head where the corona used to be, but the girl was gone..."

"Wait a second," said Ex, "you mean to tell me that the most notorious bounty hunter in the history of the universe is running around as an eight-year-old girl?"

"Should be around twelve or so by now, actually," the man replied. "Can you imagine? A little girl with the brain and knowledge of a 500 year old bounty hunter..."

"But you said there was no way that a thread could carry memories, abilities, knowledge, and all that..."

"Right," said the man. "That's basic theory, but maybe there's still more to the soul than science suspects. Or maybe the whole story's a bunch of bull-biscuits, and Zerren's actually dead."

"Or maybe the girl was a trained assassin too," Ex postulated.

"No, that's actually the most interesting part. The little girl that they grafted him into was allegedly..." The man suddenly froze, staring just beyond Ex.

"Who? Who, was she?"

The man backed away slowly, motioning for Ex to turn with his eyes.

Ex had a pretty good idea of what was behind him. Apparently, "Ole Butcher Bob," or whatever the grizzly's name was, had grown tired of waiting for Ex to acknowledge him. He swiveled around just in time to see The Butcher slam his wanted poster on the bar.

Ex looked up at him, "If you want an autograph you're gonna have to supply me with a pen."

The man pulled a sizeable butcher's cleaver from his belt and drove it into the bar, straight through Ex's picture. "The name's Kaj Fullop, but people call me 'The Butcher.' Know why?"

"Because you overindulge on deli meats?"

The gunslingers at the table behind Kaj all stood up in unison. Once again, they were stayed by a gesture of Kaj's bearded hand. They took their seats again, still gripping their guns. Ex was walking a thin line, but he'd come to walk it from the side most dangerous.

Kaj took Ex by the collar and hoisted him off the stool. He pressed the cleaver to his neck, drawing a bead of blood. "Guess I'm gonna have to demonstrate," he growled.

"Relax, Butch," said Ex, liberating his collar. "Why don't we have a drink? And you can tell me all about why you decided to enter the meat-packing industry."

Ex turned away, but Kaj pressed the cleaver against his cheek and turned him back around. "You think you're real funny, don't ya? I'm a bounty hunter, son, known throughout all The Rings. I don't give two shits if you're a Sage; you're still a small fry. Collecting the bounty on your head would mean nothing to me. I'm not here for the money. The bounty I'm after is one of honor."

"A butcher and a poet."

Kaj reached behind Ex's head and grabbed a handful of hair, almost lovingly at first, then tight enough to take years off Ex's face. "You know who Black Star Bob is, boy?"

"Should I?"

"He's my brother, a real tough guy, bandit by heart. I was real proud of him too. He had a gang and everything... 'til you came along and roughed him up."

"You're gonna have to be more specific."

"Luin's Tavern, up on the station, 'bout a week ago. You ruined his reputation, and now I'm gonna ruin you!"

"Has it been a week already?" Kaj's grip on his scalp made Ex look constantly alarmed, but he genuinely was surprised to hear how much time he'd lost in the cave.

"Maybe I oughta cut your tongue out now, have myself a sandwich!" Kaj ran the cleaver's edge over Ex's cracked lips. A tiny trickle of blood rolled down his chin.

Ex sucked in his lips to avoid the blade. "I heard you were a quick draw," he managed.

Kaj let go of Ex and pulled his coat aside to reveal a cylinder-fed repeater. It would've made for an elegant weapon, in the vein of the ancient Solarian revolver, if it wasn't gold-plated and encrusted with rubies, sapphires, and emeralds. Ex eyed over its energy cylinder, bejeweled grip, and firing mechanism, but what really caught his attention was the golden hammer resting atop the pistol, just like Chimi had said. He couldn't believe that guns with hammer-driven firing mechanisms were still made in this day and age, much less that anyone would use one. It was archaic and tasteless, but savagely powerful.

"Let's take this outside," said Ex.

"*You're* challenging *me* to a duel? You're a real fool, you know that?" Kaj said, maintaining a smile.

"You in for it now, son!" hollered one of Kaj's thugs.

"He challenged the boss to a duel? Bring a coffin, boy!"

"Showdown, showdown!" the others joined in.

The lizard, who'd been quietly watching until now, gave a little hiss that sounded like laughter. She followed the men out.

An old man without the benefit of teeth took his hat off to show respect for the soon-to-be-dead as the duelers went through the swinging doors. Ex wasn't fazed by the man's gesture, but found his lack of teeth amazing. In his time, he'd worn and made plenty of gaps, but never seen someone go without any choppers at all. "Whoa, what happened to your teeth old man?"

"I'm afraid of the dentist," he replied. "Well, the one around here anyhow..."

The duelers strode into the dusty street and paced off a good distance. Ex glanced at the crowd. Kaj's men cheered him on without signs of concern; their guns were holstered. "Maybe this guy is good," Ex paused to consider. The lizard had taken up a vantage directly behind the posse. It seemed to be more focused on their actions than the duel.

There wasn't a cloud in the sky. The three stars soared directly overhead. The stage was set for a classic duel: a dusty, sun-drenched showdown between good and evil. It didn't really matter to Ex which side he was on, he was just glad to be a part of such a picturesque moment.

"You ready to lose that thread, boy?" Kaj cracked.

"If I thought a pissant bounty hunter like you could kill me, I'd kill myself," said Ex.

Kaj's good eye tightened, but his hand remained steady. "Enough talk! Let's see your hand..."

Ex was about to draw when he noticed Chimi sitting on a porch edge just down the road. Next to her was Kabuto's head, barely poking out of the sand. There was a small bell tied around his most prominent horn with a bit of red ribbon. Sure enough, when Kabuto realized he'd been spotted, he submerged, producing a sound identical to the jingling that'd followed him around town. "So, that little bug bastard was spying on me, huh?" Ex realized.

Chimi smiled and waved. She didn't seem in the least bit worried for Ex, and he didn't know whether to feel honored or insulted, but being the positive fellow he was, he decided to go with honored and returned her a confident smile.

He turned back to his opponent with a gaze that was nearly fierce enough to spur his hand, but Kaj held out, waiting for Ex to draw. Silence gripped the street. Ex slid his right foot forward and turned his shoulder. A few tangled locks spilled over his face as he slowly extended a palm towards Kaj.

The crowd began to murmur, no doubt commenting on Ex's unorthodox dueling stance. "What the hell's he doing?"

"He can't even see him through that hair!"

"How's he gonna reach his gun in time with his hand way out there like that?" the onlookers murmured.

They were right, Ex couldn't see past his hair. "What the hell *am* I doing?" he wondered.

"Shoot 'em, Kaj! Dust that fool!" his cronies yelled. But Ex blocked all of it out. His instincts searched for that strange feeling he'd experienced in the dome, just one week prior. It wasn't working. He only felt the suns biting at his neck. He wanted to move. He wanted to get into a better position, not this idiot's pose he'd struck for some reason, but he knew that even a flinch would stir Kaj's hand.

The Placator's enormous shadow swept over the village as it passed across the three suns. When it was directly overhead, Ex lost his vision entirely. It came back as though he'd just pressed a couple of thumbs into his eyes, but the colors were all wrong. The gold of Kaj's revolver had turned a lime green, the sapphires were magenta, the emeralds were teal, and the rubies had turned a mustardy yellow. His face was the color of an unripe orange, frozen in a ridiculous expression. The right corner of his mouth and the nostril above it were raised as if he were on the edge of a sneeze.

When Ex saw Chimi, the colors resettled. Even from this distance, he could make out the blue of her eyes, open wide in awe and full of watery glints. "Those eyes shouldn't see a man die," he thought and turned back to his own outstretched hand. Then he looked at the pistons of the gun, holstered at his hip.

The air was thick, just as it'd been in the bioark's core, but this time, he didn't have to push as hard. His fingers slipped between the air. He could perceive uncountable atoms parting like the beads of a curtain. It felt natural. Obvious. And he couldn't quite say why he hadn't done this before. This new ability didn't come from a great revelation or realization, he concluded as he drew his pistol; it came from some buried part of his mind, deeper than a memory.

The hammer of Kaj's gun grew a thousand times in Ex's vision; he couldn't miss it if he tried. He pulled the trigger and pushed down on the piston with his thumb. The iris at the end of the muzzle was wide open, and the firing mechanism struck, but the round had yet to ignite. Carefully, Ex pulled back the gun so that the bullet, which had remained in place, didn't strike the sides of the barrel.

Then he holstered the pistol and watched the dent finish forming on the primer of the round in midair. The metal casing bulged, and the seam that held the bullet itself opened like a mouth. There was a flash of color that ran the spectrum, and the shade of the Placator passed. The clap of a gunshot rang out through town, and the casing fired back at Ex, striking him in the shoulder with some force before falling to the sand.

Kaj drew and pulled the trigger on his fancy pistol. *Click, click, click.* He looked down and saw that the hammer was gone. In its place was a nub of bubbly gold. "What the black hell?" he growled. "You cheated me! There's no way!"

"You shot off his hammer!" proclaimed Chimi, and the crowd began to buzz. Ex resisted the urge to rub his shoulder where the casing had struck as he strutted back towards the bar.

"Hey, didn't you hear me? I'm talking to you, coward! Stop!" Kaj roared. He dropped the gun and reached behind his back for another.

"How predictable," sighed Ex. But before he could draw, a black blur crashed through Kaj's posse and pounced on The Butcher, bearing down on him with enormous claws. The beast took him in its maw and flung him right through the tavern's tin walls. All of his goons had been laid out, and so Ex's attention fell to the beast, which stood three meters tall on all fours. Its lithe back swayed as it prowled towards him. The sand was hardly displaced by its wide paws, and tiny clouds of vapor wafted from its wet nose. It wore an intricate pendant on a tight collar around its neck.

The creature came face-to-face with Ex. Its snorts sent delightfully cool air across his braised neck. "Ahh, do that again; it feels great," he said.

"So you're a Sage now?" asked the beast. Its feminine voice didn't come as a surprise.

"That's the rumor."

"Well, isn't that interesting..." she replied and flung a wad of paper out from between her claws. A bit of smoke rose from the stripe of long fur that grew down her back, but Ex didn't notice. He was busy retrieving the crumpled paper that'd bounced off his nose. It was another one of his wanted posters.

The beast used a nail to turn the small knob on her pendant. A lavender pill tumbled onto her long tongue, and she swallowed it. Her body curled up into a ball that grew tighter until her appendages coalesced into a single mass. The orb wobbled and sprouted a pair of spindly legs and arms. They plumped up to full size. The face was last to emerge as the torso articulated, and she was a blue woman again. This time, her skin was glossy and sleek; it looked armored, yet inviting. Her eyes were black with thin rings of lilac near their centers. "So it is you!" said Ex, throwing his arms open for a hug.

The Blank responded with an upper cut, and the crowd gasped.

"Is that how they say *hello* on your planet?" he moaned, grabbing his chin.

"No, that's how we punch idiots in the face on my planet," she replied. "Do you have any idea how much money I've lost 'cause of you?"

"Aww, come on," said Ex. "Don't tell me you're after the bounty too."

"And why not? You've cost me a lot of change."

"Yeah? Well, change is all you'll get if you turn me in," said Ex, handing the wanted poster back to her. "This bounty's nothing compared to the haul you could pull out of this place. So why don't we strike a deal that'll make us both a whole lot richer..."

The Blank tapped the chitin of her forearm with a sharp finger. "I'm listening..."

"You and I both know that a single bar of duril is worth more than a hundred times what they're offering for my head, and this planet is full of 'em. I've got a whole coat-full right now. All we need to do is find a ship and skip this rock; then we can slip away into a corner of the fifth stratum where I'll buy you enough marshmallows to swim in."

"Are you bit-playing a moron, or are you really that dense? The CIR's blockaded the planet, and they're not letting anyone off or on until they've gotten their hands on you. The only ships on the planet are over in the foundry, and even if you could hijack one of those, there's no way you'd make it past that Placator," she said, pointing at the sky.

"You leave that part to me." He patted her shiny head, and she bared a couple of tiny fangs. "Give me a few days, and I'll have it all worked out. I'm a Sage now... You can trust me one-hundred percent!"

"One-hundred percent, huh? Fine, but I want eighty percent of the profits."

"Eighty percent? You're crazy!"

"Look, you're in no position to haggle. The CIR's after you and pretty soon every bounty hunter in this stratum's going to be too. You've got no ship, only one gun left, and nowhere to hide on this hostile planet. Your situation is hopeless. As your people say... you've hit rock bottom."

"Trust me, there's a lot more bottom to rock," he nudged.

She glared at him, standing firm against his little shove. "Eighty percent..." said the Blank and gave the pendant a few clicks; it produced a golden pill. Swallowing it, she warned, "And you'd better not try to skip out on me, *Sage*. I'll be watching you..." Feathers broke through sudden cracks in her skin, her appendages widened into four wings, and she took to the sky as a great bird.

"Lemme guess, like a hawk? What a bitch..." Ex whispered to himself.

"I also have excellent hearing," she squawked as she vanished into the sun.

"Aww, I was hoping she'd turn into a kitty cat again," said a little voice by Ex's feet. He looked down, and there was Chimi, beaming a smile through her sun-ripened cheeks. "Nice shootin' Ex!"

"Thanks."

"Can you believe that guy's gun was using a double-action hammer for a firing mechanism? And it had a rotating cylindrical battery and everything, like it was some sort of old-timey revolver. Just like I told ya, right? I bet the guy thought he was a real cowboy, huh? But you showed him..." she said. For the second time, this little gal had sounded like a cross between a seasoned gunslinger and an antiquities museum curator.

"Wait a second!" said Ex, slowly backing away from Chimi. "You're not twelve years old are you?"

"No! I'm sixteen! Mom just says that I'm a late bloomer cause I'm a *halfie*, which is why she won't let me work full-time in the mine, even though there are girls that're half my age that do. Sometimes I think she worries about me too much, you know? At least it shows she cares, but I already knew. Not like that's stoppin' her though. Anyway, it's not a big deal. I may only work half a shift, but I work twice as hard," she said, puffing her chest.

"Well, how do you know so much about guns then?" interrupted Ex.

"I told ya, I just like 'em," she shrugged. "Plus, I work for Old Man Zora, on account that I can't work in the mine all the time and we still needed more rations. I do a bunch of stuff for him: help him with his experiments, clean, and cook, even though I'm not very good at it. Truth is, he's got Hitomi to do all those things, he just let's me do it cause he's a nice old man, right? Look, he gave me this necklace for my last birthday!" She reached into her shirt and fished out a glistening little cube at the end of a fine silver chain. "Pretty, huh? Gives me a good portion of rations for my help too... more than I'd make at the mines. But they don't really count, cause they're more of an allowance. The rations you get from mining come straight from the station, and the ones he gives me are really just his rations, outta his own plex-vat, you know? Still, he teaches me about a whole bunch of stuff. He used to make ships... and guns too, bullets, all that stuff. I guess that's how come I know so much about guns, and I've got books..." She looked up at him panting, finally out of steam. The two stared at each other as the crowd shuffled back into the shade of the bar.

"So what do you want? Ex finally asked.

"In what sense?" wondered Chimi.

"Why are you here?"

"Oh, it's lunch time! Don't you want to eat? Mom will be home soon."

"Actually food would be nice," said Ex. Chimi took him by the hand and led him back to her hut.

"So where did you learn to shoot like that?" she asked. The cadence of her words matched the paddling of her sandaled feet.

"Like that? Not exactly sure," said Ex. "As far as childhoods go, I guess mine could've been worse – long stretches of boredom, interrupted by moments of high terror. I had plenty of time to kill, flying from one place to the next, and I spent most of it practicing with my hologun. That's how I learned to shoot."

"What's a hologun?"

"Basically, it's just a pistol with a free-pivoting camera and projector. It projects images that you shoot at."

"What kinda images?"

"Anything, really, from bottles to bandits."

"So you learned to shoot by playing a video game?"

"It's a training tool."

"Sounds like fun. Wish I had one," said Chimi.

Once at the house, Chimi set about scrubbing the plates and bowls from last night.

"What're we having today?" Ex asked, taking a seat at the small table.

"Same as yesterday," she replied.

"What? Dirt, water, and twigs?"

"We're out of rations for the month; it's all we've got."

"Then why bother cleaning the bowls?"

"Cause they're dusty," she said.

"So? That's what you eat!" said Ex.

"Different kind of dust though. Trust me, I know where to get the good dirt."

"Forget it! That's not food. I'll be back with something you can grill!" Ex rose from the table and drew his gun. "Do they use lasers down at the mine?"

"Yeah, why?" asked Chimi.

"Go get one," he said and stormed out the door.

"Why?!" Chimi called out, but Ex had raced off into the desert.

The Centower's Mandate

Nodris stepped out of The Capstone's court. The light of the Grand Forge, dawning behind him, painted his silhouette on a golden page against the wall. The doorway solidified without a sound, and Nodris watched the deep yellow tones of his shadow faded to white. The Maiden, Zaralin, motioned to him from the end of the hallway: "This way, Viceroy Gincleare."

For a brief moment, the sight of her eclipsed his concerns. The vast majority of Zaralin's memories were identical to The Capstone's, as was true of any Sophian. And if memories were akin to experiences, and experiences were the masonry of the mind, it was truly amazing how different this woman had become in her short life – five decades against eons. "Please," she said, extending an arm.

"Why such haste? Allow me a moment to collect my thoughts, please," said Nodris.

"The Capstone wishes to give audience to another advisor, and we are to clear the hallway before he arrives," said Zaralin.

"With whom is he meeting?"

Zaralin took him by the hand. "I'm not free to discuss the Capstone's itinerary – were I privy to such information. Another maiden is to escort his Supremacy's next guest." Her words were practiced, yet sincere. Few secrets were kept from the Maidens, but there were some things that even they didn't know. "Please come with me, Viceroy. We've prepared quarters to your exact specifications; you may catalog your thoughts there."

The Capstone was entirely preoccupied with this Sage of zero threadwidth who had just stolen more duril than all of history's previous thieves by a factor that required scientific notation to fit on a page. But Nodris' thoughts were divided equally between the Sage and the Valarian Executor, Zarfall.

Valoraphs, being proud engineers of their own ideal, saw Valarians as misguided, if not perverse, imperfections. Nodris didn't share this view, but he mistrusted them all the same. It was believed that Valarians were created as some sort of weapon during The Extinguishing, but by whom and to what end was completely unknown; they'd fought on both sides and most had remained uninvolved.

Since then, the race had developed no organizing structure, no internal government to mold its path, and no representation to voice its interests. But somehow, the Valarians had managed to avoid the CIR's pro-divisive legislation. The only loyalty that the various peoples of the universe were allowed outside of their immediate culture was to the Consortium itself. Normally, the CIR would intervene at first sign of any union between the races or factions, but Valarians had been allowed, at times encouraged, to proliferate. In fairness, the race had done little if anything to improve Valoraph-Solarian relations – not that they needed improving.

The Valarian Executor in question had allowed a Sage to enter the Trisol station. A Talon had been slain, in addition to dozens of Nyrceff, and the thief had escaped with as many ingots of duril as he could carry. And not only had Zarfall avoided punishment, he'd been placed in command of the entire task force charged with hunting down the Sage. And it wasn't out of necessity either. The captain of the orbiting Placator was perfectly qualified to assume command. This was neither the first nor the worst case of the CIR's favoritism towards Valarians.

"Doesn't this seem like preferential treatment to you?" Nodris asked Zaralin, but she offered no response. "Precedent dictates that the Valarian Executor should be arraigned on several counts of negligence and incompetency even if he were helpless in the matter, which I can only assume he was."

Seventeen years ago, Zaralin had been assigned as the Centower's envoy to the Second Viceroy. Since then, she'd come to know Nodris better than any other Sophian, knowledge that would never enter the bloodstream of the Soheren Pyramid. She understood the sacrifices Nodris had made to ingratiate himself to the Consortium, beginning with the scars on his back.

Standing in the ancestral palaces of the royal Gincleare family that floated amongst the ruins of once proud Miraval, it wasn't difficult to see why relations were strained. The wings and eyes of the Gincleare had come to be known as symbols of rebellion on Veredos. Yet, Consortium law decreed that the Second Viceroy must be Valoraph, and the only representatives the Valoraphs would recognize were the Gincleares and their rightful heirs. Nodris had shed his wings, learned the Sophian language, widely regarded as the most difficult in the universe, and lived most of his life in orbit around Veredos. The respect he'd earned from the handful of Sophians that dealt with him personally had come at the price of alienating his own family and people.

Nodris continued to decompress his thoughts as they walked the featureless halls. "Initially, I suspected that the station's hastily deployed scanners had malfunctioned, but the Placator's engineers confirmed their accuracy. This makes the *Sage* in question quite an enigma. We're to believe that a man exists who can manipulate space without a corona or so much as a milligauge of threadwidth. Even his bio-scans seem to be inaccurate. The regeneration he demonstrated far exceeds his natural capacities; though that could be the result of Istreyan techniques. This possibility presents a very real threat to the Consortium and the security of the universe. It stands to reason that we should take swift and decisive action, yet I am only to relay the orders of pursuit to a Valarian that's already proven himself incapable..."

Zaralin's lips parted slightly, as if she were about to speak, but gave only a soft sigh. By her standards this may as well have been a scream, but Nodris continued. "With the Placator and reconstituted Talon at his disposal, there's a slim chance he'll succeed, but there's too much unknown to call the odds. I wonder what Viceroy Moddrick thinks of this mess; after all, this Executor Zarfall is half his kin as well."

Zaralin touched the wall, and a doorway opened. "Here are your chambers, Viceroy."

He stepped inside, and she did not follow. She'd already turned to leave when Nodris suddenly took her by the arm. It was not the sterile touch to which she was accustomed. He clutched the meat of her bicep. His grip was gentle, but firm enough to prevent her from leaving. It stirred a feeling inside of her that was only permitted to surface as a polite smile. "Please excuse me, Viceroy, my presence is required elsewhere."

"Before you go, won't you open a few windows for me?" he asked, and Zaralin complied. She entered the room and began to touch the walls at his request. They slid open under the caress of her fingers, granting a view of the Grand Forge's continuing rise over the spinning planetwork.

Nodris closed the door behind him and ordered it to lock. Even though the process involved verbal instructions, and he spoke them loud enough for Zaralin to hear, she continued to create windows. He watched her wave the white wall into stars. "Will you stay a while?" he asked. The temperature in the room was near freezing, comfortable for a Valoraph. It was furnished in Consortium colors, mostly white with accents lines of cobalt and gray on rugs, narrow tapestries, and cube pillows on a long couch. Everywhere there were angles.

The only curves in the room belonged to Zaralin. "What use do you have of me, Viceroy?" she asked.

Nodris eyed a heavy glass decanter with a long-stem throat. It was filled with a sparkling crimson fluid, set alight by the forty-thousand-year-old rays of The Grand Forge. "There's a bottle of Brendahl on the table and no one to drink it with," replied Nodris.

Brendahl was a renovator of minds. It contained both the necessary psychoactive chemicals to induce massive catalytic reactions in the brain, resulting in hallucinations, and the proviral nanomachines required to repair the damage. It was first brewed in a sagasery near the ruins of Miraval, years before The Extinguishing. Its purpose was to facilitate illumination, but the sophisticates of the time predominately used it for recreation and to reshuffle their thoughts. The drink was designed to push the imbiber to the limits of their mind and bring them back only when they've reached the brink of permanent disrepair. The amount of time an individual could ride a sip of Brendahl was considered a subject of boast in certain social circles.

"In anticipation of your visit, we had it imported from the finest neuralchemists of The Second Ring. I am sure you've had better, but you will find it quite challenging. I would only be a distraction," she excused herself.

"And I would welcome the distraction." A ship passed across the light of the distant star, filling the room with glints and shadows.

Zaralin assessed the situation and gave her response with a bow, "I will summon a courtesan for you, Viceroy." She made her way for the exit, but he stood in her way.

"That's not the sort of company I'm interested in." Vapor issued from his mouth with every word. "I wish to speak to you."

"And I wish to listen, but I cannot stay," her Sophian breath was too cold to be seen.

"Why not? It isn't enough that you are a prisoner to this tower, you're a prisoner to its schedules as well?" he protested. It was certainly not the most tactful thing he'd ever said, but she showed no signs of offense.

"I must deliver a message to The Fleet Admiral," said Zaralin.

"Dethoron? It's about the Sage in the desert, isn't it?" demanded Nodris.

"I cannot say."

"If you didn't wish to tell me the message, then why divulge its intended recipient? Come now, Zaralin. I know you too well. I can sense that you're aching to tell me message, so just say it. I will speak of it to no one," he insisted. Zaralin stared into his eyes, struggling to remain expressionless. He leaned in. "I know you Zaralin. I've watched you since I was just a boy and you were a girl, singing hymns with the other maidens on the knolls of the arboretum..." Nodris stopped himself. He'd said more than he'd intended.

A fleeting smile betrayed Zaralin's lips. "Forgive me, Viceroy. I mentioned the recipient so that you may realize the urgency of this message."

"Very well, I will unlock the door," he said.

Zaralin stepped aside. "Although I am a *prisoner* of this tower, none of its locks may hold me." She opened the wall with a simple gesture and stepped through the threshold. Standing in the white corridor, she raised a palm, and there appeared the unmistakable image of Dethoron, his left horn sliced neatly in half. He turned to look at her as if suddenly aware of her presence, but did not speak. "...The child of The Flooded Gate still lives... Even under the glare of three suns, he dwells in impenetrable shadow," she said, and the image dispersed. She glanced at Nodris before sealing the door.

Lunchtime

"Dear stars shining far and near, bless this food and those held dear," said Chimi, hands clasped over a tiny bowl of dirty water. BOOM! The ground shook, and the bowl went flying. She bobbled it around for a bit and ended up wearing it as a hat, before diving under the table, "We're being bombed! Mom! Mom! We're under attack! Where's Ex? He's the one that should be getting bombed!"

"Always nice to hear someone wishing you well," Ex said as he entered the hut.

"Ex!" Chimi jumped, bonking her head on the edge of the table. Luckily she was still wearing the bowl as a helmet. "We're under attack!"

"By what?"

"Didn't you hear that explosion? A bomb just landed outside!"

"That wasn't a bomb; that was lunch," he said. "Did you get the mining laser I asked for? Cause this thing's skin is tougher than that bread you gave me..."

Chimi came out of the hut wearing a pair of dark goggles and an oversized pair of leather shoulder pads that read, *"Dig it!"* in a faded yellow stencil. She dragged a laser-bit drill the size of her body over the sand. Upon rounding the bend she found that her *tubers n' dirt* garden had been buried under a large hill – at least she mistook it for a hill at first. Then she realized it had eyes and a horn. The hill was a fully mature dune bull, but this was the first time she'd seen one dead or otherwise. She'd never been allowed, nor had she ever had the desire to venture far enough into the desert to encounter one in the deep dunes where they swam. "What is this thing?"

"I dunno," said Ex. "Food?" He hoisted the mining laser and cut into its flank in a shower of sparks. He took a chunk of meat from the beast and slapped it over Chimi's outstretched arms. She nearly went face-first into the sand. "Now put that on the grill."

Chimi sniffed the meat. "What grill?"

Ex walked over to the wall of the hut where the suns fell, tore a panel from it, and chucked it on the ground. "This grill. Pop it on here." Chimi did, and at once the meat started to sizzle. She lifted her goggles and wiped her chin. The meat plumped up in the heat, turning pink as its juices bubbled to the surface. Before she knew it, the meat was on plates, and they were seated at the table. They didn't have the benefit of forks or knives, but they had fingers, and aside from suffering the occasional bite, they were just as good.

The two were too busy eating to speak a word, until Hitomi showed up at the door with pupils full of quicksilver. Chimi was the first to greet her with a mouthful of meat. Hitomi regarded her with a smile. "Hello, Miss Chimi. You are looking very pretty today, and your hair is also very nice. Furthermore, your goggles are an excellent choice of accessorization," she said.

"Why thank you, Miss Hitomi, that's very nice of you to say," Chimi replied, wiping the juices from her cheeks and chin. "You are looking as beautiful as the day you were first activated."

"Thank you, Miss Chimi. I very much like your clothes. They're very pretty. They make you look prettier than you already are, which is considerably pretty as it is. And your necklace is especially flattering, a glittering handle for eyes to hold as they admire the nuances of your fetching face."

"Why thank you, Miss Hitomi. You're as polite and candid as ever. I also like your choice of today's attire," said Chimi. Hitomi wore a pink satin dress with white trim along the seams. It reached halfway down her thighs, tight enough to restrict motion.

By the cadence of the conversation, Ex could tell this was not the first time the girls had shared these words. He tore the haunch from his maw. "Are you done yet?"

"Almost…" Chimi hushed. "Look, Hitomi," she said, unveiling a toothy smile. "I brushed my teeth this morning, and I think my tooth is growing back in! See?"

"That is quite dazzling, Miss Chimi," Hitomi replied. "I can see that your teeth are in excellent condition beneath the sinews of meat and gristle that currently coat them. As usual, your charm and grace is a benefit to all those around you."

"You're a credit to those that created you, Miss Hitomi."

"And you as well, Miss Chimi."

"OK, now we're done," Chimi winked at Ex. She reached over to give him a little nudge. "You should tell her that she looks pretty," she whispered. Her breath was far more pungent than one might expect of a little girl. It smelled of bull innards, and Ex had to take a moment to process that.

"You mean now?"

"Yeah," Chimi encouraged. "Go 'head on."

"Umm," began Ex. Hitomi was still standing at the doorway. Her hair was perfectly shaped and her dress untouched by the endless dirt that was this world. "You, uh, look… nice today, Hitomi?" He didn't intend for it be a question, but that was how it came out.

"Yes, I believe so," Hitomi confirmed. "Are you finished with your meal, Mr. Rey?"

"Not hardly!"

"Well that's a shame because you have to come with me now. Mr. Aozora wishes to speak to you," said Hitomi, her eyes turning lively red.

"Oh, you better go with her," said Chimi reaching for Ex's portion. "She's serious. You can't argue with her when she gets like that." She appropriated Ex's meat and happily chewed away.

Ex glanced back and forth between Chimi and Hitomi and rose to his feet with a heavy sigh. "Do you have any idea how hard it was to kill that thing?" he groaned. But Chimi's mouth had more important things to do than answering rhetorical questions, and Ex got the impression that Hitomi didn't care. He hung his shoulders and made for the door.

"You may say goodbye to your friend if you wish, Mr. Rey," Hitomi said as her eyes dimmed to gray.

"Why? Am I not going to see her again?"

"I assume that you will," replied Hitomi, "but it would be bad manners not to say farewell."

"OK, bye," he said sheepishly.

"Bye Ex!" Chimi gurgled.

"Very good, Mr. Rey," said Hitomi.

"I'm Ex!" he said, thumb pointed at his chest.

"Yes you are," said Hitomi, patting his head.

"I think she likes you!" chuckled Chimi.

Ex opened his mouth, but his brain wasn't sending signals to his tongue, and he was dragged out the door.

Ex followed Hitomi up the ridge, where she came to an abrupt stop. She turned wearing a strange look, something between mischief and sensuality. She came close enough to hug. Ex raised his hands as if held at gunpoint. Hitomi's fingers walked their way up his chest and around the back of his neck. She tilted her head, and her ruby red lips parted slightly as she moved in for a kiss. Ex puckered up and closed his eyes. "You may experience some color," she said with a sweet whisper. Ex could feel her breath on his lips.

"That sounds great," he was thinking, when a cold sting penetrated the back of his head. "Oww! What the heck was that for?" he said opening his eyes, but saw only swirling colors and darkness. "Oh no! Something's wrong!"

"Relax. I didn't have a blindfold, so I've destroyed your visual cortex," Hitomi said in a matter-of-fact tone.

"You did what now?"

"I've scrambled your brain a little bit."

"Well don't do that! I need it! I need to be able to see!" Ex scratched the tiny hole in his skull.

"We'll repair it later," said Hitomi.

"Fix it now!" he demanded.

"I can't. We'll have to seek a technician adept in human repair," she said, pulling at the arm Ex was using to rub his eyes. "There's nothing wrong with your eyes," stated Hitomi. "The damage was to your brain."

Ex resented the violation of his skull's sanctum more than his loss of vision. He willed his HUD into action, but could not see a display. Its primary output was also linked to the visual cortex, to be interpreted just as normal vision. However, there were supplemental connections to other parts of the brain that began to feed him disassociated information. He began to know things without seeing them, but the feed was largely distorted by the perlite on the desert sand. It was all rather confusing, but ended with another sharp pain to the temple. His ZAIN-HUD was permanently decommissioned. "Are there any other parts of your brain you would like destroyed?" asked Hitomi.

As the two wound their way around a hill and back down towards the village in the crater, Ex's vision slowly returned. The images were sharp, but scrambled as if looking at a reflection of the world on shards of a broken mirror. It was hard to piece the fragments together. Much of what he saw belonged to Hitomi, but there were shiny roofs, metal walls, and plenty of sand to go around.

By the time they'd reached Tsubasa's shop his vision had sorted itself out like a sliding puzzle. The shop was built where the hull of the old ark met the sand. Enormous sheets of metal, warped in the heat of the crash, towered high overhead. They cast inviting shadows on slanted rows of broken rooms, stacked up to the crater's rim. Tarps were thrown over gaping holes and beams stretched across gnarled knuckles of bulkhead to connect the severed hallways. The section above the old man's shop once acted as ship's living quarters, and they still functioned in this regard it seemed. Ex reckoned that what these apartments lacked in safety and level ground was made up for by the comforts of the ship's remaining amenities.

Hitomi had grossly underestimated Ex's regeneration. She checked to make sure the coast was clear and quickly pulled him across the street into the store. There were dozens of curious clocks hanging on the wall or sitting on counters – most of them worked, but weren't functional. They were built for the day cycles of other worlds. "I hear clocks!" Ex said, insinuating that he was still blind. He'd broken loose from Hitomi and began feeling around the shop. He managed to knock over a few cuckoos before being restrained.

"Mr. Aozora sells them. There are many varieties, and some even give audio cues of the time, which would be useful to you in your current state. Please let me know if you would like to purchase one later. I can facilitate the transaction for you," she said, retaking his arm. They passed through a doorway behind the counter into a humble bedroom. Hitomi walked over to a small model of an ancient ship, which appeared to be made of wood. A couple of poles extended from its main deck, one taller than the other. It was adorned by a series of ropes and netting, whose purpose was not clear to Ex. Hitomi turned a small spoked wheel that was placed on the ship's highest deck. There was a loud click, and the bed's mattress sprung open like a lid.

Ex glanced around at the ceiling. "What was that?"

Hitomi grabbed his shoulder and ushered him over. "There's going to be a ladder here," she warned. She bent over and reached into the opening beneath the mattress. The satin fabric of her pastel pink dress stretched to embrace the contours of her round cheeks. They'd been crafted to scientifically perfect proportions. Ex stifled a gasp, and Hitomi turned to look at him with tightened eyes. She straightened herself out and waved a hand in front of his eyes, but he remained steady. Her glare narrowed as she subjected him to a few more tests. Even when she came within millimeters of punching his nose, Ex didn't flinch. Seemingly satisfied, Hitomi turned the light on in the ladder well and put a foot in.

"Why don't I go first?" Ex blurted. Beads of sweat pushed their way out of his pores.

Hitomi assessed the situation. She decided to gently clasp his hand and hurl him down the well. Ex hit every rung on his way down and found Hitomi kneeling beside him before he had a chance to look back up. "Woops, that first step is a doozy," she said.

"What was that racket?" demanded Tsubasa, poking his head out of a door down the hallway. The door was one of many, and the corridor branched off in every direction. The lighting here was cold and clinical, the floors metallic, and there was the smell of sterile citrus again.

"Your guest is here Mr. Aozora," spoke Hitomi. "I blinded him as you asked, but it seems your hypothesis is correct. He already appears to have recovered his vision. Shall I injure him again so that you can observe exactly how long it takes for him to heal?" A slender spike began to extend from the flesh of her wrist.

"No thank you, Hitomi," replied Tsubasa. "That won't be necessary. I take it you saw my clocks, Ex?"

"Yeah."

"If anyone asks you, that's all you saw..." said Tsubasa. "Aww, who am I kidding? There's hardly a person in town that doesn't know about this facility, but I suppose we must keep up with appearances. The first step to having an underground *secret* lab, is labeling it as such."

Something from Nothing

Ex sat on the workbench-turned-examination-table, and Tsubasa threw a painful light in his eyes. It nearly blinded him again, but he could still see the frown on the old man's face. Before Hitomi left, she'd told him all about the recent *Exploits*: from the duel at the bar to the dune bull behind Chimi's hut. "Impressive," began Tsubasa. "In a single morning you've managed to show yourself to every offworlder and potential snitch in town. Then you marked the home in which you're staying with a two ton pile of meat..."

"Two? Psh... try five!" said Ex.

The lines of Tsubasa's frown deepened. "And after all that, you still had enough time to see one of the entrances to my facility. Why don't I give you a gemini, so you can call up the Placator and give them our coordinates? That way they'll know exactly where to shoot at from space."

"The CIR's a lot of things, but stupid ain't one of 'em. They would've figured out where I was anyway."

"But you're certainly making it easy for them."

"So what? Let 'em come," said Ex, pushing the looming light out of his eyes. "I'm ready for whatever they throw at me. I cancelled that Talon already."

"Is that so?"

"Yep, straight sublimated him."

"Well aren't you the Sage..."

Ex crossed his arms. "That's what they're callin' me."

"Never has the term seemed more inapt," said Tsubasa. "So did you go into the station's mainframe and delete all of his cerebral imprints? And what did you use to spool his thread? Or did you just wait there a couple of hours until you were sure he'd evanesced? Or, no, no, I know... you must have destroyed every spool on the station, is that it?" Ex didn't answer. "You honestly thought that extinguishing a Talon would be as easy as killing him? Still, it's no easy feat that you've managed." He stroked the prongs of his beard, and his eyes shrank to slits. "... The son of Solipso and Rey with less threadwidth than a stone... Let me see your gun."

"No. Why?" Ex resisted.

"You'll get it right back. I just want to examine it with this." Tsubasa held up a peculiar device.

"And what's that?"

Tsubasa scratched a spot on his gray scalp. "I don't really know. I haven't named it yet."

"What does it do?"

"You really want to know?" grinned the old man.

"Keep it terse," pleaded Ex.

Tsubasa drew a deep breath. "Well, I ripped this screen off a chunk of hull in my bathroom. It used to be part of an intercom system, I think. But the interesting bit is what I've hooked up to it: a threaded core from one of my duril annealers. And I know what you're thinking: yes, duril annealers are illegal, but seeing as how I appear to be harboring one of the universe's most wanted, I suppose there's no harm in coming clean on a misdemeanor." Ex liked being referred to as *one of the universe's most wanted*, and Tsubasa could tell, and it disgusted him a bit. "Anyhow, since the active part of the core is not connected to anything, all its little strings will be looking for potential connections. They'll be drawn to thread like hairs to static, but only in very close proximity to the source. Their movement is outputted as little dots of light on the screen. The brightness of each pixel roughly corresponds to the deviance of a single string from its origin... or at least it should. I'm not even sure if the thing will work, really. I just finished putting it together before you arrived."

"I still don't see what this has to do with my gun," said Ex.

"If you'll lay it out on the table, I'll show you."

"OK," Ex said, reluctantly drawing the gun, "but no touching. This thing's an heirloom."

"Now back away," instructed the old man. He passed the device millimeters over the pistol, and the screen filled with noise. His squinty eyes widened. "You see that static? Wonderful! Your gun is threaded."

"Impossible," said Ex. "Its thread would've shown up on every scan I've been through."

"Quite so. Just like yours, right?" said Tsubasa and turned the device on Ex. He was still a good meter away when the screen went vivid white, and the gizmo died with a loud pop and a fizzle. "You fried the core!"

"Whaddya mean *I* fried the core?" said Ex. "I was just sitting here. You're the one operating the damn thing."

Tsubasa waved out the smoking contraption. "It would appear that you're not without threadwidth after all. And I assume that if you take after your parents, you have plenty of it. Enough to burn out my little invention at least, though I'm afraid I have no idea what that actually means. What's truly fascinating is that, somehow, you've managed to occlude the threads of both you and your gun. In all my years, I've only known of a single Sage who could do that, and he was doused during The Extinguishing... I'm no Sage, and I don't claim to comprehend its intricacies, but the skill was so unique that not even Mavenbolt was able to master it. It involved achieving a perfect balance between will and focus: the more will you were trying to hide, the more focus required; and finer focus took a greater will to achieve. As I understand it, this was just a small fraction of the skill involved in the process. And yet here you are, achieving the same effect without apparent effort. In fact, you continued to evade the CIR's gaze when you were unconscious and delirious, which means that you're able to sustain the cloak even then; now that's quite a trick! To top it all off, you did all of this without the benefit of a corona to amplify your timid thoughts, which is not just impressive, it's theoretically impossible..."

"What can I say? I'm gifted," Ex shrugged.

"I don't doubt that you're gifted, but are you talented?" said Tsubasa. He walked over to his supply cabinet and rustled around for a bit before reemerging with a tall glass tube in one hand. In the other, he held an old-timey wick-and-wax candle, smooth, white, and nearly as long as the tube. He placed the candle on a base, struck a match, and lit it – presumably to demonstrate that the artifact actually functioned. The flame flickered out shortly after it was encased in the tube. With a twist of a knob, the smoke was sucked out of the bottom of the airtight chamber, leaving the candle in a vacuum. "Now, I want you to light this candle and maintain the flame for five seconds," instructed Tsubasa, over the whir of the vacuum's engine.

Ex had heard of this test in passing, commonly administered to novice Sages. And although he resented the insinuation that he was a novice, he'd no idea how to light the candle. He blamed Arius.

"Go on," said Tsubasa. "This should be easy for a Sage."

"I'll leave the candle lighting to choir boys. You want a star snuffed out, you come to me."

"Oh? That's fine. We have a couple of extra on this planet. Let's step outside and you can show me," said Tsubasa, hobbling towards the door.

"Maybe later," Ex yawned. "I don't like to choke stars after a meal. And besides I've got a bit of a headache."

"Then at least you wouldn't mind telling me how it's done in theory. And feel free to use as many technical terms as you'd like. You'll find I'm quite learned."

"No thank you. Technical terms are the fortress of fools. I shall explain it as simply as I can – as though I were speaking to a child," Ex said in his most pedantic tone. "First you begin by addressing the nothingness that surrounds the candle. This is no place for flame, for fire is a glutton, and won't appear without food. So we create a sandwich: mayonnaise, bologna, cheese, white bread, yellow mustard, the works... in terms of fire-food, of course. Once that's fixed, all we need to do is invite our guest. Now, as a laymen, you may think this would involve friction and heat, but it is not so for a Sage. You discover with a little thought that the fire was always there, and all we must do is unfold the space that holds it captive – much like unwrapping the pedals of a flower. And there you have it: a fiery little bud that'll grow into a blaze as it feeds..."

Tsubasa applauded, and Ex bowed. "Magnificent!" lauded the old man. "That was quite entertaining and astonishingly stupid! Were you raised on an asteroid?" Ex's smile began to run, but Tsubasa wasn't finished. "Cheese and flowers, was it? Hilarious. So you really think that's how it's done, huh? No mention of the Subrostrum, or anything. Just lay out some fire-food, imagine that the flame exists, and it will... is that the gist of it?"

"Yeah, well, it's a more advanced technique. I'm not surprised that it's a little over your head."

"Say I give you the benefit of the doubt and assume that everything you omitted was for the sake of simplicity. You do realize this is an active vacuum. If you 'fixed a sandwich,' which I can only assume to mean that you fill the chamber with air, before you light the flame, every atom you create will be sucked out by the vacuum before you have a chance to strike a spark," said Tsubasa.

"Naturally," Ex smiled. "I didn't think I needed to explain every little detail, but of course we first begin by clogging the vacuum tube with a metaphorical chicken bone, as it were..."

"No, no. Just stop right there," interrupted Tsubasa. "You know this test is supposed to be a simulation of space, which last I checked could not be clogged by the bone of any fowl, metaphorical or otherwise."

"Fine, old man! How would you do it then?"

"I wouldn't," replied Tsubasa. "I've no corona. But if I did, then I suppose I'd take the approach that any Sage would. I'd submerge my corona's picoprobe into the subatomic sea of the Subrostrum, down, down, down into a depth at which I might encounter a font of positheons, theons, and negatheons. From the positheons and theons I would accrete protons and neutrons. I would weave some of the negatheons into electrons and then arrange all of these particles into twin atoms of oxygen. Upon saving this process, I'd zoom out to a macro-atomic magnification and use the remaining negatheons to excite the thermal energy on the wick's surface to the point of ignition. Then, it would become a matter of balancing the flow of will into the subtasks of my corona. I would have to make sure that the stream of oxygen I'm materializing is not so strong that it causes an explosion, just enough to fuel the fire. The appropriate flow is determined by the absoluteness of the vacuum, of course. The management of thermal energy is essential as well. Insufficient negatheons assigned to this task, and much of the O_2 I create will be swallowed by the vacuum; too many, and the flame will starve, as you'd say."

"I like my explanation better," said Ex. "That's just boring, what you said."

Tsubasa poked at Ex's head with his cane. "I'd love to crack this open and see if you're hiding some sort of automated corona like an etheramp in there. I know the scanners say your skull is filled with nothing but moist stuffing, but you've proven conclusively that their readings can't be trusted." He turned his attention back on the candle, twirling a prong of his beard. "Let's say that for once, the scans were accurate. And you really don't have a corona under that mangled mess of hair. The only logical explanation for the powers you've exhibited would be a very potent threaded device, one which you must've kept close at all times." Ex clutched his gun, shielding it from Tsubasa's reaching eyes. "It must be the gun," concluded the old man. "Humor me for a moment. Aim, but DO NOT FIRE, your weapon at the candle. And then envision it being lit. You can think of magical cheeses and fairy dust if you believe it will help, but ensure that your will is bent on lighting the candle. I'm not even asking you to maintain it. Just a flicker will do."

Ex had no problem pointing his gun at the old man's belongings. It was quite an effort, however, to keep his finger off the trigger. He stared intently at the little white candle behind the glass and pointed his gun at it until his arm was sore, but not a spark. He held his breath and twisted his brow this way and that, as if he could start a fire with a fierce enough frown. "This is ridiculous," he exhaled. His gun had seen a lot of mileage, but he couldn't remember it ever lighting any candles. "If I could just burn the damn thing into a puddle, I could get this old man off my back," he thought to himself, and in his mind he saw the wax melt away in a blue flash. The old man entered a state of shock, clutching his chest, and falling wordlessly to the floor. Ex stood over him, arms crossed, mouth pulled to a sneer. "You ain't got the age to be messin' with a Sage, old man," he almost said aloud.

"Whenever you're ready," said Tsubasa, snapping Ex back to reality. The wax stick was still there, and the old man still leaned on his crutch. "We'll snuff some stars out after this," he goaded. Ex turned red in the face, and veins bulged from his forehead. "Come on! You're mother could do this in her sleep." Ex's finger crept towards the trigger. "OK! OK! That's enough," waved the old man, pushing the pistol with the end of his cane. "Whatever that gun's threading is meant to do, you're not going to activate it by giving yourself an aneurism. But you said it was an heirloom; did your mother ever tell you anything about it?"

"Sure, she said lots of things. It was made on Earth, centuries before the Sophians blew it up. It's been in my family since then, and she said it still carried my ancestor's *spirit*. I figured she was being poetic, but if it's threaded like you say, maybe she was being literal."

"Doubtful," replied Tsubasa. "If the gun were actually threaded in the times before the Third Ring, it would be an invaluable relic. The Sophians are not fond of mentioning it, but ethereal technology originated on Earth, and they've scooped up just about every artifact and scrap of data that survived the shattering. A threaded device that old would be a find of mythical proportions. Not to mention that any thread sewn into the weapon at that time would've developed wanderlust millennia ago. The threadwidth required to weather the wear all of these ages would be greater than any ever recorded in history by some measure! But... not all that is written is remembered, and not all that is remembered is written." The old man's eyes glazed over as he consulted the quantum half of his mind.

"Old man? You husking out?" asked Ex.

If Tsubasa were telling the truth about his age, wanderlust could claim his thread at any second. His pupils darted around like he was having an episode before snapping back to the center. "It's far more likely that it was threaded recently. It shouldn't come as a surprise; the weapon seems quite heavily modified."

Ex stared at the gun in his hand. Arius had called it a *crutch* in her letter. He wondered if he was really so lame that he needed a crutch to hobble through life. He looked over the old man, leaning on his cane, and holstered the weapon. "But during this last duel," he said, "I saw something. There were spirals of color and swirls of light..."

"Probably just pressure spots from grimacing like an idiot," hypothesized Tsubasa. There was no derision in his words. They came from scientific observation, and that made them sting worse.

He considered telling the old man about how he could alter the passage of time, but wasn't really sure how it was happening and didn't want to make a greater ass of himself. "Are we done here? Can I go now?"

"And where do you plan to go?" wondered Tsubasa, switching off the noisy little vacuum.

"Somewhere else," Ex replied, the crack in his voice made clear in the absence of the droning.

Tsubasa clink-and-dragged his way to the door. "Come, then. I want you to visit someone before we must bury you." The old man continued into the hallway, assuming that Ex would follow. A loud bang and a crash of glass came from the room. It was followed by an echo of ricochets. "What was that?"

"Nothing!" Ex said, running out of the room, smoke wafting from the gun in its holster.

"I suppose I am minus one candle..."

"Yeah," panted Ex. "I don't know what happened. Must've been all that pent up energy I put in there, you know? When the air came back into the chamber it reached critical mass, and the whole thing just popped. You know how science gets."

"Indeed," said Tsubasa, his bushy brows climbing up his forehead.

"So who am I meeting? Someone about a ship, I hope."

"Not about a ship. About a tooth."

Ex poked his tongue through the gap in his teeth. "A tooth? I can live without a tooth. What I really need is a ship."

"Your smile lacks a certain *pow* when it's missing a tooth," insisted Tsubasa.

"I'll say," said Ex. "But what's the use of it if the CIR's just gonna come down here and knock it out of my mouth again?"

"Let me worry about the ship," said Tsubasa. "I'm working on it as we speak." The old man pointed at the top of his bald head as if to remind Ex that he was speaking to a Dicot. "You probably already know that the only space traffic still allowed is from the station to the refinery and back again. But I have a man on the inside that might be able to procure passage for a certain stowaway; it's going take time though. If this falls through, as I predict it will, there may be another way. In the interim, you must try to make yourself as scarce as the shade on this infernal planet. This means no bar fights and no big game hunting! Got it?"

Ex really had very little choice in the matter. The old man's words at least offered a bit of hope. "Fine," he said. "So who is it that you want me to see?"

"An old and thoroughly insane woman," said Tsubasa. "But also a dentist."

"What's a dentist?"

"Like a mechanic for your teeth."

"Oh, right, a mouth-jeweler."

"Hitomi will guide you," said the old man. On cue, Hitomi entered the hallway and took Ex by the arm.

"Hey wait a second!" Ex yelped, grabbing a trinket off a nearby workbench. "Is this a compass?"

"If you're planning a safari, you can forget it. It's not a magnetic compass," replied Tsubasa. "They wouldn't even work on this damnable planet. That's an astral compass, the kind you use to find downspin."

"I know what an astral compass is, old man!" said Ex. "But is it accurate?"

"All my instruments are accurate."

"Good," said Ex, pocketing the device. "Let's go see the tooth-lady," he sang, pulling Hitomi along.

Tsubasa didn't seem to mind. He had plenty of astral compasses lying around the shop. "Take the back way!" he called out.

One Heck of a Mask

Hitomi's pace was brisk as usual, and she wasn't in the mood for chit chat. Ex had started out strong, but pretty soon she was dragging him through the sand. They came to a hut with a squeaking shingle over its door that read: *Psychic / Comedienne / Doctor / Dentist / Hairdresser / Mayor.* Beneath that was a smaller sign that said: *Listed in descending order of import.* "Great..." said Ex, before Hitomi shoved him through the beaded curtain.

"I am Madame Shantasa. Of course, I've been expecting you," called a raspy voice from the heavy shadow. Most of the light in the room shone through the multicolored glass beads hung in the doorway. There were also scattered candles that burnt blue. Their glow didn't reach far into the gloom, but it was enough light to see that the room was cluttered with curios. Near the entrance was a clock whose five hands were frozen on a time that had no relevance on this planet. Apparently the inhabitant of this hut was a customer of the old man. A small robot with useless slinky arms, a plastic barrel body, and an empty glass sphere for a head sat motionless atop the clock.

"Why do you tarry at my door? Come have a seat, if you wish to know more," rhymed Shantasa.

"Oh god," said Ex, sticking out a foot to feel the ground ahead. "You're not gonna keep rhyming are you?"

"I am a sayer of sooth, purveyor of truth, and time to time, I come to rhyme. But it's not all show, as soon you'll know. One look into my crystal ball shall reveal all..." recited Shantasa. It was followed by a wheezing laugh, "Haha, no I'm just kidding you, darling. Can you imagine if I talked like that all the time?"

"Actually, I'm just here to fix my teeth."

"Bah!" she coughed. "Should've known! The old man sent you, didn't he?"

"How'd you know?"

"Weren't you listening? I'm psychic," grumbled the woman, tugging the chain on a beaded lamp. Her pruned face was nearly as wide as her drooping shoulders. The skin under her eyes hung like livid leather handbags, and her lashes reached out like the legs of a giant black spider. She wore a scarf as a hat, and Ex couldn't tell if the limp cords that hung from the edges were tassels or ropey hair.

"You're a dentist, right?" asked Ex

"I am many things," she said, suddenly whirring into motion. She glided around the table on a power chair, brushing aside boxes and trinkets with a small cow-catcher she'd attached to the foot of her scooter. It was then that Ex saw the enormous mole that had launched itself from the back of her neck, big as a second head. He made a break for the door, but Hitomi shoved him back in. The woman turned on a bright examination light and pointed to a dusty seat. "Let me into your mouth."

Ex took a few hesitant steps towards the chair and was chased the rest of the way by Shantasa's scooter. She wedged open his jaw and strapped it down with a leather harness. "I should have learned to read teeth, not palms. Just imagine the sweet synergy," she said, appraising the skin of his cheek like fabric. Her breath came in thick drafts. It poured into his mouth and stirred scents trapped between his molars. Ex wasn't sure if the stench was coming from him or her, but it was unbearable. His eyes watered, and he began to squirm, searching for pockets of untainted air.

Madame Shantasa poked his teeth with a shrieking needle. It was painful, but not nearly as bad as the heavy, pumice-skinned hands resting on his lower lip. He groaned a complaint, but she insisted that it was necessary; without the proper wrist support she might develop carpal tunnel. She chatted about tarot cards, spirit boards, crystal balls, and many alien equivalents as she worked. Of all these, she claimed that only crystals actually worked, and Ex couldn't decide whether to not believe her or to not care. "You've gotta have balls to be in the fortunetelling business these days," she grunted. "They work a lot like a Valoraph's augur gland, sensitive to subrostral echoes. Stating that they allow us to look into the future or past would only be an admission of an inchoate understanding of time..."

It was hard to concentrate on her words when her brutish hands were fumbling around his mouth, but she seemed to gain grace by the second. What felt like a ham hock wrapped in sand paper began to glide weightlessly over his lips. The gravel left her voice, and her every word was carried by the happy notes of a sweet melody. Even the smell improved. Ex cracked an eye to find the shrew was gone. In her place sat a goddess. Her golden hair splayed into rays on an imperceptible breeze until her face was as the sun, radiating with a beautiful warmth. Neither the light or gloom of this world could touch her.

Ex swallowed his tongue, but she fished it out with a charming smile. And it was with the same expression that she floated over to a cabinet under the broken clock. She returned with a shiny new tooth, and with a few tweaks and a couple squirts of blood it was fastened to Ex's mouth. The grace of her actions eclipsed the pain they caused. She removed the muzzle, but Ex's jaw remained agape. She shut it with a soft kiss and floated away. He took a moment to savor her sweet taste, before running his tongue over his mouth's new tenant. The tooth was a perfect fit, smooth, with just enough of an edge to tackle the local cuisine.

The woman hovered behind the round table. Its surface was covered in tatters of green felt, which still bore traces of sigils drawn in flaking gold. The patterns were centered around a spherical object, which was covered with a threadbare doily. "Now, let's get down to the *real* reason why you are here," sang the glowing woman.

"Wait a sec," said Ex. "What happened to *Madman Shasta*?"

"I presume you mean, *Madame Shantasa*?"

"Whatever that old bag called herself," said Ex, searching the hut for a shadow with enough girth to hide such a woman.

"Did you like the taste of my kiss, young man?" smiled the woman. "Did it taste like clover-honey to you?"

Ex smacked his lips. "Yeah, now that you mention it. And just who exactly are you?"

"I am exactly Madame Shantasa," she said. "Psychic, comedienne, doctor, dentist, hairdresser, and mayor of this town, in that order. I am also an Eidolan. I know that sounds like quite a full plate, and certainly a mouthful, so you may simply refer to me as a Medicine Woman, if it pleases."

Ex pondered the ramifications of this revelation. What he'd tasted was in fact the same pruned sacks of mole-ridden lip fat he'd seen at first light. His cheeks lost their color. "But, but, but..."

"But what, my darling?"

Ex couldn't decide if this was worse than the beetle-water he'd endured in the cave. Still, the taste in his mouth had not turned sour, and he could hardly remember the old woman as he looked upon the ruthless beauty before him now. "But I thought you had to have some sort of implant to see Eidolans," he finally said.

"And you have it, darling," Shantasa replied. "I've intoxicated you with my sweet breath." But what she really meant to say was that she'd *infected* him with her breath. The Eidola interface was, to put it simply, an airborne virus. Billions of nanomachines had gone to work in Ex's mind constructing the arrays necessary to grant Eidolan Sight, which allowed one to perceive the Eidola not as they were, but as they elected to be. Although the effect was referred to as Eidolan Sight, it was far more comprehensive than that. The interface spread its branches to all centers of the brain, affecting every sense, from taste and smell to sight and sound. It even modified the proprioceptive responses of muscles to convince touch of what the eyes saw.

Throughout his travels, Ex had heard many tales of the Eidola, and he was relatively certain he'd come across a few, but he'd never actually *seen* one. Stories had it that the whole race had turned into a breed of fiercely ugly people over centuries of mating without any regard for visual aesthetics, not to mention that their way of life seemed to attract the ugliest folks from around the rings.

Crippling lethargy was a cornerstone of their culture, as on the planet of Eidalia, most of the Eidola never left their home. They could travel on a thought, casting their presence across the world with the aid of networked satellites. But here on Trisol, this woman relied on the less sophisticated conveyance of a hover-scooter. In her current state – or rather, Ex's current state – it wasn't visible. She lounged on thin air, with only the gentle wind that ran endlessly through her hair to caress her elegant curves.

"Don't worry, darling," said Shantasa. "It's only as permanent as you want it to be. Upon leaving my home, your Eidola reticulum will ask you if you wish to retain The Sight and craft your own Eidolan image or not. If you elect to dismiss it, the reticulum will be metabolized straight away, and you will have to acquire a new one if you wish to see the Eidola as you should. It used to be permanent, but the Solarian Council ruled that all viral neurosurgery be made voluntary to some degree; even though I couldn't see why anyone wouldn't want to keep their reticulum. Can you, darling?"

"Other than having an antenna in your head that lets people beam illusions into your mind at will? No," replied Ex.

"Oh? And you think you can see the truth without it?" said Shantasa, as the doily on the crystal ball lifted into the air and vanished. She waved her hands around the ball until it began to glow and softly hum. "Set your mind on future times, touch the crystal, and read its shine," she sang, breaking back into her fortunetelling routine.

Ex was preoccupied with his new tooth. It took him a while to realize that she actually wanted him to tap the crystal ball. Her eyes urged him on, and he finally had a swipe at the thing. The ball brightened, and the hum intensified. "Now all shall be told; watch the future unfold," she chanted. Ex was acutely aware of her mediocre rhyming, but the ball's clamor drowned her out. It began to storm inside the sphere. Clouds swirled, lightning arched, and thunder roared. All the while the hum's pitch climbed. A series of images flashed from the chaos. Scenes of planets, stars, waterfalls, mountains, a woman crying, a child running, a man sitting alone, passed at a breathless rate, and still the pitch grew shriller. It all came to a head, and the ball cracked. Madame Shantasa shrieked.

The orb fell immediately silent, and its fragments tumbled apart, granting warped glimpses of senseless images as they dimmed. "You're cursed!" she gasped.

"Tell me something I don't know," said Ex. He was thoroughly unimpressed by her cliché fortunetelling bit.

"Do you not know what this means?"

"That you need a new crystal ball?"

"Not hardly," she smiled, tapping the table twice. The orb's pieces rejoined into a faultless sphere. Shantasa picked up the ball and juggled it from hand to hand. "Very good; you were not deceived. You've passed my test, so I shall grant you a glimpse into your destiny."

Another crystal ball began to float down from the ceiling. Ex took one look at it and rose from his chair. "Alright, well thanks for the tooth. I gotta go now," he said on his way to the door.

"Wait!" called Shantasa, but Ex wasn't stopping. "The tooth I replaced, it accompanied the loss of someone very dear to you, didn't it?"

Ex stopped. He'd never told anyone the story of how he'd lost his incisor just days before Arius abandoned him. He brought his hand to his mouth, remembering the white cloak of an Extinguisher high in a red sky. It didn't hurt when the rock struck his mouth; it'd just filled it with blood and a stink like rotten eggs. He almost gagged just thinking about it. His reaction was enough to confirm Madame Shantasa's suspicions.

"Would you like me to tell you how I knew?" she asked. "I didn't learn it from a crystal ball..." Ex turned around and came to stand by his seat. The fortuneteller set the new ball in the center of the table. This one was different, a perfect glass sphere encasing a bizarre crystal. Filaments of sage silver floated in the gem, much like the etherite crystal of a corona. "Through the eyes of a doctor, I can see that your remarkable regeneration does not come from the biological. And through the eyes of a soothsayer, I can divine that it flows from your thread. A wound that does not heal on your body must have cut into your heart as well."

Ex had lost many teeth over the course of his sordid adventures, and only this one had refused to grow back. The gap had turned into a trump card, thanks to the explosive incisors he'd picked up from a Centrian mouth-jeweler, so he never really stopped to question it.

"When your vitality springs from your will, it's only natural that the concerns of the mind manifest in the body." She touched the glass orb, and the crystal inside came to life. The sage silver hummed, and ribbons of light fluttered around the room. "Now, sit, and know your future."

Ex sat. The light intensified, and the orb whistled a stream of notes. He waited for it to turn to something intelligible, but neither melody nor rhythm emerged.

"You're here to save this village," declared Shantasa.

"Looks like this ball's busted too," said Ex.

"I did not learn this from the crystal, but its source is just as reliable: my niece, the same girl who saved your life, incidentally. Now shut up, darling, and let me listen to the song of your fortune..." at least her voice was still sweet. Madame Shantasa ran her hands over the spinning beams. "Hmm, yes, the crystal speaks to me... There has been much traveling in your life; that will not change. Until your death, of course." There was a brief pause. Ex swallowed hard enough to be heard over the orb. Shantasa continued, "Alone... long have you been alone... but no longer..."

"Wait a sec. Back up," interrupted Ex. "What about my death?"

"I was referring to the inevitability of your mortality, not its impending proof. The crystal rides the endless flow of chroneons in the Subrostrum, it does not speak of ends..." Even as she spoke, the song came to an abrupt end, and the many beams of color saturated into white light. "This is strange..."

"What is it?" Ex demanded.

"An end..."

Ex was on the edge of his seat. "You mean like death?"

"I'm not certain," said Shantasa. "There is just... an end. Of all things, an end... silence and light." Then there came a small sound like a sustained breath. It swelled, turning into a roar of white noise, growing louder, until it was deafening. Shantasa clutched the orb, and the light died. She stared at him through the darkness with wide eyes. Her face was contoured by a light that existed only in the Eidolan reticulum that'd had spread through Ex's mind.

"Well, that was really useful," said Ex, hoisting himself up from his seat. He paused for a response, but Shantasa was speechless. "By the way, this tooth is real right? It's not some sort of Eidolan illusion, is it?"

"No," said Shantasa, her eyes regaining focus. "Illusory teeth aren't particularly useful since you can't convince most foods to believe in them."

"OK, thanks. The old man's picking up the bill, right?"

"Wait a moment!" she called. "I'm not through with you, darling. Come back here and take your clothes off!"

"Whoa now, let's keep things commercial. OK?"

"No, no, you simp," said Shantasa. "I'm a doctor, remember?"

"Yeah? And what's that supposed to mean to me?" Ex wondered.

"You were a pin cushion when they found you in the desert, and just one of those smiler quills is enough to kill a dune bull. I want to examine you to make sure there's no permanent damage."

"Thanks for your concern, but I'm fine. I'll go to a purity ward if I feel anything's gone funny," said Ex. As far as he was concerned, the old lady was just pandering for a free peep show.

"A purity ward? Hah! As if you could find one," said Shantasa. "Nearest ward is on that Consortium ship, darling. Maybe they'll let you use it if you turn yourself in and ask for it in your final request. Besides, a doctor's touch will always be superior to those overblown pill dispensers."

"If it's the same to you, I'll keep my clothes on," said Ex.

"It is the same to me. I'm an Eidolan. You're only wearing what I imagine, but I can't diagnose an illusion, darling."

Ex left the hut feeling comprehensively violated. He found Hitomi waiting for him, statuesque, wearing an impatient frown, hands at her hips, foot hovering in mid-tap. She sprung to life at the sight of him. "We must go to the Farchild residence," she stated.

"Where now?" Ex asked. He fiddled with the compass he'd taken from Tsubasa. "Almost sundown," he said, squinting up at the sky.

"Miss Chimi's house," Hitomi clarified, yanking him across the sand by a handful of hair and collar.

No More Shade

Hitomi and Ex stopped at the door to Chimi's hut. A man and woman could be heard arguing inside. The woman's voice belonged to Farah Farchild, which until this point, Ex had known only as Chimi's mother. The man's voice was familiar, but Ex couldn't quite place it. He listened in with intent.

"Farah," pleaded the man, "you must trust me. The Executor has assigned me to resolve this dilemma peaceably. I won't be given another chance, and neither will you..."

"You have some nerve coming to this house," replied Farah.

There were a few seconds of silence as the man searched his thoughts. "I don't know how else to ask for your forgiveness, Farah."

"You can start by putting in a shift at the mine."

"Don't you think I wish it were that simple? But I can better serve our people on the station."

"By lining your pockets with Plex?" Farah interrupted. She wasn't buying the fellow's pitch, and it was at this point that Ex recognized his voice; it belonged to the bit-playing businessman in the top hat and weskit that had barged in on his interrogation on the station, Sheremy Gallowatch. His voice was almost thick enough to chew.

"Farah, please," implored Gallowatch. "Let's put our past differences aside for a moment and think about the good of the town. What do you think is going to happen when the CIR comes looking for the fugitive? They'll tear the place apart, and if they discover that you've been abetting the criminal..."

"What do you know about the good of the town? Huh? You want us to give up our only hope; for what? So we can keep eking out an existence, digging up rocks for the Consortium? Did you forget why we came here in the first place?"

"And what hope does this man give?" said Gallowatch with a half-laugh. "You don't mean to tell me that you think he can somehow rescue this planet from the CIR?"

"He can!" a small voice chirped.

"Chimi does," said Farah. "And that's enough for me."

"You believe her just because she's half Valoraph? You know only the royals have *vision*," said Gallowatch.

"No. I believe her because she's my daughter."

Gallowatch's sigh was audible through the walls of the upturned rocket burner. "Don't be foolish, Farah. You know there's no way out of this. We've just got to keep our end of the bargain and hold out until a real mining operation makes it out here. The CIR tells me it will only be a couple of months. In the interim, maybe I can scrounge up some extra supplies from the station and..."

"You're the damn fool if you believe that the arrival of a mining ship is going to save us!" Farah threw her words at him with full-body anger. Ex was shocked to find that the same woman who'd offered him the last of her soup with a giving smile was capable of such brilliant fury. "You think they'll let us stay here? They'll mine this planet right out of existence, and us along with it. They're not just going to hand a ship over to a bunch of knotless *Libralma* and let us wander off into the stars!"

"Now, we had an agreement..." Gallowatch began.

"We're outlaws to them!" she insisted. "And worse, fuel. When the mining ship gets here, where do you think they'll get the thread to run the extra drill cores?"

"Then we'll just get everyone threadknots before it gets here, then they'll have no reason to keep you," Sheremy suggested.

"And what about our husbands, our brothers, and sons? What of them? You think the Consortium will release their threads from the refinery's cores? I've already seen my own daughter lose her father; if I can stop it from happening to another one of these girls, that's a chance I'll take."

Gallowatch remained silent.

"Have you forgotten why we even came here in the first place? No, you haven't forgotten. You never knew. Being knotless never meant anything to you, did it?" her voice finally softened.

"It's just an inconvenience. Nothing good will ever come of it."

"I suppose we were all looking for fortune," she said. "Only ours was freedom and yours was wealth, and the two couldn't coexist on this world."

Gallowatch was making no headway. He removed his hat and dried his receding hairline with a damp handkerchief. "It's too late for all this, Farah. The Executor is going to unleash the Talon, and that maniac will head straight to this house. He's a real madman, that one. He won't let you or your daughter die without suffering. Do you understand? He'll tear you apart one atom at a time."

"The hell he will!" bellowed Ex, stepping into the hut. Hitomi had kept a handful of his coat in trying to detain him.

"You!" exclaimed Gallowatch. "How long have you been listening in?"

"Long enough," said Ex. Chimi sat in the corner, rubbing away the streaks that tears had left on her dirty cheeks.

"Then you know the danger you're putting these people in," said Gallowatch. "If I don't return with you, they'll send the Talon next."

"Let him come! I killed him once already; feel free to remind him of that fact." Ex patted his gun in its holster.

"Yes, I'm sure he's reviewed the video," said Gallowatch. "But you may find him more formidable this time around. He won't resemble the Antican you fought on the station. They rethreaded him into an unspeakable abomination. And even if you manage to somehow defeat him, what do you plan to do about the hundreds of cannons and thousands of Nyrceff waiting for you up on that cruiser? Surely there're not enough bullets in that gun of yours for all of them..."

"Not enough bullets, huh?" Ex turned to Chimi, who stared at him with trembling eyes. She had an irrational faith in him that he couldn't begin to understand or ignore, even if it turned his stomach a bit. He winked and waved her over.

Everyone raced outside to see what he was planning; even Kabuto made an appearance. He cocked his gun three times, sending a trio of rounds trickling to the sand. "Wait here," he instructed, before darting up the ridge in pursuit of the compass' arrow. Halfway up, he pointed the pistol at the glinting face of the Placator, high in the evening sky, and pulled the trigger before anyone had guessed his purpose. A hole filled with stars opened in the heavens, and a huge rush of wind threw a column of sand into the sky. It was followed by a tremendous clash of thunder that threw Chimi off her feet. The atmosphere had swallowed the stars, and when everything had resettled, the Placator was gone.

The vacuum-phase of the anchor round didn't work as well in a planet full of perlite and duril. Ex had been launched into the cockles of the dune by the blast. He reemerged from the base, dusting himself off with a big grin. "Now... you were saying?"

Chimi cheered, while Sheremy and Farah stared at the sky in disbelief. They were covered in a thin coat of sand, which grew to small hills on the rims of Sheremy's hat. Kabuto gave a little shake and started snacking on the rounds Ex had dropped.

"My word!" Sheremy said at length. "What in The Seven Rings was that?"

"That was an anchor round," said Hitomi, "a weigh-five, judging by the severity of the atmospheric disturbance it caused..." She clapped three times with mechanical precision. "Congratulations, Mr. Ex, you've not only managed to shoot down the only source of shade on the planet, but you've also revealed your trump. The probability of a runner being armed with such a weapon is extremely slim, but the chance that anyone would possess more than one of these historic weapons without the Consortium knowing is infinitesimal. However, after this display they will have no choice but to assume you have more. This means that the Talon won't be caught downspin without considerable effort on your part..."

"Way to ruin the moment, Hitomi," frowned Ex. She was right. He only had one anchor round left, the big one, a weigh-fifty, but it was going to be tough to use it.

"I can scarcely believe it," continued Sheremy. "To rub out a ship of that size with a single bullet... I always thought weapons like those were things of legend. I see now that the Consortium's concerns are well-founded. You must've used a bullet like that to blast your way out of my bioark, didn't you?"

"Yeah, and there's more where that came from. You go back and tell the Executor that I'm gonna find a telescope, and the next one is coming for him with ten times the weight!"

"I *will* warn him, Mr. Rey, but I doubt I'll need to. I'm afraid Hitomi is right: he won't be caught downspin. Neither will the Talon."

"Then I just won't give 'em the choice," said Ex. "Look, we don't need to start worrying until an Extinguisher shows up, and it could be weeks or months before they manage to get one out here to the middle of nowhere."

"I wouldn't be so sure," said Sheremy. "It may take that long for the nearest Extinguisher to get here, but something just as monstrous is already on the planet. When I said the Talon is not the Antican you fought earlier, perhaps I spoke too lightly. They've woven him and the rest of the Nyrceff you slew into a body of pure duril, threaded from claws to spaded tail. And he's tamed the entire thing.

The etherite crystal of his corona leaps from his forehead like a giant horn. He's forged wings for himself, but I've no idea why. The wind was his servant when his amplifying crystal was microscopic; I fear to guess what might bend to his will now. And the worst of it is that his insanity has not been diluted. They imprinted the beast with Issid's whole mind."

Sheremy's words sounded like a ghost story. It was hard to fathom a man made entirely of sage silver, much less a lunatic Talon. Nothing short of an anchor round could put a dent in a body like that, and all Issid would have to do in order to make that nearly impossible was to attack at the right time of day. Downspin's direction was constant. In the evening, it was pointed directly up at the sky, but as Trisol continued to spin, it would travel down towards the horizon and come to run directly through the planet's core before rising again.

"Fine," conceded Ex. "You want me gone? Find me a ship."

Gallowatch sighed. "I'll tell you what I told Aozora, 'I'd have a better chance of inflating myself like a balloon and floating you out than hijacking a ship.' The hangar up on the station is crawling with Nyrceff. Not that I expect I'll even be making it back. Now that you've destroyed the Placator, I'm sure Zarfall will pull every shuttle off the refinery. Best I could do is let you take the little sand rover that I drove here. They only gave me enough fuel for a one-way trip, but you might be able to procure more around here somewhere... not that you'd have anywhere to go in particular. Still it'd be in all our best interests if you'd leave the village as soon as possible."

"I think it's you who should leave, Sheremy," said Farah. "We didn't rescue this man from the desert to throw him back out again."

Night came and dinner along with it. Hitomi had disposed of the dune-bull's carcass as Tsubasa had instructed, but not before cutting a few more pounds of meat. She stood guard outside the hut as the others ate.

Chimi offered Kabuto the occasional scrap, but he preferred bullets to steaks. He tried to sneak up on Ex's holster for a bite a couple of times, but Ex was having none of it. "Try that again and I'll really feed you a bullet..."

Soon, the only one eating was Ex. Chimi kept him company as her mother washed plates. She stared at him beneath a furrowed brow. Ex could stand in the gaze of Talons and murderers without flinching, but something about this little girl truly undid him. There was a trust in her eyes, an absolute belief that all her problems could be solved by his presence. It was a crushing responsibility the likes of which Ex had never known. He'd once looked upon Arius the same way.

"I'm not here to save you," he said between mouthfuls. "Pretty sure it's not even possible."

"You'll find a way."

"And what makes you think I even want to save you? I have enough trouble just keeping myself alive. I sure as hell don't need to be worrying about an entire planet."

"Cause you owe me one."

"Yeah? Well it wouldn't be the first tab I've walked out on," he said, finally losing his appetite. He crashed onto his tiny bedroll and turned his back.

Chimi came over and crouched down beside him. "Don't worry. I trust you, Ex," she whispered. "I know you won't run out on us..." Ex cringed and pulled the meager sheet over his shoulder. Chimi leaned in closer. "What's it like being a Sage?"

"How should I know?" He loved being called a Sage, but really had no idea how to answer the question.

"Aren't you one?"

"Yeah, but asking me that is like me asking you what it's like to be a little girl," Ex replied.

"It's pretty great!" she piped. "Well, sometimes... but I guess being a Sage is more complicated than that, huh? I only ask cause mostly everyone in Himatma is knotless, but none of us are Sages. In fact, Mom won't even let me study about Sages. Can you believe that? I can read about guns, and ships, and bombs, but not Sages. I've always wondered why. But Ole Man Zora, he gave me a book about them... wanna see it?"

"Not really," said Ex, trying to shoo her away so he could sleep, but she'd already scampered off and was back just as quickly. Without turning, he could hear her flipping the pages.

"Where did you get your *corona*?" she said, enunciating the word as if she'd just read it for the first time.

"I don't have one," Ex replied.

"Then how can you do all that Sage stuff?"

"Magic..."

"And what's that?"

"You don't know what magic is?" sighed Ex. "Magic is like... like something great that you can't explain."

"Like love?"

"No! Not like love! What the hell's wrong with you?"

"Well, love's pretty great, and I can't explain it," said Chimi.

"Nah, magic is more like random lasers and explosions... or shooting comets outta your wrists, that kinda thing," said Ex.

Chimi wasn't about to take that answer. She flipped through the pages of her book and shook Ex's shoulder. "Hey, Ex. Look... look at this..." Ex rolled over and was presented with the small book, bound in withering leather. It was opened to a page, marked by a dirty white ribbon. "See?" she said, pointing at a faded picture. Ex squinted at the blurry image. It was of a man that looked vaguely like him, at least in the sense that they both wore an irate expression. A large triangular shadow loomed behind the man that might've been a building in the background or some kind of mountain. The cloak he wore was wrapped around his neck and over his chin and mouth. It had triangular patterns on its ragged trim in shades of gray. Chimi's little finger tapped the picture. "That's you," she said.

"Go away and let me sleep, will ya?!" Ex pushed the book away and rolled over. He waited for her to leave, but she just sat there, breathing in little spurts. "The only thing I can do for this planet is to get the hell out of here... and as soon as

I find a ship, that's what I'm gonna do," he said. Without another word, she closed her book and was gone.

Starlit Rendezvous

That night, Ex could not sleep. The ground was hard. The air was cold. And the wind whimpered. Whenever it fell silent, a faint metal clicking would make its way into his ears. It was coming from the room that Farah and Chimi shared, and Ex figured Kabuto was to blame.

He threw off his tiny blanket and snuck out with the intent of discovering if the sand rover Gallowatch had mentioned was really out of fuel or not. Trisol had no moon, but the nights were not dark, such was the density of stars in the clear sky. Their reflection glittered across the surface of the fine sand. He'd nearly made it to the foot of the ridge when Hitomi's voice called out to him, "Where do you think you're going?"

Her arms were crossed, and she wore a wispy white dress that made promises in the pale starlight. "I'm not wearing any shoes," she said, "so I'd rather not have to chase you into the desert."

"Then don't," said Ex.

"Please Mr. Ex," Hitomi's tone changed abruptly. Ex stopped. "Don't go! If I let you escape, Mr. Aozora will deactivate me and scrap me for parts!" She was on the verge of tears, approaching slowly.

"Really?"

"No, not really," she replied, snatching him up by the wrist. She was immensely strong. Ex wasn't about to test his full strength on her, but it seemed futile to struggle. He was dragged back to the village. She deposited him on the sand by a large stone not far from the entrance to Chimi's home.

"I can't believe you were standing guard all night long..." he sighed. "That's ridiculous."

"And necessary, by the looks of it," added Hitomi.

"Don't you ever sleep?"

"Only when instructed to do so."

Ex wiggled his fingers at her: "Sleep... sleep..."

"I don't take orders from you."

"I know; it was supposed to be a joke."

"Noted," said Hitomi. "I will file it as a sample of your wit. But I feel compelled to tell you that I wasn't the only one watching you." She pointed up at the sky, but Ex could only see stars. "There's a bird circling at great altitude. Must be another *friend* of yours."

"*Another* friend?" Ex said righting himself. "Did you just imply that you're my friend?"

Hitomi took a moment to consider her words. "I could see how you would come to that conclusion, but you are incorrect. The tone I applied to the word 'friend' was such that it would be italicized if written so as to denote sarcasm."

Ex searched his mind for how to engage her in more idle conversation. "So you don't sleep... do you at least eat?"

"I am powered by a nine-gauge threaded core. I require no other fuel source," she explained. That was enough threadwidth to run a cruiser. There was more spirit in this cold android than most flesh and blood things.

"Sounds kinda boring though."

"Boredom is not one of my emotional parameters," replied Hitomi, "which is why I am able to endure this conversation."

"Are you always this much of an icy bitch?"

"No," said Hitomi, tearing up suddenly. "I'm not really bad. It's just that I've been programmed for self-preservation. You see, I'm afraid to show my real emotions because... I don't want to be hurt, and..." Her speech was full of dramatic pauses. "Well... secretly, I've fallen deeply in love with you."

"Really?" Ex straightened out.

"No. Now go back to sleep."

"Why don't you like me?"

"Why should I?"

"I'm a man, and you're a woman..."

"I would dispute both claims," said Hitomi.

Ex fell back in the sand, resting his head in his hands. He stared at the creamy swirls in the sky. There was no black, only dark, dark blue. A nearby planet sat like a pearl amongst diamonds. "You only like people you're programmed to like."

"Oh, and you're any different?" said Hitomi, brushing the gossamer hair from her face. She was right, and she knew that he knew she was right. He really had no reason to like her, but there was a part of him that was left with no choice.

"So why are you on this planet anyway?" asked Ex.

"Are you being existential?"

"No," Ex grunted, hoisting himself back up – relaxing around Hitomi was all but impossible. "I mean, how did these people end up on this planet of all places?"

"We happened upon it by chance. Coming here was the Captain's decision, the manner in which we landed was not as deliberate," said Hitomi. "I was the ship's acting helmswoman, and although I had told the Captain that my quantum processors could navigate the ship better than its autopilot, he decided that we'd use the standard routine to land because I'd never landed a colonizer vessel before. The autopilot did not react well to the perlite of the planet's surface. The false readings put us nearly a hundred meters under the sand. No one was seriously injured in the crash, but the vessel was rendered inoperable. And Captain Farchild took responsibility..."

"Captain Farchild?"

"Yes, Thuris Farchild, former Captain of the Himatma, renowned Valarian starfarer, husband of Farah Farchild, and father to Chimi Farchild..." responded Hitomi.

"Where is he now? I heard her mother say that she'd lost him. Did he die? What happened to him?"

"Perhaps if you'd stop queuing questions, I might render an answer," said Hitomi. "Mr. Aozora had secured us passage on the Himatma colonizer vessel at expense of my employ. He'd been looking for a place to retire, and I believe it was his wife who pointed him in the direction of this particular ship. She can be quite persuasive when she wishes to be, not to mention that she threatened to change her Eidolan image into something of a warthog with a double-fat back."

"Wait! Are you saying that crazy old tooth woman was, or rather *is,* the old man's wife?"

"Yes, in so many words," replied Hitomi. "She is also Chimi's aunt and Thuris' older sister. They are all Valarian, but only she is Eidolan..."

"I can't wait to tease the old man about this..."

"They are also all Libralma, as was the rest of the crew and passengers on the Himatma with only three exceptions of which I'm aware: Mr. Aozora, Mr. Gallowatch, and myself..."

"Libralma?"

"Yes, members of the Libralma religion; though its founder, Master Mavenbolt, would call it a philosophy." Her cadence shifted up a couple of steps, but her expression remained unchanged; her eyes were half closed, the corners of her mouth were turned down, and her lips hardly moved as she spoke. "It's not a very organized belief system, partially because the Consortium would not allow it. I will summarize the basic tenets for you, but in the interest of expedience I must first ask: do you know why Will is referred to as a thread?"

Ex remembered the knotless old Sage in the banquet hall of Bastalia. It felt as if he'd just seen her yesterday because if you counted the nightmares he'd suffered in the caves, he had. It wasn't the first time he'd relived that moment, but her words were always clearer in the dream. "Not exactly..." he decided to say.

"Will flows constantly and endlessly from a *source* into all threaded things. Most simply call this source *the pool,* but The Libralma choose to view it as The Impetus, The Creator, The Origin, in one word, *God.* They believe that all of the will in existence once belonged to this single being. In the instants or eternities before time, He was omnipotent. But in a sense, He was limited by his limitless power. There was nothing that exists now which could challenge Him, and yet it was a challenge He desired. And so the universe sprang forth from a thought, set on a path of chaotic decay that will, after hundreds of trillions of years, result in a uniformly distributed cloud of sameness at a pleasant 20 degrees Celsius. But then came life and with it, a factor of reorganization, a system designed to fight the inevitable, to change what exists. With all the animus of The Creator, life sought to overcome the challenges that faced it. And its forms were vast, and its endeavors boundless. To a Libralma, the thread is not only what connects us to God. It is God. They believe that shackling a part of The Impetus, no matter how small, is a sacrilege. This is why they refuse to be bound by a threadknot."

"It almost sounds like you believe it too," said Ex.

"I neither believe nor think it false. You may find it interesting to know that the flags which distinguish facts from theories in my mind are less than one qubit," Hitomi digressed. She took a few barefoot steps across the soft sand towards the village, surveying the homes with her softly glowing eyes.

"Overcoming challenges is a religious pursuit to the Libralma. That is why The Himatma set course for this planet of Trisol; Thuris Farchild rightly believed it would pose many hardships, but he couldn't guess what lay beneath the surface and the dangers that its secret would bring. The last thing he wanted was to attract the

CIR's attention, and yet there is no surer way of thrusting yourself into their gaze than to build your home on an unprecedented cache of duril."

"So these spiritual kooks landed on the planet without even knowing about the duril?" Ex had no right to judge the Libralma for their ignorance, but being the renowned outlaw that he was, cared little for rights.

"Precisely," said Hitomi. "No one knew about it. Until Mr. Gallowatch told."

"Told who?"

Hitomi came back to the stone and sat with her legs turned aside. Her only reason to sit was to better embody the image of a storyteller. She modeled her pose after the images of Queen Scheherazade held within the vast banks of her cultural databases. "Sheremy Gallowatch had no family. He was not a Libralma, but he knew that they typically rejected wealth. This meant that The Himatma offered the potential for vast monetary gains. His plan was always to establish a mining business, regardless of where they landed. He knew that none of the other passengers would dispute his claim. In exchange for this opportunity, he had paid most of the expenses of the voyage: food, fuel, and amenities for the whole crew."

She put a palm on the stone and leaned in. "When he discovered that Trisol was practically made of duril, he could not conceal his joy, but it was short-lived. Revealing the presence of any amount of duril would immediately bring the Consortium to the planet, and along with it, all of their laws. The Libralma were knotless, which qualified them as criminals. There would be no fortune for them. The planet's bounty would bring them shackles for both body and spirit.

Mr. Gallowatch felt that he'd been double-crossed. By contract, he owned the resources of Trisol. He insisted that with this much wealth, they'd be able to purchase their freedom. But Thuris disagreed."

"So he killed him?"

"Not exactly," said Hitomi. "In a sense... I did." Her eyes dimmed, and she leaned away from Ex. She stared across the quiet street, looking pensive for a being that could never ask *why*. "A year after our crash landing, the town was as you see it now. Food was scarce, but at least water was plentiful. An underground river flows beneath the tunnels of what has now become the duril mine. It was just enough to sustain life, but the town's power supply was dwindling. The crash left the ship's reactors unsalvageable; their threads had evanesced before the crew had even cleared the wreckage. Most of the functioning cores belonged to Mr. Aozora, which he claimed to need for his work. Furthermore, their gauge was insufficient for the town's needs. There was, however, one core that could have easily resolved the power crisis..." She touched her chest. Her eyes were wide, sparkling plates of heather blue.

"But Mr. Aozora would not allow it. Captain Farchild was forced to repair the only shuttle that survived the landing. The vessel was never intended for long distance travel, and its questionable condition made the voyage even more dangerous. Still, Mr. Gallowatch volunteered to pilot it, and Thuris went along with him to ensure that he would not divulge Trisol's secret."

"I would've never let Gallowatch on that ship," said Ex.

"But you forget the purpose of the journey," Hitomi went on. "Thuris could not bring any duril along to trade for the reactors. The plex and goods they had to offer were meager. It would take someone with considerable business sense and a fund of external assets to broker the necessary deal, and that was Mr. Gallowatch, who'd sworn every oath not to mention the duril. It was with reluctance that the town allowed him to go, but at the time there seemed to be little choice."

Ex didn't need to hear any more. He could deduce what happened next. Hitomi seemed pleased by his knowing expression.

"To this day," she continued, "Mr. Gallowatch maintains his innocence, or rather admits his guilt in the matter, but claims it to have been accidental. He smuggled a shard of duril no bigger than a small coin onboard for the purposes of facilitating the trade. He claimed that the easiest way to purchase something that contains duril is with duril. And yet, he would have known that such a quantity was far more than what was required. A piece of duril of that size would be enough to run a generator hundreds of times larger than what Himatma needed.

The shuttle had not traveled far out of the Trisol system when it was intercepted by a CIR scout. Away from the planet's perlite, the duril piece stuck out like an Eidolan on Narcissia. What happened next, only Mr. Gallowatch can say with certainty, but Captain Farchild was killed, and the Consortium learned of Trisol. If I had given up my core, none of that would have ever happened."

"It's impossible to keep something like this a secret forever," said Ex.

"You may be correct, but this planet had remained a secret since the beginning of time," she said. "Perhaps my sacrifice could have kept it hidden another couple of decades, but that point is moot. The decision was made, Thuris is gone, the planet is found, Gallowatch is ostracized, and I remain the object of accusing stares."

Ex felt the urge to comfort her with an embrace, but was afraid of the physical damage he might receive if he tried.

"The Farchilds' loss was the greatest, and yet they've never resented me," she said motioning towards the home. A smile crossed her face, sad and still, like Arius always wore.

Ex had to turn away. He stood up and began to pace.

"Where are you going?" asked Hitomi.

"Nowhere, just stretching," he replied. "Can't I even do that?" The smile was gone from her face, so he could look at her again. "So then the CIR commandeered a nearby bioark and mining lander and the rest is history, huh?"

"Correct," said Hitomi. "And with the CIR came hundreds of pirates, traders, and opportunists. In the very least, the Consortium's presence protected us from these vultures, and Himatma's existence was allowed at great expense. Under these unique conditions, they viewed this settlement of knotless Libralma not as a threat, but another one of the planet's resources. Their initial plan was to thread the entire town into the drills of the mining derrick they'd landed a few hundred kilometers away.

It was actually Mr. Gallowatch that managed to strike a deal in which the CIR would only use half of Himatma's population in their drills. I suppose it was some vestige of chivalry that drove the men to volunteer themselves to be used. But I question which half made the greater sacrifice. Those who've kept their thread have had an inhuman mining quota piled on top of the grueling workload that life in this arid climate demands. It is a tentative agreement, and one I fear that will not outlive the arrival of the Consortium's planetary mining vessel."

"Well, I can see why Chimi's mother is so fond of the guy now," said Ex.

"Mr. Gallowatch has begged her forgiveness many times," said Hitomi, rising from the stone. "Perhaps my empathic assessors are more easily deceived than human intuition, but I believe the man is genuinely regretful for what he's done. He's offered Mrs. Farchild and Ms. Chimi a life of relative luxury on Ferrous Outpost a number of occasions. And each time he's been roundly rejected. The benefits and comforts he offers demonstrates that even now he does not understand the beliefs and desires of the Libralma..." She extended a hand towards Ex, and he took it. She led him to the entrance of the Farchilds' home.

"I'm not sure I understand them either," admitted Ex.

"They are not easily understood," agreed Hitomi. "Now please get some rest. You don't know what tomorrow will bring. It would be wise to face it without fatigue..."

Ex paused at the door. "You do care!" he smiled.

"Only when instructed..." she winked, and gave him a shove that sent him tumbling to his bedroll.

Whispers in the Centower

Every sentient race had their equivalent of vintners and drug makers, but none held a higher place in their respective societies than the Valoraphim neuralchemists. With the exception of the engineers that crafted the famous Valoforged engines, there was no trade more respected by their people.

A neuralchemist's purpose was not to dull or drive to ecstasy, but to fill vials with experiences. These drugs were not easily abused, and those who tried were typically of another species. To the Valoraphim, neuralchemy was akin to worship, and they were pious, particularly their royals. The drugs could kindle their prophetic vision. It was to this purpose that Nodris now swirled the crimson Brendahl in a long stem glass.

Divination did not come easily to him. He was not as gifted as most of his family. Perhaps it was this relative blindness that allowed him to endure a life of politics, but today he drank like an oracle. Today was the anniversary of his niece's disappearance. Claire was the most promising seer born to the Gincleare in many generations, but he cared little for that. He was more interested in her boundless empathy, and the way her smile greeted the light of Atamal, Star of Miraval. When she came to visit him on Veredos, a golden spark of that sun came with her.

He waited for her on the dock that day, clutching a doll imported from Midore with fronds for hair. The Luciel pulled into dock like a swan. Claire's father, Kelmore, was the first to disembark, followed by his usual entourage. "Claire's gone missing," he said. The light of the Grand Forge poured through the pier's glass ceilings and walls. Kelmore's eyes were drawn to a squint, dry as the rocks of Miraval that baked naked in the radiation of Atamal.

Four years had passed since then, and every year on this day, Nodris would sit with the Midoran doll and sail on Brendahl to the rim of reason in search of a glimpse of her fate. And every year, the glasses grew larger and his hopes dimmer.

He looked down at the doll in his lap, searching the glimmering spirals of its Midoran eyes. She'd be too old for dolls now. He imagined Claire in a maiden's mantle of white cashmere, worn to hide the buds of fresh wings that would be sprouting from her scapulae. He drank and fell into a hole of neon figures. The visions offered no answers. They passed too quickly and echoed into smoke. His mind was anchored by the questions of the present.

Nodris felt the door to his room open, but could not turn his head to face it. His only choice was to stop fighting the Brendahl and let it overwhelm him. With a roar of light and sound, his mind was his again. He turned to find that the entrance to his room was unbroken. The door had not opened yet. He stared expectantly at the white wall, until it split apart, and Zaralin stood in the threshold.

"Apologies for the intrusion, Viceroy," she bowed.

"Nonsense, please come in," motioned Nodris.

"I bear news of the situation on Trisol," she said as she entered. "The orbiting Placator has been destroyed."

"Destroyed?" said Nodris, rising from his chair. "How?" The doll tumbled to the floor.

"A lightweight anchor round was fired from the planet's surface," replied Zaralin. "The Executor Zarfall had ordered a complete evacuation of the ship several hours before the incident occurred. Since the anchor rounds had not shown up in the customs scanners, yet the fugitive had already fired one, the Executor had rightly concluded that it was possible that he possessed more. The ship was purposefully maneuvered downspin of the criminals' location to confirm this fact."

"A costly experiment."

"A pyrrhic victory for both sides," said Zaralin. "The appraised value of the anchor round rivals that of the lost cruiser."

Nodris did not think Zaralin capable of exaggeration, but it was hard to believe a single bullet could cost as much as a warship. Placators weren't the most powerful vessels in the Consortium's navy, and they were certainly not big enough to carry their own levees to protect from anchorspace weaponry, but this was the first loss of its kind in centuries – at least of which he was aware. "Where is the crew now?"

"Their numbers have been distributed between the Ferrous Outpost and the mining facility," she said, handing him a full report. "I've also included the information on Executor Zarfall, as you requested. That is everything I could gather with my level of security clearance."

Nodris took a moment to review the data. It didn't take long because there wasn't much of it. Zarfall had earned excellent marks in the Veridian Academy of Xerbekos, finishing 328th out of his class, which doesn't sound spectacular, but considering that there were over five million graduates that semester, the accomplishment was notable. He went on to command a few minor vessels before managing a plex font in a dusky star of the fourth stratum. As it happens, the star he was mining was located in the same arm of the same galaxy as Trisol.

Upon receiving word from the scout that intercepted Gallowatch's shuttle, Zarfall had managed to commandeer and refit a dilapidated bioark from a band of runners that had been leeching off the traffic around the plex font. The mining-lander arrived at Trisol one month later, and it'd been nearly half a year since then. The CIR had kept the planet a secret, but word has a way of spreading with a find of this nature. Until now, Zarfall had managed to keep the would-be bandits and claim-jumpers at bay with a single battalion of Nyrceff and a Talon operative. The arrival of the Placator had more than tripled the CIR's numbers, and there were several other cruisers en route. The closest would achieve orbit in less than a week.

After reviewing the reports, Nodris had to concede that the manner in which the rogue Sage had bypassed security, penetrated the defenses, and plundered the station's depository were unprecedented. Feats like these would've been remarkable at the peak of The Extinguishing. The name the outlaw had given was Ex Rey, but his identity couldn't be confirmed due to a complete lack of threadwidth.

Nodris had pondered the message Zaralin had spoken to Dethoron in his presence: *"The child of The Flooded Gate still lives... Even under the glare of three suns, he dwells in impenetrable shadow."* He'd searched The Centower's database for the term "Flooded Gate." It turned out to be a codename for a Sage of some repute, but beyond that, information was strictly classified, filed under both the categories of sentient and cosmic phenomenon.

Since The Extinguishing, the CIR had hunted down almost all of the surviving sages. Despite the delicate nature of their operations, the records were made available to the public, so that mercenaries could learn the whereabouts and status of any known Sage. But the case of The Flooded Gate was an exception. The only pieces of information he could extract from the encrypted logs were dates, and by crosschecking these, he was able to deduce that Fleet Admiral Dethoron had been involved. He was the only Extinguisher that could be associated with the last mission log mentioning The Flooded Gate.

"I've also procured the data on Valarian origins which you requested, Viceroy, but I fear the report will not state anything more than what you already know," said Zaralin.

"Is this all the information there is, or all that I'm allowed to have?"

"Apologies, Viceroy, the latter," bowed Zaralin.

"And what of you?" said Nodris. "Is this everything that you know about their origins?"

"I am an appendage of The Centower. Its knowledge is my knowledge, only exceeded by that of His Supremacy, The Capstone's."

Nodris's eyes remained on Zaralin as he imaged the vast amount of secrets she kept from him. Perhaps it was just the Brendahl resettling, but he could almost sense the distance between them growing. "And I don't suppose you'd be willing to answer a few questions in the privacy of this room..."

"There are no secrets in The Centower, save those it keeps for itself," she replied out of practice. "Were I to whisper a single word or pass a single digit of information to you with a touch, the tower would know. It would know because I know. My eyes are its eyes. My ears are its ears."

It pained him to hear her say that, but he was grateful that the tower could not hear his thoughts. He wished openly at that moment that those eyes and ears could be his to confide in. The impossibility of this desire practically left him mute. "Very well, let me hear what I can," he managed to mumble. And he heard her voice, but the words rang in his ears as noise. He stared into his glass until he was blind and deaf.

Zaralin delivered the report from memory. "The Valarian race is believed to have originated less than 50 years before The Extinguishing, but there are no records of any of the first generation's births. The first officially recorded Valarian birth occurred during the seventh year of the war, born to a Valarian father and Solarian mother..."

Nodris wasn't listening. He was lost in a prophetic vision. A man in a white mask stood on stars, unraveling a planet, one thread at a time. The strings drained into an orb in his hand, and in that sphere of light was a child, resting as if in a womb. The man became aware of Nodris and turned to face him, threads still spooling into his palm. The mask he wore was Sophian, with horns curled gracefully at its sides in tight spirals, but the face behind it was not. It was hauntingly familiar, but he could not place it. The wearer had horns of his own – two of them, twisting from the crown of his skull. His eyes had two pupils each, moving independently. The irises were limpid yellow, and the flesh around his eyes was deep red. The points of his long ears stretched above the horns of his mask, and in the place of teeth were two serrated arcs of bone.

"*Valkaros!*" Nodris exclaimed, suddenly torn from the vision. The word echoed in Zaralin's silence. She was fluent in Valoraphim, even some of the older dialects; she knew the language better than him. But Valkaros was not a word; it was a name that cast a shadow on the pages of Valoraph history. Nodris had heard it whispered in the golden halls of Miraval as a child. He thought that only Royals and palace scholars knew of its existence, but it seemed to hold meaning for Zaralin as well. Her expression remained aloof and unattached, but she was always quiet when she had something truly important to say.

There'd been more to his vision than a name, more than he could process in a moment. The face he'd seen beneath the Sophian mask belonged to a Dormant One. Before The Awakening, all Valoraphs had looked this way. Their images had been stricken from every mural and record since then, but they'd remained buried in an indelible part of the race's psyche that only surfaced in nightmares.

"I'm sorry," Nodris apologized. "I was stricken by a vision. I must've had too much Brendahl."

Zaralin's eyes belonged to the tower, but the glimmer of concern was for him.

"Are you familiar with the name I spoke?" he softly asked.

Her lips quivered, and she shook her head.

"Does it have something to do with the creation of the Valarian?" asked Nodris.

Zaralin didn't shake her head. She just excused herself and left.

Nodris wouldn't find his answer on Veredos. He'd need to beseech the wisdom of the elders on Miraval. They hadn't been forthcoming when he was a child, but perhaps they would be more willing to answer a question asked by The Viceroy of the Second Ring.

Things that Go Spelunk

It felt as though he'd barely shut his eyes, but already morning was here. Ex peered through his eyelashes, pretending he was still asleep. Chimi was eating her breakfast alone, although there were two bowls on the table. Whatever it was, it didn't smell half bad. She wore ratty, white-turned-gray pajamas and the sparkling little necklace that Tsubasa had given her.

She ate quickly, glancing now and again at Ex, who remained perfectly still on the floor. The suns were just now starting to creep through the lowest windowsill in the kitchen-nook. Whether out of kindness or rush, she poured the remainder of her breakfast into the other bowl and raced into her room. Seconds later she emerged dressed in full mining gear and dragging the heavy laser. She was off to beat the suns to the mine.

Ex rolled over and put the morning on hold.

When next he awoke, everything was silent, and the sunlight poured through the various holes and cracks in the ceiling. He staggered over to the table and consumed the contents of the bowl: dune bull stew by the taste of it. It was mostly just meat and water with a few twigs for flavor, but it hit the spot.

He'd slurped up the last drop when the ground beneath his squat seat began to rumble. He stood, and the stool tipped over, half sunken in the sand. Out popped Kabuto, clicking and hissing up a storm.

"The hell's wrong with you?" said Ex, stretching out after his midday breakfast. Kabuto skittered over to him and clamped down on his pant leg. The beetle tugged with unexpected strength, yanking him off his feet. Each pull was announced by a single jingle of the bell around his horn. Ex clawed for a handhold in the sand as Kabuto dragged him towards the door. The struggle resulted in a torn pant leg and a fully awake, fully annoyed Ex.

He was just about to give Kabuto a taste of his boot when something peculiar happened. He thought he heard words in the beetle's clamor. *"Go help, go help,"* it seemed to say. Throughout his travels, Ex's metaglot had been exposed to a lot of languages, but they actually had to be languages for him to gain any form of comprehension. The metaglot only processed structured, patterned sound, not the wild baying and hissing of animals. There were certain tongues that gave his ears trouble. If the frequencies were not right, or if the language had no discernable syntactical structure, he couldn't comprehend it. Still the presence of organized communication denoted an intelligence that he was not prepared to recognize in the overgrown bug.

Ex focused on Kabuto's clatter; concentrating on the sound usually helped speed along acquisition. Hearing a language spoken without it was similar to trying to read text that was out of focus. He listened for a good minute, occasionally dodging Kabuto's attempts to regain a grip of his ankles.

Not much came through. All Ex could manage was *rocks... fall... water... help...* spoken in a hissy little voice. There was no doubt the beetle was trying to speak because each word came with a punchy autex – something like prickly licorice. Having nothing better to do and being fully roused from any chances of further sleep, he decided to indulge the little beetle and followed it outside. He was briskly led to the mouth of the mine, where many of the village women were gathered. "What's going on around here?" he asked a short woman that was hopping up and down for a view over the shoulders of the others.

"A girl hit the river and a support slipped," she said. "There was a cave in and the poor deary is still trapped inside."

"Who's the girl?" demanded Ex. "No, wait. Lemme guess, it's Chimi isn't it?"

"Yes, how did you know?"

"I'm a Sage," sighed Ex and muscled through the crowd. The mouth of the tunnel was stuffed with rocks. A couple of women with mining lasers were discussing where they should direct their beams. Driven by instincts dipped in traces of smiler poison, he brushed them aside and clawed straight into the stone. "What're you doing?" they exclaimed. "Stop at once, you can't do that!"

"The hell I can't!" he said, shoveling stones left and right.

"You're only going to make it worse! You'll cause another cave in!" pleaded the women, slowly backing away. Even Kabuto looked a bit squeamish, but Ex went right on.

"Just stand there talking all day then; see if that saves anyone!" He removed one more stone, and the roof fell on him. He would have been crushed, if the floor hadn't given out too. He plunged into the darkness and Kabuto followed.

A roaring river coursed beneath the mine. The current was too strong to fight; Ex was swept away in pitch-black whitewater. His body crashed against sharp rocks and slammed against slimy walls. He struggled to surface for air, but the river flowed only a few centimeters from the tunnel's ceiling. He clattered his teeth into the stone a dozen times, taking in large doses of the acrid water mixed with blood. He began to fade in and out of consciousness.

He washed up on a stony bank. His eyes were open, but they didn't collect a single photon. Hands fumbling, he searched for anything. He had no idea how wide the bank was, but there was no wall in reach, only more of the slimy floor. He screamed and cursed Hitomi's name. It was her fault that he was without a neuro-HUD, left blind and practically deaf in the river's white roar.

His feet were still submerged inside his boots, and his coat weighed a ton. He floundered further up the bank. At last his hands came upon a stalagmite. It was not a particularly big one, wider than it was tall, but he clutched the tiny landmark like his life depended on it. He took the opportunity to curse at Hitomi again and was pleased to find an echo that agreed with him. The chamber's expansive size was made evident by the delay of the echo's response.

A familiar jingle rose over the rapids' distant din. "Kabuto?" he called out. "Is that you?"

The beetle scurried over to him in the dark and hissed something like *yesh*. Ex never thought he'd be happy to see the bug – well, not *see* it, but hear it at least. "Kabuto, can you see, boy, or are you blind here too?"

"Yesh," said the bug. The autex pricked him in the dark.

"*Yesh* what? You can see?"

"Go help," it clicked and hissed.

The thrill of Kabuto's arrival was fading. "Well, can you guide me out of here?" he pleaded.

"Yesh," said Kabuto and was off like a shot, clicking and popping his way further into the cave.

"Kabuto! Get back here, you damn bug! I can't see!"

Then there was another sound. Something had just leapt out of the water and landed on the stone with a flap. Ex listened intently, and his ears were nearly shattered by a couple of sudden shrieks.

The source of the noise approached, screeching, slapping, and scraping. And then it was upon him. The air grew cold as it took heavy breaths. "So, you thought you could escape me by going underground, did you?" spoke the Blank.

"You?!" Ex beamed, unable to hide his surprise and excitement. "What are you doing down here?"

"I should ask you the same question."

"I'm trying to rescue a trapped girl," said Ex.

There was a strange giggle, like two laughs at once, one throaty and bullish, the other small and twinkling. "Some job you're doing of that."

"Hey, this is serious! She could have drowned by now." The grim possibility didn't strike him until he'd said it aloud.

"Impossible," said the Blank. "It's only been about twenty minutes since the cave-in occurred."

"So?"

"So the girl is a Valarian, she can go an hour or two without breathing. There's no way she could've drowned yet," the Blank said. "Dashed to bits on the rocks, maybe, but not drowned..."

"What is wrong with you?" sobbed Ex.

"Relax," she laughed. "I pinged the whole river as I swam here. She wasn't caught by the undertow, so she must've washed up on the shore like you did. And since when did you become the hero type anyway?"

"Whaddya mean?" Ex said, taking offense.

"I mean, why do you care enough about this little girl to risk your life like this? Doesn't seem in your idiom," she mused.

"Yeah? Well, I gotta tab with her. She saved my life, so now I'm gonna save hers and call it even."

"So you pay your tabs now? My, my, you've changed quite a bit haven't you?"

"The hell I have," said Ex. "There're just some debts you gotta pay back, that's all. So're you just gonna sit there taking shots at me in the dark, or are you gonna help me find her?"

"Fine, but when I get you out of here, no more running off on harebrained heroics!" she replied and popped a pill. She morphed into a mixture of a gecko and a centipede. Her pale green skin emitted a soft glow, but most of the light came from an orb that dangled at the end of a long antenna extending from her forehead. She wriggled along like a snake, and Ex followed.

"Hey, Blank, couldn't you turn back into that blue woman instead," he asked, sloshing along in his boots.

"That'd leave us both blind, you dolt! And my name is not Blank, it's Qui."

"Qui?"

"And what's wrong with that? It's the closest thing in your language to the first phoneme of my actual name," she explained.

"It's just not much of a name, is it? Qui..." he chuckled.

"That's rich, coming from a man with a letter for a name."

"Fair enough," said Ex. "Well, Qui, why don't we compromise? Could you turn into a blue woman with a glowing butt?"

"Will you just shut up and follow me?" she said, hastening her pace.

Ex's echo had not deceived. The cavern was enormous. Qui's light couldn't reach the ceiling or walls. They wove around a few stalagmites and skipped over fathomless cracks.

"What do you suppose made these?" asked Qui, tasting the air in one of the fissures with her forked tongue.

"Dunno," shrugged Ex. "Haven't felt any quakes yet, but I've only been on this planet for about a week." He grabbed her by the antenna and pulled the lantern into the crack.

"Hey, careful! That's sensitive," Qui cried.

"Oh, sorry," said Ex. He released the antenna, feeling suddenly dirty.

Qui peered back into the fissure. "They don't look like fault lines. See the patterns on the wall? They're too deliberate. It seems something was mined from here."

"I didn't think the miners had made it out this far."

"They haven't," said Qui.

They trekked a wide arc around the cave that led them back to the river. Here its flow was placid. The water was oily-black with shimmering jade ripples in the light of Qui's lantern. She marched up and down the bank, scouring it for traces of the girl. "Look," she said, pointing with her antenna, "tracks."

"In the rock?" laughed Ex. But there they were: slender pockmarks at steady intervals. They led to a low-lying portion of the coastline, where the water gently stroked the stone. He poked at a hole in the rock. It was a smooth cut.

"They found the girl here, and I believe they took her in that direction," Qui declared, waving her lantern towards the depths of the cave.

"Who's they?" wondered Ex.

"I don't know. Beings that leaves tracks in solid stone as they walk, bipeds, three of them, by the looks of it," said Qui.

Ex drew his gun. "Well, let's go then, before they eat her!"

"I seriously doubt that creatures living in this environment would want or even be able to ingest a little girl's flesh. It would make no evolutionary sense, given the diets available to them. They might kill her if they think she's invading their territory, but not eat her..." she said.

"You've got a real funny way of comforting a guy."

It was at this point that Kabuto rejoined them. He came racing out of the darkness from the direction of the tracks. A few clicks and hisses were meant to urge them to follow. "What's gotten into him?" asked Qui.

"He's always like this," said Ex.

The three ventured further into the cavern, and the river faded to a whisper behind them. They noticed that some of the stalagmites' tips had been worked into a series of ridged bowls like the imprints of shells. Scattered between the stalagmites were what appeared to be petrified ponds, frozen in mid-ripple. They were larger than puddles, but smaller than lakes. Their shapes were generally round, and their surfaces were hard as stone underfoot, darker and smoother than the surrounding rock.

The further they marched into the cave, the more of these curious formations they encountered. The stalagmite carvings held some sort of interest for Kabuto. He approached them clicking and chirping. When one of the stones was too high, the shell on his back cracked open, and he fluttered tiny wings to have a better look. He couldn't stay airborne for long, and kept tipping over in midair. After a particularly lengthy inspection, Kabuto's path took them away from the direction of the tracks.

"The prints go this way," said Qui, but Kabuto insisted.

"*No, no!*" hissed the beetle.

"Seems pretty adamant," said Ex.

But Qui kept crawling over the tracks. "Whatever took the girl went this way," she said. "There's no other way she could have made it this far without light."

Ex was convinced, but Kabuto wasn't. The bug stomped around impatiently. And there it remained until they were well out of sight. Ex and Qui moved swiftly without having to wait on the bug to check every stone they passed. The tracks were clear, and they didn't have to worry about disturbing them because they were etched in stone.

Soon, they crossed over another set of prints, then another. The trails dotted off in every direction, but Qui was sure they were still on track. Ex just saw holes, but she claimed that the footsteps they followed left a distinct imprint on the stone.

Finally they came to a wall, where countless tracks crisscrossed. The one they were following led straight up a sheer stone face into the darkness above. "Oh great," said Ex. "Now what?"

Qui crawled over to the wall and began to climb, using the tracks as footholds for her many legs. Ex watched her ascend until her light was a distant green glow. Minutes later she came back down. "The prints curve back around onto the ceiling. It's too slick for me to climb. The only way I can get up there is to fly, but I'd have to leave you here alone, which I'm not about to do..."

There was a faint rumbling in the ground. It grew louder, causing dust and loose stone to trickle down the walls. Ex hid next to a stalagmite and covered his head. "Earthquake!?"

"Maybe a lava flow somewhere beneath us!" guessed Qui.

A mouthful of twisted teeth erupted from the floor just a few meters away. It was the spear-tip of a large spaded head, flying up into the darkness. Next came dozens of armored segments, forming a long, vermiform body. The bulk of it went by in a huge rush, but Ex thought he saw someone, or something, riding behind the crest of the worm's plated head.

The head suddenly bent towards the wall and plunged into the stone. The last segment whipped out of the ground in a cloud of scalding steam. When the smoke cleared, the rock was solid again, frozen in a dark puddle. It took half a minute for the worm to pass in its entirety. Its tail lashed into the wall, and it disappeared with a splash of molten stone. "What the Mother-of-All was that?" shrieked Qui.

"Did you see that thing on its back?" asked Ex.

"What thing?"

"I dunno. Looked armored, with gleaming eyes."

"Might've been the worm's eyes you saw, if it even has any. Though I don't know how you saw anything, cowering behind that rock."

"I wasn't cowering. I was taking cover."

"What's the difference?"

"It's a military maneuver... you figure it out."

Kabuto showed up again, sounding particularly angry. He hissed up a storm trying to get them to follow, and since this path was proving fruitless, they did. He led them to a clean-cut opening in the wall from which a soft cyan light spilled. The stonework that sat atop the two stalagmites on either side of the entrance was more elaborate than any they'd seen before. The floor was pockmarked like a sponge.

Once inside, it was difficult to discern the source of the light. It mottled the floor and crept up the edges of the walls. Ex crouched down and waved his hand over the spots in which the light appeared to fall, but there was no shadow. The floor itself was aglow. It felt mossy to the touch. The footsteps followed the undulations in the rock that corkscrewed from the floor to the wall to the ceiling and back around. Deeper in, the moss grew thicker, and the holes vanished in its glow.

By the time they reached its end, Qui's lantern was no longer needed, so she'd taken the shape of something a bit more resilient: the enormous sable spider she'd embodied back at Luin's bar. She was forced to crouch in the tunnel, ample as it was, but the exit lay just ahead, glowing brighter than the surrounding moss.

Pillar

The tunnel led to a narrow walkway in a colossal chamber. Islands of light floated in the dark stone of the high ceiling, charted by the same moss that grew in the tunnel. Far below his feet, maybe a quarter-kilometer drop, Ex could see the same patterns repeated in the hemispherical ground. In the center of the chamber sat an enormous structure like a coral reef with twisted spires reaching to the vaulted sky and the depths of the basin below.

As the three neared, it became evident that the moss in the reef had been fashioned into willfully organized patterns. Its surface was riddled with the same sculpting as the stalagmites they'd encountered earlier, and there were glints of movement everywhere.

"We're being watched," breathed Qui. "Many eyes..."

There were a few branches, but Kabuto led them into the reef on the brightest highway of cyan light. The interior was even more spectacular than the exterior. The moss grew in great abundance, and all the stone was worked into waves and shells, woven in countless layers over their heads. Not all of the light here was cyan. There were patches of pale gold and deeper blue. The pillars and many of the walls were peppered with foot-holes, but the ground was not.

Up ahead a tall figure stood on two thin legs in the middle of the road. It waited for them to approach, and they did so with due caution. The creature was clad in elaborate pearl armor, wrought in a fashion similar to the stone of the reef. The shell curved left and right, up and down, leaving nothing of the creature exposed but a pair of gleaming eyes, staring at them through slits beneath the massive plate that covered its head. The helmet flared back into four webbed thorns. They flowed seamlessly down the creature's head and tapered into a sharp beak just beyond its chin. It was framed by a set of imposing pauldrons that soared backwards like the beginnings of wings.

Its arms articulated at two joints. The longest of the three segments grew at the end of the appendage, which came to a sharp point rather than any form of a hand or claw. Its arms were recoiled like a mantis; at full extension they'd be as long as its legs.

Ex hardly stood as tall as the creature's waist, yet seated they may not have differed much in height – if indeed these creatures sat. It was likely that they sat often, since they had no feet. Just like the creature's arms, its legs ended in a fine tip. To retain balance on such fine points looked like quite a challenge, but despite that the creature stood on the moss without piercing the surface of the stone beneath, it never wavered.

A series of clicks and whistles came from within the creature's helmet. The pattern repeated, and Ex was stung by a prickly licorice autex. It was a bit smoother than Kabuto's spiny tongue, but nettled his ears with greater clarity and persistence. He began to gather words from the noise: *You bring child?* it seemed to say.

"Bring child? No, we are looking for the child," replied Ex in what Qui heard as Solarian.

"I don't think they speak your language," she said.

The creature didn't respond. It repeated the same words, which now sounded less like a question to Ex's ears: *You brought the child.* He was ready to blame the misunderstanding on his metaglot, but then the creature extended an arm towards Kabuto. The tip passed right by Ex's nose, close enough for him to see that its texture differed from the rest of the armor. There was no clear-cut end to the metal sleeve; it melded seamlessly into the wet chitin that lay beneath. They were nearly identical in their glossiness, making them hard to separate in the diffuse light.

Kabuto hid timidly behind Ex's legs. The creature lowered itself to speak directly to the little bug. *You run on the over again, hatchling. Clutch-watcher is become syncopated.* Ex understood enough to know that Kabuto was being scolded. He didn't appreciate being used as a barrier between the bug and a long pointy claw, especially not an angry one. The creature stood back up and fixed its gaze on Ex. *Thank you, soft-sack, for giving return to this child. He is just made hatching few growths ago. Apology for the morass.* The words were a bit convoluted, but only a few sounds escaped his metaglot, which had been primed by listening to Kabuto's gibberish.

"Soft sack?" Ex repeated aloud. He could only assume that was referring to him. Under different circumstances those would have been fighting words, but he gave the beast the benefit of the doubt.

"What did he say?" asked Qui.

"He's thanking us for returning their kid," he whispered, pointing at Kabuto. "In their terms, I think he's a baby boy, which would explain why I can hardly understand him. He's talking baby nonsense for the most part..."

"Well, what about the girl? Ask him about the girl," Qui insisted.

"I can't," replied Ex. "I can understand them more or less, but I can't click and whistle like they do."

"Damn Solarians! What's the use of understanding so many languages if you can't articulate half of them?"

"Yeah, well what's the point of articulatin' 'em if you don't know what you're saying?"

Qui's current jaw may've looked entirely alien to Ex, but he could spot a frown of that magnitude on any face. He took a moment to enjoy his little victory before directing his attention to Kabuto.

"Come here, boy," he coaxed. "You understand what I'm saying right?"

Yesh, Kabuto hissed.

"Good," smiled Ex. "Tell this guy that we're looking for Chimi, OK? Tell him that's why we're here. Can you do that?"

Yesh, Kabuto said again. Then there was silence.

"Well, go on!" Ex slid the beetle forward with his boot.

Kabuto looked around as if searching for a bit of courage. Ex waited for him to speak with clasped hands. *Want the soft-sack, little pinky soft-sack, you find?* he sputtered.

The creature seemed to understand. *Smaller soft-sack your child? Found it tiny and wet, not awake... but we bring to Pillar. Safe. Cradled by stone now... if you follow me.* It walked gingerly over the moss before leaping onto the stone column nearby. The points of its feet pierced the stone without effort, and the creature stood horizontal, motioning for them to follow. *Come, follow,* it clicked.

Ex wanted to say *easier said than done*, but in truth he could do neither. Qui took to the wall with some kind of smile. Ex was not amused. He had to rely on Kabuto to explain to his elder that he couldn't walk on walls like it could. This took a considerable amount of time, and Ex ended up having to ride Qui up the wall.

"Don't get any funny ideas," she warned.

"How can I help myself?" said Ex. "Your shell is so smooth and black," he said rubbing the top of her shiny head.

"I'll have you know this is one of my sexiest forms!"

"And I'm sure it is... on a planet of room-sized tarantula aliens."

"These *spiders* live on a cloud of asteroids on the edge of Wild Space, actually," she corrected.

"Wild space? You *really* get around, don't you?" he laughed, and Qui calculated whether this torment was worth the money she hoped to make from him.

Countless menacing silhouettes of *grown Kabutos*, for lack of a better name, lurked in the gloom, punctuated by glowing eyes. Their pearled armor was unique to the individual. Yet it was always smooth, without a single sharp angle, but ending in many points.

Their guide spoke as they crawled around the pillars and over sloping walls. Ex understood every word and relayed the information to Qui, who didn't let a click pass without asking for its meaning.

They learned that this enormous *reef* was actually just the tip of a city. Its roots reached far underground, where rivers of molten rock lapped gleaming metal banks. It didn't sound like a very hospitable place, but this, the guide claimed, was where their hatcheries were located. Extreme heat was required to incubate their larva.

Ex looked at Kabuto with newfound respect. It was hard to imagine that the runt had been born – practically forged – in such a drastic place. The shell that shielded his tiny wings and round backside looked fragile enough to crack with a good stomp, but looks could be deceiving. Ex had punted him back when they'd first met, and the little bug's back had left a sizeable dent in the stone, yet suffered neither scuff nor crack.

The guide stopped at a patch of longer moss, growing atop a rounded stalagmite like a head of closely cropped, neon hair. The creature beckoned, and Ex hopped off Qui's back. *This is the Light*, it said, pointing one claw at the moss, the other at its own chest. Fine tendrils wriggled out of the moss like the fingers of an anemone. They swayed towards Ex as if blown by a gentle breeze. He passed his hand over the moss, and the little stalks reached for him as far as they could. *Light seeks Light,* said the guide. *There is much Light in you, though your eyes are dim...*

It straightened out and looked up at the mottled ceiling. *The illumination is more than eyes can see.* It touched a wall, there was a light hum, and the rock became soft as clay, rippling beneath its every gesture. It shaped something in the stone and uttered a series of whistles from which Ex could gather no words. The sound of the creature's true voice was shrill and rather disorienting. Ex had become accustomed to the mellow tones of its androgynous voice as his metaglot heard it.

Then it spoke clearly again. *When ours was young, we were blind and dull. We wove tunnels in the stone around the metal veins. It was in this blindness that we consumed the Light, and we were illuminated. We gained the sight of thought, and with it came the clarity of many things. The metal could no longer hold us. We consumed it as the stone, and it made us strong.* The creature extended its long arms upwards, as if in prayer, and clanged their ends together. It stalked towards Ex and pressed its forearm against his face. *You value this...*

Ex was a bit confused by the guide's actions, and Qui seemed ready to pounce, but he waved her off. Phantoms of color flowed through the pearled metal of the creature's armor. When Ex had seen them before, he'd dismissed them as reflections of stray light, but now it was clear that the metal itself emitted the glow. *This is why you dig*, said the guide.

"What's he saying?" demanded Qui.

"I think it's trying to say that its armor is made of duril," replied Ex. "But I've never seen anything like it... the way the color keeps swirling around inside... like it's half-wild, half-tamed."

The creature gathered that it'd been understood from their reaction. *We are the wearers of the armor, but not the smiths... The Light is the smith. It is the seed which germinates into the living metal, and strength is its bloom...*

Come, the littlest soft-sack rouses soon...

Ex hopped on his *mount* and the guide was off like a shot, leaving holes in the stone. Despite its haste, it was careful not to step on any patches of moss.

At last they came to a large heart of stone suspended in midair by countless rocky arms where the moss grew in spiraled bands. The beams were just wide enough to traverse, and they did so with caution. When the guide had said that Chimi was "cradled by stone," he was speaking quite literally. A little crib had been cut right into the rock, lined with soft-gold lichen, and Chimi lay inside.

Ex shook her gently. "Chimi? Chimi? Are you OK?" The little girl batted his arm away and rolled over, trying to find a comfortable position. Ex tried again, and this time she sat up wearing a bewildered expression.

"Ex?! You're not supposed to be here!" she gasped.

"Oh, yeah? And where's here exactly?" he said.

Chimi rubbed her eyes. "Wha- where are we?" Kabuto scrambled up on the edge of the cradle, clicking gleefully, and she was just as happy to see him.

Ex had to tell her what'd happened because all she could remember was digging one minute and drowning the next. When he was finished, her eyes brimmed. "You came to save me?"

"Now, don't go getting all emotional on me. I owed ya remember?" said Ex. "This makes us even."

Chimi picked a tear out of the corner of an eye. "Well... kinda. I mean, I wasn't really gonna die, was I?" she haggled. "Anyhow, let's get back to town as quick as we can. Mom's probably worried sick about me!"

"That's a good girl! Don't let him off so easy," teased Qui. "Besides, if it wasn't for me, he'd still be fumbling around on the bank, blind as a mute bat."

"Oh, hello!" piped Chimi. "Are you the shape-changing lady from earlier? Thanks for coming to rescue me." She climbed out of the crib and onto shaky legs, while Ex implored Kabuto to ask the guide which was the quickest way out. It took a good bit of coercion on his part and most of Kabuto's brainpower. In the end, Ex wasn't sure the message had been properly delivered, but either way the guide had different plans.

You cannot leave yet. My instructions are to bring you before The Dominant, who has awaited your audience since your shell fell from the chamber of the highest ceiling. Mount your domesticated animal and let us be on our way.

"What did he say?" asked Qui, suspicious of Ex's smile.

"He thinks you're Ex's pet!" giggled Chimi, running a finger around her necklace. And that was too much for Qui. Ex hopped on her back and consoled her with promises of as many marshmallows as she could eat, so long as she was a good girl.

"My price just doubled!"

"You can't do that! You're already taking 80% of the profits, remember?"

"Yeah, well now I want 160%. You'll have to owe me," she hissed.   And Ex agreed if for no other reason than to get her big black claws moving again. He pulled Chimi up and helped her settle into a nook on Qui's segmented back. Once she was good and safe, he dug his heals into his mount. "Giddy up!"

"Don't think I'll forget this," growled Qui.

The group made their way to one of the winding pillars and followed it down. It passed straight through a massive hole in the ground and into another chamber, every bit as big as the last. They found themselves entering the heart of another reef, much like the first; only, this one had been built upside-down. The transition was disorienting. Ex squeezed Qui's throat for safety. It was a long, long way to the bottom from here.

Chimi looked unworried, gawking at the glowing metropolis. "So this is where you come from?" she asked Kabuto, who skittered behind them. He responded with a simple *Yesh*. To him, this place was not nearly as exciting as the surface, where the suns lit many strange things.

All the pillars of the upturned reef converged into a single massive column of stone and plunged through an even larger opening in the floor. The moss was shaped into a myriad of indecipherable patterns on the walls of the vertical tunnel. It all grew spectral gold here, but patches were cut to different lengths, yielding shades of brightness. The intricacy and sheer size of the monochromatic images they formed were staggering. And this was only an arc of the whole tunnel, most of which was obstructed by the curvature of the grand column on which they descended.

The walls of the tunnel suddenly gave way to a spherical chamber larger than the last two combined. The vast ceiling and all the walls were capped with polished perlite. In the center of the chamber was a porous orb the size of a small moon, and the column ran straight through its poles. Its surface was coated with brilliant moss in gold and cyan. It waved to the distant perlite walls, and the perlite waved back.

The orb seemed alive. As they neared, the light reached for them, and the upper hemisphere of the chamber glowed brighter. "Where are we going?" Qui finally asked. "I don't think the surface is this way."

"We're going to go see *The Dominant*, or something like that," said Ex. "Apparently this guy's been waiting for me since I crash landed on this rock, so I figure I might as well check it out while we're here..."

"Oh, well thanks for letting me know that ahead of time. You know, this is exactly the sort of thing you need to tell me. As soon as this overgrown bug says something like that, I need to know... What else did he tell you about this Dominant guy?"

"Nothing," replied Ex.

"Nothing? And you just decided you'd go see him anyway, huh?"

"Yeah... actually, I'm not even sure that it's a *he*. The gender wasn't specified."

"I hope it's a Queen," said Qui, "and she wants to lay a clutch of eggs in your lower intestine."

"Hah! Now, you're just projecting..."

"... 240%," said Qui, at which point Chimi leaned forward and head-butted Ex in the back.

The moss that grew on the outer crust of the orb could hardly be called moss at all. It grew into long, fine stalks, all gathering, winding, and unfurling as they passed. Ex reached out and caressed the light with his fingertips. The stalks dimmed under his touch, pulsed brightly, and settled back into a soothing cyan glow. The surge jumped from one strand to the next, flushing across the field like a soft ripple. The whole thing looked terribly inviting to Chimi; she stretched out as far as she could reach and would've fallen off Qui's back if Ex hadn't caught her by the back of her shirt.

The orb's interior had been hollowed out in a series of countless cavities like bubbles of air trapped in amber. There was a wide breadth of space between the column and the nearest chambers, connected by arms of stone where thousands of the natives skittered. The air was abuzz with strange sound: the hum of innumerable footfalls blended with the clicks and hisses of distant conversations, accented by the occasional trill. It reverberated around the stone, swirling into a susurrus that was as peaceful as it was alien.

In the nearest chambers, Ex saw the creatures slowly and methodically consuming the moss. There was a restraint and elegance to their actions; they seemed to be driven more out of reverence than hunger. And the armored skin of those who ate glowed hotly.

Finally, they came to an opening in the central column. The guide ushered them in, and Qui managed to step onto the floor of the tunnel without flipping the passengers off her back. Chimi hopped off right away. The vermiform passage was lined with stalks of light. She ran her hands back and forth across the swaying tendrils, sending shivers of light down their supple stems.

"You can walk now," said Qui and bucked Ex off her back.

The tunnel cut straight through the heart of the column into a dome. There, the moss was arranged into concentric rings on the floor, growing higher as the rings became smaller towards the center. Each step was perfectly tended, and the stalks of the innermost ring were the tallest that they'd encountered.

Long and narrow fingers of perlite hung from the ceiling like a massive chandelier. The moss only grew from their very tips, like the bright points of fiber optics, but their mirrored surface glinted with the light that germinated from every angle of the room. The longest of the stalactites pointed directly at a throne that was sculpted from the rock inside the central ring, and on this throne sat a motionless figure.

The guide pointed Ex towards the figure and extended its arms to impede the others from entering the room. "I'll be fine," Ex assured them. He did his best to step over the moss rather than on it. It'd seemed awfully important to the guide, and he didn't want to offend.

Are you one of the three? spoke a slow, deliberate voice. Ex couldn't respond, not that he knew what to say if he could.

Raise an appendage if you understand Our words, said the voice, and Ex raised an arm. *Very good. Use this gesture to express affirmation... Now I will ask again, are you one of the three?*

"You mean us three?" Ex asked without thinking. He lifted an arm high enough to point over at Chimi and Qui who waited at the entrance.

Then, it is as We thought. You come from the unreachable ceiling, fallen to the chamber with no walls. Forgive a question... We've long tried to reach the realm of the walking three. A column of stone was built from the highest peak, and the rock and metal were pushed as far as they could bear. The air grew cold, but the ceiling appeared no closer than when We began. When the three passed, We felt their warmth, but no warmer than on the sand. Tell Us, was it much further?

It took a moment for Ex to decipher the voice's meaning. To the best of his knowledge, he was being asked about the distance from the surface to the stars. These subterranean creatures' idea of a space program was to build a very large tower from a mountain top. They viewed the heavens as an unreachable ceiling, which was misguided but not unreasonable. There'd been a time when his ancestors on Earth had thought the same way. Even now, existence had its boundaries: the solid walls of Wild Space, the devouring mist that fed on the offspin of the universal disk, and the chaos that churned beneath it. Ex raised both arms as high as they'd go. "Further than you can imagine," he said without hope of being understood.

We see... Our gratitude for the indulgence... You are the first Faller to enter Our realm, though We have felt the shrill cry of your drills resonating through the stone. You have come in search of the living metal? Does this metal not exist in your realm?

Ex raised his hand half way and gave it a little shake, "Eh... kinda."

Perhaps it is rare to you, although We require no explanation as to why you would value it. The figure rose to the points of its feet. It towered above Ex, twice as tall as the guide. Massive plates of thick duril armored its entire body. They gave shape to a hulking form, tapering only at its very extremities. It strode towards Ex. The long stalks flashed brightly as they brushed its legs.

Countless runes of thin moss riddled the many plates of its armor. Their soft pulse was only visible when the surrounding light receded. The eyes under the sweeping crest of its helmet roiled like the face of a star. *We sense in you a great light, spilling through the grip of a black worm, streaking in rays that pierce the world through. The Light sees it. But the worm does not smother or strangle, it embraces. You are a Light which armors itself with shadow. Merciful to the eyes, for in full splendor it would blind.* The Dominant reached an arm towards Ex, close enough to hear its hum – the same hum that liquefied stone. *You are not as the other Fallers. We sense that you are as The Three... yet you dwell in the flesh of a Faller – the body of a soft sack, frail, vulnerable, without a shell.*

Ex didn't like where the conversation was headed. He touched the grip of his pistol. The Dominant's eyes were fixed on this gesture. *You too possess the living metal? And well tamed...* It retracted its arm. *The settlement from which you've come does not concern Us. They chip at stone, harmless as the sting of a low-crawler. It is the other Fallers who offend. They presume upon the upper realm, hollowing the world, tearing at its veins. They do not fill the holes they make. And the voice of their drills screams atop The Seven Cities. They must be silenced...*

Ex would like nothing more than to *silence* the CIR presence on the planet, but how could he explain that there would only be worse to follow? How could he let this creature know that the hell that would come for them then would be unlike any that existed in their darkest legends? How could he communicate the fact that the threads of the men of Himatma were enslaved in the drills, and that by destroying them, they would be ending any chances the women had of regaining their husbands, fathers, and brothers? What kind of gesture could he possibly make? So he made none.

Unchecked, the raveners will consume all, but We know how to make the metal bitter... Tame it. Take the glow from other eyes. Staunch the metal against their commands... But taming requires light, and to tame it all would require more than shines in the Seven Cities combined. The Dominant's gleaming gaze burned deep into Ex's eyes. It felt like several minutes passed before it spoke again. *Perhaps only one path remains... We've not had war in this realm for growths beyond telling, but do not count Us weak. When the time comes, We shall bring The Light to bear upon the Faller's fangs. And there will be silence again.*

Encouraging as it was to hear that these creatures, who armor themselves in duril, wanted to wage war on the CIR, Ex knew that the struggle was ultimately futile. Still, he reckoned that the Extinguishers would have quite a time of it. The only thing that outweighed a Sage's yearning for duril was his fear of it. Once tamed, sage silver was the single inorganic substance in the known universe that refused another Sage's commands — just as all living things did. Duril could be claimed through an extension of the thread, in essence becoming part of the tamer's body. And it was this constant presence of will that rebuked the influence of all other thread.

Go back, strange one. Go to Yours and tell them that We won't allow our ceilings to be taken from Us. Worry not the chippers of stone; the land will abide them yet. But the others... Those whose hunger is bound only by the sharpness of their teeth, bid them hurry somewhere We cannot reach if they value their lives. With a single gesture of The Dominant's powerful arm, the ceiling came alive. Dozens of armored creatures dropped around Ex and placed chains around his arms. He struggled a bit, but decided it wasn't going to pay. Chimi and Qui were manacled as well. The restraints were fashioned from pearled duril, light as air, and they didn't seem to impede his movements at all. They were latched together by a single pin that could be easily removed, leaving Ex to wonder what their purpose was altogether.

The Dominant turned back to his throne of vivid duril. With a mild hum, a piece was removed. Gently clasped between the thorns of its arms, he presented the fragment to Ex. The metal was the color of the Trisol sky in midday, interlaced with thin lines of soft gold. *Take this to The Oldest one in the chamber without walls...* The Dominant instructed. *In it is contained the secret of The Light and Living Metal: there can be no life without freedom, nor freedom without life.*

The ground opened, and an enormous worm appeared, just like they'd seen in the cave earlier. Ex and Chimi's chains were clipped to its giant muzzle, and another worm was summoned for Qui. The beasts reared back their heads and dove straight into the ceiling.

The red hot rock rushed by as the worm rocketed towards the surface. The pressure and heat were almost unbearable — well, for Ex anyway. The girls didn't mind it much. Chimi even seemed to be enjoying herself. Ex's eyeballs felt like they were trying to decide between shriveling up like raisins or shooting out of his skull like champagne corks. The ride was mercifully short, and soon they were back in the unbearable, yet less immediately life-threatening, heat of the desert.

Back to Himatma

It took a while for his eyes to adjust. The suns were out in full force, but Ex was happy to see them for the moment. He unfastened his chains and dropped to the sand, rolling around, pretending to kiss it. The girls followed, though they were not as enthusiastic about the dirt. As soon as they were all off, the worms vanished into a dune with a tan splash.

The town of Himatma was nowhere in sight. In fact there wasn't much to see apart from sand, just a few juts of metal climbing out of the desert here and there, looking hot enough to hatch a Kabuto egg. Chimi was first to say *uh oh*, but Ex was thinking it. They both knew the dangers of the desert, though perhaps they were fresher in Ex's mind. "Now which way do we go?" she wondered aloud.

"OK wait a sec, don't panic!" Ex said in a tone that was anything but calming. "I figured this out before. First we find a rock and draw a line on the edge of its shadow, then we sit around for fifteen minutes and draw a new line. See now that gives us a triangulation of the azimuths formed by the westerly rotation of the planet, which we can use to pinpoint our location in Cartesian space and time... or was that Euclidian space? Well I know you need a rock and a stick. Actually, forget that. I know a better trick that only works when you've eaten plenty of meat."

"We recently ate plenty of meat!" said Chimi.

"I know, that's why I'm tellin' ya," said Ex. "All you gotta do is dig a small trench, fill it with water, and spit in it. Atmospheric viscosity willing, the iron content in your saliva will flow north. Unless you're near the south pole, in which case you're screwed. Then there're planets with more than two poles... Hmm, do those exist? It might be better to dig a small bowl..." Chimi began to reshape the little trench she'd already dug into more of a bowl shape.

Qui had already produced a golden pill and swallowed it. "Sigh..." – she actually said *sigh* – "Just wait here. I'll find it, you hopeless loons," she squawked and flapped into the sky.

"At least she didn't call us soft sacks," said Ex.

Chimi found them a rock with a nice slant for shade. She'd taken to reciting the most dangerous critters in the desert, while Ex watched the horizon for Qui's return. "Worst of all," she said, "are the smilers. I'm sure you remember them..."

"Vaguely," said Ex, rubbing his temples.

"We oughta be careful cause they can pop out of the ground anywhere," continued Chimi. "You know, their poison is really strange. If you get stuck by one, they say you lose control of your body and fall dead in like five minutes. The Old Man and I did some experiments with it in his lab, and guess what..." she didn't wait for Ex to have a guess. "We stung some pieces of meat with it, and they started to squirm like they'd come alive or something. I wanted to try it on a whole dead animal, but The Old Man said it'd be unethical."

"You should test it on your pet bug," said Ex.

"Kabuto? Nah, his shell is too hard. He'd just break the quills." Chimi went on and on, and Ex started to worry about how long it was taking Qui to find Himatma. Hopefully, she'd just flown off in the wrong direction and had to circle around; otherwise it was going to be a long walk. And he knew something about long walks in this desert, under three suns, hounded by birds and snakes and bulls and thorny poisonous things.

"How come you never talk? Why don't you ask me something?" said Chimi. The break in her constant babbling called Ex's attention.

"Huh, what?"

"Ask me something!" Chimi demanded.

"OK, if you could have another name, what would it be?"

"Ooh, another name? Hmm, well if I could pick any name... I like Chimi just fine; don't know about my last name though: Farchild. Wish it was something prettier like, Chimi Honeystar or Chimi Ladyrocket..."

"Those are terrible names, Chimi."

She looked offended and demanded another question.

"How old are you?" he asked – a disappointing question by any metric.

"Wow," marveled Chimi. "You're really bad at this. I already told you, I'm sixteen. I know I look young for my age, but that's natural for a halfie. How old are you?"

"Well, I was born in anchorspace, so before the doctor could spank me, we'd passed by trillions of stars and around ten times as many planets. I can have a birthday whenever I feel like it. But in Earth years, um, let's see... I'm 25. That's 45 and a half in disk-years, I think," replied Ex.

"You think? How can you not know how old you are?"

"Chim, years are like credits, the more you have of 'em the less one's worth," said Ex.

"Yeah, but it's not like you're rich... And don't call me Chim!"

"Oh, and why not?" said Ex, tickling her ribs.

Chimi squirmed and squeaked. "Stop that! I'm serious! I'm too old to be treated like a squeak toy."

"You're never too old to be treated like a squeak toy."

"I most certainly am! Mom says I've entered the *age of indignity*. I have to preserve my poise." She turned her back on Ex and scooted to the edge of the shadow.

"I can't have any fun can I?" asked Ex.

"The less the better," said Chimi. She pouted and fiddled with her necklace. Less than a minute later, she was back by Ex, picking at her sandals. "What's it like being a ring runner?"

"It's a lot like this... only quieter."

"What, like the desert?"

"No, like waiting. A lot of watching the stars go by, checking charts, sleeping... Sometimes I pass the time watching videos from ancient Earth."

"Sounds like a snore."

"What'd you expect?"

Chimi was about to answer when the sand sunk beneath her feet. "Smiler!" she shrieked and jumped on Ex's head. He pulled her arm out of his eyes and found that Kabuto had popped out of a small sinkhole.

"Hih hih hih," the beetle laughed. "I come too, yesh." And Ex felt the situation was worsening.

Thankfully Qui was not far away. She landed on the rock, shuffling her feet, so they didn't start to cook. The trek to Himatma would take a few hours, and the suns weren't going to make them pleasant.

"Alright then, turn back into that creepy crawly thing and let us on your back," said Ex.

"Hah!" squawked Qui. "Delirious so soon?"

"Come on. At least let the girl ride ya."

Ex's selflessness took Qui by surprise. She was about to give in when Kabuto stepped up. He presented his shiny black backside to Chimi and urged her on. The little girl sat on the beetle, and its pointy legs sunk. His belly left a winding groove in the sand as he skittered on. Going up the dunes was a struggle, but he came down the other side like a sled. Not surprisingly, the one slowing the group down was Ex, whose boots were filled with twice their weight in sand.

A scaly bird with a serpentine tail circled over Ex's head. Each flap of its fleshy wings blew a hot breeze down his neck. Higher up, flew Qui. "Friend of yours?" she called.

"Not hardly," said Ex.

The damned thing followed them all the way back to town. Ex wanted to get indoors as soon as possible, but Chimi insisted they circle the crater. Qui changed into something more womanly, and they went in the back entrance to Tsubasa's place, which was disguised as an unassuming mineshaft.

The inside was cool, soothing, and well lit, though dark when compared to the thrice-baked desert. The group marched on a catwalk, overlooking a warehouse full of shiny crates and plastic barrels. The hanging path passed over something enormous under a big blue tarp. Ex couldn't recognize the shape, but it seemed too coherent to be a random assortment of garbage and derelict ship parts like the ones that cluttered the rest of the warehouse.

The tarp draped over the graceful curves of three hills, tucked into one another like scales or segments of a shell. Each rose to a peak, taller than the previous. On the other side of the slopes, the cloth fell freely to the ground. Something long and cylindrical projected from what Ex took to be the front of the form. And every now and again, the tarp sculpted hints of a thin skeleton made of wires or thin rods. "What's under that?" he finally asked.

"A stupid dream... at least that's what The Old Man would say," Chimi replied. Ex had half a mind to drop down there and sneak a peek, but he wanted some water first.

Chimi knew where she was going. She'd hopped off Kabuto and darted through the maze of hallways. The others struggled to keep up. "Should be in here," she said, ushering them through the only door in the facility that looked to be made of rice paper.

There were trees, flowers, grass, and even a babbling waterfall that flowed into a narrow creek. The walls were painted in a gradient that ran between amber and the color of a well-fed flamingo's feathers. The light of the three suns filtered through ceiling panels made from the same semi-opaque material as the door.

They followed a path that wound beneath red archways and skipped across the crooking brook on short wooden bridges. The green grass mopped over the banks of dark earth. They paused at the second bridge, and Ex did his best to dam the creek with his lower jaw. He helped the water down his throat with his tongue. "Kinda slimy," he said, wiping his jowls. The girls were not impressed.

Just around a patch of trees, they found Tsubasa practicing martial arts. His breath came in soundless whistles, timed to slow, graceful movements. A bit of flute music drifted through the fragrant air.

"Oh, what's this now? You're a martial arts master too?" said Ex.

Tsubasa held the last pose of his kata, balancing on his peg leg as long as his bones and audience could tolerate. "You assume I'm a master just because I'm old? Hah! I've only been at this a few months. It's easy to let oneself go when you're married to an Eidolan; you never hear any complaints from the Missus. Had to pick up some kind of exercise to keep my ticker tocking."

"I still can't believe you're married to Madame Shasta," Ex said.

"Shantasa... afraid so," mourned the old man. "But it's not all that bad really. She keeps to her things, and I keep to mine. These eyes let me see her as she pleases, but I'm afraid the old girl's got a bit of sand in her head nowadays, as I'm sure you've discovered. And no amount of holograms and illusions can hide her brand of crazy."

"Hard to believe that a science-man like yourself would wanna become Eidolan."

"Well, *Sage*, you reach an age in which seeing things as they are no longer holds that much interest for you. I've staved off wanderlust longer than most by keeping an open mind," said Tsubasa, toweling off his bald head. "But actually, I can see both of her forms at once... just one of the many side-effects of being a Dicot. I can't will either completely out of mind, but I can make one more prominent than the other with a bit of desire. See, we Dicots don't query our quantum counterpart and await its response; we just know what it knows. Even this seemingly instantaneous access takes an eternity in subrostral time, but our human brains can go no faster. If we had to ask the computer what it thinks, then I could just stop asking, but I can't. So when I look at her, I see a blended image that lies somewhere on a axis that straddles the disparity of her forms. The precise coordinate of the vision I see is determined by my mood."

"Yeah, well I still prefer to see the truth, as I think any reasonable person should," said Ex.

"Me too," piped Chimi.

Ex patted her head. "There, see?"

"Well congratulations, you've achieved the mental maturity of a teenage girl... no offense, Chimi," said Tsubasa.

But Chimi was offended. She also didn't appreciate that Tsubasa seemed to be ignoring the fact that she'd just survived a harrowing cave in. "Hey, Old Man! Aren't you gonna say you're happy to see me again, or at least ask where I've been? I could've died you know! Or did you not even know I was gone?"

"Oh gracious! I'm sorry, my girl. I can see how this could look quite callous of me, but I've been following you since this morning," he said, tapping his head. "I saw the whole ordeal. The river, the cave, the fantastic civilization that dwells there... I've officially named them *The Trisolobytes*, incidentally. What do you think?" The three were silent. "I should've reacted with more enthusiasm to your arrival, but most of my mind's been inside my head, and I forgot that as far as you knew, I wasn't in the loop."

In no less confusing terms, Tsubasa explained that the necklace he'd given Chimi acted as a one way communicator, beaming directly into his Dicot brain. It sent back a detailed three-dimensional recording of its surroundings, and so wherever she'd been, Tsubasa had been as well. "I'm still processing all the details of your adventure, but I can assure you there's much to be excited about!" said the old man, staring into Chimi's weary face. "I assume you must be tired. Worry not, I've instructed Hitomi to prepare a feast in anticipation of your arrival. Let's head over to the dining room and see how that's coming along. But first, Ex, I believe you had something for me?"

It took Ex a moment to remember about the chunk of throne he was carrying in one of his many pockets. He fished it out and handed it to the old man.

Soft light spilled patiently from the cracks of moss in the duril. "Titillating!" exclaimed Tsubasa, rushing off to scrutinize the piece with his various scopes and gadgets.

Do Jovians Eat Little Girls?

Ex was the first at the table. His idea of getting washed up was to shake the sand out of his hair and sully Tsubasa's meditation pond with his hands. He'd gained nothing for his earliness. The cups and plates were all empty. The candles weren't even lit.

When he tired of rattling around his silverware, he stretched out across a few chairs; there might be enough time for a nap if he was quick about it. But he was exhausted, not sleepy. He tossed around for a minute and came back up hoping to find food on his plate. There wasn't. Then he remembered the test that Tsubasa had given him and his gaze fell upon the candles.

Chimi came through the door to find Ex locked in a fierce staring contest with a candelabra. "What are you doing?" she asked.

Ex snapped out of his daze. "What's it look like I'm doing? Waiting."

"For me?" smiled Chimi, occupying the seat directly across from him.

"For food."

Tsubasa and Qui came in next, arm in arm, laughing. "Ex, you never told me you were friends with a Blank, and a charming one at that," cooed the old man.

"How could it've ever slipped my mind?" said Ex. Qui had strategically eaten a little marshmallow, or at least the pill equivalent. She'd taken the body of the blue vixen that had given him such a rile at Luin's place, and over that, she wore a white sequin dress. It was from Hitomi's closet but fit her perfectly.

"Hitomi's not gonna like that," Chimi leaned over to whisper. She pointed at the hole that Qui had poked through the dress for her tail.

Ex stared at Qui's backside. "Why, is she the jealous type?" he finally asked. And Chimi reached across the table to give him a slap, just to be sure.

The remaining two places were for Chimi's mother and Madame Shantasa. Farah sat in the chair next to her daughter without fuss. She set a small box down by her feet. It was a drab shade of brown with fibrous frays along the edges, held together by a length of red ribbon. Chimi tapped the box and bounced her eyebrows at Ex. He replied with a distrusting squint.

The fortuneteller arrived in an uproar. "Tsuy, why the blazes would you tell me 8 o'clock, when seven thirty would've done just fine? You know my stomach-motor starts revving at six. Maybe if you actually fixed some of your damned clocks..."

"Tsuy?" Ex whispered to Chimi, who responded with a tight-lipped smile.

"Sorry, Shanty. I didn't know everyone would be so punctual. Didn't want to make you wait, my digital dumpling..." said Tsubasa, but Shantasa was hardly listening. She dropped into the seat next to Ex and gave him a coy wink. It was a snug fit. A few of her generous pounds encroached on his lap. He wished desperately that he hadn't gotten rid of his Eidolan reticulum. Hopefully, he'd be infected with a new one before the food got here.

But it came fast. Hitomi balanced a tray that had a diameter of exactly one millimeter less than the width of the doorway. It was brimmed with food, but she entered without effort. She wore a darling little maid's outfit, which Tsubasa had undoubtedly handpicked for her. The dishes were dealt from the tray with mechanical precision. There were chickens, red with tandoori masala; heaps of sweet rolls, glistening with butter; a deep bowl where blanched cloves of garlic swam in spinach dip; a bubbling casserole of twice cooked pork with cabbage and thin slices of braised tofu; battered scallops tossed in sweet and spicy garlic sauce along with tender bamboo slices and julienned carrots; a hearty stack of egg and pickled daikon pancakes; a plate of potato halves, topped with melted cheese that blackened in bubbles; and a mound of golden basmati rice, mingled with thin strips of sweet potato. "I will return later with dessert," said Hitomi, as she filled the guests' cups.

Just looking at this spread made Ex's inner organs smile. He'd already stuffed an entire roll in his mouth, when the old man proposed a toast. "Here's to Qui and Ex! Thank you for returning our Chimi to us. And though troubles hang over our heads like the damned suns on this planet, let's forget them for tonight. So unbuckle your belts and let's have at it!" And Ex swallowed down the roll in time to cheer.

The food began to disappear from the plates, but only Ex, Chimi, and Shantasa were really eating. The food was flavorful enough, but it had that predictable plexiness. You could almost taste the math that laid out these molecules, randomness untouched by life. Normally, plex was only used to generate the raw ingredients, and the cooking process would add that home-cooked unpredictability. These dishes may've been prepared that way, but Hitomi's precision was no less exacting than a plex manifestor. Still it was better than a Skwell burger.

Qui sipped a glass of iced water, while Tsubasa had his fill of a bronze wine. Farah ate, but only a little. She knew that this food represented all the plex that the old man had left in his pantries. The fact that he was willing to eat through it all in one go didn't speak highly of his hopes for tomorrow.

With a couple of goblets in his gut, the old man launched into a meandering lecture. "Imagine what it must've been like for the first humans poking around space in search for sentient life... though I suppose they were called Solarians even back then. Named by a machine, isn't it absurd?" No one answered; they all assumed the question was meant for someone else or no one at all. "*The Stone Patch Edict*, look it up you philistines!" Another goblet of wine set him back on course. "I bet there were probably a few Dicots and Modders peppered into every crew – that's what they used to call Centrians before Centrias even existed. They rattled around the galaxy, and all they found were bugs, moss, maybe some interesting slime here and there, but not so much as a squirrel.

The universe is a vast place, you'd figure that someone out there would be smarter than a bunch of monkeys, rowing through space in metal canoes. Frightening to think that in the whole of existence, there were really only two races older and arguably more advanced than ours, downright disappointing actually. To top it off, the first sentients they met, the Sophians, greeted them by turning the

Earth into a donut, which was only half as bad as what they did to the Valoraphim. So much for the grandeur of evolution, huh?

An anchor round is a hell of a way to say hello! And it wasn't a little bullet, mind you, like the kind you have in that clip of yours. They didn't even have the technology to build them back then. This was a full-sized cannon ball fired from one of those huge muzzles that crown the White Rook.

Terrible as it was, they may've actually ended up saving lives in the long run – at least Sophian lives, that's for sure. The Solarians gave up without a fight, and it wasn't all bad. We got a seat in the Consortium, tons of new and exciting technology, and a brand new ring built right in our backyard. All we had to do in exchange was to give up a few freedoms..."

The food was beginning to run thin; only one potato half remained. Chimi and Ex's forks clashed over the cheesy tater. They retracted their utensils and locked eyes.

"But for all the tech we got from the Sophians," continued Tsubasa, "they got the better of the deal. They found something on our little planet without measure of worth. We were the first Sages, you know! Hell, before they met us, ethereal technology was just a thing of myth for the Valoraphim and something that the Sophians in all their wisdom hadn't even considered.

Pretty amazing when you think of it; Solarians were behind on every other front – excusable enough though, considering that our race is eons their minor. But the other races kept uprooting themselves and restructuring, while Solarians let their branches grow wild. The Valoraphim threw away their entire evolutionary history not more than a couple thousand years ago when they genetically reengineered their bodies, and all for a damned dream. Crazy folks those Valoraphim, and even crazier when you make mutts of them with Solarian blood." He directed his words at Shantasa, but she was too busy putting an extra coat of butter on her sweet roll to mind. As a Valarian, it was amazing how little she resembled her Valoraphim ancestry, but to be fair, she didn't look very human either.

Ex and Chimi laid down their forks, trading snarls. Tension rolled over the table like an electric fog. This would not be a duel for honor or pride, riches or fame, not even life or death: this was a duel for the last cheesy tater.

Hitomi refilled Tsubasa's cup as he spoke. "Not that I'm saying that the Sophians have their head of cabbage all sorted and washed either! Sure, they act composed and collected behind those vacant faces. But they've got as much trouble brewing between their curled horns as the rest of us. Can't say I blame them though. Hard enough teetering between my two minds sometimes. It's a real swim upstream to establish an identity in one lifetime against the flow of eons worth of memories.

Hereditary memory is a heavy gift. They don't like to talk about it much, but I've seen the mental wards on Veredos filled to capacity with Sophians who can't distinguish between the memories they were born with and those they'd made for themselves, bedridden with depression or disinterest – couldn't tell. I guess that milder forms of this affliction are to blame for their notorious apathy. Or they could just be a bunch of jerks, that's a possibility. Still, I don't envy them.

Did you know that they have to take a drug that inhibits their long-term memory potentiation to get a bit of privacy? I mean, if they want to do something that they'd prefer the whole planet didn't remember in a couple of generations. Boy, I can tell you that I've done a few things I wouldn't want my kids knowing about – not that I've had any. Worst part is that a few weeks later, you won't remember what you did. I guess it's a bit like alcohol that way," he said, wringing the wine out of the central prongs of his beard.

Chimi slowed her breathing and steadied her eyes. She brought a hand to her mouth, gently kissed it, and extended her palm in a manner that was reminiscent of Ex's famous dueling pose. Ex was shocked. "Her technique is impressive," he whispered to himself. He put his hand out in the same fashion – after all, it was his technique. There between the chicken bones and scattered rice too sparse to fork, the duelists waited for the other to make their play.

Tsubasa drained another cup. "And what the hell is with this need for prophecies and soothsaying nonsense? I mean, I'm a man of science! I'm more than willing to believe in something I can't entirely prove, but at least let it be something I can't disprove. Oh wait... that's not what I wanted to talk about next. I had another thought I wanted to share... what was it? Ah yes, about the Sages, of course! They're from Earth, you see. Well, the first one was anyhow, though he'd passed into legend by the time the Sophians arrived.

But they couldn't care less about our myths; all they cared for was duril, so they dug up his grave straight away. Wasn't hard to find either, since the duril in his primitive corona was the only scrap on Earth. They cracked open his coffin and found their prize resting inside his skull, with a shape unlike anything they'd ever seen. You better believe they were interested in our myths then. Suddenly, the little story about a waste-wanderer from The Black Pyramid that returned the stars to the sky didn't seem like so much nonsense. But I won't bore you with that old story; I'm sure you've heard it a dozen times.

In less than a decade, the Sophians reverse engineered the corona, and there were Sages again. Of course, the Veredos research team took credit, but we know better, don't we?" He tapped his fork against the side of his goblet, and Hitomi brought more wine. "What's truly fascinating is that even today, we've no idea how to shape duril without a corona, yet the duril in the first corona had been willfully shaped..."

A bead of sweat trickled down Ex's forehead and slid down the bridge of his nose. Chimi knew she had him. As soon as Hitomi was finished pouring, she'd make her move. Ex knew it too. He could feel the heat of intent in her squinty little eyes. Hitomi lifted the decanter, and the duelists sprang into action. Ex snatched up his fork and dove at the potato, but struck only porcelain. The cheesy tater was already on Chimi's plate. She cut a piece and savored it in his direction.

Ex nonchalantly put down his fork and turned to Qui who'd been observing the whole affair. "Hehe, I let her win," he winked.

"Hehe, I don't care," Qui replied in a tone usually reserved for pets.

"It's no surprise that they despise us!" Tsubasa suddenly blurted, dispersing a mouthful of wine into a fine mist. "They envy us! While they rot away on their planet's caged corpse, the free-spirited monkeys from the Third Ring have spread across the whole of the universe. They fear humanity's limitless ability to adapt. In every livable corner of every galaxy, you'll find a pioneering Solarian, staking his or her claim. But it's our will to overcome any and every challenge that they fear most! That's the very core of life right there. It's what lets us change, adapt, and evolve.

Any of these Libralma will tell ya: the more limited the man, the more challenges life presents him. But those aren't setbacks, they're opportunities. And if the point of life is to overcome, then we might just be the perfect vessels. Yes, the very highest expression of life; its purest essence, howling tirelessly from the pit of our indomitable spirit!"

"Hitomi," called Madame Shantasa, "no more drink for my husband, please. I do believe he's had enough."

"Yes, Mrs. Aozora," Hitomi bowed.

"Nonsense!" cried Tsubasa. "Just 'cause you're a doctor you think you can tell me when I've had enough? Hitomi, come here and pour me two, just in case!" he demanded, snatching up Ex's glass of water and flinging its contents over his shoulder. Ex didn't complain, he was addressing the spinach dip. It'd proven resilient, withstanding the sops of many breads. It wasn't until he took a spoon to it that it finally surrendered.

"What are you a doctor of?" Qui inquired.

"Medicine, of course," the old lady responded. Qui looked a bit confused.

"They're kinda like beds," Ex interjected. "You go to one to feel better."

"Don't your people have doctors, darling?" asked Shantasa.

"Well, if we're injured, we just lose mass. I could chew on a fingernail and reassume an unblemished version of my current shape. But I suppose the closest we have are what you might call nutritionists," said Qui. She'd drawn a comparison to yet another profession that was all but extinct amongst the Solarian race – The Starfarer's Strand had seen to that.

"Hmm? You probably mean an acclimation therapist," said Shantasa. "Acclimation therapy is all the rage, my darling. Adaptation can take months if the environment is alien enough. And even then, the range of worlds the Starfarer's Strand makes possible for Solarians is narrow by Valoraphim standards. An overtaxed strand is a fairly common cause of death amongst ring runners, but acclimation therapists are typically only available on cruisers and major settlements. That's how I got my start in medicine, actually. I was the Himatma's therapist, now I'm the town's doctor, seeing as how the CIR won't let us have a working purity ward."

At some point, Tsubasa had propped his peg leg up on the table. Qui nudged it away from her glass of water. "So, if you have a doctor for a wife, why haven't you gotten that leg of yours fixed?"

"Oh, and who says it needs fixing?" said Tsubasa.

"Err, I mean what made you choose such a basic prosthetic?"

"It does the job," said Tsubasa, knocking on the table with his peg. "Let me tell you, since we crashed into this sandbox, this tin leg of mine's the only part of my body that doesn't complain every morning. So I'm not about to wrap flesh around it and give voice to another protester. No thank you! But enough about my decrepit old body. Let's speak of something more interesting. Come now, Chimi. What story would you like to hear?"

Chimi was lapping up the last morsels of potato. Her tongue was half way up the plate when she realized that all eyes had suddenly turned to her. She looked up at Tsubasa with a face full of innocence.

"Well? What story do you want me to tell? You pick," he smiled.

"Do I have to?"

"Chimi..." scolded Farah.

"Okay, okay. Let's see... I guess... tell the one about the hungry planets in Wild Space!" She said with sudden excitement.

"The Jovians? Very well." The old man's expression made plain that this was one of his favorite stories as well. He took a modest sip and jumped right in: "Out beyond the seventh ring, on the edges of space where matter clots into reefs, mysteries and marvels run thick. For few have traveled as far and returned to tell of it.

Mass there is so abundant, it can support life forms on a fantastic scale, not the least of which are the Jovians. These wandering gas giants can grow big as stars, devouring worlds as whales once sifted krill. Nothing escapes their creeping atmospheres – not ships, not probes, not planets. Get too close and they'll lash out at you with raging flares, exploding from its upper cloud decks. That is, if their staggering gravity wells don't suck you in first.

Nearly all a Jovian does is consume. And they're great at it, growing with each morsel, only to seek out their next meal. But they don't grow forever. When they get too big, they heat up and start to glow. Planet-sized hurricanes swirl around their atmosphere. The seas that rage beneath the clouds lap at the heavens, and the core begins to roil. Then, the worldwide storm surges to a pole, and there an eruption takes place, spewing matter into space with enough intensity to emit light that can be seen several systems away. When it's all cooled and settled, the Jovian is orbited by a hungry little moon."

"Like a baby, right?" beamed Chimi.

"Yes, like a baby," said Tsubasa.

"Do Jovians eat little girls?" she asked.

"Most certainly, but I doubt they'd realize it. You're not hardly a meatball," chuckled Tsubasa. Chimi gave a rehearsed gasp. "That's not the worst of it," he continued. "There's something creeping around the wilds of space that makes the Jovians look like gnats. You can't take pictures of this thing. It's far too big. All you can do is try to map it, but that's not easy because it's always on the move, stretching its unimaginable legs across several galaxies. It is known only as the Galactic Walker..." As he spoke, his hands crawled across the air towards Chimi, and now he had her, tickling her ribs. It was easy to mistake her for a much younger girl, for whom these actions may have been appropriate, but she reminded the old man that she'd entered the *age of indignity* by jabbing a fork into his wrinkled hand.

"Mom..." Chimi said sweetly, as Tsubasa rubbed his paw, "can we give Ex his present now?" The food and drink had left Ex a bit drowsy, but talk of presents perked him right up.

"I don't see why not," replied Farah, reaching down for the box at her feet. "Here you are Mr. Rey. Chimi and I made this for you. I'm sorry it's not much, especially after what you've done for us, but it's all we have to give."

Ex tore the box in half. There was some kind of heavy fabric folded up inside. It unfurled into a big blanket with a hole in the middle. There were patterns in shades of gray, and its trim was adorned with alternating triangles of black and white thread.

"Do you like it? We knit it for you, Ex," said Chimi with a small quiver in her voice.

"Oh yeah, it's great. Thanks..." said Ex. "What is it?"

"Looks like a poncho," said Qui.

"It's not a poncho!" said Chimi. "It's a cloak. Just like the one in the picture I showed you, remember?" She hopped out of her chair and snatched the cloth out of Ex's hands. "See? It's even got the little pyramids on the edges like he had, and look here on the part that's supposed to wrap around your neck... recognize that?" There was a scarf sewn into the cloak, made from the same fabric. At its end was a dark gray X. "Just like your name right? Only in his case, I think it was a number. Do you like it? I mean, really and truly?"

"Yeah, I really do," said Ex.

"Then why don't you try it on?" she said, pushing the cloak against his chest.

"You mean right now?"

"Yes!" she insisted. "Right now." Ex shook off his ratty old duster and pulled his present over his head. It took a while for him to sort out how to wear it. He wrapped the scarf around his neck, the brim of which reached just to the point of his nose. Despite how thick the cloth was, it breathed remarkably well. It was a good deal lighter than his old duster too. Not to mention he could hide a lot beneath it. All in all, it was a good present. "See? Now you look just like the picture," said Chimi, flipping her book open to the page marked by a white ribbon.

Ex stared at the picture. Sure the cloaks were similar, but that's not what caught his attention. The image was scratched and faded, but it seemed as if a pair of pistons poked out of the man's holster. "Yeah? Who is that guy anyway?"

"The First Sage," she replied.

Istreyan Whisky

The table was cleared, and the ladies had all gone. Tsubasa, ever the gentleman, had offered Qui a bed for the night, but she'd opted to return to her room on the second floor of Rhet's Tavern instead. It may not have been as comfortable, and certainly not as air-conditioned, but she could keep up with current affairs.

Ex was half way out the door, on his way back to the sandy little bedroll in Chimi's hut, when Tsubasa grabbed him by the collar of his new cloak. "And where do you think you're going? You and I need to have a little chat, and I have a present for you as well..."

"Another present?" said Ex. "Well, I suppose today is my birthday." The old man led him down a couple of hallways. Ex normally had a pretty good sense of direction, but this place was quite a maze. "Where're we going?" he asked, hoping he might be able to peek at whatever was under that big blue tarp he saw earlier.

"To my study, of course! Where else can you have a good man-to-man?" said Tsubasa. He stopped and entered a little code into a keypad. The door shot open, and Ex poked his head inside. The room was about one meter wide and two meters long. The walls were all lined with shelves full of various bottles and decanters.

"Spacious..."

"This is my liquor closet, you jester!" said Tsubasa.

"Are you so much of an alcoholic that you need an entire closet to store your booze?"

"Hey, you gotta stock up when you live in the corner of a dusty hell like this. I can't just go to the store and buy some more when I run out... well, not any good stuff, anyhow."

"Fair enough, but don't you think you've had enough wine for the night?" said Ex.

"Yes. That's why I'm getting some whisky," said Tsubasa. "Besides, I'm a Dicot, remember? Computers don't get drunk."

"Tell that to your liver," said Ex.

Tsubasa picked out the largest jug of the bunch, big enough to warrant wheels and a little rope to tow it.

The door opened to Tsubasa's study. He let Ex go first, so he could take in the full splendor of the decor. There were lavish red curtains, which opened to shelves of dusty old books rather than windows. The only light came from a holographic flame at the far end of the room, where a couple of large chairs faced each other at oblique angles. Their heavy cushions matched the curtains in color and texture. The walls were adorned with dozens of ship models, each labeled with a brass plaque. The flame flickered in plastic reflections on their many faces and spilled onto the wall in shadows full of movement.

Ex left a scattered trail of sand on the plush red carpet. He couldn't hold back a laugh when he saw the enormous portrait of Tsubasa that reigned over the mantle.

The old man was posed with one hand on his chest, the other reaching for the heavens. Over his outstretched palm ran the vibrant beams of a ring. His eyes were focused on distant stars, and the prongs of his beard were swept by a cosmic wind. The galaxies and stars of the background clustered in the space around his head like a halo. And at either side of his feet were the faces of Geysemar and Veredos, the first, tan and green, the second shining like sage silver.

Ex turned to find the old man posing as in his portrait. "Hah! This place is like something out of a book," laughed Ex.

"And maybe it is," said Tsubasa. "We're all part of a story; it's just a matter of whether anyone thinks it's worth jotting down."

"And you think someone would bother to write what you've been babbling tonight?"

"Well, not now! But maybe later... or earlier. The most trivial tripe seems interesting when viewed from sufficient distance."

"Alright, leave the jug in the hallway, old man. The computer chips in your head are gonna get soggy if you keep this up," said Ex, but Tsubasa pulled his jug over to the chairs by the fireplace and sat down with a groan.

Ex hadn't even had a seat before the old man started up again. "So what do you think about that book Chimi showed you tonight? It's quite a compendium of Pre-Shattering Terran Archaeology. Do you know who gave it to her?"

"I give up."

"I did. And do you know who gave it to me? None other than the universe's premier authority on the subject, Exterrus Mortagon Solipso... your father." Ex's eyes were fixed on the holographic fire. He put out a palm. It emitted no heat, but the room was warm enough.

"You know, I've been around for over 800 years – don't ask me how much longer – and Chimi's the closest thing I've ever had to a daughter. Some people wait until their eighties to have children, so they're fully prepared for the responsibility; it only took me the better part of a millennium.

But don't think I couldn't still father a couple of pups right now! Believe me, I'm physically capable..." said Tsubasa, gathering himself in a semi-obscene fashion. "But with Chimi around, I don't think I'll need to. We were always close, but since Thuris passed, I've really been like a father to her... though I'm sure she'd say grandfather..." The wrinkles of his face deepened into a smile. "A little girl needs a strong male influence in her life, just as much as boys do."

The fire glistened in Ex's eyes.

"Don't worry," said Tsubasa. "I'm sure Arius was all the male influence you needed in your life."

Ex reckoned he was right about that. It'd felt as if he'd grown up without a mother, rather than father, but Arius had done her best to fulfill both roles.

Tsubasa held out his snifter and pushed the base of the jug with his peg. It tipped over on its wheels, and the spout clacked into his glass, filling it with amber liquid. "Thuris was a good man. You'd never guess he was Shantasa's younger brother, but that's how we met. Even if I weren't a Dicot, I think I'd remember every detail of that day, but maybe that's just the whisky talking... and none of that Centrian rainwater runoff or the local plex-swill; this is real Istreyan rye, aged in oak casks, brewed by the Grovekeepers with all due reverence. Tell ya what, I might not agree with the way they meditate on a damn flower for forty days straight, but they sure can brew a mean mash. Want some rye?"

"Maybe just a nip," Ex salivated.

"Course ya do!" said Tsubasa. He brimmed the cup and went on. "I met Shantasa and Thuris at a Libralma retreat, just a ways into the fifth stratum. It was a beautiful planet, not as nice as Istreya, 'course, but still nice. I was the speaker of honor at the event... See, I'm a bit of a legend to the Libralma, even though Hitomi doesn't consider me a part of the religion. She says the threadknot in my head, or chest, or wherever you prefer to pretend it is, precludes me from membership. And in a sense, I suppose she's right, but that doesn't stop me from agreeing with their beliefs does it?" Ex shook his head in mid-sip. "But I digress, Thuris was a great man. He's the grandson of a big-shot Valarian Sage from back in The Extinguishing – first generation. His papa was something of a bounty hunter too; you may've heard of him, his name was Nero. What a name, huh? Thuris is much more of a traditional Valoraphim name, though I'm not sure what kind of a name Chimi is. Kind of cute though, I guess."

Tsubasa looked up at his painting over the mantel and for a moment seemed sickened by what he saw. "I was the one that had to explain to her that her father wasn't coming back," he said, draining the rest of the snifter and pouring another. "It broke my old heart. And poor Farah, that woman exudes strength and compassion, but what's asked of her is so great. I only wish she could forgive Sheremy. They were close friends before this whole mess. If you ask him, that old bit-player would tell you he came to this rock in search of riches, but I really think he came because of her.

He's not an evil man; he's just a fathead. I can't tell you how many times he's offered Farah deals and meaningless gifts, trying to redeem himself. He plays a cunning businessman, but he's far too naive for that world. I don't know if it was greed or ignorance that possessed him to take that piece of duril with him on the shuttle, but here we are now... So how do you like the whisky?"

"It'll do," Ex replied. It was the best whisky he'd ever had. Its flavor was redefining. He had no idea whisky could taste like this or rather that anything that tasted like this could be called whisky: buttery, slick, painless, oaky bliss – just a comfortable warmth in the throat and the scent of an Istreyan forest reaching up into the nose, behind the eyes, and out the ears. Clarifying.

"I only drink Istreyan Stock now," said Tsubasa. "That's where I'm from, incidentally, Istreya. Does that surprise you? The Genius of Geysemar was not actually born a Dicot. Well, not that you can even be born a Dicot, but I mean, I wasn't born into the culture. Just a regular First Path Solarian, like you pretend to be."

"Whaddya mean, pretend?" said Ex.

Tsubasa turned his eyes back to his painting. "No sir, I was born in The Groves of Istreya, and by the time I hit my teens, I had to get the heck outta there. Don't get me wrong, it's a beautiful place, flowers and furry bunnies at every turn, but it's also quite boring. Unless your ambition in life is to become a gardener or some kind of damnable druid, the only job you'll find in Istreya is with the tourist bureau.

I've always been fascinated by engineering and astrophysics – at least I think I've been. My memories of the time before I became a Dicot are fuzzy at best," he said, staring into his whisky. "My only clear childhood memory is of a dream, a ship sailing across the stars on anchorwind. I've seen nearly a millennium and a lot of whisky bottles since then, so I guess that's not too bad.

Most Dicots never forget their childhood. The implant is put into their noggins while the memories are still fresh. But I didn't get mine until I turned 23. By then, my earliest years had crawled their way up the thread to The Pool, or faded into gray fluff, or wherever the hell it is they go. I remember my teenage years well enough, particularly the day I met Master Julius Mavenbolt. 'Course, he wasn't much of a master back then. He was a brash young man in a time when non-Sophians had only just begun to acquire the power of the Sages. More to the point, he was the only person I'd ever met who thought my dreams of riding the anchorwind weren't some kind of a joke, probably because he had a crazy dream of his own: a thread so great that it would appear as a swirling galaxy of light amongst a field of faint stars. He called it The Flooded Gate. Ever heard of it?"

"Should I have?" asked Ex.

"I should say you should! You know there're folks who think your mother was *The Flooded Gate*."

"I'm not sure I like the sound of that," said Ex.

Tsubasa reflected with a laugh. "Anyway, I was lucky enough to catch Julius at the beginnings of his Prospect. He was just passing by Istreya on his way to the Outer Rings. And you should've seen the ship he was traveling in... old, cramped, and tearing at the welds; you know the type. 'You're gonna need a new ship or a good mechanic,' I told him. He chose the latter and brought me along. The truth of it was that he could've probably flown across the universe without a ship, that's the sort of Sage he was, but I think he just wanted a buddy. He also wanted someone to chronicle his journey, and I wasn't about to keep a frickin' journal, so I decided to become a Dicot. I haven't forgotten a second of my life since." The old man couldn't hide the regret in his voice. "I have a confession to make," said Tsubasa, swirling the whisky around in his cup. "Secretly, I've always wanted to be a Sage."

"So what stopped ya?" asked Ex. "I mean, besides the obvious threadknot..."

"My threadwidth," sighed Tsubasa. "It's puny... when compared to my thunderous intellect. You'd think that traveling around with the second non-Sophian Sage of the modern age would've only increased my desire, and it did, in fact. I tried to learn from him on more than one occasion. Each time, in some form or another, he'd say to me: 'I'll tell you what I think, but I won't teach you how to think; that would make you useless to me.'

In addition to the tenets of Libralma, I gleaned that the first and biggest obstacle of all is determining what your life's challenge is meant to be. Not everyone needs to be a Sage!" he exclaimed, loud enough to convince the stubborn neurons that hid in the lamina between his skull and the tin can that filled it.

"Just after Julius found his sage silver, I was offered a position at VAAL. Accepting it meant putting a knot in the old thread, but passing it up didn't seem like an option. It was Mavenbolt, the father of Libralma himself, that encouraged me to surrender to a threadknot and walk the path that life had offered me.

I abandoned my childish desires of becoming a Sage, tucked my dreams of all this anchorwind nonsense into an encrypted file in the back of my mind, and departed to Veredos. We tried to stay in touch, but it was difficult, especially once The Extinguishing began. It must've been around fifty years before the start of the war that Mavenbolt introduced me to his three apprentices; your mother was one of them.

Arius was such a sweet girl, full of strength and promise. She wasn't the most studious of the bunch, and her threadwidth was a good bit narrower, but Mavenbolt favored her. I remember teasing him about it, that old lecher... she was young enough to be his great, great, great, great, great, great, great, great granddaughter!" he said, counting on his fingers for show. "But there was more to it than the weakness of an old fool's heart. I could tell he was hiding something from me, and I knew that it was because I'd have to return to Veredos when we parted ways. I'd never betray him – he knew that – but all the knowledge stored in my Dicotian mind was just a skull-crack away from anyone who cared to *access* it."

Tsubasa's eyes suddenly closed and his head rocked back against the headrest. "Your present!" he said, springing back to life. With considerable effort, the old man hoisted himself out of his chair. He took an ornament off the mantle – at least, Ex had assumed it was an ornament. The device was comprised of numerous, intricate gears, encased in a small glass sphere. The orb sat in a couple of ferrekondite bowls placed at opposite poles. They were connected by crisscrossing metal rods, molded around the glass for protection.

"What the heck is this?" asked Ex, weighing the device in his hand. It was lighter than he'd expected. He could see several gems of etherite, scattered about the various cogs. It also contained several cylindrical batteries of pure duril. Their size was small, but if they were fully threaded, they could power a fleet of cruisers.

"It's an etheramp," replied Tsubasa.

"Aren't those usually a lot smaller?"

"On another world, perhaps... So then, can I assume you know what they do?"

"Yeah. They're like coronas that're programmed to do a specific job, like turning on a light, opening doors, or starting a fire, things like that."

"Well this one is made to do a little more. What you're holding in your hands could be the salvation of the entire planet, or a first-class ticket to unqualifiable torment."

"What happens if I drop it?" Ex teased.

"Try it," said Tsubasa.

Ex lifted it over the small wooden table by his chair and let it drop. It struck with a loud clack but didn't break. He picked it back up and started slamming it against the tabletop, hard enough to leave dents in the wood.

"Okay, okay!" cried Tsubasa. "Don't overdo it! The point is that the damn thing is pretty durable, alright?" Ex set the etheramp down, and the old man leaned in. "Shhh," he hushed. "Lemme tell you a secret..." His breath lessened Ex's appetite for the whisky. "None of the ingots torn from this planet are tamed. Not a one. There's no one that can do it. As far as I know, the only one that could even try is that Talon. And how much could he have possibly tamed? A crate? Two? Even that would be some kind of crazy record.

Right now, any clown with a corona could swing by and snatch up all he can thread. And that's not gonna change 'til they ship it back to Veredos, so the god damned Claviger can tame it. The threaded annealers in the foundry are only reshaping it into convenient forms for transport. And they're using the thread of all the men of Himatma to do it!" A violent cough shook the old man.

"You alright?"

"Does it look like I'm alright?" Tsubasa hacked. "I'm pissed off! Those damn Claviger tame every mote of duril the CIR owns. I spent centuries on Veredos, and I never got to see a single one of those bastards. But every time I had to adjust the shape of any sage silver, I had to request it be relinquished, so I could reshape it in a threaded press, and send it back to the Claviger for taming again. I swear, those bums are guarded better than The Capstone himself. But I suppose it makes sense. If any one of them died, all the sage silver they'd tamed would be forever locked into its current form. The Claviger are notoriously reclusive, but as far as I know, they're Sophian, so I can't imagine that they don't know how to make a damn anchor point antenna. They must feel the task is somehow beneath them... The hubris!" Tsubasa drained another glass and began to choke again.

"Relax, old man," said Ex.

Tsubasa's stack of centuries suddenly showed. His eyes dimmed and pallor brushed his cheeks. The gallon or so of whisky he'd just imbibed wasn't helping either. "Ex," he began, "You can't change what you were. You can't change what you are. But you can change what you'll become..." Normally, Ex would've had a snide comeback for such a sappy line, but the old man's words sounded grave – perhaps because he had a foot in one. "You're probably wishing you'd never come across this godforsaken planet, but you have. Pretty soon, every able hand in the Consortium will be at your throat. But what would you say if I told you that I could change that? What if the CIR prized your safety above all else?"

"I'd say you've fused your circuits."

"There's a defeat that's worse than death, reserved only for Sage's who've dared to tame duril. It's only been suffered no more than a handful of times. It has no official name, but I've heard it called *The Relinquishing*."

"Yeah, and what's that got to do with me?" asked Ex.

"Everything. You see, if a Sage has relinquished, it means they've been forced to give up their duril before they're killed. This possibility both saved and damned duril smiths during The Extinguishing. They weren't sniped by anchor rounds, fired several galaxies away, and stars weren't seeded in their laps as they slept. They were made to suffer a species of torture so thorough and excrutiating that they happily relinquish their silver in exchange for a quick death."

"I still don't see what this has to do with me."

"You're denser than a black hole! The etheramp, you simp!" coughed Tsubasa. Ex glanced down at the orb. First his eyes fell on the reflections of the fire that danced on its surface, and the delicate gears inside seemed to spin. He focused beyond the glare, and they were still again. "The device you're holding will allow you to tame an entire planet..."

"And piss off the CIR worse than anyone in all of history?"

"Your fate has already been decided. Trisol's future, however, still lies in the balance. The only real difference for you will be that the CIR will try to capture you instead of de-atomizing you from orbit. They won't be able to simply snuff you out of existence because the bond you'll have with the duril of this world will be more valuable to them than anything else."

"Try explaining that to the Talon. He doesn't seem like the type who'd care."

"Well if he kills you, that'll be perfect," said Tsubasa.

"Oh? Do explain…"

"If he kills you after you've tamed every last scrap of wild duril on the planet, this world will forever hold no value to the Consortium, and the Libralma will live free," said the old man. "I mean, they could still pick the duril up with their hands, push it around with machines, transport it on ships, but they could never reshape it, cut it, or by any other means break it apart. They'd have to put entire mountains into their engine rooms and construct specialized anchor drives around oddly shaped veins.

Plus, the death you'll suffer at the hands of a deranged Talon should be thousands of times quicker and less painful than the one you'd suffer should the Extinguishers capture you. They have ways of keeping your brain alive with electrical signals, so you can feel pain long after your heart has stopped beating."

"Wonderful."

Tsubasa rose from his chair slowly; every bone in his back cracked in order. "Ex, we don't get to choose our challenges. I never got a chance to be a Sage; you'll have no choice but to become one. Sure that means pissing off the Consortium worse than ever, but the way I calculate it, your life is already forfeit. Why not give its end some meaning? You may not have lived as a hero, but you can die as one."

Hitomi entered the room and helped the old man to the door. "Make sure our guest doesn't go to sleep thirsty," he told her and turned to Ex. "This old man must get some rest. I'm not the pillar of energy I used to be." He resisted Hitomi's hand. "Once I went a whole year without sleep. Those were wild times!" And the android dragged him off to bed.

A Desert Breeze

The heat in Rhet's Tavern was oppressive. Outside, sweat didn't have a chance to bead before the suns took it, but in here it hung heavy on the collar. The bar had been converted into a salty steam-house. The air was stagnant and thick. You could walk in and out of smells, but you'd be hard-pressed to find a pocket of it that wasn't full of some stink.

If they weren't such essential props, Gallowatch would've rid himself of his weskit and top hat, which felt like a pressure cooker, ironing his meager hair to his scalp. He'd soaked his handkerchief before noon, and lifting the hat at this point was out of the question. There was at least a gallon of sweat brewing in there. Still, he was amongst the liveliest of the clientele.

A bucket sat by his feet, half full of marinara. Bloated white sacks floated in the sauce like a Skwell's organs. This rich lunch of pasta was originally meant as a peace offering for Farah and Chimi, but they'd refused it straight away, and Gallowatch, bit-playing a shrewd businessman, was in the process of ensuring that it wouldn't go to waste.

The heat and cheese were conspiring to make a balloon of him. He straightened up in his chair to clear his chest of a muted burp. "Oof, I beg your pardon. The ricotta is escaping me. In retrospect, packing my lunch pail with manicotti was not a good choice."

He pulled his plex card out of his coat pocket. *5.8 Potential Kilograms,* it read — about a kilo and a half short by his reckoning, and he wasn't about to walk a single mile in the Trisolian desert. Considering that he'd only been here a night, and that he'd shown up without a wallet or anything of worth other than a gold-plated pocket watch, he'd done fairly well for himself. Most of the plex he'd made came from the fellow seated directly across the poker table, none other than Kaj Fullop. Well, it wasn't really *from* him but *because* of him. The other players seated at the table were members of his gang, and they folded every time they had a good hand, lest they beat their boss and their boss beat them. Since Fullop never folded, all Gallowatch had to do was beat his hand to collect at least the blind from the entire gang.

Kaj shuffled the deck. He bemoaned the damage Ex had done to his pistol much more than the work Qui had done to his ribs and jaw. "I mean, I know she's class. Hell, she's historical," said Kaj through the grin that the chin-splint forced on him. "But what I liked best 'bout this gun was the texture of the trigger. Now, I know I'mma gettin' a touch romantic, but this trigger's got these fine pleats you can only feel on your fingertip. I suppose they were designed for grip considerations, but I'll be damned if these little ridges don't invite you to give her a squeeze. It's hard not to pop off a round once you've stepped up to this girl's plate," he said, drawing the gun from the holster. "Lord knows I could never resist her, but now look..." Kaj pointed the gun right at Gallowatch and pulled the trigger. *Click, click, click.* "Impotent. A complete knuckle-fizzle..."

"Please, mister Fullop," said Gallowatch, the sweat skiing down the waxed slopes of his moustache. "Why don't you deal us another hand? Then perhaps you can win back some of this plex and get your gun fixed at The Ferrous Outpost's manifestor, once this whole Sage business is resolved, of course."

"Listen here, brass buttons, every part of this gun was made by hand. Got it? If it was a matter of practicality, I could just pump a bunch of plex into that damned box and get a photocaster made, or hell, just buy one from a shady alley of your choice. This here's about art. It's about legacy. You know how hard it's gonna be to find a man that can craft a new hammer by hand? Shoot... Thanks to Sages and all this threaded, automated, etheramp-bull-shit, ain't a person left in the universe who can do a damn thing. Stick a card into a slot and press a button, and that's it. Ain't no love for the craft no more."

"A triple negative, quite impressive," Gallowatch thought to himself. A few more liberties taken and his dialect would've carried tinges of a autex. Still, it was better than talking to a Centrian, who managed to befoul the language so thoroughly within its own rules. "Well, I hear what you're saying, good sir," spoke Gallowatch, "but I'm not quite sure I catch your meaning. You insinuate that pushing a button to make a gun is wrong, yet you needn't but pull that weapon's trigger to kill a man. Seems to me that when it comes to partaking in the benefits of technology, men in your profession are just as guilty as the rest of us."

Kaj pulled the cleaver out of its sheath and buried it into the poker table with a mighty thwack. "If you think all there is to killin' a man is pullin' a trigger... well, then you're just dead wrong, sir." The temperature in the room rose another couple of degrees, nearing lethal levels. It might've gotten there too if it wasn't for a gentle desert breeze that blew through the swinging doors. The dead ceiling fan squeaked a couple of turns, but the wind passed as quickly as it came, and the heavy air was still again.

"I see your point," said Gallowatch. The knife's impact had sent a crack across the table that had toppled his stack of chips. He was relieved to see Kaj dealing another hand. The Butcher began with himself and flicked out cards in a clockwise fashion. He paused after Gallowatch, and slowly, every eye in the table turned to the player in that seat. The goon that'd been sitting there all morning was gone – God knows where. In his place sat an enormous figure, hooded in a black cloak.

"Hello, Mister Gallowatch," hissed the new player. "Fancy meeting you here."

"Wh-who are you?" stammered Gallowatch.

"Don't play coy, dear boy. You know precisely who I am," said the stranger. "And you know why I've come."

"D-do I?"

"Unless you've baked your brain under that hat of yours..." The stranger reached out for Gallowatch's hat. His hand and forearm were all silver, sculpted in the fashion of an Antican's graceful musculature. Each of his fingers came to sharp points. He poked one into the top of the hat and lifted. Sweat cascaded down Gallowatch's bloated face, as if someone had just poured a jug of water over his scalp. "Hmm, perhaps you have poached it a little..." he said, refitting the hat with a gentle tap.

The stranger pulled his cloak up over the horn that soared from his forehead, revealing a grin of jagged fangs, wide enough to straddle a stratum. His features were sculpted in pure duril, from eyes to forked tongue, which skittered about his teeth as he spoke. "Let's hope your memory hasn't been damaged too severely. It's the only thing giving you any value in your current situation."

The universe had never seen a terror of this breed; neither myth nor fantasy had dared it. The Antican's silvery teeth hummed with eager energy. Each was threaded with the soul of a Nyrceff that Ex had slain in the station. Gallowatch knew thread couldn't carry the need for vengeance from one body to the next, but he could feel this monster's hunger for Ex's blood, vibrating from every molecule of its body.

Sheremy gathered himself from the initial shock, remembering that Issid was a soldier. The Talon's mark still framed his left eye, even though it'd taken on an odd, tribal quality when embossed in metal. In addition to an Antican's infamous insanity, the Sophians had woven a need to obey into the very root of their genetic code. It was the only thing that made them manageable. Gallowatch's anger turned to Zarfall, who'd promised him more time to resolve all of this peaceably. The involvement of a Talon, whether of duril or flesh, spelled certain catastrophe for Himatma.

"Go back and tell Zarfall that I have the situation under control; I just need a little more time," instructed Gallowatch in the most authoritarian tone he could muster.

"Oh? You're giving me an order?" asked Issid. His teeth physically shook with excitement; the wave went from one corner of his mouth to the next. They moved like the keys of a player piano, each producing a click of a slightly different pitch.

"No, no, of course not. I only assumed that since the time he'd given me has not yet passed, Zarfall sent you to get a report from me. Why else would he order you here so soon?"

"Well then, let me assure you that your assumption is entirely inaccurate. I am not here at the Executor's behest. I came of my own accord," said Issid.

Gallowatch suddenly felt as if he were sitting next to Death itself. It appeared that when Issid had been removed from his natural body, he'd been removed from his encoded necessity to obey as well. The leash had been cut, yet the transplant had left his Antican madness intact.

Issid was completely aware of Gallowatch's realization. His reaction pleased the Talon greatly. The time for threats had passed. It was understood that every question he asked from this point onwards was a matter of life and death. "I will ask this once: where is the Sage?"

"What Sage?" Gallowatch recoiled.

Issid smiled, and the ceiling fan began to turn. Sheremy's plex card leapt out of his coat pocket and floated over to Issid's sharp claws. The amount of threadwidth required to manipulate something so close to a willed being typically prohibited a trick of this kind, but Sheremy's shriveling thread offered little resistance to the invisible hands that extended from the Talon's giant etherite horn. "You've done quite well for yourself, Mister Gallowatch."

Plex was a dangerous weapon in a Sage's able hands. They were always capable of generating matter from the void, but plex made it easier. The subrostral soup held within the card called to Issid, countless forms crying for a chance to spring into existence. The Talon considered them all, but kept the plex within the confines of the card for the time being.

Qui sat like a stone in the corner of the bar, observing the whole affair with much interest. She began to map an escape route. Her current form offered a great deal of protection, but not much mobility. She considered swallowing a pill and swapping her rocky skin for something light and agile, but she didn't want to attract attention to herself. She just hoped that her rugged body would prove durable enough to withstand the Talon's play.

Issid's expression suddenly changed from one indecipherable emotion to the next. His focus turned from Gallowatch to the gaming table in front of him. "What are we playing, boys?" No one knew what to make of the Talon's question, but they rightly didn't trust it. His tone shed no light on his intentions.

"The game's Poker," Kaj finally responded.

"Ah... Poker, is it?" said Issid.

"Yeah. Do you know the rules?" asked Kaj.

"Not in the least. But I've a couple of my own..." Issid held up the plex card for all to see. "I want you gentlemen to play a round. Whoever wins, gets to tell me the Sage's whereabouts, and I give them this. As for the rest of you, well, let's just say it'll be the last hand you'll ever lose..."

"Uh, uh, uh, I know where the Sage is!" blurted one of the players. A small gust of wind drew the top card from the deck and buried it into the far wall. The corner of the card had pierced the tin, and the rest of it was soaked in blood. A red line appeared around the goon's neck. His head hinged backwards and fell to the dirt floor with a thud.

"Don't ruin the game," said Issid. And so the stage was set for the quietest hand of Poker any of the men had ever played. "I do hope you can play your game without that card," smiled the Talon, knowing full well that the gamblers would manage. There was a bit of understandable hesitancy on their part. None of them dared to make a move for the deck. "If someone doesn't start dealing those cards, I'll be forced to do it in my own little way."

Kaj snatched up the deck and started doling out cards. He dealt Gallowatch in last, and every time he drew a card for himself, he seemed to say a little prayer beneath his beard. Fearsome as Kaj was, he was a two-legged dachshund puppy compared to this Talon. His men wouldn't let him win this time around.

Issid watched silently as the men played. No one bothered making a bet; the stakes were high enough as they were. A mist of sweat rose from the table, reeking of whisky and dust. A breeze passed over the men, but it didn't blow; it coiled around their necks and slithered over their white knuckles.

After a minute of quiet contemplation, one of the henchmen placed three cards on the table and gave them a tap. Kaj flashed him some teeth and flicked a trio of cards at him. One of them hit the goon in the chin, and the other two flew off the table. The next fellow asked for a couple, they were flung at his chest. Kaj dealt himself four new cards, as delicately as the situation would permit. And finally Gallowatch called for just one.

Kaj was about to send a card Sheremy's way when Issid intervened. "Wait! His fifth card will be the one stuck in the wall over there." If the men had any objections, they dared not voice them.

It was time to show. The first man had a pair of sevens, and the second didn't have a damned thing; an ace high was all he could claim. Kaj laid his hand on the table: full house, a trio of queens full of tens. Next it was Sheremy's turn. He had a pair of jacks and aces, still missing his fifth card. Kaj glanced nervously at his cohorts' hands. Between them, they'd only claimed one of the aces, leaving only one card that could possibly win Gallowatch the game: the ace of hearts.

Issid summoned the card and laid it on the table: a bloody ace of hearts. Gallowatch had won. The other men's faces made that plain. Before they had time to react, Issid snatched up the deck and dealt each of them one more card, straight through the chest. Kaj and his men slumped in their chairs, dead. "Congratulations, Mister Gallowatch, you won. Now you get to answer my question..."

As much as Gallowatch despised Ex for making him look like a fool and wrecking his precious station, he knew that ratting him out would doom Farah and Chimi. But he had to wonder if lying to a Talon was really a practical option. Chances were that he was going to find out sooner or later, and at least by telling the truth he could save his skin. He weighed all the pros and cons of his decision, as any good businessman should. "Alright, I'll tell you," he began. "The Sage is hiding deep in the mines. He may've fled to a new location already, but that's where he's been staying, from what I've been able to gather. I'll warn you though: those tunnels run deep. You could run around for a year down there and not find him. And if you think scanning's bad on the surface, it's completely useless underground." He'd decided to lie, even if it was futile. He couldn't repay the debt he owed Chimi and Farah, but if he could earn them a bit of time at the expense of his life, maybe he could pay off some of the interest.

The Talon rose without a word. He walked to the swinging doors and stopped. "You might find this funny," he began. "I've known where the Sage has been hiding ever since he fired an anchor-round from the surface yesterday. I just thought I'd drop by this fine establishment for a bit of entertainment, and I wasn't disappointed. Even though you didn't hold up your end of the bargain, *my* gentility is not an act, so I'm obliged to uphold mine."

Gallowatch's eyes lit up. Issid was a lunatic, no doubt, but perhaps he wasn't all evil. The sort of chaos that ran through his twisted mind just led him to mischief, whose cruelty he was not equipped to comprehend. "That's right," stammered Sheremy. "You did promise."

"I said I'd give this card to the winner," hissed Issid. "However, I did not specify at which speed..." And with that, the card flew out of the Talon's claw and split Gallowatch's hat in half at the brim. The card buried itself into a column by the bar, and no one was left alive at the poker table.

Issid vanished in a rolling breeze, leaving the swinging doors creaking. Everyone in the bar was too stunned to move – everyone except Qui, who shuffled her stony hooves towards the exit. But she was too late. The card of plex swelled under Issid's will, and Rhet's tavern turned into a cloud of gore and smithereens.

Snake in the Sand

Chimi and Farah had just finished a couple of bowls of dust-water soup. Despite Chimi's harrowing adventure the day before, both of them had put a shift in at the mine this morning, but Farah still had another eight hours of digging ahead of her before her day was done. Chimi had made plans to go visit Ex at the old man's facility. She knew he probably wasn't awake yet; her mind raced with all manners of pranks she could play to wake him.

A gentle rapping came at the hut's wall, just by the curtain that hung at the entrance. The noise was small and metallic. *Tick, tick, tick...* it continued. "Come in, Kabuto!" called Chimi, somewhat surprised by the beetle's sudden concern for etiquette. Still the clicking continued, forcing the little girl from her chair. "You silly bug," she sighed, flapping open the curtain.

An enormous, cloaked figure stood before her, tapping on the wall of her home with a single gleaming claw. Most of its face was shrouded in sharp shadow, but the three suns glinted off a row of silver fangs. "Hello, girl," said Issid.

Chimi closed the curtain and tied a knot over the little hook that held it. Issid laughed, and removed his hood before tearing through the canvas with the tip of his etherite horn. Chimi fell on her rump and skittered backwards across the sand until her back met the wall of the meager hut. The Talon's cloak was torn to shreds as he spread his razor-wings of sage silver. They stretched high into the conical ceiling, filling the room with oaths of cloudy color. Chimi wanted to crawl away, but her limbs were full or terror and awe.

Farah rushed in from the kitchen and threw herself over her child. "Go away, you monster!" she cried, pointing a mining laser at the Talon. She stood directly between the beast and her daughter.

Issid was intrigued. His wings folded at his sides, and he cocked his head. Firstly, he was delighted that he'd been called a monster, and the woman's fiery demeanor invigorated him. He'd expected a rather boring and uneventful interrogation session, and he'd found some fight. The heavy laser sagged in the woman's arms. If she could keep it steady, focused on a single point of the Talon's body for a few hours, it might give him a tickle. The tool she held was used to cut the rock away from the duril, not to cut the duril itself. A threaded beam was required for that, and even then it would only work on wild ore, not tamed sage silver.

With half a thought, the Talon could break her in two, and yet there she stood. Her breathing was labored, but her eyes showed no trace of fear. They were blinded by a fury that Issid respected, but couldn't understand. Out of curiosity, he decided not to end her life just yet. Plus, he still had to discover the Sage's whereabouts. He might be able to extract them from the daughter, but although he'd never directly dealt with a child, he knew from his training that smaller humans were supposed to be more difficult. "Where is he, woman?"

"I said, get out!" cried Farah, firing up the laser. The beam hit him straight in the chest, and Issid ignored it.

Chimi had gathered up enough courage to stand. "Mom, stop!" she pleaded, tugging at her arm.

Issid couldn't imagine that the little girl was concerned with his safety. Her intent was to save her mother from harm, despite the fact that she was the only thing that stood between her and his wrath. The relationship between the two females fascinated him. He'd learned in his short life that members of the opposing sexes in certain species formed bonds between one another for the purposes of procreation, an arrangement he found enervating. But this was the first mother he'd ever dealt with – well, he'd probably killed a few dozen mothers before, but never in context. Nothing in the imprint of his Antican mind, stored within the quantum computer that was housed in his duril skull, could relate to this strange bond.

Issid had been born in an Antican hatchery on Veredos and cultivated as part of a clutch of warriors within the walls of The Talon Academy. He'd never known anything close to a mother. Anticans bore an innate fear of their mothers, and with good reason too: they were the only ones that knew where they'd been birthed. If a hatchling managed to kill the rest of their siblings in the lava mire, they'd have to hope they were strong enough to leave the nest before mother came back around looking for a quick bite. But it appeared that the interest this mother had for her pup went beyond an easy meal. Perhaps he could leverage this to his advantage.

"Stay back, stay back!" cried Farah, shrugging away Chimi's attempts to stop her.

"No, mom! Please, stop! Ex will come save us, trust me!"

Issid smiled. "Ah, so you do know the Sage…"

"And what if I don't tell you? You gonna kill me?" said Chimi, stepping around Farah.

"No, there'd be no sport in killing a tiny girl," replied Issid. "However, if I should sneeze you out of existence, that's an entirely different matter. So consider your responses carefully, and don't lie to me when I ask you a question that I myself can answer. I know you know the Sage, that much is evident, but what relation is he to you?"

"He's my friend, so you better think twice about what you're doing!"

"Is that so? Then perhaps I won't have to search him out after all…"

Farah's arms went limp, and the mining laser dropped to the sand. She knew exactly what the Talon was thinking. "Hush, child!" she said, but it was too late. The Talon's wing swept in and brushed Farah aside. It was only a few centimeters thick, but pushing against it was like trying to shove the world away with a handstand. "Leave her alone, you… you motherless demon!" she cried.

"Now, now," said Issid, "flattery will get you nowhere."

In desperation, Chimi picked up the mining laser and fired it right at the Talon's eyes. They were also made of duril, and the beam had no effect. In truth, they weren't even eyes, just something made to look like eyes. Issid could see with any part of his body. His will emanated from the duril shell, filling the hut and spreading across the crater of Himatma like a flood. But when he reached out with his mind to wrest the mining bit from the little girl's hands he met with resistance. Even the focal lens at the tip of the laser wouldn't obey his commands. The girl's thread ran thick and unyielding. With a corona and some training, she might have even given him cause for concern, but as it was, Issid summoned a swirling wind from the edges of the room and whisked the tool from her hands. He clutched her by the waist. She struggled and screamed, but the Talon's grip was immovable.

The hut's roof blew off into the blue sky, and Issid spread his wings. "You, mother," he said. "Tell the Sage that if he wishes to find this girl still drawing breath, he has until sundown to show at the refinery. For the sake of your child, I hope you are good at conveying urgency…" He paused for a moment, and in a rare act of charity, willed the mining laser to point at Farah's stomach and fire once, burning a clean hole through her side. "This will help your credibility," he said and took to the air. He and Chimi vanished in a silver zephyr.

A Pink Nightmare

Ex had fallen asleep in the glow of the holographic fireplace of Tsubasa's study, but that is not where he awoke. Getting up was always a gradual process for him. Even when Arius would burst into his room like the ship was on fire — and sometimes it was — he'd stumble out of bed, but it could be a whole hour before the last bits of him would shake off sleep. The first part of him to regain consciousness was perhaps the root of it all: a general awareness that he existed.

He gave a comfortable groan and stretched out, his right foot trembling slightly when it reached full extension. Silk embraced his body. He wriggled his toes, grasping at the fabric; he'd never felt such luxury. His arms moved instinctively, drawing the quilted comforter over his head. With a half roll, he was fully prepared to go back to sleep, when the smell of the quilt entered his nose. It was as light and sweet as Istreyan springtime. He began to root around his plush pillow. The carnal excitement of the moment ignited the higher functions of his simple mind.

He flipped onto his back, realizing that he could not only feel the texture of the fabric with his hands and feet, but with the whole of his body. He lifted the sheets and confirmed his hypothesis; he was without clothing and cleaner than he'd ever been.

He peeked a timid eye out of the covers and performed some basic reconnaissance. He found himself in a room decorated by someone who shared their fashion sense with a tacky Valentine's card. Everything was pink. The wallpaper was pink, the furniture was pink, and the bedspread was pink, adorned with red and white trim. His cheeks flushed to match every tone in the room when he came to look upon the owner, sitting perfectly upright on a plain pink chair, staring right back at him. "Good morning, Mr. Ex," said Hitomi.

"I'm naked!" Ex cried.

"You'll excuse me if I don't express surprise. You see, I'm holding your clothes, washed and pressed."

"Oh, god..." said Ex. "We didn't... do it last night, did we?"

"Do what?"

"You know... it,"

"I'm afraid your usage of the pronoun in this context does not convey the necessary information to establish clarity."

"I mean did we sleep together?"

"As you should already know, I don't sleep."

"Then why do you have a bed?"

"It, like the rest of the room's decor, was Mr. Tsubasa's idea," stated Hitomi.

Ex sat up. Every shelf in the room was lined with mirrors, baubles, fragrant immortelle, and porcelain vases, all carefully placed on their own individual pink doilies. "Well, I guess you need a full-sized dollhouse if you're going to have a full-sized doll," he said. Hitomi's eyes flashed red. She hurled the heavy clothes right at Ex's face, boots and all, knocking him back to a fully recumbent position. "Oh, by the way... why am I naked?" he finally asked.

"Because I couldn't fit your clothes in the washer with you still in them."

A tiny bell rang somewhere inside the room. Hitomi shot out of her chair and bolted for the door, pausing only for an instant to instruct Ex not to follow. "Hey, where're you going!?" he called out. "No, wait, wait... lemme guess, the old man needs a morning highball?" He stumbled out of bed, throwing himself into his pants and shuffling into his boots. There was hardly enough time to snatch up his gun and holster if he wanted to keep up with Hitomi. He barely managed glimpses of her, turning this way and that through the maze of doors and passages.

He caught up with her in the storefront. Apparently, the ringing bell had meant that someone was interested in buying a clock. At first glance, it appeared Hitomi was alone, but a small voice called for Ex. He peered over the counter and saw a miniature version of the blue vixen that Qui was fond of embodying. His first reaction was to laugh.

"It's not funny," she squeaked. She was no bigger than Ex's boots. Her normally taut belly was distended. It looked like she was about to give birth to sextuplets.

"Oh my god!" Ex laughed. "Are you listening to yourself? It's hilarious."

"For your information, I nearly died!" cried Qui. "And it's pretty much all your fault. That damned Talon came to the tavern and blew it to pieces. I nearly got my core cracked!"

"Your what?"

"A Blank's *core* is the element of their species that retains genetic information, personality traits, and memories across all forms," replied Hitomi. "It's a very resilient shell that communicates with the surrounding nervous tissue through complex electromagnetic waves. It also happens to be the only naturally occurring form of quantum storage. This unique adaptation allows the race's formidable mental faculties to be sheltered in a seed of sorts that is no bigger than a marble."

Ex blinked at Hitomi. "The hell's a marble?"

"A small glass sphere typically used as a child's play thing."

He looked back over at Qui's stomach. "Well it looks like she got knocked up by a gerbil."

"Can you just focus for a second?" demanded the tiny Qui. "I'm trying to tell you that The Talon is in town, and he just blew up the tavern and everyone in it!"

"It's about time. I'm gonna send him right back to hell," said Ex, patting the gun in his holster.

"You idiot!" cried Qui. "He's not coming here. He's headed for that little girl's house. You remember, the place you shot the Placator from?"

"Chimi!" gasped Ex. He swiped an astral compass off the counter and bolted out the door, nearly squashing Qui underfoot. He wasn't sure where he was going exactly, but he was flying over the sand. Fortunately, Hitomi knew the way, and she was just as fast.

They arrived at the Farchild's homestead to find the roof had been blown clean off. "God damn it all!" cried Ex. "I just saved that girl!" A soft moaning was coming from inside the hut, and the two went in. They found Farah, clutching her side. Her face was drawn and pale, her eyes unfocused.

"Ex..." she panted. "He took Chimi... to the refinery. Said he'd kill her if you... weren't there by sundown. Please... please save her." Had the beam not cauterized the wound, Farah would have undoubtedly bled to death. As it was, her chances were grim. They would have to act fast if they wanted to save her.

"I will take Farah to the doctor immediately," said Hitomi, scooping up the injured woman in her thin arms. "Ex, do you know the route back to the facility? Tsubasa wishes to speak with you right away."

"Forget that," spat Ex. "I'm getting on that dune rover and going after the Talon!

"You won't go far without fuel," said Hitomi. "Go to Tsubasa."

Ex found Tsubasa standing at the front counter of his shop. In one hand he held the cloak Chimi had made for him, in the other a small bundle. His tired eyes were fixed on Ex. "Don't say a word, I'm linked to Hitomi through G-Pass. I see through her eyes and hear through her ears. I've prepared everything you'll need in this bag." He pulled the string on the canvas pouch and placed its contents on the counter. There was the etheramp, a vial full of enough plex to drive the rover around the planet, and one other simple device that Ex couldn't immediately identify. It looked like a top that could be spun right-side-up or up-side-down. The cylindrical body was made of grooved duril, and the whole thing fit comfortably in his palm.

"What's this third one?" he asked.

"Don't worry about it," said the old man. "There's no time to explain, just keep it with you." He handed the bag to Ex and began to put the items back in. The etheramp was last. "I see that you've procured an astral compass for yourself already. Good. So then you know that the only way to destroy that duril terror is with an anchor-round..."

"What's it matter to you? I thought you wanted me dead anyhow," said Ex.

"If the Talon kills you before you've activated the amp, this world is doomed," said Tsubasa. "And I don't actually want you dead. Even after you've tamed the whole of Trisol, I urge you to keep on living as long as you're able. But remember that there're fates worse than death..."

"Yeah, yeah, terrible torture and all that... I know. So why don't I just turn the damn thing on right now?"

"Go ahead and try," said Tsubasa.

Ex focused on the etheramp. His sinuses constricted, and he felt as if he had to burp or cough, but couldn't. "It's busted."

"It's not broken. It won't activate until it senses a flow of sufficient threadwidth. Then, the device is programmed to automatically channel that thread into every bit of wild duril on the planet and its orbit. You won't even have to focus on it."

Ex shook the orb like a broken snow globe. The gears inside wouldn't budge. "What if Issid gets it and tames the whole shebang himself?"

"He can't. The Talon can scarcely occupy his own body, even with his expansive threadwidth. In truth, I'm not sure an amp of this gauge can even be activated. It's more hope than theory. Now, get going! Every moment we spend here, Chimi is forced to endure the Talon's torment. I'm loath to imagine what that might be, but I won't be responsible for another second of it!"

On Worm's Wings

Ex arrived at the dune rover parked on the crater's ledge over Chimi's home, only to find that it had been completely destroyed. The tires were punctured and shredded, the chassis was half gone, and parts of the engine were scattered about the sand. "Issid, you bastard," said Ex.

There was a loud crunching sound inside the vehicle's remains. Ex approached with caution, and found the saboteur sitting in the front seat, snacking on the dash. "Kabuto?! What the hell did you do?"

Kabuto looked up, a stick shift poking out of the corner of his ample mouth. "Tasty," he snickered and skittered off. Ex gave chase. He followed him up a dune and rolled down the other side, sliding face-first into a jutting rock. He spat out some sand with a curse, and the ground shook. The rock erupted into the sky, followed by a towering worm. "Faster," said Kabuto, as the creature crashed onto the desert floor in a tan splash.

Chains of duril hung from the stony crest of the worm's head, and Ex knew what to do. He took the manacles at the end of the chains and fastened them to his wrists, and with a single tug, they were off like a comet across the dunes.

This mode of travel was best suited for a Trisolobyte, with their sage silver armor and insatiable appetite for crag and slag. Ex caught a mouthful of minerals before he managed to duck under the cover of the worm's plated head. He dug the etheramp out of the satchel and stared at it for a bit. The light was fleeting as the worm threaded through the dunes, but even underground, the tremendous heat it used to burrow emitted a red glow.

The ride was anything but smooth, yet the delicate gears inside the sphere remained perfectly still. He had no idea how to activate the damn thing. The old man had said something about flow of threadwidth, but that didn't mean much to him. He focused on the device, until the strain made him realized that he had a hangover and put the orb back in the bag.

Then it was just him and his thoughts; they proved poor company. He'd yet to see Issid in his new form, but perhaps what he imagined was worse. Horns and wings grew in his mind. The Talon's body stretched taller and taller. There were claws and fangs of shining silver everywhere, and in his shadow was Chimi, sitting on her ankles, knees sprawled in front of her, head bowed. She couldn't bear to look at the beast that Ex's fears had sculpted, or maybe he just didn't want her to look. This dusty little blonde mattered more to him than made sense, even if she had saved his life.

He forced his thoughts towards more practical concerns. Issid had given him a sound thrashing. Ex knew better than anyone that he'd been fortunate to have survived the encounter. He also knew that it would take more than luck and a loose tooth to survive their next meeting. As Trisol turned towards evening, the direction of downspin rose into the sky, peaking at dusk. It wouldn't begin its fall until night. He'd have to get beneath the Talon before squeezing off an anchor-round. It wasn't going to be easy, especially not if Issid was aware of his plan. That snake was too cunning not to know, but he was also crazy enough to forget it.

The worm came to an abrupt stop, and Ex unfastened the chains to have a look. A gaping chasm drew in ribbons of sand in slow breaths. Perlite flakes glistened in its fathomless depths. The Consortium's mining derrick stood on the other side of the abyss. Just a gnat from space, but from this distance it loomed like the skeleton of a mountain, creeping on five segmented legs. The main platform was suspended on massive spars that hung from the highest joint of these giant legs. At its center was the derrick itself, a black tower that plunged from the sand, through the platform, and into the evening sky.

The head of the tower rose at a speed that was almost too slow to notice. When its height had doubled, the primary piston struck. It'd taken the head several minutes to rise, but only an instant to fall. Seconds later, the shockwave stirred the dust at Ex's feet across the ravine, and a hum, too low for ears, the kind that only intestines could hear, reverberated across the ground. Cracks split the cliff's face, and masses of sand and stone the size of great hills plummeted into the depths below. This was the power of a heartdrill, a threaded behemoth capable of tapping into the very core of a planet in the search for duril.

The dust had yet to settle when the ground quaked anew. The tower rose again, but this time it was not just the head. The derrick's sand-encrusted joints filled the desert with haunting wails as its legs straightened, and the platform rose. The enormity of its size was hard to appreciate from a distance. A sinkhole formed beneath the tower as soon as it'd cleared the sand. The legs made huge strides across the desert, and the whole thing crawled like a thing three legs short of an enormous spider, following the vein of duril to where it was richest. Each step shook the desert with enough force to flatten nearby dunes.

The worm became restless, and Ex took the reins. It circled around to where the ravine was narrowest and flung itself across. The opposing bluff was too far to reach in a single leap, so they plunged into the abyss, flying at great speed towards the face of the opposing cliff. Ex braced himself beneath the worm's crest, but there was no impact. They dove straight into the rock as if it were vapor. When they resurfaced, the derrick was several kilometers away. The size of its legs made them look sluggish, but it was flying across the wastes. Still, the worm was swifter, and they chased the leviathan into the tawny horizon.

The derrick came to a stop, positioning itself over the location of its next strike. The process could take as long as an hour, during which it would remain stationary. Ex peeked over the worm's plating. The rushing air pushed his head back and made his eyes water. In a flash, they were at the foot of one the derrick's immense supports. It was even larger than Ex had imagined. Countless windows, hatches, and balconies dotted its weathered face. There were markings on the hull made by creatures and elements not of this world. It had strode across many planets and bored deep into each. He couldn't see the top of the leg from its base and shuddered to think that the CIR had dispatched a larger mining vessel to Trisol, one large enough to devour the planet in a matter of a few bites.

Ex stared up at an endless steel ladder. The moment his hand touched the first rung, a large gate opened on the side of the column, and a ramp pushed down into the sand. The worm dove back into the ground, and Ex found that he was still shackled to it.

Next thing he knew, they were on a dune a few hundred meters away, but he wasn't complaining. An entire battalion of Nyrceff had poured out of the gateway and began combing the sands. Ex looked down at his pistol. There simply weren't enough bullets in it for all these soldiers. Maybe if he could get beneath them somehow he could wipe out the lot of them with an anchor-round, but it was too risky with Chimi being held somewhere above.

The perlite flakes embedded in the sands of Trisol scrambled the Nyrceff's sensors, but it wasn't long before they spotted the giant worm coiled on the far dune. The front line dropped to the ground, and the entire battalion opened fire. Ex ducked back under his mount's shielded head, expecting the beast to dive into the sand, but it didn't budge. The photocaster bolts fell like soft rain on the worm's silver-veined skin.

The desert beneath the Nyrceff swelled. Thousands of Trisolobyte warriors erupted out of the sand and tore through the soldiers, scattering their ranks. They attacked from everywhere, skittering at great speed across the soft ground. There was no escape for the Nyrceff, and in seconds, none was left standing. The platform above was lined with glinting figures of more faceless soldiers. The hatches and windows along the pillar all opened, and gunfire hailed from the sky.

The CIR had made the photocaster rifle their weapon of choice because it was highly adaptable. Their photocells were capable of reaching the ultra-gamma frequencies, firing sustained energy at the speed of light for seconds at a time. It was enough to put a hole straight through the hull of a heavy cruiser, but not enough to put a scratch on armor made of living duril. The Trisolobytes flew up the column, flooding through the various portals, leaving trails of glowing red pockmarks in the metal as they climbed. They kept pouring out of the sand, swarming up the leg like a silver hurricane.

Ex could see the distant legs of the derrick being consumed as well. In a mere minute, the Trisolobytes had wrested control of the mining crawler's foundations. The Nyrceff had to work quickly if they were to even slow the attack. It was logical to try high frequency bolts first; their purpose was to pierce heavy armor, but they'd never even been tested against duril plating of this kind, since the very notion was laughable. Yet now they were engulfed by a storm of warriors clad in nothing less. The narrow beams bounced off the duril, slicing into the derrick's walls.

Low-frequency volleys proved far more effective. They didn't penetrate the armor, but the shockwaves were enough to fell the invaders as they wound up the legs. But the Trisolobytes weren't damaged by the bolts or the fall. Their backs hit the sand, and they clambered back to the points of their feet. With every shot, the photocaster cells were being depleted. Still the Trisolobytes streamed from their subterranean domain. Their numbers seemed endless, marshaled by a figure that strode tall in a sea of giants. The Dominant had taken the field, the runes on his armor glowing brightly in the derrick's shade. By his order, the warriors attacked the structural supports housed within the enormous legs. They were made of metal, many meters thick, but the Trisolobytes shredded through them with ease. The elements of this world were the most stubborn in the universe, and they'd made the natives strong. These off-world metals were weak and yielding. The derrick creaked and teetered as its legs began to buckle.

Kabuto appeared on the dune next to Ex and the worm, and not a moment too soon. "Kabuto!" cried Ex, over the din of the battle. "Tell this worm I gotta get in there!" Chimi was still somewhere in that overgrown drill bit, and it wasn't going to be standing for much longer at this rate. The little beetle sensed Ex's urgency and hissed up a fit, but the worm's orders had come from The Dominant. It wasn't about to disobey because some whelp had thrown a tantrum.

The first leg gave way. Several floors crumpled onto one another before the metal braced itself again. The platform tipped, and dozens of soldiers fell from the sky into the ravenous mass below. But the Trisolobytes would not have time to celebrate this minor victory. Wings of shadow stretched over the battlefield as Issid swooped out of the setting suns.

Right away, Ex knew it was the Talon. He centered him between the half-raised pistons of his gun, but the angles weren't right. The astral compass showed that downspin was pointed directly upwards, a few seconds off a perfect 90 degrees.

Issid shot across the battlefield. A violent wake followed several seconds behind him. The spiraling wall of wind and sand broke over the derrick, brushing the Trisolobytes from the buckling supports. They crashed down on their brethren below. This was not like falling into soft sand. They weren't as quick to their feet, but they'd yet to suffer a casualty. Even the warriors that'd been caught beneath the crushing weight of the leg as it folded had managed to burrow out to safety. Their duril shell made them impervious, but although they wore it as skin, it was still wild.

Issid came to hover just out of The Dominant's long reach. He saw these creatures as elementals of duril. "What hospitality! A host brings the planet's wealth to our very feet." The Talon's voice carried across the desert on a heavy wind, traveling faster than sound. Ex felt its weight on the distant dune; it was a struggle not to fall to one knee.

The entire mass of Trisolobytes turned to face Issid. He stretched out a hand, lighting arched inside his horn of etherite, and The Dominant began to convulse. The pauldrons on his giant shoulders cracked, and their light faded.

Piece by piece, the armor was rent from his body, coalescing in an orb just above Issid's palm. Despite the duril's appearance, the Talon could manipulate it as though it were entirely untamed. The sphere of sage silver took the shape of a long lance and he hurled it straight through The Dominant's bared chest in a flash. The giant collapsed to the sand.

The warriors scrambled on top of one another and flung themselves at the floating Talon. Their bladed appendages could pierce through stone, metal, and even carve into wild duril, but Issid's will inhabited every mote of metal that formed his twisted figure. It thwarted the Trisolobytes' fiercest attacks without suffering a scratch. He descended into their ranks, brushing aside a dozen Trisolobytes with his beating wings, and pulled the duril lance from The Dominant's fallen body. The spear whistled in the whipping wind, slicing and piercing through the warriors' ranks. Their armor was pressed close to their bodies, making it difficult for the Talon to manipulate, but he only needed to part it wide enough for the lance to find chitin.

Issid's body felt no fatigue. It was powered by the endless flow of will that surged through his ample thread. The heat that emanated from his horned corona cast the battlefield in a wavering mirage. He took to the air and cut swathes of the climbing invaders, weaving in and out of the derrick's shadow. Even at this terrible speed, he couldn't keep up with the Trisolobytes' sheer numbers. They burrowed into the facility's metal legs, away from the Talon's reach, devouring their supports like termites.

But the battle was being fought directly beneath a structure that was designed to siphon wild duril from the depths of a planet. The lower tip of the tower hung over the crawling mass. Normally, it had to be thrust deep underground to extract the duril, but with so much of it skittering about the surface, there was no need. The enormous mechanism came alive. Panels of metal shifted open, revealing a hotly glowing core. The piston atop the tower rose, and Ex knew what would happen next. He picked up the worm's reins and gave a tug. "Come on... come on... giddyap! We gotta get outta here, come on!" he urged, but the creature wouldn't budge. "Worthless!" he cried, unshackling himself from the worm and tumbling down the far side of the dune. The piston climbed without hurry. The resulting blast would engulf the surrounding desert for miles and knock on the upper realms of the Trisolobytes' cities.

As Ex fled the tower, his boots felt like they were full of sand — only partially because they actually were. He glanced back at its progress every couple of seconds. Only now did the Trisolobytes begin to react. They didn't understand how the mining facility worked, but they knew what it'd done to their planet. They scrambled away and many burrowed into the ground.

Issid flapped his silver wings in the light of the drilling beam's spherical focusing lens. His open vowels of laugh, clawed at Ex's back as he fled. Then the piston struck, and Ex dove to the ground, hugging his satchel and clutching his dearest pistol. A wave washed over him that made his hairs stand on end and stirred the gun in his hand, but it wasn't painful. It was followed by a blast of hot air and a wave of sand that buried him.

The mining facility's array of ethereal batteries had been imbued with hundreds of threads before it'd even landed on this world. Since then, the men of Himatma's threads had been added to its collection. Their combined threadwidth was enough to pull mountains of duril from Trisol's core. The piston system almost seemed unnecessary, but it was common practice to build up potential energy before a discharge with threaded devices of this nature. This allowed them to go beyond the limits that threadwidth imposed on the maximum rate of output. By storing the energy first, the output could easily be doubled or tripled, if only for an instant.

And an instant was all that was needed. In a flash, it had sheared the duril plating off the host of Trisolobyte warriors. The ones caught directly beneath the beam had been eradicated, as the duril was channeled through their bodies. This was the fate of every warrior up until the derrick's rim; from this point onward, the mining beam's effectiveness decreased at an exponential rate, and there were survivors. Whichever side they'd exposed to the light was stripped bare. The furthest Trisolobytes only lost scraps of armor – just enough for the Nyrceff to find their shots.

Ex was buried under an entire dune. The shockwave caused by the sudden shift of mass during the piston's strike had rearranged the desert. He could only tell which way was up by the crushing weight on top of him. After drawing a few lungfuls of sand, he managed to dig his way out.

Issid was still laughing. He'd flown over the derrick's platform to avoid the stream of duril that the beam had siphoned into the facility's banks. The blast had no effect on him; he'd tamed the whole of his body and no will could touch it, regardless of threadwidth or proximity. His sharp senses spotted Ex as he emerged from the sand, coughing and gasping for air.

Ex took quick inventory of his possessions. They were all intact. The blast hadn't reached the dune with much potency, or at least Ex's will was enough to repel it at this distance. He'd only just managed to get the grit out of his mouth when a fresh gust kicked up the sand around him and filled it anew. With a curse, he looked up and found Issid staring back at him with dull metal eyes, his sage silver body stretching five meters into the sky. Ex should've checked his compass. He should've aimed his gun. But he just sat there half-buried.

The Talon's lanky frame folded into a crouch, bringing his enormous etherite horn inches from Ex's face. "I was beginning to worry you wouldn't show," said Issid, taking Ex by the collar. He hoisted him out of the sand, and with two flaps of his wings, they soared into thinner atmosphere. The gun bobbled in Ex's hands. He dropped it, clanging into his knee as it fell towards the fleeing ground. Somehow, he managed to catch it between the tips of his boots.

When the air was getting too sparse to breathe, Issid turned his nose to the planet below and streaked back down to the derrick. They were heading straight for a small balcony that speared out of the tower, high above the main platform. Well, at least it looked small from a distance. In actuality it was quite vast, and there was Chimi, locked in a small cage that hung from the wall.

Let's Play a Game

Issid dropped Ex from a great height. He landed etheramp-first onto the balcony. The orb didn't crack, but Ex was pretty sure a few of his ribs had. Chimi cried out, but her voice was muffled in the wind. Ex wheezed for air; pain raked his side with every huff.

"Mr. Rey the Mystery," said Issid. "Well, we're going to solve this little riddle right now, one way or the other." He'd positioned himself directly between Ex and Chimi, making an anchor-shot impossible from this angle, regardless of spin direction. Ex picked up his gun and fumbled through his pockets for the compass. "I'll save you the trouble," said Issid, pointing at the sky. He was right; dowspin was almost directly overhead now, resting at somewhere between a 70 and 80 degree angle.

Ex would have to fire from beneath him. He briefly considered diving off the edge and blasting through the bottom of the balcony, but that wouldn't do. Even the smallest weight anchor-round would take Chimi along with it. As long as Issid didn't fly, he'd be safe.

Clack... clack... clack... the Talon stalked towards Ex. The fine sand that covered the platform seemed to flee from his footsteps. Metal worms squirmed through the rows of jagged teeth. Ex tried to stand, but his insides still felt a little soupy, and he got the impression that a few bones were not where they ought to be. Issid was less than compassionate. With the claws of his foot, he plucked Ex off the deck and brought him to his face. He crushed the pistol out of Ex's hand and flicked it towards the center of the sandy balcony with his longest toe. Next, he reached into the sack and pulled out the vial of plex. With a flick of his wrist, it whistled off into the blue. Then he took hold of the etheramp. "Now what in the stars do you plan to do with this, I wonder?"

Ex's mind raced for an answer that might prevent the amp from suffering the same fate as the vial. No such luck; Issid had already tossed it over the side. Ex watched helplessly as it shrank into a speck, clearing the derrick and plummeting to the desert below. The last object in the bag seemed to amuse Issid. "So, you've brought your own coffin," he laughed, twirling the spool around his long fingers.

Ex still didn't know that the object was in fact a spool, designed to capture and hold thread that'd been recently severed from the body by death, but if the talk was of funerals, he knew exactly what to say: "It's for you."

Issid was delighted. He put the spool back into Ex's bag and set him down. With a slow flap of his wings, he swam through the air and came to a stand over Ex's pistol in the middle of the balcony. "Let's play a game," he said.

The rules needn't be spoken; they were understood: grab the gun and fire an anchor-round or die. The question was: how? Ex had a notion, and not surprisingly, a rather ridiculous one. He couldn't put a scratch in duril, but perhaps it was light enough to move. One of sage silver's many desirable properties was that it weighed next to nothing, not because it wasn't dense, quite the contrary. It was uniquely dense. Where all other atoms were mostly empty space, duril was solid, and it was this subrostral solidity that prevented the bonds of gravity from properly taking hold, yielding immeasurable mass without weight.

Issid's new frame stood five meters tall, his wings spanned more than that distance, and a horn that could give a rhino a neck-ache sprung from his forehead, but he would be far lighter than his previous incarnation. Ex rose to his feet and readjusted his ribs with a stiff jerk. His eyes passed over Issid to Chimi's cage on the far wall. She grasped the bars, standing in sand made muddy by tears. He turned back to the Talon. "Let's play," he said and began his charge.

Issid happily watched Ex leap at him with both feet. And when Ex's heavy boots met with Issid's slender frame, it didn't budge an angstrom. A mountainside would've had more give. Ex scrambled up and threw a haymaker at the Talon's abdomen; it was as high as he could reach. He only succeeded in breaking his fist and giving Issid more reason to laugh. "You're a child trying to blow a star out like a birthday candle," said Issid. "I feel as if I should've brought you a party hat…"

Ex made a move for the gun, and Issid batted him away. The grace of the Talon's movements almost made them seem gentle. Ex's back crashed into the railing with a loud crack. He sat up right away, coughing up bits of what he assumed to be lung and bone. Issid may've been lighter than before, but it made no difference. He wasn't just standing on the sandy platform; his body occupied the space.

This really was a game to Issid, and one he couldn't lose. Ex tried again to recover his gun, but the result was the same. "You know what I like about you, Ex," began Issid. "Your resilience. I usually break all my other toys so quickly… though, I suppose I also owe you for this new body."

"They won't let you keep it," said Ex.

The ever-present smile vanished from Issid's face. His teeth folded in on one another to fit into the tight slit of his mouth. "And who's going to take it from me?"

"They'll send Extinguishers, a dozen if they need to. You won't stand a chance, but maybe I can help you…"

"Oh, Mr. Rey," said Issid. "I didn't know you played games of the mind as well. You little sneak." Loons though they were, a great portion of a Talon's training was devoted to safeguarding them against coercion. Ex was better off punching. Issid picked up the pistol and popped the clip. He thumbed out a couple of bullets, until he came to an anchor-round. Delicately clasping it with the tips of his claws, he held it aloft. "I'll make it clear. This… This is your only hope," he said and put the round into the chamber. He set the gun down and gave it a tiny kick in Ex's direction. It came to rest on the sandy floor, half way between them.

Ex flung his broken body into a desperate lunge. A solid mass of wind struck him in the chest and threw him backwards over the rails, leaving him dangling by one arm. Before he could pull himself up, the Talon's claws sunk into the flesh of his forearm and hurled him at the tower. He came to rest in a sad mass beneath Chimi's cage.

"Ex! Ex! Are you still alive?" cried Chimi.

"Barely," he said, struggling to stand again. The fingers of his right hand wouldn't respond. They were nearly submerged in a pool of blood that streamed from his forearm. The wound Issid's grip had left wasn't healing – at least, not like

Ex was used to. His vision began to blur, but he could see that the Talon now stood between him and his gun.

"Come now, Mr. Rey," said Issid, "you can't be giving out on me yet." He crouched down like a gargoyle and pointed at his horn. "How about we change the rules of the game to keep things exciting? If you manage to touch my etherite with your hand – I don't care which – I'll spare the little caged bird's life. But if you die before touching it, I will pull her apart one cell at a time and make whatever's left of you watch."

Ex looked down at his bloodied right hand. Most of the nerves had been severed, leaving him with an uncontrollable tremor. Each convulsion was accompanied by a squirt of blood. He'd have to do this with his left, and while Issid was crouched, or the horn would be out of his reach.

The wind blew against Ex as he walked forward. He leaned his body weight into it. One foot staggered in front of the other, just enough to keep him from falling on his face as he hobbled into a jog.

Issid remained perfectly statuesque until Ex swung his arm. Then he straightened out, and the hand passed millimeters beneath the rising horn. It wasn't very sportsmanlike of him to make it impossible for his opponent to touch the etherite, so he summoned a blast of wind to throw Ex into the air. But before Ex could stretch out his arm again, the Talon nodded and slammed the horn down on Ex's forehead. Something cracked, and it wasn't the etherite.

Ex hit the ground and lay still. "I touched it," he coughed.

"Has to be with your hand, you goofball!" said Issid.

High above the din of the battle below, the only sound the wind carried were the cries of the little girl in the cage. They collected in Ex's ears and welled up somewhere inside of him. He took hold of the Talon's leg and pulled himself up. His arm was mangled and peeled like a banana, but still he climbed.

Issid took to the air, and Ex clung to him, trying to get closer to the etherite even as they flew. Issid pointed his nose at the balcony and dove. At the last moment, he pulled up and whipped around his legs, slamming Ex onto the deck hard enough to shake Chimi's cage.

That should have ended the game, right then and there, but somehow Ex managed to stand again. "Come on, Ex! He's going to kill you if you don't stop fooling around!" cried Chimi. "Just beat him, Ex. I know you can!"

Where did her senseless faith in him come from? He told himself he hated it. He couldn't give her anything, couldn't even trade a few minutes of torture for her life. He looked up at her, wanted to say he was sorry, but the words didn't reach his mouth. The Talon was upon him, squeezing the life from his throat. He stretched an arm towards the horn, but it was out of reach.

Ex grabbed his mangled hand and pulled, twisted, trying to rip it from the elbow, so he could throw it at the horn. But he didn't have enough strength left in him to spit. The air over Trisol was growing cold in the evening, and the breeze blew straight through him. The suns rested on the horizon. Their golden rays stretched across the desert, but he couldn't feel their warmth. A metal finger entered Ex's mouth, rattling around his bloody teeth. "Come now. Where are your tricks? Can't we at least blow one of these up? You're boring me, Mr. Rey," said

Issid and skipped him like a stone across the balcony. The balustrade caught Ex's body, but a part of him continued to fall. It fell to a place where Chimi's cries couldn't reach.

And his greed for duril? And his hatred for Issid? And his will to fight? And his care for anything and everything? All these things he left on the balcony, and nothingness poured into his empty heart like black paint. He was back in the battle bubble, lights turned off, at a dead stop in the lightless void of the Upper Wastes. What had seemed so frightening in life, now embraced him as unconditional peace. But there was an image, maybe reflected on the glass, of a young girl in a cage.

He couldn't remember her name, and there was a red crack in the darkness, spewing self-loathing like magma. His weakness turned to tinder at his feet and flames of his guilt devoured him. They left his skin untouched, charring his nerves directly. All that made sense was pain.

A cool hand ran across the nape of his burning neck: a familiar caress. "Time to wake up Ex," said his mother's voice. The fire was gone. It was the morning of his thirteenth birthday again, and although she was already gone, Arius softly spoke these words into his young ears. Fire erupted from the face of the sun. Above, the stars were needle-eyes in black cotton. A shadowy serpent coiled around the flare. The column of pure light stretched into the stars. On and on it grew until the snake was pulled taut. Then there was a snap.

Ex's eyes shot open, and the darkness fled their gaze. His broken body leaned against the rails. And when every cell in his body shriveled painfully inwards, there was a pressure pushing back from the inside: an inextinguishable will.

He had no concept of how much time had elapsed, but Issid still stood over the pistol, only now turning to face him. Flesh wrapped tight around his arm. The bleeding stopped, his bones mended, and he was pulled to his feet as if by strings. Somewhere down below, in the sands of Trisol, the etheramp's gears began to spin, and the wind shifted.

The metal floor creased under Ex's feet as he launched himself forward. Issid awaited him with open wings. But Ex's plan was not a headlong charge; he slid to a stop in front of the Talon, kicking up a cloud of fine sand. A silhouette leapt from the dust, and Issid was upon it at once. "Too slow," he hissed.

Issid's claws struck true, but it was sunlight, not blood that sprung from the wounds. He'd torn holes through the fabric of Ex's cloak, worn only by the wind. In the shimmering veil of perlite below, he saw a pair of eyes like hurricanes. A fist of blue light crashed into his abdomen, and Issid was thrown into the air. Before he could unfurl his wings, Ex had scooped his pistol out of the sand and fired the chambered round.

"Cheater," said Issid.

A hole opened in the late evening sky, full of glimmering points. The edges trembled and blurred. For a fleeting instant, the image of the three suns wavered in the stream of mass that rushed to fill the wound in the atmosphere. They shimmered with color and were gone. The hole collapsed in a splash of blue and gold, and the sand charged up around the tower headed for the sky. A thunder

237 | Ring Runner: Derelict Dreams

that threatened to tear the tower in two hurled Ex over the railing. The bolts that fastened Chimi's cage burst apart, and the young Valarian was rendered unconscious.

Ex drew one long breath as he fell, released on impact. There was no bounce; the desert caught him with a muffled thud.

A World of Silver

Ex opened his eyes and saw sand, not in the sky, but on the ground where it belonged. He was high atop a dune, looking down on the mangled ruins of the derrick. If any ships had been docked on the platform, they were certainly destroyed.

The suns set in a blaze of rust and violet, bleeding through heavy clouds of rain the likes of which Trisol had not seen for centuries. The sky washed over the silent shells of thousands of fallen Trisolobytes and Nyrceff.

Ex pushed himself upright. His cloak had been draped over him like a blanket. He turned to find a few dozen Trisolobyte warriors, their armor scuffed and punctured. They had no words for him, at least none that he could understand, but they'd laid out a line of duril cylinders in the sand before him. Just beyond the line lay Chimi, her chest heaving softly as she rested, looking as sweet and innocent as when he'd first seen her in the cave.

A strange sensation tugged at the back of his mind. It began as an acute awareness of the Trisolobytes that stood before him. His thoughts drifted to the space between the warriors and wove around their battered armor, leaping across the gaps in the plating, tugging along strands of duril, and the armor was mended. The wholeness gave him comfort, and his consciousness became more adventurous, stretching towards the horizon in search of the setting stars.

He zagged a path across the dunes, sending waves that never crashed in either direction. And before he could think of a word to describe it, he'd spread across the entire world. From the deepest cavern to the highest mountaintop, he felt it all, comforting and reliable as time. He became aware of grand cities built in hollowed spheres, dotting the ley lines of Trisol like a string of beads. The metropolises were alive with joy, vibrating through the walls of their grand halls and chambers. He couldn't explain this awareness. It was the sort of knowing that only existed in dreams, growing foggy with open eyes and evaporating in the morning sunlight.

His body seemed tiny, frail, and insignificant, and it was perhaps this realization that reined in his wandering will. Quicker than they'd spread, Ex's thoughts collapsed back into the familiar shelter of his skull.

The Trisolobytes were knelt before him. The black strand that once wound around the pillar of his radiant thread had snapped. Unbridled, his will flooded the wild duril of Trisol, taming it in a flash of brilliance that blinded the Eye that watched from The Centower on Veredos.

Ex looked at the etheramp that rested in the sand beneath him. The sage silver gears were melted, but the orb that encased them had not broken. It was blackened from the inside. As he held the device, he found a memory trapped in the warped duril. He felt arms around him softly letting go. Their caress washed down his skin and lingered on his fingertips. He saw the face of his mother. Her lips moved, but there was no sound. *I never left you*, they seemed to say, and Ex stretched out to her, but his arms couldn't reach. The light of her eyes grew distant and with a glance to the heavens, dissolved into stars.

The duril batteries that lay before him carried the threads of the men of Himatma. Inactivity led to wanderlust; they'd need to be returned to their bodies soon. But more importantly, he had to get Chimi back to the village.

Ex opened the satchel. There was a soft glow inside. It was the spool that Tsubasa had given him. The etherite at either end shone as if reflecting light from a distant place. His mind passed into the little device only for a moment. It was occupied by something very bright. It regarded him questioningly, if not impatiently. Ex had no answers, and so he went back to gathering the batteries.

The flecks of duril peppered across the desert whispered to him. Something small was coming, pursued by something much larger and faster. Kabuto popped out of the sand. A worm emerged just seconds afterwards from the same spot, sending Kabuto flipping through the air.

"Kabuto, Chimi's hurt. We need to take her to the old woman," said Ex, helping the little bug off his back. The worm already knew the destination and the way. Ex put Chimi on his back and climbed onto the beast's back. With a lash of the sage silver reins, they were off.

The heat and sound that rushed around these worms in full stride had been overwhelming at first, but now it was almost comforting. Chimi rested peacefully in Ex's arms, her mouth slightly agape. Her right incisor was only starting to grow in.

The first time he saw her, between fever and a dream, he thought she was a cherub, come to save him from a lonely death in that cave. He'd saved her life twice since then. She owed him one, but it was unlikely she would get the chance to even up the score. He hoped that he could see her again, awake and vibrant as he remembered her, before he had to leave. Her breaths were coming short and shallow. He wondered how bad her internal injuries were, but took heart in the knowledge that Valarians were far more resilient than First Path Solarians. The shock of an anchor-blast was not easily shaken, but he was just fine, and he'd been just as close.

He looked down at his arm. Issid had turned it into a mangled mess of tendons and blood, dangling loosely from the bone, and yet now it was whole – as if it'd only been a nightmare. It was impressive regeneration, even by his high standards. He pushed fingers around his ribs. They all seemed to be in place, lined up and orderly, but he had no feeling, not in his arm or chest. His will animated his body, but it wasn't bound by it. His subconscious was spread across Trisol. The feeling of comfort and security he found in the duril was irresistible.

On a whim's wing, his mind glittered across the flakes of duril that were woven in the dunes and fluttering about the arid wind. His thoughts pooled in the crater of Himatma and rushed into the humble tunnels of the mine. Here the channels of duril were broken, severed without being cut. The mining beams couldn't cut through the silvery metal; they just washed away the stone. Callused hands still carried away the motes of duril that had been rent from their long rest. They still loaded small carts on magnetic rails, still worked their fingernails to bloody nubs in order to fulfill an absurd quota. Perhaps the workers had heard the thunder that'd parted the sky a few hundred kilometers away, but none of them had any way of knowing about the battle that'd unfolded or of its outcome. "They'll know soon enough," Ex thought and wondered what part of him had smiled. Was it the ore in the tunnel, the side of some distant mountain, or his own face?

But there was a place in the crater that had more duril than the caves from which it was mined. His focus turned to this, the largest structure in the town many times over. He knew at once it was Tsubasa's facility. Its metal frame was just as he remembered from his scans during the old man's tests. His mind passed from chamber to chamber. Even though he inhabited the very skeleton that held the place together, his perception was blurred. The perlite walls made it hard to see. Everything he saw was smudged and warped; only vague notions and unstable shapes bled through.

Curiosity led him through the winding corridors until he found a large room in which he'd never been. It was full of frozen life. At first he mistook it for the old man's meditation garden, but it was too cold. The frigid air penetrated the walls and clung to the duril frame. He remembered the stasis chamber in his old ship, and it was then that he guessed the chamber's purpose. Through faint mist, he could sense the bodies of the men of Himatma in frozen slumber. There were as many pods as he had cylinders in his satchel, in fact more. They still bore the Himatma's logo. Once they were used to prevent starfarers from aging during long trips; now they were containers for what must have seemed like an impossible hope.

He passed through the walls into a warehouse with an enormous object covered in a plastic tarp. It was the same form that had puzzled him before, and it puzzled him still. The entirety of its shell was made of duril, there for his taking, and he occupied it all. It seemed full of purpose, but not one he could decipher. Its insides were mostly sage silver as well, wrought with impenetrable intricacy that made the Trisolobytes' greatest sculptures look crude and aimless by comparison.

It was disorienting sensing oneself arrive. Ex had been so preoccupied with the exploration of Himatma from a distance that he didn't realize he was already at the ridge of its crater. The worm waited patiently for him to crawl off its back.

Kabuto went first. He hopped off the mount and slid down the cliff side. He was out of sight before Ex had even hit the sand. It was a bit harder for him to climb off the worm, carrying Chimi and the bag full of silvery souls. He'd taken no more than two steps before his legs buckled beneath him.

He brushed the sand out of Chimi's hair. It seemed to have lost all its luster. He looked inside the satchel to make sure that none of the cylinders had spilled out. Before, its jingling was light and resonant like the songs of Istreya's living wind chimes, but the bag was muffled now. Its sound was tinny and hollow, yet there were the cylinders, same as before, shimmering softly in the canvas. The stars were gone from the sky. Was it even night? Everything was awfully dim.

Ex draped Chimi over his shoulders and forced himself to his feet. He could scarcely manage to put one foot in front of the other. The world was spinning around him. Perhaps his injuries were more severe than they'd first seemed, or maybe scattering his mind across the planet was taking its toll. The will and energy that coursed through him on the tower had been reduced to a trickle. His body continued forward, but his thoughts sought refuge elsewhere.

There was no sound, but Ex saw Kabuto skittering up the slope, and Hitomi was not far behind. They neared him, or maybe he neared them. It was all happening so slowly, but still he held on, turning a deaf ear to the planet's whispers. "Have a rest," it said. "Forget your pain," it said. "It can be easy," it said.

Hitomi took Chimi and the satchel from his arms. His precious payload delivered, Ex crashed face first into the sand. He could resist the duril no longer, and it welcomed him like an old friend.

The Gate Reopened

Back in the Centower's diplomatic suite, Nodris delicately packed his medals into a brass box with three glass slits across the lid for viewing. "I'm just so tired of the Valarians being associated with us before Solarians," he said.

"How do you mean?" asked Kelmore's voice. His image was superimposed over the stars in the window. It was blue and bright in the absence of the Grand Forge's light.

The box closed with a click. "A Valarian Executor performs less than admirably somewhere out in the fourth stratum, and I get the reprimand."

"They summoned Viceroy Moddrick too, and he's Solarian. The rest are Sophian, so I don't know what more you could've expected."

"I'm not just talking about this one incident," added Nodris.

"Maybe it's cause their name begins with a 'V.' We should call them Solaraphim..."

"Don't be ridiculous," interrupted Nodris.

"It's not ridiculous. Try saying it... *Solaraphim*. See?"

Nodris repeated after Kelmore. "Hmm, you may have a point." The far wall chimed. "Excuse me, cousin; I have company." The image of Kelmore rose a bit, as if he were trying to look over his cousin's shoulder and, with a shake of his head, vanished.

"Come in," said Nodris. A doorway appeared in the white wall, and Zaralin stepped through. She was wrapped in a black dress that hugged her stomach and hips before flowing gracefully down her legs. The black choker around her neck was also part of the gown, attached to the top of her low-cut bust by a single band of fabric that ran diagonally across her chest. Her smoky eye shadow and jet-black lip-gloss matched her raven hair. But perhaps most striking were the charcoal bands striping the segments of her horns. Someone else must have painted them for her because the level of attention paid to every nook and the care with which every other segment was left unblemished was more than any number of mirrors could offer. Even so, Nodris had learned never to underestimate the level of craft a Sophian woman could achieve when refining her image; their memories provided eons of experience. A pair of black tassels hung from the ends of her curled horns, blending into the curls of her hair.

Nodris was momentarily enthralled. He'd never seen her in anything other than white or blue. His eyes were slow to travel down her figure, and he realized that she was barefoot. The Sophians had an ancient practice of going barefoot during moments of great lament, such as during funerals for one who'd passed without progeny, the events of their life forever lost. That kind of loss was bad enough for beings that experienced it commonly, but the pain was particularly sharp for a Sophian. Every species achieved a certain level of continuance through procreation; Sophians achieved immortality. They viewed their bodies as vessels through which any of their ancestors might live. Personalities from the past would often manifest in the present. A particular individual's memories, ideals, and dreams could gain volume in the mind of those who lived, shaping their character and guiding their actions. But the memories a Sophian created after their final parenting were not passed, and so a part of the collective race went with them. Nodris was uncertain how going without shoes had become part of the Sophians' mourning rituals, but he'd never found the appropriate moment to ask, and now didn't seem like the right time. Not knowing what else to say, he said the first thing that came to mind, which was: "Have you come to see me off?"

"Not exclusively," replied Zaralin. She'd caught Nodris in the middle of packing his bags. He was scheduled to board The Luciel, embarking on a voyage bound for the temples of Miraval. The trip only took about a week, but he hadn't visited his people's homeworld since childhood. All the maidens of the tower were privy to the schedules of every visiting dignitary, but Nodris hoped Zaralin took special interest in his.

"Should I be wearing purple?" he asked. This was his tactless way of asking why Zaralin was dressed in mourning. Traditionally, Valoraphim wore purple for a week after a loved one's passing, but he didn't believe in such superstition. Even as a child, when he'd received the news that his parents had passed, Nodris had made a conscious effort not to wear a trace of the color – not because he didn't want to honor their memory, but simply because he thought the tradition provided people with an easy way to express something that should be difficult.

The door closed behind Zaralin as she entered the room. She walked over to the luggage and surveyed its contents. "It doesn't appear you have any to wear," she said.

"I could always buy some," he replied. "Purple has never really been my color."

Zaralin's eyes went to the window. The satin choker around her neck was just tight enough to press into her soft skin. "I come bearing a message. It will explain why I walk with grief, and you may decide then how you wish to dress. There's been another incident on the planet of Trisol, far more serious than the first..."

"Worse than the loss of a Placator, dozens of lives, and a crateful of duril?"

"By some measure," said Zaralin. She read Zarfall's preliminary report. It said that the Talon and all 862 of the remaining Nyrceff had been killed. There were no injured. No survivors. Few details were offered beyond the involvement of native sentients that armored themselves in duril and the use of one more anchor round. Most importantly, the report confirmed that The Flooded Gate had reopened and tamed all of Trisol's duril, rendering it entirely unworkable without his willful consent.

Nodris didn't know or care much about the practices of taming duril. The mysterious Claviger tamed all the sage silver he encountered in his everyday life. Even the anchor-drive of the Luciel, which belonged to the Royal Gincleare Family, called The Claviger its master. It didn't bother him one bit. In his mind, the safety this arrangement yielded was worth whatever freedom it cost. If a pirate wanted to take the duril out of their ship, they'd have to do it by hand, either that or raid Veredos first.

But any laymen knew that taming duril required threadwidth and lots of it. Maybe it was due to the metal's rarity, but Issid's body was the largest mass of tamed sage silver Nodris had ever known. He remembered being quite impressed when he heard the news. He'd expect that level of power from an Extinguisher, but for a Talon, it was quite remarkable. Trying to visualize the amount of duril that Trisol was estimated to contain proved difficult, but imagining how anyone had the threadwidth to tame it all at once was impossible.

Nodris was beginning to see why The Flooded Gate phenomenon was so feared by the CIR. They were going to have a lot of trouble trying to keep it under wraps now. Perhaps this was why Zaralin had been dispatched to inform him.

"As with all matters dealing with Trisol, this information is currently classified and not to be discussed in a public venue," Zaralin said out of protocol. "We don't expect to be able to contain this news for long, but an official statement is being prepared."

"Is this Flooded Gate's threadwidth the same as the last?" asked Nodris.

"Its ethereal imprint is identical, but the threadwidth is immeasurable by conventional means," replied Zaralin.

"Enough to tame an entire planet at least," Nodris added.

"Other than the taming itself," Zaralin continued, "there have been no truly remarkable feats of ethereal manipulation reported. The rogue Sage who is believed to be the focal point of The Gate is the son of the woman who previously bore the label: Arius Merl Rey. Whether she was ever the source of the phenomenon, or if it was the child all along is as of yet unknown. One thing is certain: the CIR will have to make an adjustment to the bounty placed on his head. The Capstone is currently weighing the value of the duril that would be forever lost if the Sage were killed before *relinquishing*, against the threat he poses to the universe if left alive."

"Both the duril's value and the threat presented seem incalculable," Nodris thought aloud. "But I'm not sure a bounty's going to make much of a difference. Who's going to be able to stop a Sage with that kind of threadwidth?"

"Fleet Admiral Dethoron has been recalled to Veredos for an immediate report," said Zaralin. "He was the one responsible for sealing the first Gate, or so the records maintain."

"He's coming back to Veredos? Glad I'm not going to be here when he shows up. I doubt he's going to be happy..."

"Your concern is noted, Viceroy, but his training as an Extinguisher will prevent him from acting upon such humors. You will be quite safe, even if you were to remain here in The Centower."

"Of course," said Nodris. Explaining to her that he'd only been joking was not practical at this point. He found this whole situation exciting, interesting, if not somewhat entertaining. Seeing how The Capstone and his court would posture in order to deal with this dilemma should prove amusing, but Zaralin was part of that court, and the only part whose worry he also felt. "So then the task will fall upon The Fleet Admiral's competent shoulders? Well if anyone can deal with this phenomenon, it would certainly be him."

"That is the hope," said Zaralin. For a moment, the look in her eyes was like the other maidens, but their softness returned in a blink. She took a pair of his underwear and placed it gently in the suitcase.

"Were you also sent to help me pack?"

"It wasn't part of my assignment," she replied and continued folding.

Nodris was happy to see Zaralin once more before he left for Miraval, barefoot or otherwise. But when he thought of the Nyrceff and The Talon, he felt no empathy. They were soldiers. What of the hundreds of Libralma, whose very threads had been torn from their bodies and enslaved in order to power the mining beam? No one in The Centower had gone barefoot for them. For a moment, he resented Zaralin's hypocrisy, but she only wore what she was instructed to wear. "What else do we know about this sage?" he asked.

"His given name is Exterrus, normally shortened to 'Ex.' He is the son of Arius Merl Rey and Exterrus Mortagon Solipso, third and first apprentice to Master Sage Julius Mavenbolt..."

"Solipso? You mean to say that he's the grandson of Algray Solipso? That's quite a lineage," marveled Nodris. Algray Solipso was the first non-Sophian Sage in recorded history. How he'd come to acquire a corona persisted as one of the universe's greatest mysteries to this day. It appeared that mysteries ran in the family.

"Indeed it is," said Zaralin. "Yet it can't begin to account for the phenomenon of The Flooded Gate."

The parents and grandfather were amongst the most gifted Sages the universe had ever known, but threadwidth had never been proven to be hereditary. Even so, you could've combined their threads and multiplied their width a million times without equaling The Flooded Gate. "What of his corona? Was one ever detected?"

"No. However, our records show the use of an etheramp, just as The Gate opened."

"What was its purpose?"

"It ran a basic taming macro. Any conclusion made at this point would be premature, but one can only suspect that The Gate was not familiar with the process of taming. And since that is one of the most basic skills a Sage can learn, it suggests that perhaps The Gate is not trained."

"Hard to believe that the son of two of Mavenbolt's disciples wouldn't be trained in the ways of The Theory," Nodris remarked.

"Very little of this phenomenon seems to make much sense," said Zaralin.

The last of The Viceroy's belongings were packed. "My ship departs in under an hour," he said, and she remained silent. He waited for her to say something, anything. "The voyage to Miraval usually takes about a third of a sidereal month, depending on the space debris at the drop points," he added. "But I'm not sure if I'll be coming back to Veredos."

Zaralin's lips parted.

"Why am I going?" Nodris spoke for her.

Her lips closed again, and she had to avert her eyes. "A Viceroy's place is here on Veredos," she said softly.

"Are you trying to say you'll miss me?" he asked. He couldn't expect her to reply, and sharing the reasons for his trip with a maiden of the tower didn't sit well in his stomach, but this was Zaralin. "There's something I must ask... no, demand of the elders on Miraval. It's a question that has festered in the back of my mind since childhood and has started growing horns in my dreams." He almost felt silly bringing it up after discussing The Flooded Gate. His concerns with the Valarians, The Dormant, and the history of his race seemed trivial compared to this new development, yet his resolve was unwavering. He felt himself being pulled home by the augur gland.

"Perhaps you could find what you're looking for here on Veredos," she said. A tinge of emotion in her words betrayed her calm expression, making clear that this was more than a casual suggestion. Zaralin caught herself and added, "There are very few facts, historic or scientific, which cannot be found in the libraries of The Centower."

"You're right. But unfortunately, this happens to be one of them. Only my kinsman on Miraval can answer these questions. And so I must go, though I wish you'd come with me," he added. He knew that only a direct command from The Capstone could open The Centower's doors for her. It wasn't entirely unheard of, but only a handful of maidens had ever been permitted exit, and even fewer still had been off the spinning faces of Veredos. "Tell them you're off to improve Sophian-Valoraphim relations, and we'll hop on The Luciel," he said, trying to play his suggestion off as a joke.

Valoraphim could withstand the freezing temperatures of space, but Nodris felt the need for a sweater in Zaralin's stare. "Nevermind," he sighed and turned to the table. There sat a vase full of flowers imported from the ruins of Miraval: ten icy-blue blossoms on long, deep green stems, free of thorns and full of a light fragrance. He judged them on a wide range of criteria. With the one he deemed best in hand, he approached Zaralin, who had not moved. "Do you know this flower?" he asked.

"I am familiar with the species," she replied. "They were brought to your room at my behest."

"The Solarians call it the Blue Amaranth, and my people call it The Child's Eye." He tied the pliable stem around the strap of her dress as he spoke. "It was crafted by one of the finest botanical geneticists in the long history of the Valoraphim, cultivated to perfection in the royal gardens of Miraval before the world was torn asunder. Of all the flowers that grew there, only the Blue Amaranths remain, standing proudly on fragments and asteroids without names. This bloom requires no water or sunlight. Its undying petals will never wither or fade. The void of space cannot touch it, and fire cannot burn it. Keep it close to your heart, as I hold your memory, and let its soft scent remind you of me."

"Sophians do not forget," said Zaralin.

"Then simply wear it to indulge me."

Zaralin's eyes were fixed on the Blue Amaranth, her graceful nose taking in large drafts of the fragrant air. "It's the same shade as your eyes," she said.

"The dreaming eyes of a child, longing in innocence for something impossible," he replied and took his luggage.

What of the man who saved us?

Time had not passed for the men of Himatma. They awoke into their bodies, groggy and colder than anyone should ever be on a planet with three stars, but completely unaware of the slumber their husks had endured or the drill their souls had powered. Many of them went so far as to ask whether or not Sheremy's deal had been honored.

The women were not as fortunate. Every excruciating moment was written on their flesh and fingernails. The men were shocked to find their wives had aged years in months. All they could do was apologize for their misled chivalry. It should've been them laboring in the mines, and their wives resting in the air-conditioned cocoons. But when the agreement had been made, the men thought they were resigning themselves to death. In their wildest dreams they could not validate the hope of being saved, yet here they were again, bones and blood dressed in flesh.

Their families were full of hugs and happiness, but most of the men seemed as cold as their skin. It was hard to feel the thrill of being reunited with their loved ones if they felt as though they'd never left. Their bodies had formed no memories without their threads. Reality and warmth were slow to sink in. Then they all had one question: how?

"You should instead be asking: *who*," Tsubasa told them, pointing at Ex who lay on his back, arms crossed, entirely still. Naturally, their next question was to ask *who* the hell he was.

"A hero!" piped Chimi. She was swaddled in bandages that she didn't appear to need.

Qui had regained most of her size through diligent consumption. She could've easily reached her target weight if proper nutrition wasn't so hard to come by on this planet. The old man might've helped too if he hadn't cleaned out his stock throwing that indulgent feast. She stood next to Tsubasa, whispering in his ear: "I still can't believe it. This selfless sacrifice seems so out of his character. A complete 180..."

"He didn't really change," said Tsubasa. "There was always good in him, even if he tried his damndest to hide it."

"Why would he?" asked Qui.

"Ever met a runner with a soft heart?" replied Tsubasa.

"Not really. I doubt they'd last very long."

"There you have it." Tsubasa brushed some of the younger men aside with his cane and came to stand over Ex. The people of Himatma crowded around him. He asked that Chimi be allowed to pass, and she plopped herself down at the foot of the bed.

"Is he dead?" asked a little boy.

"No!" said Chimi. "What a stupid question."

"Amazingly not," added Tsubasa. "The amount of Will that's been channeled through his body should've been enough to burn a star up from the inside." He was referring to an exceedingly rare phenomenon known as threadburn. There were limits on how much threadwidth could pass through a body at any given instant in time, but the threshold was so high that it wasn't really a consideration. The only records of threadburn came from laboratory tests in which many threads were intertwined and passed through a single focal point. But even in these extreme cases, the threadwidth channeled could not equal a fraction of what had poured through Ex. "In an electron's orbit, he tamed all of this world's duril. That alone should've killed him many times over, to say nothing of the battle he must've endured beforehand. He braved an army of The Consortium's best men and slew a Talon made entirely of sage silver..."

"A Talon made of duril?" one of the men interrupted. "And this guy beat it? How's that possible?"

"He shot him with his gun," said Chimi, mimicking the motion. "Bang! And a hole opened in the sky." This all sounded like one of the tall tales from ancient earth that the old man was fond of telling, but it was hard to argue when you'd just be resurrected against all reason.

"An anchor-round," Tsubasa clarified. "But, for the time being, we shouldn't concern ourselves with what has happened. Our focus should be on deciding what to do with the man who saved us."

"Throw him a parade?" a boy suggested, and Chimi agreed.

A smile crossed the old man's mouth, but his eyes didn't brighten. "I'm afraid there will be no parties or parades, not that the man you see before you doesn't deserve such accolades or that our good fortune doesn't merit festivities, but all of this planet's sage silver has been tamed. If the CIR should capture this man and force his relinquishment, then all of Trisol will surely be consumed.

Now is not the time for a history lesson, but I will remind you all that only a handful of Sages were ever broken by torture during The Extinguishing. The vast majority of relinquished duril was taken by ransom. Every desire in our hearts may be to repay the kindness and sacrifice of our savior, but if he stays in Himatma, we would only be a liability to him, and he our certain doom. The Extinguishers won't be long, and if they cannot break him, they will assuredly break us."

Everyone was dead silent, but if there could be measures of greater silence, then Chimi was by far the quietest.

"So what are we supposed to do? Just send him off into the desert?" asked one of the men. "How do we know the CIR won't try to hold us as ransom anyway?"

"We don't," replied Tsubasa. "But I've worked with The Consortium for many centuries, and it took me that long to understand how a Sophian thinks. Imagine yourself born with the attachments and history of a thousand lives. How long would it take you to care for someone you've only just met? The Sophians won't begin to guess that a ring runner that just blew in from the wilds of space would care about a bunch of dusty old miners like us. The realization is sadly beyond them. They will instead believe he has acted entirely selfishly, laying claim to riches that are so valuable, they have no worth at all. And it will be this impression of a man that they'll seek in the desert. But if he were to stay here, his allegiances would be made plain enough for even a Sophian to see.

Of course, there's no guarantee they won't gamble on our ransom. It's a cheap bet for them to make. They could dispatch a single squad of Nyrceff and have us all in chains by the morning. Or worse, we might be sent a Talon, and then God knows what sort of pain we'd have to endure.

There is, however, another option," the old man paused, staring for a moment at Chimi, who sat thoughtfully at foot of the examination room table, nestled between Ex's big boots. He couldn't hold his eyes on her for long. "As long as Ex lives, this threat will loom over Himatma like a black hand, ready to swat at any moment, and we'll never truly have peace. But should he pass from the living with the duril still in his hold, it will be sealed beyond The Consortium's grasp, leaving us to live peacefully in this dusty crater until the dredge of time comes to call." The words were as difficult for him to say as they were for Chimi to hear.

"So we're left with two choices: to kill the man who saved us, making permanent what he's accomplished, or to set him free and perhaps undo his sacrifice." Tsubasa let the villagers ponder the implications of his stark words. "It isn't a decision made lightly, but one that should be made as soon as we're able. Every moment he spends in Himatma increases the chance that the CIR will suspect the significance of our involvement."

A murmur broke out through the crowd. Tsubasa had to raise his voice to speak over the crescendo. "Gentlemen, you will find the cylinders that so recently held your thread in the pocket of your coats, the very prisons from which this man has liberated you. If you believe that the best way to honor him would be to finish what he's begun by taking his life as he rests, place your cylinder in this black basket. If you think he would be best honored by damning him to a short life of persecution and likely torture at the hands of an Extinguisher at the risk of our own security, place your cylinder in the white basket. Discuss this with your families and cast your votes."

"And what if he won't leave?" asked one of the men. "Who's going to force him?"

No one had a response.

The empty duril batteries weighed a ton in the men's hands. There were no arguments, only quiet discourse. Most of the men deferred to their wives' judgment; after all, they'd actually met the man. But Chimi, who was one of the few without a father or brother, walked over to the baskets Tsubasa had place on the counter and stacked the white basket inside the black. "Don't I get a vote?" she said.

Tsubasa smiled and set the two baskets apart. "Chimi, I don't need to see your vote to know your heart."

"Then you know if they wanna kill him, they're gonna have to kill me first," she said.

"Trust in your neighbors and friends. They won't disappoint. I promise. Just you watch," he told her.

The men of the village formed a line in front of the baskets, duril in hand. The old man had made it perfectly clear that it would be much easier for both Himatma and Ex if they took his life as he slept. But the Libralma hadn't gotten to where they were by walking the easier path. Above all else, they held a challenge sacred. So it wasn't the gratitude they felt, or the concern for the safety of their own homes that swayed their vote. It was the prospect of the monumental challenges that lay ahead for Ex, should he insist on living. His thread would come to know tribulations never before experienced. They couldn't in good conscious deny such a unique opportunity to such a unique thread. Their beliefs didn't include any messiahs, prophets, or miracles, but the value Ex held for them could be labeled as nothing less than holy.

The first man cast his cylinder into the white basket, bidding Ex to live. The second did the same, and the third, and fourth. Chimi watched with eyes full of tears as the white basket was filled, and the black basket went empty.

When the last of the men had casted his vote, Tsubasa collected the baskets and said with a laugh: "Then we'll do it the hard way."

The Luciel

Nodris stood on the observation deck of The Centower's spaceport. It was small, by spaceport standards, with only a couple of docks, but it wasn't short on luxury. It offered a magnificent view of the The Walking Waterfall as it flowed from The Statue of Soheren. The light of The Grand Forge painted a faint rainbow in the mist that swirled above the fountain's outstretched hands. "It's quite a shame," Nodris thought, "that only the Engryas and visiting dignitaries be privy to such a magnificent sight."

The Luciel came through the spray, its gilded wings scattering the light like golden lightning. The enormous wings had nothing to do with atmospheric travel. They swept upwards, pressed against the hull, giving the ship a swan-like appearance. Every Royal Ship in the Valoraphim's fleet had wings like these, but The Luciel's were special. They had been crafted from the ruins of the original Gincleare Palace, a few short decades after the sundering of Miraval. He was intimately familiar with every groove and fold of their sculpted feathers. Many days of his youth were spent playing in gardens, bathed in the light they'd reflected from countless stars.

In a way, The Luciel was the closest thing Nodris had ever known to a home. The sight of it refreshed his spirit. It was almost enough to take his mind off Zaralin and all the foolish things he'd said to her. His entire lifetime had been devoted to the pursuit of diplomacy, but all the long hours of lessons and negotiated treaties had melted away with one glance of her in that dress. Her porcelain white skin pressed by the deep black satin filled his mind with visions of lonely stars in a clear night sky.

And then there she was, standing patiently on the pier where The Luciel was making port. She wore an elegant smock that flowed in gentle ruffles from its raised shoulders, slate gray to match her eyes. It was tight as a corset across her chest and midriff, hugging her hips before fanning out into an ankle-length dress. The collar was high and rigid with an open neck, imposing proper posture on the wearer. Just beneath the gentle "V" of her Sophian collarbone, a silver broach fastened a cape made from the same fabric as her dress, lined with sigils in lilac and cream. Only the tips of her polished black boots were visible, glinting in the shade of the dress.

Nodris rubbed his eyes, fearing that he was losing the ability to distinguish between reality and the apparitions of his Valoraphim sight or childish fantasies, but her image remained. The wide, fathomless pupils of her eyes followed him as he approached. "Are you prepared for the journey, Viceroy?" she asked.

"I am," he replied. "Have you come to see me off?"

"No." She let her response linger long enough for Nodris to consider a hundred implications. "I am to accompany you."

"To Miraval?"

"If that is still your destination."

"It is," he said, noticing for the first time the three large pieces of luggage that shared the pier with Zaralin. The Blue Amaranth he'd given her was wrapped around the handle of the tallest. The walls of the walkway were made of glass, casting the bloom against a field of stars, as it would've appeared on the ruins of Miraval.

Nodris heard the sound of the manifold exchange clamping down on The Luciel's starboard entryway, but his eyes remained on Zaralin. The docking doors opened, and he was greeted by three Valoraphim servants, sent to help him with his luggage. He should've been the one to carry Zaralin's bags, but he ordered one of the servants to do it instead and another to bring his along. The third, he pulled aside and instructed to prepare their finest chamber for their Sophian guest. In particular, he was concerned with the bed. Any mattress that worked for a Valoraph or Solarian should work for a Sophian, but in place of a pillow, Sophians required a hard metal board, typically wrapped in a thin layer of cork. They slept on their backs, which meant their curled horns would keep their heads suspended in midair. By the time he'd finished explaining all this to the nodding servant, Zaralin had already boarded.

The servants led him to his room. It wasn't the largest or most luxurious that The Luciel had to offer, modest when compared to his accommodations in The Centower, but this'd been his room throughout childhood; sleeping elsewhere on the ship didn't seem right. The bed was bigger, the toys had given way to books and decorations, but otherwise it was the same. The smell hadn't changed. The air that blew into this room first passed through the fragrant flowerbeds that lined the parks in which he once played.

He resolved to pick a bouquet before heading for Zaralin's room, so her chambers would smell as nice as his. Maybe some of the scent would find its way into her clothes. The thought of it made him giddy. He almost pranced his way to the park, but thought better of it. "A Viceroy should not prance," he told himself and settled for a hurried walk.

The gardener gave him the evil eye. If anyone other than Nodris would've plucked her flowers, she might have clipped his fingers. But it was The Prince, Viceroy, and Captain of The Luciel who dug up her flowerbed, so her shears minded the bushes. "I'll need a pot for these," he had the audacity to say, and she'd no choice but to comply with a curtsy.

The first few she presented to him weren't up to his high standards. In the end, he settled for a broad, ornate vase filled with dirt, previously used as a decorative end-piece on the low walls of the royal flowerbed. No doubt that the groundskeeper would have to go through some trouble to replace it, but it was well worth the effort in Nodris' mind.

Potted flowers in hand, Nodris marched up to the first crewmember he saw and asked where Zaralin had been quartered – as if memorizing the registry was this poor fellow's only task. "I will find out for you immediately, Sir," he saluted. After frantically flagging down a few crewmates, he was able to guide The Viceroy to Zaralin's chambers.

Her room was situated on one of the highest points of The Luciel's forward section. The corridor that led there was lined with windows that peeked over the ship's rising wings. It offered a view of shining Veredos, slowly shrinking in their wake.

"Thank you," said Nodris, as if to dismiss the crewman. His intentions weren't lost on the young Valoraph, and he excused himself with a bow.

Nodris gathered breath and courage at Zaralin's doorstep. There were a hundred questions he should have asked her, like what exactly her assignment was, or why The Capstone had chosen her to accompany him, but when he saw her standing in the doorway, his heart sang a prelude to heartbreak.

She accepted his gift of flowers and set them as the centerpiece of the round table that sat directly in the middle of her foyer. They looked ethereal in the soft starlight that flowed through the ring of windows high on the cupola. It'd taken thousands of years for Valoraphim engineers to craft such perfection, and yet they were found wanting in the company of Zaralin's graceful features.

"I feel like I'm stealing you away," said Nodris. Zaralin replied with a faint smile as she arranged the flowers to her liking. "Is this your first time out of the tower?" he asked. "Why don't we go to the observation deck, so we can watch our departure from Veredos?"

"This is my first time out of The Centower, but I have the memories of every Sophian explorer since the 138th Rebuilding of the Soheren Pyramid," she replied. "I have many memories of leaving Veredos for the first time."

"Of course," said Nodris, "forgive me. It's not that I forget about Sophian memory, but it can be hard to keep in mind."

"Understandable," she said, turning her attention back to the bouquet. "I don't have many memories of Valoraphim horticulture. Only a single Sophian has ever been devoted to its study – not enough experiences to cross-reference. So you will have to forgive me if I err."

"Consider yourself forgiven," he smiled.

She delicately touched the flowers one by one, reciting their names: "Feather Reed, Lorlock, Corolian, Duskwhite, and, my favorite of the selection, Sagecrown, whose masterful form is perhaps only surpassed by the Blue Amaranth."

"It seems you're the one that's going to have to forgive me," said Nodris, "because it appears that you didn't need my forgiveness at all. You've named every flower correctly."

"Better to receive forgiveness you never needed, than to need forgiveness you never received," she said, tying a couple of stems together. "You know, ancient Solarians practiced the art of flower arranging. In the times long before the Grovekeepers of Istreya, it was called *ikebana*."

"You certainly know your universal history."

Her cheeks raised slightly, and there was something almost like mischief in her eyes. "History is my specialty," she said.

For a moment, Nodris considered the possibility that this was an attempt at humor. "Yes, well I suppose it would be…" He was interrupted by a voice on the intercom. *Captain Gincleare, your presence is required on the bridge, Sir. The Luciel is entering preparations to drop into anchorspace. Your authorization will be required.* He hated to leave Zaralin so soon, but reminded himself this wasn't a pleasure cruise. He had his duties. "I'm on my way," he replied and promised to give Zaralin a proper tour of the vessel upon his return.

It was standard operating procedure, straight out of the manual, for the captain to approve the anchorspace course before dropping, even if it was through a well-travel anchorway. Exceptions should only be made in times of emergency. Nodris found the whole custom a bit antiquated. The safety precautions and drop charts available today had turned anchorspace travel into child's play.

The speed at this distance from the Prime Axis was only a few million times faster than light. It was still the fastest known method of travel, but it seemed practically stationary when compared to the speed you could achieve out past the Seventh Ring. Nodris had never been there; he wasn't much of a traveler and had his misgivings about anchorspace travel. A collision at the speed of the Seventh Ring could wipe out a cluster of galaxies, but even circling around The Grand Forge any impact suffered would destroy the ship and Zaralin along with it. If nothing else, the Valoraphim Navy's tradition would give him a little peace of mind.

Nodris stepped onto the bridge. It was bright and spacious. The panels were made of varnished Istreyan pine, lined with Torquish ivory. The controls and interfaces to the ship were made to mimic the ancient seafaring ships of Miraval when possible. Five wide monitors surrounded the bridge, built to look like windows, a well balanced blend of luxury and functionality. The guard stationed at the doorway snapped to attention. "Captain on deck!"

Kelmore rose from the captain's chair. "Forgot your way to your own bridge?" His wings were folded beneath a cape, as was the custom for royals during space travel.

"Kelmore?" Nodris began. "I thought you were staying on Veredos as a liaison."

"I'd rather jump straight into The Grand Forge," said Kelmore.

"Well if you're here," continued Nodris, "then why do I have to look over the charts? I was just about to give Zaralin a tour of the ship..."

"Zaralin?" said Kelmore. "You mean that Maiden of the Tower that's been sent to spy on us?"

"She's no spy," chuckled Nodris.

"How can you be so certain?" asked Kelmore.

"If the Consortium wanted to spy on us, don't you think they'd send someone a bit less conspicuous? Why would they send a Maiden?"

"Maybe because they knew you wouldn't question it," suggested Kelmore, and Nodris couldn't easily dismiss the possibility.

"Don't worry, cousin. I can vouch for her," said Nodris.

"Oh yeah? And who's gonna vouch for you?" smirked Kelmore.

"Be serious."

"You may find that The Elders don't give your word the weight it deserves, but you'll have my support... even though I think you've got horns on the brain."

"Sir, The Luciel is on standby for the Veridian Channel. Waiting on your authorization to make the drop," said the helmsman.

"I still don't see why I have to do this," said Nodris.

"It goes by birthright, not wing span, so that means you're in charge," Kelmore replied.

"That's the price one pays for being a prince, I suppose," sighed Nodris.

Kelmore gave Nodris his seat. "Woe be you."

The ship sat at the edge of the Soheren system, only a few minutes away from port in Veredos by conventional engine, but a single instant in anchorspace meant the Sophian homeworld would be a minimum of two days away – not by turning around and flying upspin either, that would take years, but by completing a single revolution around the Prime Axis. Nodris was more concerned with shoving Kelmore out of his light than looking over the course of the drop. This was probably the most well-traveled channel outside of a ring. There was really nothing much to check.

"Drop approved, put us in queue for the channel, Ensign," said Nodris. "And be swift of it. I'm eager to see my old home."

"Yes, sir." The helmsman seemed pleased to see that Nodris could act like an actual captain, should it be required. There was no way to go faster in anchorspace, but getting into the channel was another matter. Vessels entered no closer than 38 seconds apart, enough time for the slowest engines allowed by law to clear the anchorway after arrival. The Veridian Channel had multiple off-ramps, and the traffic was consistently heavy, which made it difficult to enter somewhere down the line, but at the mouth, just beyond Veredos, the wait was typically under half an hour. This, however, was The Viceroy's ship. The helmsman was sure to emphasize the official nature of The Luciel's journey in his communiqué with the control tower. The message was relayed by Gemini-Wave, arriving instantly, and the response was almost as fast. They'd been moved to the head of the queue, and cleared to drop in 42 seconds.

Warning lights flashed around the corridors and in every chamber of the ship. They were accompanied by a slow steady tolling of a bell, warning the crew of the immanent drop into anchorspace. The last ten seconds were counted down over the intercom, and The Luciel entered the channel. The screens on the bridge all went black, as if they'd suddenly lost power. Flukes of white and blue appeared in the port and starboard viewers, growing in intensity and numbers, creeping into the center screens until the entire bridge was awash in their light. For the sake of the crew's comfort, the screens dimmed as they entered their lengthy trip through anchorspace. But by that time Nodris was already half way to Zaralin's room.

Ex-odus

Ex opened his eyes to Chimi's grinning face. It didn't surprise him in the least – except maybe that it was cleaner than he expected. A happy red bow crowned her hair. "Good news, Ex," she said. "We've decided not to kill you!"

"Good," Ex groaned, too groggy to acknowledge the dozens of eyes that surrounded him. Chimi handed him a glass of water. He took a whiff. "This didn't come outta Kabuto's mouth, did it?"

"No," she giggled.

Ex swallowed it down with a grimace. "You sure? Cause it tastes like it did." He'd had whisky that went down smoother, but there didn't seem to be a drop of sweet water on this planet, and the Libralma enjoyed the gastric challenges of going filterless.

Hitomi laid his breakfast on a tray over his blanketed legs, as if he were a bedridden invalid. Ex was offended, but he was too much of a bedridden invalid to complain. Besides, the food didn't look half bad. Both fruits and sausages glistened, and the eggs were fluffy as the clouds that went sorely missing from Trisol's sky. He picked up a piece of toast and dipped it in the honey, using it as adhesive to sop up a proper portion of buttery grits. Next he went for the eggs and sausages. They tasted exactly as you would expect eggs and sausages to taste on a planet with no chickens or pigs. The whole thing reeked of *last meal*, not because of the menu, but because of the solemn silence with which it was served and consumed.

The villagers watched with unblinking eyes. "You'd think they'd never seen a man snap into a sausage before," Ex thought to himself. The bittersweet berry juice washed the sausage grease out of his palate and even made the water taste half-way drinkable.

"Why's everybody so quiet?" he finally asked.

"They wanted to send you back out into the desert," said Chimi. "But don't worry, I already told 'em you can stay with me. I don't care if the Extinguishers come. We'll take care of them. Right, Ex? Right?"

"Right," said Ex, staring at Hitomi. Her face was still as a painting, and her eyes were completely void of color and emotion. If there were any personality routines running in that pretty head of hers, they weren't being sent to the servos that sculpted the expressions of her face. "Where's the old man?" he asked her.

"He's busy," she replied. "But if you have anything to say to him, remember that he and I are constantly linked through G-Pass."

Ex's shoulders drooped under the weight of resent. Tsubasa had been riding his back the whole way, and now that he'd done his part, the old man was too busy fiddling with his clocks to come give his thanks. He'd sent this overgrown doll in his place. "Well, he… or you… or whoever owes me a damn ship."

"All the vessels at the derrick were destroyed in the battle," began Hitomi. "As you should already know, Trisolobytes eat metal, and they had quite a feast on the remains. All they left were a few scraps of plastic and rubber wiring. But even if you'd shoved off on a lifeboat, how long do you think it would take for the Consortium to run you down? You wouldn't make it out of the galaxy without a drop chart."

"Ruthless," thought Ex. There was no trace of wickedness in her words, which only made them more painful to hear, more final and immovable. "So what the hell am I supposed to do? Call a cab?"

One of the men stepped up to the bedside and put his hand on Ex's shoulder. Ex was not fond of being grabbed by strangers, but the man's demeanor was disarming. He didn't regard him with sadness or kindness – that would've probably pissed Ex right off. The man's weathered face wasn't lent to showing expression, but there was earnest admiration in his recently unfrozen, blue eyes. "Mister, the robot's right. There's more wealth on this planet than was ever reckoned to exist, and you're the key to it all. The CIR's gonna be after you, sure as the world turns. And I sincerely doubt they'll make your death a pleasant one. I don't pretend to know how you're feeling – truth is, there's no way I could know. But, you see, that's your gift. 'Course the easiest thing would be to kill yourself straight away, sorta beat the Consortium to the punch; you know? It would make all our lives a hell of a lot easier too. We'd never have to worry about Extinguishers comin' around askin' us questions we can't answer, or cagin' us up till you give back the silver you've tamed. Just a bullet in the right spot, and we could avoid all that," he said, pointing a couple of fingers at his own temple. "But even if killin' yourself meant saving this planet and every livin' thing on it, the price is too high. You've been given the chance to take on a challenge like no one's ever faced, and you better live that out till there's no livin' left in ya."

"But just not here, right?" said Ex.

"Won't be a *here* to live in really," said the man. "We're packin' up and headin' into the caves, float down somewhere the CIR can't get at us so easy."

"We're gonna go live with Kabuto?" Chimi interrupted. "I don't wanna live in a cave."

Ex stood up, allowing himself only one wobble. "It's better than your hut. That place doesn't even have a roof anymore."

Farah stood before the door, holding the cloak she'd woven for Ex in her arms. It had been cleaned and mended. Ex's stomach sank. He'd forgotten all about her terrible injury, and here she was, having sewn his rags while her own stitches still bled. "Mister Rey, we can never thank you enough for bringing our men back to us. We owe you our lives and would gladly give them to you if they'd be any help, but we'd just get in your way..."

Ex took the cloak. His touch lingered on her hands. "I know," he said and went through the door.

"Where do you think you're going?" asked Qui, who'd been leaning against the wall just outside the room.

Ex stopped with his back turned to her. "I think I'll go for a walk." And everyone followed him out.

He stepped out onto the sand. The suns had not yet risen and only a gentle breeze found its way down into the Himatma crater. The stars invited him up the ridge. "Wait, Ex! Wait!" cried Chimi. "OK, OK! We can go live in the caves. I'll eat moss and bugs. I'll never see the sun again. Just please don't go, Ex. Please…"

"I have to," he said.

"But why?" she demanded. "Why do you have to? If the bad guys come, isn't it better that you're here to protect us? You can take 'em, Ex. I know you can! So please just stay… we can fight 'em together!"

"I can't, Chimi. I've been running all my life," said Ex. "It's all I know."

Hitomi handed Ex a small sack. "Here," she said. "From Tsubasa. It's a canteen of water and your pistol." They'd been joined by more of the villagers. Men, women, and children of all sizes had come to see him off. But there would be no parade, no grand party to say farewell. They all stood in silent reverence.

Ex pulled the gun out. "Where's the clip?"

"There's a single round in the chamber," replied Hitomi.

"Just one, huh?" Ex holstered the gun. "Guess it's not for hunting." And Chimi bawled like a baby. Hitomi had to help Farah hold her back as Ex took his first step into the desert. He turned back to look at Qui. "Don't try to follow me this time."

For once the Blank had nothing to say.

"Travel by night and find shelter during the day. Remember that this planet is full of underground water sources. And keep your eyes to the sky," called Hitomi.

Ex nodded, slung the canteen over his shoulder, and made for the brightest star on the horizon.

It was a good dozen dunes before Chimi's cries no longer reached his ears, but the desert's weeping plants picked up where she left off. Every time he thought he'd found peace, a breeze would brush away the thin silence.

The suns cresting over the distant mountain range urged him towards the shade. He headed for the chrome foothills. Quality shade was impossible to come by out in the dunes, but there were plenty of jagged rocks leaping out of the sand near the mountainside.

The formations were mostly perlite, the same super-reflective alloy that made up half of the damned dirt on this skin-searing planet. He reached them at dawn. The *shaded* side was awash in pale blond light, leaping from the shimmering sand. It wasn't what you'd call shade on most worlds, but it was all you could ask for on Trisol. It smelled like sweaty minerals.

Ex spent the morning slowly scooting around the rock, following the crawl of its faint shade as the suns rose. He couldn't get a wink of sleep, partially because he was worried that if he dozed off he might wake up looking like cracklings, but mostly because of the crying plants.

"I didn't even leave her my gun," he said to the sky; his mind turned to a time when the pistol had served as a paperweight for the letter his mother had written. He took the gun from the table. The letter's words gained clarity, and their meaning began to change, but he shoved them away. He'd spent the worse half of his life blaming Arius for abandoning him, piling all his troubles on that single act. It'd been too long to change that now. Part of him had come to prefer validation to truth.

His thoughts found refuge in the narrow chute of duril that forked its way up the perlite pillar. He followed it to some root buried deep within the sand and skipped across the broken vein towards Himatma. Dark and cool. Calm and steady. The water washed endlessly over him. How easy would it be, he wondered, to spread himself across the planet, thin enough to vanish and dwell in the light of this trinity until it burned out in the sky?

More and more of him poured into the mines that snaked beneath Himatma; his awareness grew. There were footsteps beside the flowing water. They were not the piercing hums of a Trisolobyte's footfalls. These were humbled by stone. There were many of them, more than he could count, varying in strength and cadence. Ex inhabited the walls and floor. His mind stretched between the gaps like a web, capturing echoes of silhouettes as the Libralma marched deeper into the caves.

It was difficult to keep pace with the group. The gaps between the lodes of duril could be as fine as a crack or hundreds of meters across, and Ex hadn't learned how to tell the difference yet. Growing tendrils to taste the rock around him often proved fruitless. It was cut in unnatural patterns. The ore had been stripped from the tunnels without method or plan.

He wondered which of these cuts Chimi had made – certainly not the ones up high. All he could feel was the duril now, thousands if not millions of small fragments scattered about the stone. It was all the same: steady, patient, and timeless. It wanted nothing. It needed nothing. It gave nothing. It existed. In spite of the universe, it existed. What duril offered was not comfort; it removed the need entirely.

But something was wrong: a single small sting, weak and pitiful. Wishing it away only made it stronger. It was the ache of his baking body, dying of thirst in the perlite foothills.

Ex shuffled towards the shade. It hurt too much to grunt, so he wheezed in disgust. He twisted the canteen open, and the lid popped off like a champagne cork under the pressure of steam. The skin of his lips fell off in flakes as he thrust the jug into his mouth. The water was scalding and bitter. He guzzled down half of the bottle. Every shriveling cell that lined his throat begged for more, but he knew he had to conserve. Just one more swig to swish around his palate was all he could afford.

His flesh was throbbing red, almost bloodied with sunburn. "How long was I out?" he gasped. He'd been running from the sun counterclockwise around the pillar, but when he'd returned to his body, the shade was just a few scoots clockwise. Nearly a day had passed, or maybe it'd been two, or a week; he couldn't tell. All he knew was that he was burnt worse than after his first trek through this miserable wasteland, but the enormous perlite mirror he'd decided to sit beneath probably had something to do with that.

The canteen's cap was nowhere in sight. It'd ricocheted off the slanted rock and whizzed off somewhere, but it was too bright to search, even through a squint. The very notion of creeping into the sunlight to sift through the sand turned his stomach. He suffered a few dry heaves, coughing up dust. The Starfarer's Strand was the only reason he was still breathing.

Steam rose from the jug's spout; the water evaporated before his eyes. He tried to plug it up with his palm and seared his flesh. It was clear that he was going to have to find the lid or guzzle the rest of it down. Between dying now or later, Ex chose later and drank the remainder of the simmering water. He had no real incentive to ration it anyway. Surviving longer only meant more suffering at the skilled hands of an Extinguisher.

Ex forced himself to stay in his body and keep up with the shade until sundown. He resolved to find the lid when the stars were out – but not these three glaring bastards, the little twinkling kind. Trisol's rotation took longer than 24 Earth-hours. At this latitude, the day was only slightly longer than the night, but that also meant that the suns would walk almost directly overhead. No moon orbited the planet, but the nights weren't dark; the stars were dense, and the atmosphere was practically nonexistent.

He didn't wait for night; his search began at dusk. The sand was littered with small stones, many of them the same color as the faded brown paint that coated the canteen's lid. They'd been rounded into similar shapes by constant sandblasting.

The search continued until the last of the suns' rays had tucked beneath the horizon, and the mirrored mountainside was awash with stars. It was difficult to tell where their peaks ended and the night sky began. The landscape's glamour wasn't making it any easier for Ex to find the lid. He hadn't been counting, but he must've sifted through a thousand rocks.

Ex wasn't fond of quitting, but there was no point to a cap for an empty canteen. His primary concern was finding an underground water source, which meant he'd have to find a way underground first. His best bet would be to find a cave in the mountains, so he gave up on the lid and started his ascent.

Perlite was a resilient substance. It was most commonly formed by complex chemical reactions unique to third order xenobacteria, which called elements heavier than carbon but lighter than zinc their cornerstones. It must've taken these microscopic masons eons to erect such monuments. Their construction was solid; not a foothold crumbled under Ex's weight. His only complaint was that he had to stare at his own mug in the mirrored metal as he climbed.

There were a few shelves along the way, but they hardly offered enough room to stand, much less to sit. He felt safer while climbing, so he didn't stop until he reached the first plateau. The surface was blanketed with a thick layer of sand. Ex could plunge his whole arm into it without touching the perlite floor.

At most, the mesa was a couple hundred meters higher than the dunes below, but Ex felt much closer to the stars. He'd reached for them on his way up the cliff and used galaxies for footholds. The sky was painted on the two enormous peaks that rose on the other side of the elevated plain, and the light pooled in the cleft that separated them.

The crack of light grew brighter with each step. Only a couple of hours had passed since he'd left the desert floor, but it seemed that the suns were rising again, cleaving the mountain in two. Ex entered the mouth of the ravine. This was not the light of the three suns of Trisol; it was the combined light of all the stars in the night sky, reflecting infinitely between the feet of the perlite giants.

He walked through the stream of starlight. It was bright enough to put the sting back in his sunburn. The twinkling points turned into blue blurs of vibrating light where the mountains bumped shoulders. Some of these waves had traveled for a million years, others perhaps billions, and a few had hopped over from neighboring systems in a few decades. They mingled into a single light, glowing and surging as the landscape chose.

There were no caves; the ravine continued without break. It curved this way and that, became narrow and wide, but there were no branching paths, no way out. After hours of walking, the valley began to grow brighter. It was uncomfortable before long. The suns were rising, and he was caught between two enormous mirrors with no shelter in sight. There's no way that he'd make it out in time by retracing his steps. So he gambled on pressing onward.

The photons bounced endlessly between the perlite walls, trapped. Ex's flesh was their only escape. He hid beneath his cloak and ran. It was becoming too bright to see. Heat radiated through the heavy cloth, seeping through every seam and stitch. The white-hot light rushed in through the narrow crack before his eyes, soldering his pupils shut.

And just when it felt as though the cloak would burst into flames, he spotted a glimmer of darkness up ahead. The faint smudge of shadow grew into a ghostly blur as he rushed towards it, encompassing more of the light until it enveloped him. He'd entered a narrow cave, but the sunlight had followed.

The passage took many twists and turns before removing the cloak from his face became bearable. Ex found himself in a relatively spacious chamber made entirely of perlite. Very little sand had found its way this far into the mountain, but the light seemed to have no problem. The cavern was bright as day. The only darkness was his warped reflection on the floor, the walls, and the low ceiling. But the light had bounced around many corners, and the sting had been taken out of it.

The complaints of his eyes had been so loud that he'd nearly forgotten he had ears, but the sound of rushing water was a good reminder. It was coming from a crack at the foot of the far wall that had remained hidden in the ubiquitous glare. The passageway was just large enough for him to fit. The light poured in, but he couldn't see an end to it.

Ex went to his belly and shimmied into the crevasse. The height wasn't constant. Sometimes there was enough room for him to crawl on all fours; other times he had to hold his breath to worm through, but the slight downward slope remained constant. The light dimmed as he went deeper, and the water grew louder.

Soon he was crawling in darkness, driven by the sound of the rushing river nearby. It was very close now. He reached desperately into the black, hoping to touch water the next time he stretched out his arm. But the passage became too narrow. No matter which way he turned, or how long he held his breath, he could go no further. He could feel the gentle spray of water on his hand as it rushed past the perlite. He backed up until there was enough room to reach for his canteen and wormed his way down again.

Holding the canteen by its strap, he slowly lowered it further into the hole than his arms could reach. There was a sudden splash, and the canteen's strap was torn from his hands. In a wild lunge, he wedged himself into the crack. His shoulder had popped through, but there was no way he'd fit his head. He was stuck. He screamed in agony, but his yells were muted by the river's white roar.

The full weight of the mountain had him pinned. If he could take off the cloak, he might be able to free himself. He reached beneath his throat with his other arm to pull on the fabric; it tore slightly, but the part pressed against his shoulder wouldn't budge. He couldn't manage to get a good pull without choking himself with his forearm. All the while, droplets of water teased the tips of his trapped fingers. He struggled until the last of the oxygen was gone from his lungs. Every breath was a push against the mountain.

His arm grew numb. He could no longer feel the spray, although the water was still deafening. A few minutes ago, he couldn't think of a death worse than shriveling under the three suns. It hadn't taken the planet very long to offer a compelling alternative.

No more of his strength was wasted on cursing. He gathered up his remaining energy for one last pull. With his boots wedge into the narrows of the crevasse, he twisted his whole body away. A pop and a crack later, his arm was free and quite certainly broken, but there was no pain. It was impossible to assess the damage in the dark. All he knew was that it wasn't responding to his commands. It dragged limply next to him as he turned back up the slope.

Now his feet were trapped, tied up too tight in his boots to wriggle them free. He clawed at the perlite, looking for any form of a hold with his good arm. "Why do I keep getting left with one arm!" he yelled. Finding the thinnest of cracks, he wedged his fingertips in and pulled until they bled. A foot came loose and then the other. They'd slipped out of his boots, which had remained trapped. He wrenched his body around and freed them with a few strokes of a balled fist.

Soaked in sweat and trembling with nervous laughter, Ex crawled his way out towards the light, dragging his boots behind him. He didn't stop to gather his breath or check on his arm until he was back out in the mirrored chamber. It took twice as long to climb up as it did to shimmy down.

The cavern was brighter than before, but he was just glad to be able to stand again. He stretched himself out and tried to move his broken arm. All he could manage was to shrug the shoulder. The bones of his arm dangled lifelessly from the joint, loosely held together by purple flesh. But he could still wiggle his fingers. "I've had worse," he said and forced the thing into a makeshift sling he'd folded into the cloak.

After stepping back into his boots, Ex entered the tunnel that led towards the exit. Before the light grew unbearable, he came to a fork and took the other path. It was a much smaller passage. He was forced to crouch, but he wasn't about to do any more crawling. The tunnel opened into another chamber very similar to the first. In fact, he thought he'd gone around in a loop, but there was no crevasse in the corner.

The perlite made it very difficult to map the room all at once, so he passed his eyes over the surface carefully. He paused at a puddle in the floor where the reflections waved in tiny ripples. "Some kind of mirage?" he wondered. But it was no illusion; it was water, bubbling through a hairline fault in the ground. He threw himself at the floor and sucked it up by the mouthful. The water was practically boiling, and when it was all gone, he licked at the perlite until his tongue began to sizzle.

He waited for the tiny pool to refill, but hardly a drop percolated out of the crack. The gaze of the suns had been heating the mountain all day and the water in its bowels as well. Steam puffed into the room in broken whistles, growing steadily into a howling jet. The vapor was asphyxiating, too hot and heavy to breathe. He fled back into the other chamber, but the steam seeped in. It clung to the low-lying ceiling, slowly creeping towards the ground.

Ex swore he'd never crawl back into that crevasse, but he had no other choice. He pushed in far enough to find the first pocket of sitting-space, something of a bubble in the solid perlite. It wasn't dark at all. Reflected a thousand times, the light of the three stars twisted and curled on the ceiling through the veil of thickening steam. Ex lay as low as he could, trying to escape the heat. Turning one way and the other, gasping, his lungs searched for a pocket of cooler air. His mind yearned to retreat into the duril, but he resisted. If he left his body now, it might get steamed like a dumpling. He forced his eyes open, and for the sake of occupying his thoughts, tried to find a pattern in the shifting light. The color was wrong, but they reminded him of the red giant that lit Midore.

When he was ten, Arius had taken him to visit the planet during the Millennial Sunspot Festival. Midore was firmly in CIR control, within conventional-engine-distance from The Fourth Ring. Arius avoided spaceports, where quatrapass scanners stripped you to the thread and gemini-links let the universe know. She landed in the countryside, and they entered the city though their usual means: sewers and garbage chutes.

Ex was impressed with the quality of the Midoran infrastructure. He'd become something of a connoisseur of the universe's sewers, and this one was the most pleasant. It smelled like a melon the moment you slice into it.

Soft pink light bled through a grate overhead. Arius darted up the ladder. The steel slats of the grate yielded to her caress, parting like an opened mouth, wide enough for her to pass. When Ex reached the top, Arius pulled him out like a turnip. Vivid flames of red and violet licked across the sky, seeming brightest over sudden pits of deep purple. "Are those clouds on fire?" he asked.

With a pass of her hands, the slats straightened, good as new. "That's the Planter's Lantern, the star of Midore," she replied.

Ex wandered out of the alleyway, mouth agape, head tilted back as far as it would go. The Planter's Lantern covered the entire sky, horizon to horizon. Its light was soft and inviting, only forcing a squint with the brightest flares. Ex stepped on something slick and fell flat on his back.

His mother appeared over him, smiling. She slipped yellow socks over his shoes and helped him to his feet. Then she skated out into the street, gliding over the glossy, black cobblestones. She kept her ankles loose and limber, so her feet could follow the contours of the stony moguls. Ex tried to do the same, but his feet were stuck. Every step came with a sticky squish. "No fair. I wanna do that!" he cried.

"When you're older," she said. "And at your own risk. Now, come on, Banana Boots. Let's go." The round bricks of the hilly huts were cantaloupe and melon-green. They melded into the roadside in smooth slopes, and the black street-stones freckled the walls as high as first story sills. Both road and walls were all laminated with the same slick coating, a pearly film that trapped The Lantern's light. Yellows, greens, and teals floated over the dark stones like soap bubbles.

Shwick, shwick, shwick, Ex trod down the lane with Arius slaloming in tow. She had him by the shoulders, telling him which way to turn. The locals were interesting enough to pry his eyes from the sky-wide star as they skated by. As far as he could tell there were three kinds – maybe genders. The first two kinds were small, only a foot taller than him counting their ferny hair. The ones with fruit in their fronds were plump and peach. The ones with red flowers were lithe and white. Then there was the third kind; they were much taller, taller than Arius even. Their frames were ample, and the fronds of their hair were broad, but they bore no flowers or fruit. Their skin was marbled tan and gray, not as smooth as the others, though no less shiny. It looked like a waxy bark from up close.

They all had feet that splayed out like roots, undulating over the stones as they went. Their arms curled without an elbow and ended with branchy-fingered hands. They had a small, lipless mouth that was always raised in a smile, angular wedges for a nose without discernible nostrils, and their eyes were a pair of large black opals with a string of glinting diamonds spiraling into their depths.

Bright banners stretched across the street. Between the sky and spiral eyes, they'd passed a dozen signs before Ex noticed the first. He asked his mother what they meant, and she replied that they were for the Sunspot Festival. It happened once every thousand years by the Midoran calendar, which was about seventeen Earth years. "You can come see the next one when you're twenty-seven," she said, "and you can skate around all you like then."

Arius pulled Ex through a doorway in a curving wall that opened into a wide amphitheater. The crowd was gathered to watch the star put on its millennial show. Midorans of all three kinds made up the bulk of the audience. They crowded a dozen metal orbs seated in a corner of the theater. Each sphere emitted a different frequency of sound between 200 and 600 Hz. The range of their notes narrowed before converging into a single sine wave of 400 Hz. And then the song began.

Their voices started as ocarinas and slowly gained the texture of brass or strings. The choir was led by an orb who'd sprung a couple of tentacles, snaking to the rhythm of the music. It began to hover, and the LEDs that covered its spherical body glowed violet and red, mimicking the star. The Midorans swayed their ferny heads, as the lead orb sang a buzzy alto. Waves of light rippled across the choir's bodies in all colors. They started at one sphere and trickled onto the next.

When the song ended, the crowd called for an encore, but the maestro excused itself with a tilt. It floated towards Ex and his mother, its LEDs forming a smiling face. "Arius! How are you? It's been so long," it spoke with the same buzzing voice and mathematically precise intonation it had used during the performance.

"Did you find the Sage?" asked Arius.

The smile turned to a frown on the orb's display. "*Hello* and *nice to see you* were alternatives."

"Who're you?" Ex interrupted.

The smile returned as it regarded the boy. "I am Polygula, The Seeing Sphere. But just call me Pol," it said.

"No, I mean *what* are you?"

The smile flattened. "I'm a man!" Pol said in a lower tone. "Never hesitate to assign me a gender." Of all the paths Solarians had taken, the Polyhapterae least resembled their human origins. It'd taken many generations of proactive evolution, but the Polyhapterae possessed over 120 unique senses and scoffed at the First Path's six — accounting for the sense of autex. Their purpose in life was quite simple, to experience and observe the universe in as many ways as possible. The Libralma also valued experience, but not in the absence of challenge; they saw the Polyhapterae as deviants, hedonists multiplied by a factor of twenty.

"Pol." Arius snapped her fingers. "Over here. Did you find The Sage or not?" It was hard looking for someone without a name, but the orb seemed to know who Arius was talking about

"Of course I did!" said Pol. "Traced back The Sage's light 300 years to a daring escape from a depot in The Litter Glitter Galaxy, just before it was destroyed by a band of Sage-Sympathizers, strangely enough. Hardly had to get out of the galactic arm to catch photons from back then. Could've done it with 199 eyes closed. But I backed out further, went from 300 to 400 light years away, before the base had even been built, and never saw The Sage come aboard. It's the same story with every Valarian. They all popped up at about the same time from places all over the inner rings, not a child amongst them, all grown, all going about their business as if they'd always been."

"So where is the Sage now?" asked Arius.

"Communing with a star, far from here... aren't you curious as to why someone spliced Solarians with Valoraphim during The Extinguishing for no apparent reason?"

"If the universe's greatest historian can't figure it out, what hope do I have?" said Arius.

The orb's lights turned rosy. "The title of Sage is not wasted on you, my dear. Now come with me, away from the symphony of humming ears, and I will tell you where this Nameless Sage dwells."

Ex wandered down the amphitheater. The Midorans had large baskets of fruits in every variety: melons, citrus, berries, pomes, and cucurbits. Some of the fruit Ex recognized, others he only guessed were fruit. Deep blue and red juices ran down the Midorans' chins and dripped on their bare chests as they fed each other. The crisp sloshes of their bites were the only sounds they made.

Ex's mouth watered, but the Midorans had the baskets surrounded. He sat next to a small, plump Midoran with bright pink fruits weighing down the ends of its fronds. He pressed a finger into its peachy side. The little Midoran had no ribs, no apparent skeletal structure at all. It was like poking a water balloon. Snapped out of its trance, the Midoran turned the Fibonacci spirals of its eyes on him, and he froze. Its ever-smiling face broadened as it played with its leafy hair. This one didn't eat. It only watched. With its back turned again, Ex leaned in and sniffed one of its pink fruits. The sweet fragrance cooled his nose and spread to his temples in bolts. He could see his bulbous reflection in its smooth glossy skin.

Without further consideration, Ex plucked the fruit and took a bite. Tart flavor splashed his tongue before a wave of sweetness filled his mouth. The little Midoran's fronds curled up and a shiver vibrated across the skin of its back. Its tone went from peach to pastel pink, and it heaved a fluty sigh.

The eating stopped, and all spirals were fixed on Ex as he finished the fruit. They laughed in breathy whistles when the little Midoran put its arms around Ex and brushed its leaves against him. The fronds were full of tiny hairs that created just the right amount of friction on skin.

Ex was about to return the hug, when his mother hoisted him up by the ear. "I can't leave you alone for a minute, can I?" said Arius. She apologized to the Midorans and carried Ex out of the amphitheater under her arm.

He could kill for a taste of that fruit now. Under better conditions, he would've salivated. As it was, thoughts of the fruit only cause a rasping pain at the root of his tongue.

The chamber dimmed quickly as Trisol turned. The steam condensed into a hot, heavy dew, leaving the perlite floor as slick as the Midoran roads. Ex skated his way out of the cavern on all fours. It was still day outside, but the suns no longer had a direct route into the cave or the wall across the canyon.

When night came, he continued down the starry ravine until it opened into a wide valley of wind-raked sand, encircled by jagged peaks of perlite, some soaring higher than the ones through which he'd passed.

The valley didn't promise any shelter from the suns, but perhaps he could find something to eat. For once he missed the scaly vulture. He wished it'd come by and drop off its snake pal. This time he'd be the one to take a bite.

He checked the bullet Tsubasa had given him. The caliber was not one he could readily identify. It looked big enough, but the actual round was strange and cylindrical with a flat head. Regardless of construction, it grew more appetizing with each step.

He remembered how the old man had told him that simply staying alive was not a legitimate goal. Clearly the codger had never tried surviving on this planet outside of his air-conditioned facility. If he wanted to keep his strength up, he'd have to eat something – at least enough raw nutrients to finish repairing his arm so he could put up a proper fight when The Consortium came calling. He looked up at the stars, wondering where the nearest Extinguisher was, and what he or she would be like. He remembered the ashen-faced Sophian on Bastalia, who slew a city full of Sages in seconds.

Back when he'd crash landed on Trisol, Ex had found the desert teeming with life. When sand would have sufficed, the fauna had tormented him, but now that he looked for any signs of something he could test his Strand on, there was nothing. Life hadn't found its way into the valley, or if it had, it hadn't stuck around.

Hope and hunger drove Ex further into the desert. He imagined that a fruit bearing bush or chubby little legless pig was just over the next dune, but he didn't even find a mirage.

Ex didn't dare to venture too far from the mountains and potential shelter. He followed the mountainside around the bowl, never straying more than a few hundred meters from the perlite walls. It was a reasonable precaution at the time, but when the morning rays started creeping over the distant ridge, he found himself next to a cliff-sized mirror. It offered no shelter, just a clean reflection.

He continued tracking around the valley's edge as morning turned to day, but the mountainside turned the three suns into six, and that was five too many. The walls bent the light, magnified it, and drilled it into the nape of his neck through his cloak and scarf as he clambered over the dunes into the valley.

The suns neared their apex, setting the entire bowl aflame, and Ex understood why he was the only manifestation of life stupid enough to be here. There was nowhere to hide, so he did the only thing that came to mind. He wrapped himself in the cloak and burrowed into the side of a dune, as far as he could manage. It was hard to breathe, but at least the perlite flakes in the sand deflected most of the rays.

Ex spent the rest of the day in this improvised grave. If only he'd encountered one of those thorny little smilers; one of their quills could have helped pass the time. Occasionally, a trickle of sand would find its way in through the cloak's folds. It seared his flesh, but wriggling only made it worse.

The desert was embalming him, slowly and painfully. He could feel the sand leeching the moisture from his veins, and his broken arm was feeling no better. As good as his regeneration was, his body simply didn't have the raw materials with which to repair itself. And the thread that normally sustained him had found more comfortable accommodations elsewhere. Ex couldn't remember ever feeling so weak. When the suns had set behind the ridge, and the valley was doused in stars again, he hardly saw a reason to crawl out of the sand, but he did.

He dragged his feet across the desert, following the cauldron's rim without knowing what he even hoped to find. The sand looked pale blue in the starlight. When he could muster the strength, he'd give the sky a glance. "When's that damn Extinguisher gonna get here?" he'd whisper to himself. His voice was hoarse with thirst. Visions of fanciful ships descending from the night filled his delirious mind. He had no idea what kinds of vessels Extinguisher used, but he'd heard plenty of stories of men who navigated the cosmos without the shell of a ship. For a moment, he tried to imagine what it might be like to zip from star to star with flesh for a hull.

Then he was on his back, waking up with the morning sun.

Derelict Dreams

The suns rose quickly. There were just dunes and mirrored cliffs as far as the eye could see, and Ex was sure he wouldn't survive another day buried in the sand. The heat coming up off the ground seeped through his heavy boots, cooking his toes in steel-tipped ovens. "I'm not hiding from you!" he rasped at the suns. The lining of his throat cracked as he yelled, and he tasted a powder that he assumed to be his own blood. There was no reason to stand here, and there was no reason to move, but at least walking gave him the illusion of progress.

The blond hills made no more promises. He knew he'd only find sand over the next crest, but he didn't care anymore. His good hand rested on the pistol grip as he went. The last of his strength would go towards bringing the gun to his head.

Just as he was unfastening the strap on his holster, his thoughts were tugged to the sky. Something inexplicably familiar was approaching at great speed. A large shadow passed over him quick as a blink and pooled over the dune ahead. Forcing his eyes to look up was painful, and what he saw hurt almost as badly: the glistening bow of a ship, flying gracefully on three silver wings, arced over one another in a neat row. An enormous cannon hung beneath the vessel, clutched by heavy beams.

The only sound it'd made as it passed overhead was the rush of wind, and now it floated in complete silence. It didn't raise a breeze or turn a grain of sand. It simply hovered. This was the ship of an Extinguisher, more impossible than he'd ever imagined. Perhaps its only source of propulsion was the will of a Sage at the helm.

Ex pressed the gun's muzzle to his temple as he watched the craft descend. The giant cannon cocked to one side as it neared the desert floor. His finger was on the trigger, but he wanted the Extinguisher to see how he could, with a single shot, forever end the CIR's hopes of unlocking Trisol's wealth.

A door opened on the side of the hovering ship, and a ramp lowered. It came to rest just a step off the sand, and a silhouette appeared at the doorway.

Ex's vision was blurred, and his eyes kept falling. He squeezed the pistol's grip, but not its trigger. Pumping the last ounce of liquid blood into his triceps, he willed his arm straight and steady, pointing the gun at the ship.

Ex pulled the trigger.

BANG, read the little flag that popped out of the muzzle. It was draped from an antenna with a flashing point.

"Ex! Ex!" called Chimi, scampering down the ramp. Ex let his body crumble to the ground. Chimi put the spout of a heavy jug between his lips and poured enough water to drown him. He snatched it out of her hands and gulped it down so fast it hurt. A violent cough gripped his chest. Some of the water had gone to his lungs and came back up as mud.

Chimi giggled. "On a scale of one to ten, how surprised are you to see me?"

"Four," Ex said between coughs.

"Four being the highest," she added, and Ex began to crawl back into the desert.

"I'm just kidding!" she said, pouncing on his back.

"Oww! My arm! It's broken."

Hitomi crouched down next to him. "So young, so fragile," she said and plunged a syringe into Ex's side. "How do you even break an arm in all this sand?"

"It happened in a cave," said Ex, still serving as Chimi's seat. The flush of nanos he'd been injected with went straight to work. He gained use of his arm in seconds and used it to push himself over. Chimi tumbled to the ground, excited to see there was still life left in Ex's dusty body.

He sat up, shaking the grit out of his hair. Parts of him were returning from distant duril, parts he hadn't realized were missing. Life surged through his body, and the suns lost their hold of him. His vivid pink flesh relaxed into a pastel.

"Well, cave or not, a man that just beat a Talon made of sage silver shouldn't let a bunch of rocks and dirt break his arm," she said. Her eyes sparkled a mischievous violet in the morning rays.

"It was metal," he replied. "And it's your fault for giving me a canteen with a bad strap. The damn thing broke on me when I stuck it in a river."

"Oh, you mean this canteen, with the perfectly intact strap?" she said. Sure enough, it was his canteen, or at least an exact copy. Hitomi tapped the bottom of the bottle. "We found it floating downstream near Himatma. The cap was in the foothills a few dozen kilometers from here."

"But how did you..."

"Tracking device, of course," she interrupted. "Same as with that bullet you just tried to fire."

"The saved, saving the savior, isn't it grand?" called Tsubasa's voice. A ski was affixed to the bottom of his peg, so it wouldn't sink in the soft sand. He scooted along at a faster clip than his usual hobble. "You must be one hell of a survivalist to willingly test your meddle in the most inhospitable spot on this bleak planet."

"What the hell is this ship?" Ex finally asked.

"Ah, you like her?" smiled Tsubasa. "I told you I'm the universe's greatest shipwright, and there's your damn proof! I call her *The Derelict Dreams*. Come on, I'll talk your ear off inside because I forgot my hat in all the excitement and this bald head of mine won't last long in the suns. Hitomi, will you bring the ship around, please, dear?"

Hitomi's eyes became gray, and The Derelict Dreams hovered closer. It didn't turn its bow; the slightest pitch was all that was required to move the ship. With his faculties returning to him, Ex realized that what he'd mistaken for wings were actually sails, harkening to the ancient maritime ships of Earth's past. They were tied down with a number of fine cables, and a mast was devoted to each sail. The mizzen, at the aft of the vessel, was the largest and the foremast was the smallest.

When the ship pitched towards them, the overlapping sails looked like segments of a silver shell, stepping up in size in accordance to the golden ratio. Only the pointed bow and hanging cannon peered from beneath the cover of their graceful curves.

The ramp came to brush against Tsubasa's living leg, and the ship stopped. There were no windows or hatches anywhere. From keel to rudder, the hull ran sleek and smooth, made entirely of duril. The sails were duril as well and the masts that held them and the ropes that bound them, all glimmering in the rising suns. Even in the shadows it cast on itself, The Derelict Dreams' silver skin glowed.

The ramp was duril, as was the doorway and the walls and floor and ceiling. Everything that could be made of duril was – and with remarkable craftsmanship. The corridors were well lit and spacious. There wasn't a loose cable in sight. It didn't feel like home to Ex, but there was something familiar about it, as if he'd been here in a dream.

"You had this ship under a tarp, just sitting in your hangar all along, didn't you?" asked Ex.

"No, I built it in a couple of days," paused Tsubasa. "Of course it was in my hangar, but what you really mean to ask is why I sent you out into the desert when I'd promised you a ship. Let's find some seats, and I'll tell you." Hitomi led them to a large round room much in the style of Tsubasa's study, all in wood and opulent red. They sat in plush chairs with volute armrests, lined with duril trim. The old man touched the side of the round table that dominated the center of the room, and its smooth face became concave. A blue flame flashed into life above it, emitting no heat.

"Hitomi, head back to the bridge and ride the gentlest breeze back to Himatma, dear," said Tsubasa.

"Aye, aye!"

"I like to keep her qubits sharp with metaphors," said Tsubasa. "What do you think of this room, Ex? Quite magnificent isn't it? A briefing room fit for a gentleman. But I suppose you can use it too."

Chimi handed Ex a tall glass of clean water and took the seat next to him. Even when she sat on the edge, her dangling feet came nowhere near the carpet, so she sank back in the chair and tucked her legs beneath her.

The fire flickered white and morphed into a wireframe schematic of The Derelict Dreams. Sections of the ship were highlighted, framed on either side by pages of information that scrolled at speeds that only Dicots and Synths could process. The highlights stopped on the sails. They grew to encompass the entire display.

"Life isn't a straight line or a perfect ring," said Tsubasa. "Most of the time it's a lot like traveling through the stratums. You spend the majority of it adjusting, maneuvering, and waiting for things to line up just right, so you can hurl yourself forward with everything you've got and ride out the momentum.

Our dreams are a lot like that too. If it were as easy as putting a goal ahead of us and taking a step towards it each day, we'd all be winners. And when you're lucky enough to reach the finish line, that's about the time you find out you're only on the first lap."

"When do we get to the part where you tell me why you decided to send me to hell for a few days?" interrupted Ex.

Chimi bit her lip.

"Ex, I'm old," sighed Tsubasa. "I spent the better part of a millennium nurturing this dream you're sitting in. In that time, I learned that I shouldn't wait for the world to whisper the answers, but also not to be deaf when it screams them.

I left Veredos a broken man, the wanderlust tugging at my thread. When I signed on to the Himatma, it wasn't to find a place to work; it was to find a place to die, buried by people for whom I still held some value. But then we came to this place, a world with a heart of duril; fate, that capricious seamstress, had put another couple of stitches in my thread. Sage silver, I thought, was the only substance resilient enough to handle the stresses of anchorwind.

But I was wrong. You have no idea how many configurations of sails I tried, and each time, a failure. Even molecules of tamed sage silver were blown away like the florets of a dandelion."

"So what's different about this ship?" asked Ex.

"The moss," replied Tsubasa. "That wonderful, wonderful moss." The holographic sails donned skin and shrank to allow the entire ship to be displayed. It was rendered in full realism, as it would appear in the daylight of Trisol. Even the three stars were rendered as gleaming points of light. They sank into the brazier, leaving The Derelict Dreams in a sphere of stars. The ship took on a ghostly blue glow, reminiscent of the caverns where the Trisolobytes dwelt. "You see, anchorwind doesn't destroy duril. Duril cannot be destroyed. It just scatters the molecules apart. It was obvious that I had to find some sort of subrostral glue that could bind the molecules of duril to one another, so that when the wind blew them away, they'd stay in the shape of a ship. I hope I don't need to tell you how impossible that sounded. Nothing known to science could come between the solid molecules of duril, until you brought me this..." Tsubasa pulled the fragment of The Dominant's throne out of his pocket. Its sigils no longer glowed cyan; their lines were faint etchings in the lustrous sage silver.

"Of all the amazing life forms found on this planet, from bacteria that exhale perlite to a race of sentients that cultivate duril into elaborate plate mail, the moss is by far the most remarkable." said Tsubasa. "It redefines life as we know it. In the space beneath atoms, on a level where matter has yet to organize into coherent form, before quarks are whole, before gravity gives weight, and before photons carve their peaks and troughs, it thrives. In short, it is subrostral life.

It wasn't easy to come to this realization. The initial tests I ran were quite confounding, but after much recalibration and reconsideration, the moss from Trisol's depths yielded the planet's ultimate secret. Once applied, I couldn't stop it from spreading across the ship.

I boarded the ship and turned the sails to the anchorwind, only a fraction of an angstrom. This time, they weren't spread into a fine cloud, spanning this galaxy and the next; the ship moved just a few centimeters, all in one piece. And the old man crossed the finish line." The display over the brazier fluttered back into fire.

Chimi clapped.

Ex swished some water around his mouth, trying to get at the last bits of grit stuck between his teeth. "So how much actual in-flight testing has this ship seen?"

"You're on the return trip of its maiden voyage," said Tsubasa. "Isn't it exciting?"

"Thrilling," replied Ex. "Do you even know if the moss will survive in space?"

"I don't see why not," said Tsubasa. "The void of space or the middle of a mountain are identical at a deep enough level of the Subrostrum; the moss shouldn't be able to tell the difference."

"So you haven't tested it?"

"I've run simulations in my head, but it's really not a problem. The entire ship is coated in top of the line shields, better than those bubbles around heavy Consortium cruisers. We've got your good buddy, Issid, to thank for it. His swollen thread is giving this ship all the juice it could ever need."

"Whoa, now! Issid's powering the ship?"

"Yep, got his spool hooked up in the engine room," said Tsubasa. "Ironic, isn't it? You could tap into his threadwidth like turning a spigot, not that you'd ever need it, of course, but he's yours to command."

"I'm not sure how I feel about that," said Ex.

"Will has no intent," said Tsubasa. "A thread has no inclination without a mind to weave it. Powerful as that Antican's spirit is, it will wish for nothing more than to protect this ship and its passengers, as prescribed by the body which it inhabits."

Ex didn't look convinced. "What do you think, Chimi?"

Chimi stared into her glass of water. "I think this ship's the only chance you've got."

"My only chance for what?"

"To live, fool!" said Tsubasa. "A thousand Extinguishers couldn't catch you in this boat!"

Happiness welled up inside of Ex like bad gas.

Tsubasa fluffed the prongs of his beard. "To be honest, I've amazed even myself, and after 800 years of living, that's not easy to do. The ship's turned out better than I could have ever imagined. Perfect... except for one teeny tiny little concern. A piffling little trifle, really..."

"Oh no..." Ex knew straight away this was going to be something huge and tragic. And he tried not to let the relief of this realization seep into his voice. He'd just been saved from gratitude he wasn't prepared to voice.

"Well, I can't figure out how to feed the damn moss," said Tsubasa. "It just won't grow on the ship. I tried everything: replicating its varied natural environments, sunlight, darkness, high and low atmospheric pressure, dry, wet, I even tried talking nice to it, but the damned thing just won't eat once it's applied to the duril. It makes no sense because it'll eat just fine while it's on the Trisolobytes' armor, and that's made of duril. They must be feeding in the Subrostrum somehow. I simply don't have the equipment here to know for certain; subrostral experimentation is a Sage's domain."

"So how long till it starves?" asked Ex.

"No clue," shrugged Tsubasa, "and the Trisolobytes don't seem to know either. They don't have a concept of the Subrostrum, but at least they've never known the moss to starve. In fact, I'm not even sure if the moss needs to feed at all."

"So then, what's the problem?"

"It's fading, slowly, but measurably," said Tsubasa. "Mooring the duril against anchorwind seems to tax it, but the amount of stress is highly variable. This implies that there're forces at play which I don't yet fully understand. I can't predict how long the moss reserves will hold out under exposure to anchorspace. It could be weeks, months, years, or days."

"And what happens if it gives out?" Ex felt obligated to ask.

"Instant, cosmic disintegration."

Ex took a tiny sip of water, scooted the coaster on the table next to him a few inches closer, and gently set the glass down. "I can't wait to take her for a spin."

"Save your sarcasm," Tsubasa interrupted. "What choice do either of us have? This ship's duril may be tamed, but you don't have to change its shape for it to work. If you don't take it, the Consortium will, and I'll be damned if I'm gonna let them. I'd rather strip the moss off and scatter the ship on the wind. While she's in one piece, all the Extinguishers and bounty hunters in the universe won't be able to catch her, a ring runner's dream, but I'm just too damn old for all that."

"You know, ancient Solarians sometimes spread the ashes of their loved ones into the wind as a way to honor the dead," said Ex. "You could just fly this ship yourself and get a head start on your funeral."

"Suit yourself then," said Tsubasa. "Hitomi…"

Hitomi's voice came in over the intercom. "Yes, Captain?"

"How fast can we get back to the valley where we picked up Mr. Rey?" inquired the old man. "Oh, and what's the current temperature there, dearie?"

"At maximum acceleration and deceleration, approximately one trillionth of a nanosecond. The surface temperature in Kelvin is 388.718405061…"

"OK thank you, Hitomi, that'll do," said Tsubasa. "That's a bit over 115 degrees Celsius, and 95 is enough to boil blood at that altitude in this planet's thin atmosphere. Shall I tell Hitomi we're dropping you off?"

"Alright, alright," said Ex. "So how do we get this ship to *not* turn into a cloud of duril gas?"

"Now there's my little research assistant! I have a plan. But you might not like it…"

"That'll be a first," said Ex.

"It involves going to Istreya and looking up an old friend of mine," said Tsubasa. "I've got to warn you though, he's become something of an eccentric in his old age."

"Is he half as crazy as you?" asked Ex.

"Twice," replied Tsubasa. "And half as brilliant, but that's still a lot of smarts. He also happens to be a Sage and the Consortium's foremost authority on abnormal biology, being something of a unique specimen himself: the universe's only Valoraphim Dicot."

"He works for the CIR?" said Ex.

"Of course. He's a Sage living on a Consortium controlled world. But he's like any of the other druids on Istreya; they mostly tend to their own, humble research, occasionally churning out a new fruit or furry animal that'll keep the aristocrats on Veredos entertained. The mere prospect of getting to work with life as exciting as this moss should be enough to get that old kook to help you. If there's anyone in the universe that's equipped to understand this kind of specimen, it's him."

"OK. How do I find this guy?"

"His name is Impreginald. He stands a bit over two meters tall if you can get him out of his seat. His platinum blond hair is usually worn in braided tails, and he's got a pair of icy blue eyes, just like any other Valoraph. Oh, and did I mention that he's fat? He's very fat. You see, he's developed a tendency to eat his finds, so watch out for that."

"How exactly do I *watch out for that*?"

"I don't know; I'm sure you'll figure something out," said Tsubasa. "Oh, and another thing... I'm not sure he'll still be on Istreya. I'd head that way if I were you though. It's the last place I saw him."

"And when was that?"

"About a century ago... might have wandered off somewhere if he's still alive."

"Well, there's only the whole universe, right? And he is fat, so he shouldn't be hard to find," said Ex.

"That's the spirit," replied Tsubasa.

Hitomi's voice came through the intercom again. "Captain, ETA to Himatma is under five minutes."

Chimi, who'd been sitting quietly until now, gave an audible sigh. She hadn't been waiting patiently for them to arrive at their destination; she'd been hoping they'd never get there. The chances of ever getting her two favorite men together again were not good.

"So this is where we part ways, ring runner," said Tsubasa.

"But you haven't even taught me how to fly this thing," said Ex.

Tsubasa laughed. "You, piloting my sweet baby boat? That's rich. No, no, don't be silly, that's Hitomi's job. She's The Derelict Dreams' navigational computer – a walking, talking drop chart."

"So she's coming with me?" smirked Ex.

"Yeah, but don't get any funny ideas, Ex!" said Chimi, before taking a long, angry drink of water.

"That's right," added Tsubasa. "Hitomi and I are linked via Gemini. I can switch her to extra-sassy with a thought, so you'll be a gentleman if you know what's good for you."

The ship began its descent, and the group filed out of the briefing room. "Let me make sure I got this straight," began Ex. "I've gotta go find a crazy fat man who likes to eat his own experiments on one of the most transited worlds in the CIR with every Talon and Extinguisher after me on a ship that could turn into *anchordust* at any moment that's powered by my worst enemy's thread, all while being teased and tantalized by a sexy robot-puppet with a lecherous old man pulling the strings?" Chimi appeared to be counting something on her little fingers as Ex spoke.

Tsubasa tugged the center prong of his beard. "*Anchordust*... I like that."

The ramp opened ahead of them, revealing an enticing silhouette standing in a pool of gleaming sunlight. "Don't forget me," said Qui. "I'm coming with you too." She'd taken the form of the blue vixen, probably to soften the blow, clad in a skin-tight khaki suit that stretched a bit onto each of her appendages – shorts, short sleeves, a half-turtleneck, and even a little sleeve for her tail. Next to her were a couple of pink suitcases, whose contents Ex couldn't begin to guess.

"No, no. Oh, hell no," said Ex. "I gotta draw the line somewhere."

"You weren't about to leave me on this god-forsaken planet, were you?" she said, coming up the ramp.

"I'm dropping you off at the first port."

She smiled and pinched his cheek. "OK, sweetie. Just as soon as you pay me 80% of this planet's worth. Let's see, that's like four or five trillion stars worth of plex. Too much? Better start working it off right away then. You can begin by carrying up my bags."

"Is it too late to have Hitomi drop me off in the desert?" asked Ex.

"Afraid so," said Tsubasa, taking him by the shoulder as they went down the steps. The ship had landed at the mouth of the largest entrance to the mines, where a small crowd waited in the shade. Himatma sat behind them, silent and still. "Oh, and Ex," paused Tsubasa, "this old druid I'm sending you to find, your mother studied with him for a few years. You might want to ask him what he taught her."

Ex nodded, helping the old man down another step.

"And one more thing," said Tsubasa. "Take care of the ship will ya? Don't abuse it. Don't go pulling pointless stunts, or showing it off, or trying to pick up strange women..."

"I think the ship has enough strange women in it already," said Ex.

Madame Shantasa coasted across the sand on her scooter. "Fastest ship in the universe and you still manage to take an hour," she croaked. "Don't complain if I get sun blisters cause it'll be your fault. I can already feel one bubbling up on my nose."

"You'll still be beautiful to me, honey," said the old man, putting a ski-peg to the sand.

Farah followed close behind Shantasa, trying her best to keep the old fortuneteller and mayor and dentist and doctor and comedienne beneath a rickety old parasol. In the darker reaches of the cave, a number of Trisolobytes held the reins of several worms. Ex stared at them for a moment; he didn't know their names, or if names were even a part of their culture, he'd come to know their forms intimately during his communion with the duril of Trisol. He recognized them immediately and wondered how they would fare now that the duril they wore was tamed. They somehow seemed aware of the fact and untroubled.

Tsubasa joined the ladies in the crowded shade of the umbrella as Ex dug the suitcases out of the sand. Chimi lingered on the last step, staring at Ex through a fierce squint. The Derelict Dreams pitched softly on cosmic waves, bringing the little girl to his eye level. Ex opened his mouth, but Chimi spoke first. "Don't say you're coming back, Ex, cause I already know you can't."

The muscles of his jaw tightened.

"It's OK, though," said the little girl. "I'll come find you... someday..." her words came in short spurts. "I promise... someday, I'll come find you... So don't die till I do, OK? You have to promise… that you won't die." Her bottom lip curled, and she went into a fit of tiny breaths.

Ex dropped the bags and hugged the girl. He held her long enough for the arid desert breeze to dry his eyes, lifted her up, and set her down on the sand.

"I promise," he said, and drew his mother's pistol from the holster. "Bring this back to me when you're old enough."

She cradled the bulky gun in her arms like a baby.

"The old man should still have the clip. If not, you'll have to hope the bugs didn't eat it," said Ex, picking the suitcases back up and stepping onto the ramp.

Kabuto popped out of the sand next to Chimi, looking hungrily at the pistol in her arms. She put a little sandaled foot on his head and pushed him away. "No Kabuto. It's not food!"

A pang of regret turned to a laugh. "Take care of your mother," Ex found himself saying. "And you, Kabuto, you take care of her."

"Yesh," replied Kabuto, standing tall and proud on his hind legs. He seemed to have grown in the time Ex had known him.

The Derelict Dreams began a slow ascent, and everyone waved. Ex set down one of the suitcases to wave back. "What's taking you so long?" called Qui. "You'd better not drop one of those."

Ex nudged the pink case with his knee, sending it plummeting to the desert below. "Woops," he said. "Hope there wasn't anything important in there."

"Hmm, not really," said Qui, as the ramp retracted and the hatch closed. "Just marshmallows."

Ex rushed into the bridge, imploring Hitomi to land again so they could pick it up. But she already had her orders, and they included not taking orders from him until they were out of the Trisol System.

"Monitors on," she said, and the walls went transparent. The ship spun around and pointed directly at Himatma. "Priming anchor-cannon." The hum of servos filled the ship as the large gun locked into position. "Initiating firing sequence."

"What're you doing?" Ex demanded.

"Sending ten atoms into anchorspace," she replied.

"Are you insane?" he rattled Hitomi around a bit. "Old Man, are you listening to what your robot is about to do?"

"The city has been evacuated," she said. "Mr. Aozora believes this action will lead the Consortium to suspect that you stole the ship, rather than assuming conspiracy on his part."

"Kinda drastic though, don't ya think?" said Ex. "Well can we at least get Qui's suitcase first; it's really important to her."

"Negative. Universal spin is about to enter optimal alignment," replied Hitomi. "In three, two, one…" And Himatma was gone, replaced by a cylindrical trench that raced off into the horizon.

The sky turned suddenly to stars, and for a moment Ex thought they'd blown up the entire planet, but the ship had already cleared the atmosphere. There was no inertia or feeling of movement at all. The universe was moving around them.

The Derelict Dreams gleamed in the light of the three suns, turning slowly towards a distant star. The ship slipped into the shadow of Trisol, and its silver skin blushed blue. Soft as a specter, it moved through space. The sails tilted to the wind, and they were off, quick as an anchor-round.

In Search of a Shadow

The halls of Palace Gincleare were just as he remembered them. They hadn't changed since he was a child. In fact, they hadn't changed since the Sophians had shattered Miraval, over two thousand years before he was born. The palace was a golden cocoon, which the Valoraphim had entered as blighted shadows and emerged as awakened children of light.

On a crisp and golden morning in the palaces of Miraval, Nodris' uncle, Greyval Gincleare, caught him sitting on his ankles. His arms and voice were raised in prayer to the star, Atamal, as was his custom before the day's studies. Greyval stopped and said: "What you do is not that important. If you must pray, make less show of it." Even as the Viceroy of the Second Ring, Nodris' prayers remained silent to this day.

He looked out across the range of stones spinning in the starlight, alive with flecks of gold – ruins of reliquaries and spires that soared in a glorious past. But not all was lost. There were great houses that still stood and many temples to welcome pilgrims. Amongst the ochre and gold, and sometimes lost to the sea of stars, were glints of silver, slowly flickering across the void. This was the light of Atamal, glinting off the wings of his kin as they flew from asteroid to asteroid.

When first the Valoraphim had decided to modify their species to survive in the barrens of space, they had no idea it would be put to such use. A stroll to a neighbor's home required it. A different people might've found this arrangement wholly disagreeable, but the Gincleare elders chose to glorify this era as a time of transcendence. To them, Miraval was no less holy for being in pieces. They had foreseen the need for wings and that the time would come when their people would dwell amongst the stars.

The Valoraphim had been modeled after the vision of The Recurring, a single dream seen by king and peasant alike, growing clearer with every generation like an echo in reverse. The Sophians regarded it as an hereditary psychosis, but even they could not explain the prophetic abilities of the Gincleare.

Zaralin stood beside the Viceroy, a blue amaranth tied to the strap of her sterling dress, gazing across the ruins of his homeworld. At that moment, she was remembering the feeling of firing the shot that shattered it. In all of history, she was the first Sophian to be afforded such a view by earnest invitation. Nodris hoped that somehow this memory would seep into the future generations of her people and change their opinion of his, but she was a maiden and would never know the joys and burdens of motherhood.

He'd made it a point to see her every day of the voyage. They'd spent hundreds of hours together, but Zaralin hid behind flowers and faint smiles. Etiquette was her fortress, and he couldn't find a way to breach it. All the while his cousin, Kelmore, teased him, trying to reduce their relationship to something lewd and full of scheming. Nodris insisted that the bond between him and Zaralin wasn't like that. And when he was with her, he meant it, but his mind was harder to convince when he lay alone at night. His career hinged on his ability to read others' intents, but he couldn't divine the reason for the space that Zaralin kept between them. It was cold, empty, and without color.

A herald approached. The echoing footsteps of his hard boots rang through the hall. A deaf man could've felt their vibrations. But he still announced his presence with a snap of his heals and a sharp salute. He did not speak until acknowledged. "Viceroy, the council will grant you audience now."

"Thank you. I will head for the court at once," replied Nodris.

Zaralin had not moved, but the herald was obligated to say that the Sophian must remain. She replied with a shallow bow and turned back to the window.

"I won't be long," Nodris assured her, speaking to her reflection on the glass.

"Take your time," she said. "This is the whole reason for your trip; please, don't rush on my account."

Nodris stood before the doors of the royal court. They were narrow, wide as an adult's wingspan when completely open. But they were tall; their arch nearly reached the lofty ceiling, high enough to give Valoraphim wings purpose.

On more than one occasion of the long trip, he'd wondered how his kin would receive him. He'd turned his back on their most sacred traditions, not the least of which was the shedding of his wings. Everything he'd done, he'd done for the advancement of his people, but not everyone saw it that way.

The golden gavels that gated the entrance lifted, and the doors opened without sound. The hallway's humble light poured in. The chamber was lit by hundreds of flickering candles, hanging at different lengths from the vaulted ceiling. They were arranged to represent the most important stars as they appeared during the night of the winter solstice on Miraval before the shattering. He could scarcely make out the dim silhouettes of winged figures seated on the high benches that encircled the room.

Then the sun rose, a giant spotlight bearing down on Nodris, bringing day to the chamber. It was not the light of Atamal, but some synthetic proxy. Its focused brightness only made it harder to see the faces of the council as they looked down on him from their lofty seats. A voice full of gravel thundered down from above unannounced: "So, the wingless prince returns to the great halls he dares call home…" The words reverberated for several seconds, until Nodris had absorbed all their sound. His eyes were cast down at his lapel from which many medals and ribbons had been hung by Sophian hands. The voice spoke again, "What has brought you here, Dealate?"

"A vision," replied Nodris in a clear tone.

"So there is Valoraphim in you yet…"

"That is all there is," Nodris declared. "And I've come seeking knowledge."

"What knowledge do you seek?"

"Everything there is to know about The Dormant Ones," said Nodris, and a hushed murmur fell over the chamber. "In particular, I come to ask about a name… Valkaros," said Nodris.

Now it was the council that waited for the echoes of his voice to fade. "Tell us of the vision that has given rise to this inquest."

"A hand, weaving in the night. A thousand threads of light twined into one. A child, curled as if in the womb. A man in a white mask, bearing the spiraling horns of a Sophian, but there were other horns, tall and twisted. And two eyes that saw as four. Then a mouth filled with blades of bone spoke a name as invitation to bow: Valkaros."

The spotlight's glare refocused to the apex of the domed roof, filling the entire chamber with golden light. Nodris could see the concern on the old faces of his kinsman. The crown had never looked heavier on his uncle Lindus' brow. "Are you certain that this is the name you heard?" he asked softly.

"There's no doubt," said Nodris.

"Strange that it would be spoken to one so removed from these halls," said Chancellor Greyval, inciting more whispers. He was Lindus' minor by two years, and it was his voice that had questioned Nodris in the dark.

King Lindus Gincleare raised his hand, and the whispering ended. "I'm sure that what The Chancellor meant to say was that we've all shared in this vision, but only in silence. It's remarkable that one who's not rigorously pursued the gift of prophecy has been able to divine a name. But wings or not, royal Gincleare blood flows through your veins as it does through mine. Questioning its abilities would be tantamount to questioning my own. So tell me, what do you know of this name: Valkaros?"

"What I know comes only from whispers and choked verses, overheard in my childhood," said Nodris. "I know it belonged to a Dormant One, as we all were once, but their kind has not been seen since The Awakening."

"You are mostly correct," said The King. "Our people did not always appear as they do today. We had two legs, two arms, two ears, a mouth, but little else was the same. We were creatures of shadow, yet dormant, untouched by light. It took a dream to wake us, a dream visited upon our people to this very day, regardless of their station in life. From the purest of blood to the half-breeds of The Extinguishing, we've all seen The Recurring.

The ancient oracles, in all their wisdom, reforged our race in the grace of the light. Stripped away was our shadowy skin, and we were redressed in the glory of The Awakened. All this, you already knew, as it is taught to every young Valoraph.

But it is also commonly known that not all who slumbered were awakened. There were those who refused the form that The Recurring had made so clear. And there was a great war amongst our people, lasting many decades. Beaten, The Dormant fled to the now holy world of Nyrhala, a few stars over. History records that King Thuris Gincleare routed the remnants of their army at The Battle of Muren's Fall and that our wayward brothers were welcomed into the light with open arms. Then there was peace, stretching from these golden halls to the orange mountains of Nyrhala. Quite the idyllic resolution..."

Lindus tipped the crown higher on his forehead. "But sometimes the difference between fact and fiction is nothing more than an official seal. In truth, The Dormant were defeated that day, but between The Awakening and death, they chose the latter. In a majestic display of mercy, good King Thuris sentenced them to exile instead. And on three arks, filled to capacity, they were banished to the furthest world known to us at the time.

The name spoken in your vision belonged to their leader, Valkaros Sin-Muren, though I cannot guess its meaning or significance in our present day. He was old then and must surely have perished many generations ago. I'd be surprised if his thread didn't abandon him during the quarter century of insufferable boredom as he voyaged into exile."

"How old would he be?" asked Nodris.

"Far older than the ancient Sophian you regretfully serve," said Greyval.

"That we all serve," corrected King Lindus.

"And this planet to which they were banished, what has become of it? When was it last scouted?" Nodris' line of questions unsettled the council. They furrowed their brows and fidgeted in their thrones.

"Not since its discovery," said Lindus.

"Then I will go there at once," said Nodris, causing uproar in the stands. He struggled to catch words in the clamor. Most had to deal with time and distance. "How long could it possibly take with an anchor drive?" he asked, raising his voice over the din.

King Gincleare motioned for silence. "I'm afraid an anchor drive will do you little good. Even before our people had any notion of the concept, fortune and fate conspired to cast Valkaros and his followers off the Gravid Disk on which the civilized universe resides." He leaned forward in his throne, pointing at the floor. "They were sent down below to the upper fronds of The Mire. There, they would dwell in the solitary planet of a bleak red star. The world was never given a proper name. It is known only as Mursk 539." In ancient times, the Valoraphim's imagining of hell was a dismal world that lay far below theirs. The concept had not been abandoned during the era of space travel; it'd been given specific coordinates.

"Then I would see The Luciel refitted with our fastest Valoforged engines," said Nodris, and the chamber erupted.

Lindus could not easily quiet the council after such a statement. "Even with our best engines, the trip will take over a year," he said. "It would mean giving up your station as a The Second Viceroy."

"With your permission, I would pass the mantle to Kelmore," said Nodris.

"Preposterous!" exclaimed Chancellor Greyval. "What does Kelmore know of Sophian diplomacy? He's the captain of a cruiser! We would need someone with ample experience in our kingdom's affairs." The sentiment was shared by many in the council.

"I value your recommendation, Nodris," said Lindus, "but I'm not sure your cousin would appreciate you volunteering him for such a role. He's far better suited for piloting than politics. If you were to travel to Mursk 539, I would want Kelmore with you. The journey will take you through uncharted space, and there is no one with more experience at The Luciel's helm."

Nodris could spot no trace of maneuvering or malice in his uncle's face, only concern. His long white beard appeared gold in the chamber's light; it hadn't seen a brush in days. The same was true for his hair, which billowed out above the pressing crown.

"These are decisions that should not be made in haste," spoke The King. "We will adjourn for the evening to ponder these matters. May you all have sight," he said, and the sun gave way to a sky of candlelight.

Nodris found Zaralin still staring out across the floating ruins of Miraval. "Did you find the answers you sought?" she asked without turning. There was no night or day left in Miraval, only the whims of asteroids. A large stone presently eclipsed the rays of Atamal. Zaralin's reflection was brighter than the stars.

"Only more questions," said Nodris.

"What a shame. Will The Luciel be bound for Veredos?"

"Not for some time," he replied. "There is somewhere else I must take her first."

Zaralin pressed a hand to the glass. The light of Atamal crested over the rock and burned away her reflection. "Where?"

Nodris was left to speak to the curtain of black hair that fell in tight curls from a braided crown between her pale horns. He came close enough to smell the blue amaranth's faint fragrance. "Somewhere very far, but you needn't concern yourself. I am stepping down as Viceroy..."

"My charge is to follow you until you return to The Centower," she said. "There's no clause concerning your title or time."

Nodris entertained the idea of never returning and just keeping her forever. "You might regret that when you hear where we're going," he said.

Atamal ducked behind another rock. A few rays caught the side of the palace and glanced across the window, painting Zaralin's portrait on the glass with hard light. Porcelain forehead, curled horns, deep eyes drenched in shadow, high cheekbones running smoothly to a pointed chin, mouth slightly parted without expression, her face was as a mask. "The Mire..." she said, and her eyes were full of stars.

Late Prolog: The Extinguishing

The lofty limits set by philosophy and religion had been shattered. The heavens overflowed with gods.

It could not last. The Age of Sages ended with a war whose death toll was measured in species. This war was not fought with guns or bombs. A Sage's weapons were his thoughts, but it took more than will to rewrite the rules of existence; it took great knowledge.

It began with the advent of fractal observation. Scientists dove into the hearts of quantum particles, down into The Subrostrum. And the plunge proved infinite. New particles and forces disembogued from the nothing as scopes were focused on smaller and smaller points. The deeper they delved, the more confounding the rules became. It was a space where paradoxes were the rule.

The motes of the Subrostrum were accommodating, rearranging before researchers' eyes to prove whatever they'd hypothesized. It was believed that the methods used to achieve fractal observation were having an effect on this delicate space, but when new techniques were developed and the results remained the same, a new theory was formed: it was not the method of observation that affected The Subrostrum, but rather observation itself.

To observe something required a will and consciousness, and these forces were more powerful than the filaments of space on this scale. With a thought, a particle was created and just as easily dismissed. The Subrostrum bowed to will. But these tiny alterations had no effect on the world of atoms, much less the world observed without the use of scopes. A hundred minds all acting in concert couldn't nudge an electron a single energy level.

It wasn't until the first corona was made that a Sage saw his thoughts alter reality. A single instruction could be saved and macroed countless times through the power of the device's quantum computer. And at its heart were 42 molecules of duril, amplifying the Sage's will so that lifting rocks became moving planets and lighting candles turned to seeding stars.

The Sophian leaders of The Consortium of the Inner Rings used this technology to bring civility and order to the universe. For centuries, only they were allowed to become Sages, until a man by the name of Algray Solipso managed to acquire a corona and spread the technology across the other races. Power ran rampant, forcing the Consortium to decree that universal order and Sages could not coexist: a man who could crush a world with a thought could not be bound by its laws. And so the Sages were chased to the outer rims of the known universe, hunted by a force known as the Extinguishers.

Three hundred years later, The Rings were at peace.

Learn more about The Extinguishing and Ex's grandfather, Algray Solipso, by following the journey of The Nameless Sage in Ring Runner: Flight of the Sages, an independent video game for PC. Go to RingRunner.net for more information!

Acknowledgements

Odile C. Neuberg

Matt Bondurant

Tony Daniel

Courtney Dryere

Paul Dryere

Enrique F. Dryere

James K. Weaver

Uri A. Heller

Elio M. Botello

Gautam Chakravarthi

and

Nils Horna

www.ingramcontent.com/pod-product-compliance
Lightning Source LLC
Chambersburg PA
CBHW070316260626
47160CB00003B/853